the One

RUSS UNDERWOOD

This book is dedicated to my wonderful and loving wife Mary. Her support, encouragement, and inspiration made completing this work possible.

A special thanks to the following people:
My editors for this book Mike Garrett,
Deb Wright, and Holle Abee.
My cover design team at Damonza.com

Chapter One

———·••●••·———

I HAVE TO HURRY. . . . I have to hurry. . . . I have to hurry! This thought kept racing through Ethan's mind over and over again. He was speeding home as fast as he could, pushing the limits of his jet-black BMW X-7. He found himself consumed and possessed by this thought and was driving as if his very life depended on it. He was weaving in and out of traffic, taking every opportunity to move ahead of each car in front of him, like a race car driver relentlessly pursuing first place at the finish line.

He felt that no one was going to stop him from making it to his house by three o'clock, not the cars, not the traffic lights, not the stop signs, not pedestrians, not anything! After all, today was his tenth wedding anniversary, and he couldn't wait to get home and surprise his wife, Emma.

The weather on Ethan's drive home that spring day in South Georgia could not have been more perfect. It was April fifth. The sun was shining brightly, fueling the flowers' and trees' burst of new growth for the spring. The sky was as blue as the deepest, clearest ocean, and the air was filled with the sweet smell of blooming jasmine. Spring had arrived in South Georgia, and it was a welcome sight for him after three long months of freezing temperatures, overcast skies, and the bareness and starkness on all the vegetation that only winter brings. He genuinely felt that it was as if this most perfect day had been created just for Ethan's anniversary and the surprises he had planned.

Having run the final two stop signs on the road to his home, Ethan picked up the pace even more. He weaved wildly through the parked cars on the narrow street. I have to hurry. . . . I have to hurry. . . . I have to hurry! Finally, he wheeled into the driveway as if on two wheels, then screeched to a stop, and a sense of relief covered him. He saw Emma's car. He had made it home before Emma left to go to the gym. He wasn't too late, but now he knew he must find her and surprise her.

Ethan and Emma lived in a typical Southern upper-class golf course community. It was located in Kinderlou Forest, which Ethan believed was the most prestigious subdivision in Valdosta. The neighborhood was a masterpiece, complete with gated entrances, perfectly manicured grounds and common areas, and the most impressive golf course south of Atlanta.

Ethan's career as a hedge fund manager had blossomed and given them plenty of money for the finer things life had to offer. The management fees he received from his clients were flooding in. He had a knack for selecting and managing investments, and his investors rewarded him handsomely for it. After all, they were receiving higher investment returns than at any point in their lives.

His investing prowess had allowed Emma to be a housewife and devote substantial time to their church and several charities, which he felt she thoroughly enjoyed. Ethan relished having her there when he came home each day, too. Their home was a large two-story Southwestern-style home. It was over five thousand square feet, yet was warm and inviting, both inside and out. Emma had selected the décor on the inside, and despite the home's sprawling size, each room had a coziness and comfort about it that everyone who visited commented on.

Outside, the hand-laid stone was placed perfectly throughout the exterior to complement the light tan stucco siding, and the stone and stucco blended together to appear as one. The home was complete with a large kidney-shaped pool in the back yard, along with a massive cool deck and an outdoor cabana that could have been a small home itself, complete with bathroom, kitchen, and a small bedroom.

Finally, there was an elegant black wrought iron fence surrounding and protecting the pool, yet it seemed to blend in to its surroundings. The whole yard and house flowed effortlessly to the eye. In summary, Ethan believed the house and yard were perfect.

Ethan parked the car and jumped out almost before the engine shut off. His flowing brown hair flapped in the warm spring breeze. Ethan Phillips was above average in height, standing 6'1", and had a handsome face that was sharp, chiseled, and strong all at the same time. By any human measure, Ethan was attractive and had a presence about him when he entered a room.

Men and women alike would find themselves staring at him almost as if doing so was beyond their control. His bright hazel eyes and tanned olive complexion captivated anyone he met, especially women. His chest, biceps, legs, and butt were all sculpted like granite, as he took great pride in his health and appearance. He worked out six days a week and thoroughly enjoyed the benefits of being fit and healthy.

His appearance was statuesque and striking. Ethan could have easily been a model, but he had no time for such things, as making his investors filthy rich was his passion.

Ethan threw open the back driver side door and quickly reached for the one dozen bright pink roses, Emma's favorite color, of course. He hastily double checked his coat pocket and was relieved the white envelope with two airplane tickets to Hawaii was still safely inside. Hawaii was a bucket list item for them both. They had always wanted to go, but never seemed to find the time.

Ethan had also made reservations at their favorite Italian restaurant, Luciano's, a small but romantic venue in downtown Valdosta. They loved the cuisine and atmosphere there, but they had been so busy lately they had not been able to eat there in over six months. Ethan had called ahead and spoken to the maître d and arranged for the small orchestra at the restaurant to play a medley of their favorite songs. He had thought of everything.

He still had time to catch her before she was dressed and had left. I have to hurry. . . . I have to hurry. . . . I have to hurry! Ethan reached to open the door inside the garage and nearly yanked his shoulder out of socket. That was odd, Ethan thought. He knew Emma always had the door unlocked when she was home, despite Ethan's plea for her to be more careful. Well, Ethan reasoned, Emma had finally taken his advice and decided to be more safe when home alone.

Undaunted, Ethan quickly unlocked the door and sprang into the kitchen expecting to see Emma, but his wife was nowhere to be found. He roamed through the downstairs section of the house, eagerly calling her name. "Emma? Emma? I'm home early, honey!"

He listened intently each time, but heard no response. Finally, as Ethan made his way to the foot of the wooden spiral staircase leading to the second floor, he could hear music coming from upstairs. Emma was upstairs, he decided. He briskly ascended the circular staircase, as he had so many times before, and with each step he took, the music grew louder and louder.

As Ethan reached the midway point of the staircase, he paused as he recognized the tune. It was Julio Iglesias, her favorite artist, singing "When I Need You." It was *their* song. It was the song they slow danced to on their first date twelve years ago. Emma must be just as excited about our anniversary as I am, Ethan thought. He hadn't heard her play that song in over three years. She was just as thrilled as he was about their special day and no doubt had some surprises for him, Ethan thought hopefully.

Ethan reached the top of the staircase, turned sharply to the right, and glided quickly to their closed bedroom door. He grabbed the door knob and burst into the bedroom like a Jack in the Box, calling out happily, "Emma, I'm home early, honey! Happy anniversary!"

Just as the last of these words rolled off his tongue, his heart plunged to his feet like a massive anchor being released from a docking freighter. His body turned as white as a ghost, and he felt as if all eight pints of his blood were sucked out of his body at once by a giant vacuum. Ethan stood in shock and horror. There in front of him was his wife, naked, straddling another man and in the middle of having sex.

Emma had also taken great care of her body and appearance. It was so painful and anguishing for Ethan to see her cascading blonde hair and sculpted body straddling another man. Stunned and heartbroken, Ethan turned his attention to the man Emma was on top of, the co-conspirator in this sordid affair. The man was Chris Jeffries, the investment analyst in the hedge fund Ethan had started with local Valdosta investors. Until that moment, Chris was a man Ethan had considered to be a good friend.

Emma blurted out, "What are you doing home?"

Her first words weren't I'm sorry, please forgive me, or it's not what you think, Ethan thought. Ethan was furious and felt pure rage building inside at the sight of what he had discovered. It was a sign for the first time to Ethan just where exactly he stood with her in their relationship.

Ethan called on all of his restraint and resolve and somehow managed to remain calm and replied, "I came home early to surprise you. After all, today is our tenth wedding anniversary, but I can see you had other plans for celebrating it."

∽

Initially, Emma was shocked and frustrated at having her interlude with Chris exposed by Ethan. However, the gravity of the moment now began to sink in with her. Emma, now feeling guilt, shame, and embarrassment, could barely muster any words and began sobbing loudly. She only managed to blurt out, "We never meant to hurt you!" These were the only words she could manage to speak. She was still in shock at having her affair exposed. Emma knew that she had to work fast to hopefully diffuse this situation and salvage her marriage.

∽

Chris was terrified with the thought of what Ethan might do. "Please forgive me! It was a mistake, and it won't happen again! I promise!" Chris blurted out, shaking, with fear evident in his eyes. He was also trying to diffuse the situation. He wanted to do or say whatever he had to in order to prevent Ethan from taking any drastic action.

Ethan and Chris had been friends for over four years. Chris had been grateful to Ethan for hiring him right out of college. To show his appreciation, he worked very hard for Ethan and as a result was often at Ethan's house for hours at the time. In the process though, Chris had developed feelings for Emma. These feelings, however, had blossomed into much more.

∽

Emma, finally catching her breath from crying, said in what she hoped was a convincing manner, "I'm sorry, too, honey. Please just let me explain everything! It's not what it looks like!" Like Chris, she, too, was worried what Ethan might do. She knew he was slow to anger, but when he did get angry, it was like a nuclear bomb going off. She also knew Ethan kept a shotgun in their bedroom closet.

∽

Hurt beyond words and utterly devastated, Ethan paused for what had to seem like an eternity to Emma and Chris, and he carefully considered his words before saying anything. After processing all he had seen, Ethan looked up from the floor and said, "I think it's best if both of you are gone when I get back. You have one hour before I return, and God help you if either of you are here then."

Ethan continued, "Emma, we're done. Pack enough of your clothes and personal items to last a while. Don't return here ever again. I'll have all of your clothes and belongings sent to your new address. You've broken our covenant with God and with each other! You make me sick! You both make me sick! Get out of here! And go to hell, both of you!" With his tirade complete Ethan turned, slammed the bedroom door, and stormed away. He then flew down the stairs and hurried into his car.

Ethan was broken, and it seemed like his perfect life had evaporated in an instant. Fighting back tears, he pulled out of the driveway and began driving. Where had it all gone wrong? Ethan questioned. How could she do that on *our* anniversary, of all days? The questions just kept coming. And how could she have a sordid sexual affair with *my* friend, in *our* house, in *our* bedroom, while playing *our* song on *our* anniversary?

Ethan could control the tears no longer, and they overcame him and began streaming down his face. As fast as he wiped them, the tears came pouring out. Ethan began sobbing bitterly, replaying over and over in his mind what he had just seen, trying desperately to understand why he hadn't seen any signs of the affair sooner.

It was such a total shock to him. "I'm so stupid!" Ethan screamed out loudly in the car. The image of his wife of ten years entangled with another man in their bedroom in the throes of passion was burned into his brain, as if a cattle hand had taken a branding iron and seared the image permanently into his memory. Ethan knew he could never forget that image and never forgive Emma for what she had done to him.

He was devastated and hurt, and he would never, ever let another woman do that to him again, he decided. The pain was too great, and Ethan thought if he couldn't trust Emma, there was no way in the world there was any other woman walking the Earth who could be trusted, either.

Chapter Two

Three years later. . . .

LIFE HAD RETURNED close to normal for Ethan, or so he thought, except he hadn't been able to bring himself to date anyone again. The thought of dating still made him sick. He and Emma had divorced, and the divorce went as well as could be expected under the circumstances. Emma had left Valdosta and moved to Atlanta with Chris. The shame and embarrassment of what she had done and with who was the gossip all over the small Southern town. Emma had gladly left town with Chris, asking only for a divorce settlement of fifty thousand dollars cash. She left the house and all of their assets to Ethan.

During the divorce, Ethan came to understand just how unhappy Emma had become and how eager she was to leave him and her old life behind. She had been hiding her feelings and her affair from Ethan for over three years. He never saw her affair coming, and that bothered him greatly. Perhaps he'd been blinded by his work and oblivious to Emma's needs, or perhaps Emma had just changed, or worse yet, she was never really the woman Ethan thought she was.

Whatever the case, it was clear now that Emma had shut down emotionally, hidden all her feelings from him, and fled to another man. However, Ethan resigned himself to the fact their divorce was for the best.

Emma informed him after the divorce papers were signed that she and Chris would be married in two months. That fact didn't surprise Ethan, though, because he had come to understand that Emma's relationship with Chris was far more than a casual fling. He discovered that Chris and Emma were very much in love and had been for quite some time. In fact, Emma also let Ethan know after the divorce was finalized that she had been planning to leave him the next month after he caught them.

The three years since the divorce, though, had seemed to ease much of his pain, Ethan thought. Time, it turns out, does heal many wounds, he had convinced himself.

He had remained in Valdosta, but had sold their home and purchased a small pine tree farm a few miles farther out from town. He had also built a cozy three-bedroom cabin there. It was two thousand square feet, but decorated with a rustic elegance throughout and was warm and luxurious. Being out from town and isolated had allowed him the time he needed to heal, and the cabin also proved to be an excellent home office.

Since the divorce, Ethan had thrown himself into his hedge fund and was making more money than ever, and so were his investors. He had also built a strong friendship with one of his investors. His name was William Francesco. Everyone called him Willie and he was a retired multi-millionaire real estate tycoon from Atlanta.

Willie had made a fortune buying and selling real estate during the Atlanta real estate craze. He had exited the real estate market at just the right time and took his wealth south to Valdosta to retire and settle into a simpler life with his then new bride, Ann.

Ann was fifteen years younger than Willie, but they both seemed as happy as could be. They had moved to Valdosta because Ann wanted to come back home to the friends and family she grew up with. Willie welcomed the slower pace and quickly blended into Valdosta society.

Willie was a short, round man with silver-gray hair and bright blue eyes. The years had been kind to Willie, and he still had most of his hair and few wrinkles for someone seventy years old. He had a sharp wit and terrific sense of humor and was outgoing and gregarious. It was easy to see how he had succeeded in life. He met people so easily and effortlessly and could instantly connect with almost anyone.

After a long day of managing investments, Ethan was relaxing and having a glass of chardonnay at his favorite local hangout, The Landing. Willie was to meet him for drinks and great conversation. As Ethan sipped on a glass of wine at the bar, he heard a voice call out from behind him. "Hey Captain, how's it going today?"

It was Willie, and he never used Ethan's name in their greetings or conversations, but rather always referred to him as "Captain." It was a sign of Willie's affection for him, Ethan reasoned. "Well hello, Willie! How are you doing today?" Ethan responded.

"Captain, if I was any better, I just couldn't stand it. Ann and I are getting ready to go to Hawaii, so I'm on cloud nine." Willie responded.

Hawaii . . . that was where he and Emma were to go before that horrible day in April a little over three years ago, remembered Ethan, but he didn't let his thoughts dwell on that fact and quickly responded, "That's great, Willie! I know y'all will have a great time, and I hear the weather is awesome this time of year."

"Well, I hope so, Captain. I'm as nervous as a cat in a room full of rocking chairs about all that flying we'll have to do to get there. I've never liked to fly, but Hawaii is going to be a blast. So, I'll just load up on wine and valium before we take off." Willie said, laughing out loud so anyone close by could hear. Ethan knew his laugh was contagious, and he saw that others nearby in the bar couldn't help but laugh, too.

Ethan, though, had known Willie long enough to be able to sense he was nervous about the trip. "I'm sure you'll do fine, Willie. You've flown many times before, so just relax and enjoy the ride and the destination. It beats working, and flying is safer than driving, anyway," Ethan responded to try and reassure Willie.

"I can always count on you, Captain, to try and make me feel better," Willie responded.

Their conversation then naturally drifted to business and the hedge fund Ethan managed. Willie was the largest investor in the fund and had been the first to pledge money to Ethan. Willie had also been responsible for recommending and referring almost all of the local investors in the fund to Ethan.

⚓

Willie saw a lot of himself in Ethan, and the two had instantly formed a bond and connection when Ethan first met Willie and pitched the hedge fund idea. Ethan was like the son Willie had never had nor taken the time to have. The older man had been so consumed with money and real estate that children had passed him by and landed him two ex-wives in the process.

An hour or so had passed, and after discussing investment options, investment returns, and potential new investors, Willie guided the conversation to Ethan's personal life. "So, Captain, who are you courting now?" Willie questioned good heartedly.

"Now, Willie, you know I'm not dating anyone. I don't have the time or stomach for it," Ethan calmly countered.

"All work and no play make Jack a dull boy, Captain," Willie quipped back. "You need a little filly in your life to keep you straight and take trips with and a gal to have a family with," Willie continued.

❦

Ethan began to get uncomfortable with where the conversation had drifted. Willie hadn't delved into his dating life this much since they met. Ethan had shared with Willie the whole sad story about Emma early in their friendship, but Willie had always kept his conversation on Ethan's dating life at a superficial level. Something was different about Willie today, Ethan thought.

"Willie, you know my story, and you know the hurt I endured, and I don't trust women. Anyone around here who dates me is only doing so with dollar signs on her mind," Ethan curtly responded.

"Look, Captain, I know how you feel about all of that. All I'm saying is think about it and just put yourself out there and date a little. It's not going to hurt a thing to let the badger out every now and again. Just go have a drink or two with one of the dozen eligible darlings in Valdosta who are chasing you! You're a great guy, and I know there's someone special out there somewhere waiting on you, Captain," Willie offered.

"I know you mean well, Willie, so we'll see. Well, it's getting late, and I need to get home. I have to look over some earnings reports before tomorrow. Thanks for the drinks tonight. Next time they're on me," Ethan said, trying to close the uncomfortable turn the conversation had taken and slip out on a good note with Willie. After all, Willie was his largest investor, and he didn't want to make him angry.

"Alright, Captain. I'll let you off the hook this time, but I'll be hitting you up again about it. You're too great a catch to stay unhitched. And I'm gonna hold you to paying the tab next time, too! I guess I'll just plan on seeing your bright, shining face at our investors' meeting next week, right?" Willie responded kindly.

"Sounds good, Willie. I'll see you then for sure. Take care, and tell Ann I said hello," Ethan said as he walked out of The Landing and headed home.

Chapter Three

HAT NIGHT AND the next day, Ethan pondered the whole evening with Willie. Their conversations had always been dominated by business, people they knew, life experiences, and their friendship. Willie had never shown that much of an interest in Ethan's dating life. Even two years ago when Ethan had shared with Willie all that had happened with Emma and the divorce, Willie had just listened and been a sounding board. He hadn't offered any opinions, thoughts, or wisdom, but had just listened and let Ethan get everything off his chest. Willie had never judged Ethan, nor anyone, for that matter, and that was why he and Ethan connected so well.

Everyone in Valdosta knew what had happened between him and Emma, and even his male friends, all of whom were married, treated him differently now. It was as if he was marked with a scarlet letter or something. Even though they all knew the tragic story, it was as if they blamed him for the divorce and assumed he must have caused his wife to cheat on him, then leave him. If he were a real man his wife wouldn't want to have an affair in his own home with someone half her age, then divorce him was the message his friends subtly conveyed to him.

Ethan could sense these thoughts in his "friends" each time he was around them. The condescending looks, the smart remarks, and the lack of real understanding of his situation were prevalent everywhere. His friends were superficial and shallow, and over time, he grew to resent them so much that he rarely mingled with them at all now.

Ethan so enjoyed Willie because he had none of the traits his friends did. He was true and honest and didn't have a judgmental bone in his body, and Willie had more money than anyone outside of Atlanta and didn't need or want to mooch off Ethan. This was another quality Willie had that many of Ethan's friends did not. He would always be there for Ethan, and Ethan would likewise always be there for him.

So what had possessed Willie to urge dating so much last night? Why was he so bent on me dating again? Why did he keep pushing it even when he knew I was uncomfortable? Willie had never done that before. Something just didn't seem right, Ethan thought.

As he was replaying the evening with Willie, his thoughts were interrupted by his cellphone's ringing. It was Greta Walker, Ethan's administrative assistant. "Good morning, Mr. Phillips. The earnings call with Harris Environmental needs to be moved up from two o'clock today to twelve o'clock, and the company wanted me to make sure I let you know. They would very much like you to listen in on the call," Greta shared with Ethan in her typical professional manner.

Greta was sixty years old and completely gray headed, but an elegant and classy woman, with black-rimmed glasses and a soothing voice. She was always dressed like the consummate professional secretary. She had a quaint beauty and laid-back temperament. Greta was extremely thorough with her job and always professional with Ethan and investors. She had been a godsend to Ethan the ten years she had been with him, and he couldn't ask for a better administrative assistant. She could often read his mind and complete tasks before Ethan even asked.

"Hey, Greta. Yes, I'll definitely make that call. Thanks for the update. Is there anything else going on this morning?" Ethan questioned.

"No, sir. I'm almost done assembling the quarterly investor packet, and I should have that ready for your review tomorrow," Greta responded.

"That's perfect. Thank you for having it completed so timely. I'll have plenty of time to review it and get it back to you to get to the printer before the meeting next week. If you need me, just call. I'm here at the cabin reviewing earnings reports," Ethan advised.

"Yes, sir. I will keep you updated, and please let me know if I can be of assistance in any way," Greta calmly replied.

"Sounds good, Greta. Goodbye."

The day passed quickly for Ethan with the conference call, then reviewing the five earnings reports from companies his hedge fund was already invested in. It was painstaking work, but often some of the most helpful and insightful information was buried in the earnings reports. Ethan had a knack for finding problematic details and grilling management about it. These questions and management's responses had often guided him in his investing decisions and had proven to be one of his many God-given abilities.

It was about ten o'clock in the evening, and Ethan had just enjoyed a glass of chardonnay and settled into bed for the night. All of the day's work and his morning workout had gotten the better of him. He soon gave in to his exhaustion and faded off to sleep.

The next thing Ethan knew, his cellphone rang and woke him from a deep sleep. He groggily looked over at his phone to see it was Willie's number, and with sleep still in his eyes, he glanced at the clock that glowed two fifty-five a.m. What in the world did Willie want at this hour? Ethan wondered. "Um, hello, Willie. What's going on?" Ethan questioned with his voice cracking from being in a deep slumber before the call.

"Ethan, I'm so glad I got you! This is Ann," Willie's wife answered. The fear and borderline panic in her voice was immediately obvious to Ethan. Why was Ann, of all people, calling at this hour? Ethan wondered.

Chapter Four

"IT'S WILLIE. THE doctors think he's had a heart attack!" Ann responded, now beginning to cry uncontrollably.

"Oh, no! I'm so sorry, Ann! I'm on my way! Are you in the emergency room?" asked Ethan, with fear and concern in his voice.

"Yes, I'm in the waiting room. Please hurry." said Ann. Ethan noticed she barely got the words out of her mouth for sobbing and crying.

"I'll be there in fifteen minutes," Ethan calmly and reassuringly replied.

"Thank you, Ethan," Ann responded gratefully through her sobbing.

Ethan hastily threw on the first pair of slacks and the first shirt he could find. He then pulled on his socks and slid into his shoes in seconds. In two minutes he was out the door and headed to town in his SUV. Ethan drove into town just as fast as he had that day in April trying to get home to Emma. He hoped this time he wouldn't be just as devastated when he reached his destination.

True to his word, he sprinted through the automatic doors in the emergency room a quarter hour after he hung up with Ann. Frantically he searched the waiting room, then running to him from his right, he saw Ann.

Ann was an elegant woman with shiny blonde hair and bright blue eyes that rivaled Willie's. She was average height for a woman and was slim thanks to her daily aerobics routine. Her typical bright and shining face wasn't present, though. Ann's eyes were swollen and red from all the tears she must have shed for Willie, Ethan thought. Her face was gloomy and haggard from the lack of sleep and worry about her husband's condition. "Ethan, I'm so happy you're here!" Ann said gratefully as Ethan watched her throw her arms around him.

"I'm sorry it took so long. Please sit down and tell me what happened to Willie," Ethan replied in a calm and caring tone. He then sat beside her in the waiting room.

"Well, Willie and I went to bed just as we always do. Then about midnight, Willie got up to go to the bathroom, and when he came out, he fell down trying to get back into bed. He called out my name, and I jumped up and ran to him. I could see he was short of breath, and his color wasn't good. He was also complaining of pain in his chest and left arm. I instantly thought heart attack. I quickly gave him an aspirin because I had heard that helps right after a heart attack. He wasn't very responsive, so I called 911. The ambulance came soon after, and we've been here since," Ann recounted as Ethan watched tears resume streaming down her face.

"What have the doctors told you?" Ethan questioned intently.

"Thankfully, Dr. Johannsen, who's a friend of Willie's and in your hedge fund, is the cardiologist on call tonight, so Willie has gotten the best care possible. Dr. Johannsen updated me about thirty minutes ago that Willie did have a heart attack, but that he felt like the surgery was a success. He said Willie should be fine given time and plenty of rest," Ann replied with Ethan detecting the first hint of comfort in her voice.

"I can tell you Willie is in excellent hands with Dr. Johannsen. Have you been back to see him, and could I see him?" asked Ethan anxiously.

"I've seen him, and he's sleeping comfortably. Dr. Johannsen let me in to see him once the surgery was finished. He put a stent in the clogged artery and expects Willie to have a full recovery. He said that by my giving Willie the aspirin when I did, it helped reduce the damage to the heart. God was just with me in that moment, I guess. He'll be moved out of surgery to ICU shortly, and you should be able to visit him in about two or three hours, if you like," Ann told Ethan, now appearing to have finally calmed down from all that transpired.

"Okay. Thank you so much for calling me. Is there anything I can get for you or do for you in the meantime?" Ethan asked, hoping to be some help to her.

"No, Ethan. Thank you, though. My Mom and Dad are here to take care of me. Please just talk with Willie when you can. He was asking for you at the house before the EMT's arrived, and they and the nurses both said he's asked for you several times since. It'll mean so much to him to see you tonight. He really needs to talk to you," Ann responded, almost pleading it seemed to Ethan.

"I'll definitely do that as soon as they let me in. Thanks again for calling me," Ethan said graciously as Ann returned to wait with her parents.

Ann's last comment seemed strange to Ethan. It was as if she was telling him he *must* talk with Willie tonight. Was she not telling him everything about Willie's condition? Was Willie about to die? Why did he have to talk to Willie *tonight*? The questions kept coming to him as they always seemed to. Ethan was such an analytic. He couldn't help but analyze this situation or any situation, for that matter.

Time flew by quickly in the waiting room while Ethan was replaying and studying all that happened the night before and all Willie had said to him over drinks. As he was going over these questions in his mind, a nurse came out of ICU and spoke to him. "Mr. Phillips, you can visit Mr. Francesco now. He's still recovering from surgery, but is alert, so you can have fifteen minutes with him. But please don't get him excited or upset," cautioned the nurse.

"Okay, no problem. Thank you," Ethan politely replied.

As Ethan entered Willie's room, he heard a familiar voice from the bed. He looked to his left and there lay Willie. He was swollen from the surgery, but his color was better than Ethan expected. His hair was sticking out in every direction, from all the chaos he had been through that night, no doubt. Oxygen tubes were draped on his face to help him with each breath. The usual gleam in his eye was still there, but much more faded and weaker than usual. "Hello, Captain! How do you like my hotel room?" said Willie. Ethan could see Willie was weak and barely able to muster a smile.

"The Ritz, it's not, Willie. How are you feeling?" Ethan responded wryly, trying to keep the humor going to distract them both from Willie's condition.

"I'm going to be fine, Captain. I just wanted a little excitement for Ann tonight, I guess. Something to break up the routine," said Willie, whispering and chuckling softly.

Ethan couldn't help but chuckle too. Willie's sense of humor always made him laugh, regardless of the situation. "I'm glad to hear you're going to be okay. Dr. Johannsen said it was a heart attack," Ethan explained.

"Yeah, it was, but it was a mild one. They went in and inserted a stent and said I should be fine if I take it easy," Willie said. It was obvious to Ethan that Willie was trying to reassure him he would be okay.

"That's great news. I've been so worried about you since Ann called me. You're a great friend, and I'm glad you wanted me here," Ethan replied.

"You're a great friend, too, Captain. And I did want you here. We need to talk," said Willie weakly and with a serious tone. Ethan could tell the conversation was shifting to unfamiliar territory as Willie was seldom this serious when talking with him. What was coming next? Ethan wondered nervously.

"Ethan, this little event and some other things that happened have really gotten me to thinking about a lot of things, mainly about you," Willie began. Ethan was already shocked and speechless. Willie never used Ethan's first name when talking with him.

Willie continued, "You're an excellent hedge fund manager. You're a natural, and you give it everything you have. But I think you're missing out on a lot life has to offer. I don't think you're completely happy. You need to relax and enjoy yourself a little. Take it easy for a while, take a trip, and recharge those old batteries of yours. If you don't, you're going to flame out."

Ethan cringed because he was sure Willie was about to revisit the dating topic again. "I don't have time right now to do that, Willie. The investor meeting is next week, and there are at least a dozen new companies I need to evaluate to put some of the fund's excess cash to work. Maybe I can do that in a few months," Ethan cautiously countered.

"Nonsense, Captain. I can get all of the investors to agree to delay the meeting because of my little hiccup today. You know the other investors won't want to meet without me. We always have one hundred percent attendance," Willie explained.

"That's true, but what about the company research? I can't just put that on hold," Ethan responded.

"Take it with you. You can take a few hours a day, do your research, and relax the rest of the time. You need it, and you know it. You're all work and no play, and that'll make you a dull, burned-out boy. Please do this for me, as a personal favor. If not, I'm not too proud to get Ann in here, too, and we'll double team ya," Willie said. Ethan noticed him manage another smile and continue to labor to talk.

"Alright, Willie. I give in. I'll take a week and relax a little, but just as a favor to you, of course. But I'll have to figure out where to go. It's been a while since I've been on a vacation anywhere," Ethan cautioned.

"Nope, got that covered, Captain. I've got an old real estate buddy from Atlanta who has a house in Rosemary Beach, Florida. It's about fifteen miles due west of Panama City. It's relaxing, and you'll love it. My buddy's house was available, and I reserved it for you starting tomorrow. All you gotta do is pack and go," Willie said. Ethan sensed Willie trying to muster excitement despite his weak condition.

"Wow, you're serious about this, aren't you? That's thoughtful, but I can find a place. Besides, I'm not going anywhere with you in this condition. You and Ann are good friends, and I want to be here to help out," Ethan countered.

"No, Captain, you need to go to Rosemary Beach. Ann and I will be just fine. We have her parents and several friends from the church who'll be glad to help out. You go enjoy yourself, and I'm sure I'll bug you plenty about helping me when you get back. Trust me, you'll thank me for going. Just promise me you'll relax," Willie advised.

"Alright, Willie. I'll go to Rosemary Beach. This is generous of you. I can't thank you enough," Ethan responded.

"Good! It's settled, Captain. Who knows? You may meet 'the one' down there, too," Willie said optimistically.

"I don't know about that. I think I'm better off staying single for quite some time. Maybe when I retire I'll look for someone then," Ethan quipped nervously and hoped Willie was too weak to delve further into his relationship status.

"Captain, one thing I've learned in life is that when it comes to good ol' Cupid, he's not an earnings call or an investor meeting that you can plan on your calendar. He strikes when the good Lord tells him to," Willie said with a gentleness and caring Ethan was used to from his friend. "Now, get out of here and enjoy yourself; I insist. I'm gonna be fine, and Ann will help me mend my ticker while you're gone," Willie added.

"I don't feel right just leaving town for a vacation right after you've had a heart attack and surgery, Willie," Ethan replied with worry in his voice.

"Captain, I'll be able to heal and recover much faster knowing my best friend is relaxing and enjoying himself for the first time in a long, long time," Willie told him. Ethan could see that Willie was fighting back tears.

Ethan was stunned to hear Willie call him his best friend. Willie had many friends, and most had been his buddies for twenty or thirty years or more. Ethan was touched, and he felt the exact same way about Willie.

"I consider you my best friend, too, Willie. Our friendship has been such a blessing to me, and I'll do as you ask," Ethan responded, now fighting back the emotion of the moment himself. He didn't want to cry in front of his best friend. Ethan wanted to project strength to Willie.

"That's great! You've made me happier than a turtle on an escalator!" Willie blurted out. It appeared to Ethan that Willie was mustering the last of his strength at that moment.

Sensing Willie was nearly completely spent, Ethan knew it was time to leave and let his ailing friend rest and recuperate. "Alright, I'll let you rest now. I'm going to call and check on you while I'm gone, though; you can count on that. Get well, Willie, and remember I owe you a round of drinks at The Landing, too," Ethan replied, smiling.

"I will, Captain. Go let the old badger loose for a few days, and I'll be here when you get back," Willie said, exhausted from the conversation. Willie could fight it no more and succumbed to his fatigue, with his head gently tilting to the side, and he began to fade off to sleep. With that, Ethan whispered goodbye, eased out of Willie's room, and left the hospital to go home for a few hours of sleep before leaving for Rosemary Beach the next day.

After Ethan got home, he pondered over yet another curious conversation with Willie. He was deeply touched that Willie considered him his best friend. Ethan felt likewise. He couldn't help but feel honored that Willie wanted so much to help him and give him a vacation. He knew he needed it, but he had just not made it a priority. Willie had seen that fact and stepped in to help, just what a true friend would do, Ethan felt.

As Ethan began to drift off to sleep, he chuckled at Willie's comment about finding 'the one' at Rosemary Beach. No chance of that, Ethan mused, and chalked Willie's comment up to delirium from the pain medication he was taking. He knew he had too many other things to worry about right now.

Chapter Five

HE DRIVE TO Rosemary Beach the next day flew by for Ethan. Maybe it was because he was driving like a speed demon as he usually did, or maybe it was because his mind was filled with thoughts of Willie and his condition and all he told him. Willie had been acting so peculiar lately by bringing up dating, then sharing in ICU all he had with him. He was flattered beyond words that Willie considered him his best friend, but the whole conversation and Willie's sudden obvious concern for him on a dating level was puzzling.

Ethan felt like there was something Willie wasn't telling him, and he wondered what it could possibly be. Was Willie sending me down here so I wouldn't see him die? If Willie considered me his best friend, then why hadn't he already mentioned it? Why wait until now of all times to tell me I'm his best friend? Should I ask Willie about all of it and see how he responds? He had so many questions and so few answers. He was on vacation now, Ethan reasoned, so it was time to just relax for a change and try to put it all to the side for now.

As Ethan's thoughts began to clear, he realized his GPS had him only a couple of miles from his destination. He continued on Back Beach Road until he came to the traffic light for State Road 30A and Rosemary Beach. Ethan didn't really know much about Rosemary Beach. He hadn't even heard of it until Willie mentioned it to him, so he didn't know what to expect. He knew Willie had a taste for the finer things in life, and he could only assume that this must be a nice vacation spot and a luxurious home.

Ethan casually made his way down State Road 30A into Rosemary Beach. He was completely amazed at what he saw as he entered there. Lining the two-lane road were sand live oak trees surrounded at their base by saw palmettos. The trees, with their short but full canopies, draped gently over the road and provided relief from the bright May Florida sunshine.

As Ethan continued down 30A, he noticed to his right were long rectangles of open lawn, along with expertly spaced sidewalks and crosswalks dissecting the grass. Children were playing kickball, bocce ball, corn hole, and other games on the lawns. Adults could also be seen lounging on towels in the afternoon sun, watching the children frolic and play, yet at the same time getting their last rays of sunshine for the day.

He approached and stopped at the second traffic light, gazed to his right, and saw Barret Square and the perfectly manicured park area in the center. It was Rosemary Beach's town square and was surrounded tastefully by shops and restaurants. His GPS, however, guided him to the left at the traffic light, and he turned into a street made of perfectly placed brick pavers. There was no asphalt or concrete, just pavers providing Ethan and all who came a sense of home.

As he continued around the south side of Barrett Square, he passed another park area to his left that also blended into the surroundings, then as he reached the post office on his right, at the top of a small hill he stopped his car briefly to take in all that he saw. Ethan was blown away.

He gazed down Main Street and the slight decline of the narrowing street of pavers and saw a small, quaint little town with three and four-story buildings lining each side of the road. Each building was unique, and each had a shop or a restaurant on the bottom floor. He guessed condos or homes were on the upper floors.

Many of the buildings also had balconies that hovered gently above the paver-clad sidewalks. It was easy for Ethan to see the New Orleans, Dutch West Indies, and Charleston influences in the architecture. All the buildings contrasted greatly with the traditional beach town, yet seemed to be a natural part of the landscape. Ethan had never seen anything quite like this in America. It reminded him of another place he'd been. What was its name? he pondered intently.

"I've got it!" Ethan cried out inside his car, then turned quickly to look around, hoping no one was watching him talk to himself. The little town reminded him of Austria. It was as if someone had taken a small Austrian village and picked it up, buildings, streets, and all, and set it down here in this place. It was so unexpected; it seemed so out of place, yet it was so inviting to him. Instantly, Ethan found the cares of this world leaving his mind as he gazed at what was in front of him.

Just then a loud honk rang out from behind. Another car had pulled up behind him and was in no mood to wait on Ethan to finish daydreaming. "How embarrassing. I hope no one saw that, either," Ethan said aloud to himself in the car. "I need to watch out. If I'm not careful I'll end up talking to myself," Ethan continued, then as soon as he spoke these words, he laughed out loud at himself. He *was* talking to himself as he often did, particularly when in deep thought.

Recognizing the need to move ahead, Ethan eased down the street, taking in the shops and restaurants on either side. He observed the wide paver-lined sidewalks with the tables and chairs neatly spaced on them in front of each restaurant. This little street was a welcoming place of activity and social life, with people scurrying around on foot and bicycles, both in the street and on the sidewalks.

As he came to a stop sign at the bottom of the hill, he noticed an elegant hotel to his left, The Pearl. The Pearl, as he would discover, was a four star boutique-style hotel known for its chic guest rooms tastefully decorated with artwork from local artists. The white and black paint covering its walls and balconies were just as unique and inviting as the rest of the street. An interesting name for a hotel, Ethan thought, and decided he would have to find time to satisfy his curiosity and check it out before he left.

Turning left off Main Street, Ethan continued a short distance before turning back to the right onto Hope Town Lane, then arriving at his house for the week. This was going to be a great place to relax for a few days, Ethan thought, as he pulled into the garage on the first floor.

Once Ethan made his way up the stairs from the garage and into the house, he was completely floored. He was overwhelmed with a spacious four-bedroom home with a large great room and massive kitchen. There was also a luxurious master bedroom, complete with its own master bath. In addition, there were three other bedrooms and two more full baths, as well as a half bath. The home had to be at least thirty-five hundred square feet and could easily accommodate six to eight people, Ethan thought.

Deep brown hardwood floors ran throughout the house except for the kitchen and bathrooms, and they shined brightly with the reflection of the afternoon sun. In the kitchen and bathrooms, large white ceramic tiles were used and served to break up the hardwood floors and add a touch of elegance. There was also a fully stocked wet bar complete with wines from several countries.

The home was decorated by someone with expensive and sophisticated taste, Ethan decided. The interior had a European and Mediterranean décor, and the artwork, vases, and furniture all appeared to Ethan to be French, Italian, or Greek.

As Ethan then ventured onto the second floor deck, he was breathless at the view. The home faced the Gulf of Mexico, and it was just steps from the boardwalk leading to the beach. He estimated it would take no more than two minutes and he could be on the beach. To his surprise, he looked below from the deck only to see a small private swimming pool for the home directly beneath him. Awesome, Ethan thought. I can't wait to take a dip in there tomorrow, he continued thinking.

After surveying the home and all its amenities, he was impressed beyond words by both its size and the décor. The fine paintings and pictures lining the walls were intriguing to look at, as were the elegant vases and numerous books scattered throughout the house. There was also a fully stocked refrigerator and pantry. This would be a great place for a honeymoon, Ethan thought.

Just then Ethan caught himself daydreaming and wondered where in the world that last thought had come from. He wasn't even dating someone, let alone engaged, he mused. "Why would one of my first thoughts of this place be it being an ideal honeymoon spot? How could I think that when I haven't dated someone in three years? And why would I even have a thought of marriage when the idea of simply dating someone makes me sick?" Ethan muttered aloud to himself.

The questions again took over his analytical mind and thoughts. Pushing away the questions, Ethan brought himself out of his thoughts. He put his luggage in the bedroom and then decided to check out the refrigerator.

After finding some fresh pineapple and green tea in the refrigerator, Ethan made his way to one of the many windows. This window in particular overlooked the western green, and from it he could also see the adjoining homes. The western green was a spacious grass area where kids played and rode bikes. He could see children running, laughing, playing games, and in general enjoying life.

As he continued to gaze out the window, he noticed all the homes were side by side, yet didn't appear crowded. Just like the town square and the town itself, everything seemed to blend and meld together so naturally.

He then made his way back to the second story deck. Ethan decided this would be a great place to unwind each evening with a glass of chardonnay and enjoy the breaking waves and beach and watch the world go by. This is the perfect location for me to relax this week, Ethan thought. As much as he had fought the idea of a vacation with Willie, he was now grateful to be here and in this house. Ethan decided he owed Willie a huge favor and would have to make it up to him when he returned to Valdosta.

After surveying the house, Ethan determined his next order of business was to unpack and put away all of his clothes so he would have that task over and done with. Within thirty minutes Ethan's car was unloaded and all of his clothes and personal effects put away.

Now that he was unpacked, he was overcome by intense hunger. He decided to explore the town briefly, and then stop by Wild Olives, a bistro on the north side of Barrett Square, for a quick bite to eat. There was just something about the name that piqued his interest when he saw it on his drive in.

By the time he'd finished eating, then exploring Rosemary Beach on foot, he returned to the house and discovered it was well after nine o'clock. Ethan decided to officially start his vacation and opened a bottle of chardonnay from the bar. He poured himself a glass and moved onto the deck to sit and relax. Darkness had now overtaken Rosemary Beach.

As Ethan gazed around this replica Austrian village, he could see the gas streetlights flickering along each street, lighting the way for those venturing out. He could hear the sounds of children laughing, running in the dark, and playing hide and seek and other games. He could also barely hear the sound of a guitar strumming a Jimmy Buffet tune from one of the local main street restaurants just around the corner.

Located to his right was The Pearl hotel. The lights from it were shining brightly against the darkness, and the sounds of its customers on the rooftop bar making merry and enjoying each other's company were muffled but audible. The gulf waters coming ashore could be heard robustly breaking against the sand just one hundred feet in front of the deck. The wind was blowing gently but steadily to keep the temperature cool and inviting. It was a perfect evening to sit back and relax, Ethan felt.

Ethan finished his wine and made his way back inside for a refill. He poured one more glass of chardonnay and returned to the deck to let the sounds, the breeze, and the sights be absorbed by his mind and body for just a little while longer.

A second glass of chardonnay in one night was unusual for him, but not because he feared getting drunk. Quite the opposite was true, as his body had tremendous alcohol tolerance. No, it was all the sugar and calories that wine contained that prevented him from enjoying it more. How could he maintain that chiseled physique if he gave in to drinking three or four glasses of wine in a night? Ethan had determined.

After another thirty minutes or so of soaking up the ocean and Rosemary Beach's evening atmosphere, he decided to head to bed. He needed to review earnings reports first thing in the morning so that he could spend the rest of the day relaxing. After he changed into comfortable shorts and a T-shirt, Ethan lay down in the spacious California king bed and immediately drifted off to sleep for the night.

The next morning Ethan slept in until eight, which was unusual for him. As he got out of bed he decided that between all the driving yesterday and the stress and late night with Willie, all the sleep he had gotten last night was long overdue and necessary to recharge his batteries.

After he ate a modest breakfast, he changed into his workout clothes. He didn't see a gym within the town or town square, so he drove back out to Back Beach Road and found one. It was higher priced than he was used to in Valdosta, but the weights, cardio equipment, and Olympic swimming pool were much nicer than his gym back home. Ethan finished his typical Wednesday workout, came back to the house, showered, and then began to pore himself straight into reviewing the earnings reports.

He became engrossed in the paperwork, and, before he knew it, he had reviewed the information for five of the new companies he was interested in. He had also made several pages of notes and comments. In the process, he had allowed five hours to pass by. "Oh no, I've almost let the day get away from me, working on my vacation," Ethan mumbled to himself.

Not wanting to let any more of the day go to waste, Ethan headed out on foot to explore more of the town and town square. It was a lovely day, with the temperature in the low eighties, the wind gently blowing, and the sun bright and high in the sky. He strolled down the paver-lined sidewalks and in and out of all of the shops along the way. The street and its surroundings erased from his mind all the earnings reports and Willie's condition and odd behavior. Everything he had been worrying about fell by the wayside.

In the town, Ethan managed to find a few souvenirs for Willie and Ann and even found a few items for himself. He glanced down at his watch and was shocked to see it was seven-thirty. Where had the time gone? Ethan wondered. It seems like I just started walking around an hour ago, he thought.

By this time Ethan had grown quite hungry from all the walking in town. He estimated he must have traveled at least two miles that day between shopping in all the stores and strolling through the neighborhoods and admiring all of the homes in the planned development.

As he headed down the hill toward The Pearl hotel and his house, he came to Edward's Restaurant. This was the place where he had heard the guitar playing the night before, and the same artist was playing again tonight. Ethan glanced at the menu on the street, and between it, the music, and laid-back atmosphere, he decided to give the place a try.

The weather that night was ideal, so he asked for and secured the last vacant table on the sidewalk. As he sat down and looked around at the architecture, he felt like he was a thousand miles from home and all things familiar. Ethan, now starving, became absorbed in the menu and quickly made his selection. A ribeye steak and baked potato would do nicely, he decided. This would be enough food to satisfy his hunger without blowing his diet wide open, he thought. A petite waitress with long red hair and a pleasant manner then appeared and asked "Good evening. Can I start you off with a drink tonight?"

Ethan smiled in return to the waitress and said "Yes, I'd like a glass of your house chardonnay. Also, I think I'm ready to order too. I'd like the ribeye steak with a baked potato."

"Certainly sir," the waitress said while smiling. She then leaned over in front of him to gather the menu intentionally revealing her considerable cleavage and said with a flirtatious grin, "Is there anything else I can get for you?"

"No, I think that will be it," Ethan responded with a smile. He knew she was trying to flirt with him. However, she was half his age and he was only interested in relaxing this next week.

I'll get that order in for you right away and hurry back with your wine," she replied with yet another flirty smile and a wink.

She then gathered the menu, and soon returned with a tall glass of chardonnay. This was a great way to end the evening, Ethan thought, with a smile of contentment beaming across his well-tanned faced.

As Ethan enjoyed his wine and was observing all the people on the busy street, suddenly his attention was drawn to his left. There, gliding down the hill, was the most beautiful woman he had ever seen. She was average height and had a perfectly curved body and the face of a goddess, which he could not look away from. Ethan was immediately in a trance.

He'd seen many beautiful women in his day, especially since his divorce, but none ever held his attention. *This* woman captivated him. Her long, flowing dark brown hair gently bounced up and down from her graceful gait in the black high heels she was floating down the sidewalk in. Her stride was smooth and elegant with each passing step. He could even pick up the clicking sound of her heels as they struck the pavers.

The black cocktail dress the woman wore molded to her perfect figure and subtly revealed every curve of her sexy body. The dress gently danced around her frame with each fluid stride. Her light tan complexion, completely without wrinkles, appeared so soft and supple. Ethan could also see her rich, full lips even from a distance, with light red lipstick inviting him to come kiss her, he thought. Then there were those eyes, those gorgeous, deep brown eyes. Even from fifteen yards across the street he couldn't miss them. They were mesmerizing and so trusting. She was an angel from heaven, he decided.

"I must be seeing things," Ethan stuttered quietly to himself, still unable to look away from her. This was the most alluring woman he'd ever seen, and he couldn't take his eyes off her. Had she been watching him, she would no doubt have run for her life, fearing he must be a stalker to stare her down like that, Ethan thought, yet he couldn't stop gazing at her.

As she made her way down the street and was almost directly across from Ethan, she glanced up and looked across the narrow thoroughfare directly at him. For a moment Ethan lost his breath, and his heart seemed to stop. She instantly had a power over him just by looking at him, then just as quickly, she turned back to gaze in front of her and continued her glide down the street. In an instant, she was gone.

After a minute or two had passed, Ethan came out of his trance, but was left feeling like a Star Trek alien that Mr. Spock had performed a mind meld on. His brain was mush, and all he could think about was her. After a few more minutes of dreaming about her and replaying what he saw, he slowly began to regain his mind and emotions. Even though he'd never met her, she somehow seemed familiar to Ethan.

I have to meet her, he thought, and suddenly Ethan jumped up, left his wine and food, which had just arrived, and scoured the western green and nearby streets and walkways searching for her. He frantically scanned the area, but to no avail. She was gone. Just that quickly she had walked into and out of his life. He guessed he would probably never see her again.

Once Ethan had spent about ten minutes of searching, he realized he had abandoned his meal and quickly made his way back to his table to eat. What am I doing chasing her down? Did she even see or notice me? Wouldn't she think I was crazy if I had been able to find her? The questions ran through his mind. She had looked right at him and didn't smile or wave or acknowledge his presence. Ethan decided she probably never saw him. He was invisible to her, he reasoned.

Ordinarily, being unnoticed by a woman wouldn't cause Ethan a minute's worry, but *she* was different. Her whole aura was different. She was so beautiful, yet projected a sense of trust like no one he had ever seen, Ethan believed. Finally, after another ten minutes of daydreaming about her, Ethan returned to the present, finished his meal, and paid the check.

As he walked back to the house, his rational mind took over his thoughts. He must have just been tipsy from drinking the chardonnay too quickly on an empty stomach, Ethan mused. The wine just made her seem prettier than she was, he continued rationalizing. She hadn't noticed him when she passed by. Besides, she couldn't be trusted anyway Ethan felt. He couldn't trust any woman after what Emma had done to him, he continued thinking.

In the morning the wine will have worn off, and all of this will have passed, Ethan surmised, as he entered the house and lay down in his bed. Instantly, he drifted off to sleep with his mind was now free from pondering about this beautiful woman.

Chapter Six

HE NEXT DAY brought the same routine for Ethan as the day before. He rose at eight and immediately went to work out, then returned home. He then immersed himself into reviewing the earnings reports once again. Today, however, he kept much better track of time and spent only three hours working and stopped just after lunch. Weary from the tedious review of the reports and fed up with the solitude and isolation yesterday, he decided to venture to the beach today.

It was just a short walk to the whitewashed boardwalk, then to the waves rolling into the surf. As Ethan strolled down the wood planks, he noticed green and white umbrellas and chairs lining the beach and decided he would rent one for the day.

After paying the fee, he made his way to his umbrella with a small cooler in hand. Refreshments would make the afternoon pass more smoothly, Ethan thought. After all, he was on vacation and needed to relax. A week of drinking a few extra glasses of chardonnay wouldn't hurt him or his physique, he rationalized. He could always work out that much harder when he returned to the grind back in Valdosta, he felt.

Rosemary Beach, it seemed, was already weaving a spell of relaxation on him that was a new experience for Ethan. He put down his cooler and laid a towel over the chair, and as he sat down, he spoke to an older couple immediately to his left. "Good afternoon. It's a great day to be on the beach, isn't it," Ethan said warmly in his South Georgia drawl.

"Good afternoon, kid. Yes, it's a great day for the beach and for a few refreshments," said the man as he gently raised a beer.

"I'd have to agree with that, for sure. I'm Ethan Phillips, by the way," Ethan countered with a gentle, warm smile across his face as he extended his hand to shake.

"Nice to meet you, Ethan Phillips. My name is Michael Fredericks, and this lovely lady to my left is my wife, Janine," Michael said in a hospitable tone. "We're from New York, well that is, we live and work in New York. I'm originally from Topeka, Kansas," Michael added.

"And I'm from Dallas, Texas. Big D, I call it," Janine chimed in with that unmistakable Texas twang. "We love coming down here every chance we get. It's just so peaceful and relaxin'," Janine continued. "You here for business or pleasure, sweetie?" Janine asked curiously.

"It's definitely pleasure. It's my first vacation in over three years. It's long overdue, I think," Ethan replied.

"I should say so, sweetie. Everyone needs to cut loose, relax, and kick up their boots every now and then just to keep their sanity," Janine added.

"That's what my good friend tells me all the time, and I guess I'm finally taking his advice," Ethan replied, now truly believing that statement, thanks to Rosemary Beach.

"So are you down here alone, Ethan?" Janine asked.

"Why don't you just jump right into the man's personal life, Janine?" Michael blurted out. Ethan could see he was visibly exasperated his wife had asked so bold a question to someone she just met. Ethan took it all in stride, though.

"It's okay, Michael," Ethan added reassuringly. "Yes, ma'am, I'm here alone this week. I've been divorced now for about three years," Ethan replied, then felt odd that he just shared that information with total strangers. He rarely mentioned his divorce, but somehow Michael and Janine seemed to put him at ease.

"Well, honey, you're too good lookin' to be at Rosemary Beach all by yourself; I can tell you that! This is one of the most romantic places on the planet, and it's a shame you're here wastin' it alone," Janine replied in her Texas accent. It was clear to Ethan that she was a woman who spoke what was on her mind, but did so in a way that wasn't offensive.

"There you go offering unsolicited advice again, Janine. You're going to make Ethan wish he hadn't sat beside us," Michael added with Ethan picking up on an elevated level of concern in his voice this time. Ethan could see Michael was frustrated with Janine's comments.

"It's no big deal. I'm not bothered by it. Janine is probably right," Ethan added reassuringly, trying to prevent Michael from getting upset further. "By the way, I'm from Valdosta, Georgia, but you've probably never heard of it and have no idea where that is," Ethan added, trying to change the subject and keep Michael and Janine from arguing.

"Really! That's a huge coincidence. One of my best friends from college lives in Valdosta and is a cardiologist there. His name is Karl Johannsen. Maybe you've heard of him?" Michael replied. Michael seemed to Ethan to be shocked to meet someone from the same town Karl lived in.

"Are you serious?" Ethan questioned, with surprise on his face. "Dr. Johannsen is an investor in a small hedge fund I manage for a group of local investors in Valdosta, and he also just operated on my best friend, Willie Francesco, before I came here," Ethan added.

"That's amazing! I just talked to Karl last week, and he has told me all about Willie. He thinks the world of both him and Ann," Michael responded and it appeared to Ethan he was elated to have made a connection to his good friend, Karl.

"And Karl's wife, Eva, makes the best homemade brownies," Janine interrupted. Ethan could already tell that she had a habit of trying to change the direction of the conversation and usually succeeded, at least, temporarily. "In fact, just about everything she cooks is delicious. We eat with them anytime we visit," Janine continued.

"So you've visited Valdosta then?" Ethan questioned.

"We sure have, sweetie. Several times. We usually stop by there after comin' here each year," Janine replied.

"It's incredible that you know Dr. Johannsen, and not only know Valdosta but have visited there," Ethan said, stunned at the likelihood of meeting people from so far away who knew people from where he lived and had visited his hometown.

"They're really good friends and have been for both Janine and me for too many years to count," Michael added. Ethan could sense the obvious affection Michael had for Karl and Eva.

"When I get back home, I'll have to let Karl and Eva know I've met y'all. They'll be shocked, too, I think," Ethan added.

Just then Ethan heard a loud cellphone ringing close by. It was Janine's phone chiming away, playing "Yellow Rose of Texas" and could easily be heard for over twenty feet. "Hey, sweetie. What's up?" Janine answered, using words like "sweetie" and "honey" interchangeably with people's names. "What? Aw crap, you've got to be kiddin' me!" Janine blurted out, clearly frustrated.

Ethan then observed the people on the beach within the sound of her voice smile and chuckle under their breath at her comment. "Okay, we'll be there in just a few minutes. Don't worry about botherin' us; it's alright, sweetie. We'll see you in a few. Bye," Janine added.

"What's the matter?" asked Michael. Ethan sensed worry in his voice.

"It's Anna. She needs us to come watch the baby while she runs up to the pharmacy to get a prescription filled. Her sinuses are drivin' her nuts, and she's run out of her medicine," Janine replied.

"Okay, honey. We'll head on back then. Ethan, I hate we can't stay and continue our conversation, but we better go see about our daughter, Anna, and the baby. It was great meeting you and chatting," Michael said, smiling.

"It's alright. I completely understand. I've very much enjoyed talking with you and Janine, as well," Ethan replied, grateful to have had contact with such nice people today.

"Here's my card, kid," Michael said as he handed Ethan a shiny business card. "Call us if you want to have dinner one night while you're here, and maybe we'll see you more here on the beach, too," Michael added.

"Thanks, Michael. I'll definitely keep that in mind. I've enjoyed meeting you both, and I hope Anna will be okay," Ethan responded with sincerity and concern.

"Thanks; talk to you soon," Michael replied as Ethan watched him finish loading their beach bag.

"Goodbye, sweetie. Take care, and I'll be on the lookout for a date for ya!" Janine waved and yelled over her shoulder as she headed toward the boardwalk.

Oh, great. That's all I need, a blind date down here, Ethan thought. No doubt Janine was filling in for Willie in his absence, Ethan decided, and now managed a small chuckle.

For the next few hours Ethan continued to relax and sip on the wine he'd brought down to the beach with him in the cooler. He reflected on his new-found friends and the conversation. It was such an incredible coincidence to meet people here who lived in New York, but were best friends with the doctor in Valdosta who had saved his best friend's life. They were nice people, and he felt like he made an instant connection with them, just as he had with Willie. It was so strange to just happen upon them at the beach and for them to know Karl so well. Perhaps it was the wine, but for now, it just seemed like too many coincidences to continue to think about at the moment.

Ethan turned his attention to watching the surf and all the kids and adults having fun and soaking in the relaxation that the ocean brought. His mind now unavoidably drifted back to the woman he saw yesterday. He replayed over and over in his mind her brief appearance. She was so beautiful, yet there was something else about her that captivated him, but he couldn't put his finger on it. Where was she right now? Would he see her again? Would he get to speak to her? Most important, was she married? In his trance yesterday, Ethan had completely forgotten to notice if she was wearing a ring.

Suddenly, out of nowhere, his rational, analytic mind assumed control of his thoughts. You don't need to waste any time thinking about her. She's probably married, and after all, she didn't even notice you yesterday, so you obviously made no impression on her. Remember, she can't be trusted and will only let you down later. These were Ethan's thoughts now, and they seemed easier for him to deal with, quite honestly.

His rational, analytic side was safe and comfortable and an area he had lived in the last three years. These thoughts about the woman he saw were triggering other feelings inside him that he didn't know how to process and handle.

All of his thoughts and daydreaming had nearly let the afternoon completely pass by. It was almost six o'clock now, and Ethan packed his cooler and went back to his house to shower, mill around town, then eat.

The water from the shower head felt so soothing and relaxing as it washed away the salty air and sunscreen from his bronzed skin. The warm water covered him like a blanket and brought him back to a state of relaxation. Ethan quickly shampooed and bathed, then just let the water fall gently over his head like a warm South Georgia summer rain. The steady stream helped him feel recharged and alive again and also washed away some of the lingering effects of his afternoon wine.

He then finished his shower and got dressed. He slipped on a mint green pullover shirt and khaki shorts and stepped into his sandals. Ethan looked sharp with the pale green shirt contrasting his dark brown complexion. His muscular chest and arms were subtly bulging inside the shirt. His fit physique was difficult to hide, and he did get some satisfaction from tastefully displaying to the world all the hard work he put into his body's appearance.

By now it was seven o'clock and, dressed and out the door, Ethan drifted around town trying to decide where to eat tonight. There were several options nearby, and he strolled and scanned each menu trying to make a decision. Ethan decided to give Restaurant Paradis a try tonight. It seemed to him to be an elegant, classy restaurant, and the outdoor menu had several entrees that were appealing. He went inside to get a table and finish the day with a nice meal.

"Yes, sir. Can I help you?" the maître d asked politely.

"Yes. I'd like a table for one," Ethan replied.

"I'm sorry, sir, but our last small table was just taken. I would expect it will be about thirty minutes before we have an opening. Would you like to wait at the bar or outside, perhaps?" the maître d asked, trying to accommodate Ethan as best he could.

"I'll just wait outside, if that's okay?" Ethan inquired.

"Yes, sir, that will be fine. We'll call you when the table is ready."

Summer Davis had just finished showering and getting dressed and was putting on the finishing touches of her makeup. The red sundress covered her lightly tanned body and fit like a glove, flattering her perfect figure tastefully. She always dressed well, and tonight was no exception.

Summer felt like she might have dressed a little too formally for her stroll around town the previous night in her black cocktail dress and high heels. I don't know why I'm getting all dressed up again, she thought. There's just not any good men left out there who are romantic and know how to treat a woman and her son, Summer thought almost hopelessly. Well, I can at least have a great meal and go on a date with my precious little man, she decided.

Summer was staying at Rosemary Beach, too, in the flats across the street from the beach. She had discovered the town through some friends of her sister several years ago and immediately fell in love with the area. Summer was here on her annual summer vacation with her son, Jake. Jake was twelve going on twenty, but the two of them got along fabulously, and she enjoyed it so much when he stayed with her. They loved each other very much and had formed a lasting mother-son bond.

Summer made a nice living as an event planner in Thomasville, Georgia, but found herself also coordinating events in surrounding towns to make a decent living for the two of them. Life hadn't been easy since her divorce, but she was committed to building a new life for herself and Jake, and by all accounts, she had succeeded.

Her thoughts were suddenly interrupted. "Hey, Mom, Chad from next door just came by and wants to know if I can eat with his family tonight and go look for crabs on the beach after we eat," Jake asked hopefully.

"No, baby. I was going to take you out to eat tonight since we ate in the condo last night," Summer responded, hoping the lure of eating out would sway Jake.

"Aw, Mom. Can't we eat out another night?" Jake pleaded.

"Well, I guess we could, baby, but I was really wanting to take you some place nice tonight. You know, a date with my favorite little man," Summer replied with a gleam in her eye and smiling widely.

"Please, Mom, pretty please," Jake continued to plead. "Chad has his X-box here, and he's getting Toby, Chance, and Jacob to come, too. And we're gonna play a game of kickball before we go crabbing" Jake added. Summer could tell that Jake was hoping all of this information and his sorrowful pleas would be successful in swaying her decision.

Summer thought for a moment, and as difficult as it was to say yes, she decided he would have more fun tonight with the boys. Jake was reaching the age where he wanted to spend less and less time with her. She knew it was part of the natural order of things, but it was still hard for her to accept. "Okay, baby. That'll be fine. I want to go with you to Chad's house and talk with his parents first, though," Summer responded, hiding her disappointment at having to eat alone.

"No problemo, Mom. Let's go!" Jake yelled as he grabbed her hand and rushed her out the door to Chad's house.

Summer met Chad's parents at their condo and satisfied herself that Jake was in good hands, then returned to her flat. Now she couldn't decide what to do. Maybe I should just put on comfy clothes and stay in, she thought. No, I'm all dressed up, and I'm going to have a great meal and a nice glass of chardonnay, she convinced herself. There's no point in just sitting around here tonight. Jake will be with Chad until eleven o'clock, so there's no excuse not to get out and enjoy myself, Summer decided.

She made her way to the street and began the short walk to the town center. As she walked, she was trying to decide what she wanted to eat. The only thing that sounded good to her was a nice filet from Restaurant Paradis.

Chapter Seven

"MR. PHILLIPS, TABLE for one. Mr. Phillips, table for one," Sebastian Lawrence, the maître d at Restaurant Paradis, called out in a smooth and calming voice. Sebastian was tall, at six feet four inches and slightly heavy set with a shiny bald head and an expertly groomed black beard and mustache.

"Yes, here I am. I'm Mr. Phillips," Ethan offered anxiously.

"Sir, your table is now ready, and you can be seated. Please follow me," Sebastian politely responded, then promptly led Ethan to a cozy table for two in the corner of the restaurant. This would be the perfect place for his quiet little dinner tonight, Ethan thought, as he made his way to the table.

The restaurant was elegant and tastefully decorated on the inside. It had been difficult to tell from the appearance on the outside, but he now decided it had been well worth the wait. The chandeliers made from wine barrels were a particularly nice touch. The atmosphere was festive, primarily from the lounge, but not overly so. The interior of the restaurant reminded Ethan of the wine country he had visited in Italy. There were oil paintings lining the walls with scenes from different places in Italy, and the color of the walls and tables and chairs reminded Ethan of the old country he had visited as a teenager.

"I hope you enjoy your meal tonight," Sebastian politely added after seating Ethan, then he returned to the front of the restaurant.

Just then, his waiter for the evening came by and introduced himself.

"Good evening. My name is Vladimir. How can I serve tonight? You like a glass of wine or a drink?" he asked graciously, but in broken English.

"Good evening, Vladimir. My name is Ethan Phillips. Yes, I'd like a glass of wine. Bring me a glass of the house chardonnay, if you don't mind," Ethan replied.

"Yes, sir, coming right up. Please look over menu, and let me know if you have any questions. I recommend either the Gulf Coast snapper or cast iron filet," Vladimir offered with a smile.

"Thank you. I'll certainly think about that," Ethan said, smiling back at Vladimir. "Do I detect that you have an accent, Vladimir?" Ethan asked, knowing the answer to the question.

"Yes, sir. I'm from Georgia," Vladimir replied, smiling and Ethan sensed Vladimir was clearly proud of where he was from.

"Oh that's awesome. I'm from Georgia, too, but the U.S. state and not the country," Ethan added with a smile.

"Very good, Mr. Phillips. We have something in common," Vladimir responded. The bright smile he now had on his faced made it clear to Ethan that Vladimir was happy a customer had taken time to delve into his life.

"We do, indeed," Ethan quickly replied with an approving nod.

"We are comrades, so to speak. I'll be back with bread shortly, Mr. Phillips," Vladimir replied, smiling, and with that he retreated to his other customers, then into the kitchen.

Ethan soon had his wine and leaned back in his chair to enjoy both it and the surroundings. He observed this was a relaxing restaurant. It was a little more upscale than the night before, but still warm and inviting, just as Edward's had been. He was very impressed thus far with the dining options at Rosemary Beach.

As Ethan was enjoying the atmosphere, he caught a glimpse of a couple to his right. They were totally engrossed in conversation with each other and laughing and smiling repeatedly. Seeing them caused his mind to drift back again to the mystery woman from yesterday. Who in the world was she? Did she live here in Rosemary Beach, or was she just visiting? Would he see her again before he left and be able to meet her? The same questions leapt from his brain just as they always seemed to when he was deep in thought.

She was so beautiful, but it was more than that to Ethan. Pretty women he had seen many, many times, but there was something else about her that caused him to continue thinking about her and want so badly to meet her. It was frustrating to continue dreaming about her, Ethan thought. Oh well, he decided, it was nice to just have been able to see a woman so captivating, and he resumed soaking in the atmosphere and enjoying his wine.

ఎస్

Summer crossed 30A and was soon at Restaurant Paradis. This walk would get kind of sweaty in the middle of summer, she thought. It was a cool evening with a soft breeze that had provided her ample comfort during the walk. Once Summer reached the restaurant, she quickly found her friend, Sebastian, the maître d.

"Well, hello, Summer, darling! It's just fabulous to see you again!" Sebastian said warmly and affectionately and Summer noticed him reach his arms out wide to give his good friend a big hug and a kiss on each cheek.

Summer had known Sebastian for over three years. She had met him on one of her trips to Rosemary Beach, and they instantly connected and became fast friends. Sebastian had subsequently asked Summer to plan his and his partner Eric Williams' reception in Rosemary Beach for their union last year. Summer did so, and it was a grand event. Since that event, every time Summer would see Sebastian he would thank her repeatedly.

"Hey, Sebastian! How are you?" Summer replied, happy to see her good friend once again.

"Honey, I'm living the dream; what are you talking about?" Sebastian replied, waving and snapping his fingers in excitement. Summer could see he was obviously happy with his life.

"That's awesome. I knew the two of you were a match. I enjoyed planning your reception last year. I think that's been my best event yet. I've put pictures of it all over my website for publicity. I hope that was okay?" Summer asked cautiously, but knowing both Sebastian and Eric didn't care.

"Shoot, you go right ahead, honey. That's the least we can do to show our thanks for that posh soiree you planned for us!" Sebastian added with his usual smile.

"Thank you," Summer calmly responded with an equally big smile. "How is Eric, by the way?" Summer questioned.

"Honey, he's fabulous. We've been working on finishing our pool house. You'll have to come over for martinis and see it when we get done," Sebastian added excitedly with a wave and a smile.

"I'm so glad. I'm sure it'll be gorgeous when you finish it," Summer went on to say.

"So, do you need a table tonight, honey?" Sebastian asked curiously.

"Yes, I do, if you have one. I hate I'm getting here so late, but Jake threw me a curveball just before we were about to leave and wanted to eat with a friend. So, I had to get him squared away before I could come," Summer added, clearly frazzled and frustrated with arriving so late and without her son.

"Let me take a look, honey, and see what Sebastian can do," he replied and sprang inside to survey his tables. As Summer was waiting, she began thinking about the filet she would like to have tonight. She was so hungry and had her heart set on it. She hoped Sebastian could find her a table. Just then she saw him come breezing back outside to update her.

"Honey, I just used my last free table and I'm full tonight. I've got reservations now until we close, but I have an idea for you, boo," Sebastian said, raising his eyebrows and giving a wry smile at the same time.

"You look like you're up to something, Sebastian. What is it?" Summer replied dryly with concern in her voice. She could tell he had something up his sleeve and the Lord only knows what it was, she worried.

"Sweetie, you're no bar fly, so the lounge is out, but I do have one of my tables for two with this delicious-looking man eating alone. I think you should eat with him. And no, he's not married. I've already looked him up and down, honey; trust me," Sebastian said. Summer could easily see the gleam in his eye when he said that.

"I don't know, Sebastian. Maybe," Summer said, clearly hesitant.

"Don't worry, honey, I'll keep an eye on you two lovebirds, and if you need me just give me a wink and I'll get you out of there pronto, sweetie," Sebastian said. Summer knew he was trying to assure her she would be just fine.

"In that case, okay. As long as he isn't rude, I might make that work long enough to eat. Can I see what he looks like first? I don't want to eat dinner with someone who's creepy or a stalker, ya know?" Summer said with a small smile and a hint of concern still across her face.

"Sure thing, honey. Follow me and we can check him out around the corner up here and see what you think," Sebastian said. Summer sensed excitement overtaking his voice.

"Okay, you lead the way," Summer replied, anxious about what this man would look like or act like. As she peered around the corner of the partition leading to the dining room, she gasped. It was *him*. The man in front of Edward's yesterday. She had seen him yesterday, but didn't want to stare. After all, a lady doesn't do such things, she believed.

She had seen him notice her and had hoped he would come across the street and introduce himself or at least casually wander in behind her at the Havana Café and say hello. Summer had even slowed her gait as she went by to make sure he saw her.

Snapping back to reality now, she couldn't help but stare at him. He was so handsome, so elegant looking, yet appearing gentle, caring, and approachable. Also, how could she not notice his body? He had tan arms, and his muscular chest pressed firmly against his shirt. She quickly decided she had never seen a man like this before.

"See, I told you, honey. Don't you just want to eat him up?" Sebastian asked, obvious to Summer he was satisfied with his matchmaking skills.

"Yes, I think that table will do nicely, Sebastian," Summer replied, still staring intently at the man.

"You got it, honey. Let me go get you in the door with him. Stay right here," Sebastian responded intently. "Summer, Summer," he asked.

Summer found herself in an obvious daydream. "Um, sorry. Yes, that's fine. I didn't hear you," she said, trying to cover for her daydreaming about the man.

"It's okay, boo, I'd be dreaming about what I was gonna do to him, too," Sebastian added with a wink and a smile and headed off to the table. She watched him walk quickly to the man's table.

"Sir, I have a small favor to ask. There's a lady here alone who's had a rough time getting here, and I'd like to ask if she can sit and eat with you, if that isn't too much of an imposition? I don't have any free tables the rest of the evening for her. She's a personal friend of mine and a lovely woman, and I think you would enjoy her company," Sebastian politely asked.

Ethan was caught off guard by Sebastian. He wasn't sure he'd ever been presented with such a request before. He had been deep in thought about the woman from yesterday and didn't expect such an interruption. After giving it brief consideration, Ethan replied, "Well, okay, I guess it'll be alright. Just as long as she isn't drunk, loud, or rude. That would kill the peaceful evening I'm having so far."

"Sir, trust me. I don't think any of that will be an issue with this lady. I'll bring her over shortly," Sebastian replied confidently.

What have I gotten myself into? Ethan thought. I'm always playing the part of the Good Samaritan. I hope I don't regret this.

Ethan watched as Sebastian disappeared to retrieve the woman, then reappeared and, to Ethan's complete surprise, the person following him to his table was *her*. Ethan was speechless. As she approached the table, Ethan somehow managed to stop staring at her and stand up to greet the gorgeous woman.

"Mr. Phillips, I'd like to introduce Ms. Davis. Ms. Davis, this is Mr. Phillips. I'd also like to thank you both for doing this for me. To show our thanks I will send over a complimentary bottle of wine. What would you like?" Sebastian offered. Ethan observed that Sebastian seemed to have a beaming smile across his face.

"A bottle of your best chardonnay, perhaps?" Ethan asked, raising his eyebrows as he smiled and asked Summer.

"Yes, um, that will do quite nicely, I think," Summer responded and Ethan noticed a small smile from her in return.

"Very well. I'll send it over immediately. Enjoy your evening, and thank you again," Sebastian offer and winked to Summer where only she could see. Sebastian then retreated and resumed his duties at the front of the restaurant.

"Let me get your chair for you, Ms. Davis," Ethan offered and made his way around and seated her.

"Thank you, Mr. Phillips," Summer replied cordially.

"Please, call me Ethan. My father was named Mr. Phillips," Ethan countered jokingly with a wry smile.

"Okay, Ethan. I'm Summer," she replied, smiling back at him.

⊷

"Summer? Well, that's a wonderful name. I'm glad to meet you," Ethan replied with the sincerity in his voice obvious to Summer.

"Same here. Have you already ordered, Ethan?" Summer asked, hoping the answer was no. She already was imagining how nice it would be to spend the evening eating and talking with this gorgeous man.

"Yes, I had just ordered a few minutes ago before you sat down. I just love a good steak, so I ordered the cast iron filet," Ethan responded.

"That sounds wonderful, actually. I think that's what I'm going to get, too," Summer said, smiling.

"Alright, let me get Vladimir's attention." With that, she observed Ethan raise his hand and motion to their waiter across the room.

She saw Vladimir walk over briskly and ask, "Yes, sir. What can I help you with?"

"The lady would like the cast iron filet for her entrée," Summer watched Ethan boldly assert to the waiter. She was caught off guard but pleased that he had just jumped in and placed her order without asking.

"Madam, you like anything else?" Vladimir asked.

"No, I think between that and the bread that will be plenty," Summer politely responded. Vladimir then quickly retreated to update the order with the kitchen.

"I didn't mean to blurt out your order like that. I hope I didn't offend you?" Ethan volunteered.

"Oh, no. It's okay, really. I had already said I wanted it, so it's fine," Summer added. She thought how nice it was for Ethan to place her order for her and flag down the waiter. She wasn't used to being treated with such respect and manners.

"Well, that's good. I'm glad I didn't," Ethan said. Summer noticed that he seemed unable to keep from smiling at her which pleased her greatly.

❧

Until their food arrived, they made small talk about the weather, where they were staying, the local restaurants, and how lovely Rosemary Beach was. Ethan had noticed Summer wasn't wearing a wedding ring, which thrilled him. He also made sure his ring hand and finger stayed clearly visible to Summer so that she could hopefully see he wasn't married either.

As they were talking, Ethan kept his eyes glued on Summer. Her eyes were like magnets drawing him in to her, and she was so very beautiful. Their food had now arrived, and they began eating. Their conversation drifted to a slightly deeper and more personal level.

"So, Summer, are you in Rosemary Beach for a while?" Ethan questioned, trying to ease into getting to know Summer more.

"Not as long as I'd like to be, that's for sure. I'm just here with my son for the week," Summer added, smiling.

"What's your son's name?" Ethan asked, keenly interested in her response.

"His name is Jake, and he's twelve but thinks he's twenty," Summer replied, now chuckling.

Ethan couldn't help but laugh, too. "That's a great name for a boy, very masculine. What does he like to do?" Ethan continued, wanting to know more about Jake.

"He just loves baseball. That's his favorite sport, but he likes basketball a lot, too, and like all kids his age, he's all about playing X-box," Summer replied. Ethan noticed that she rolled her eyes at the X-box comment. Ethan surmised that Summer could not relate to the fascination that young boys or adults, for that matter, had with an X-box.

"Ah, yes, most of my married friends back in Valdosta who have little boys make the same complaint. They have a time getting them off it and outside to play," Ethan told her, continuing to maintain eye contact with Summer. He just loved looking at those gorgeous brown eyes.

⏤

Summer, too, maintained eye contact as she was also attracted to Ethan and was flattered he had such an interest in her son. It was unusual for a man to be interested in Jake, she thought. Most of the men she had gone out with since her divorce had shown little interest in the boy.

"At least with Jake, he does like being outside a lot, so I usually don't have to fight with him to get him to go out and play. He usually gets tired of playing X-box after an hour or so," she replied, happy her son was like that.

"That's great. He sounds like a great kid. What do you think of the filet?" Ethan asked.

"Mine is wonderful. I just love a filet, and this place never disappoints. I love this chardonnay, too. You picked a good one. How's your steak?" Summer added with a wide smile.

"Thanks on the wine. I figured if I chose the best the house had, even I couldn't go wrong," Ethan said, laughing softly. "My steak is great. I think it's the best filet I've ever had," he added. "I'm glad I chose to come here tonight for both the food and the company," Ethan continued happily.

Summer was glad she had come, too. She was enjoying Ethan's company and conversation and, of course, she enjoyed just looking at him. Summer was enamored with Ethan. She found herself getting lost in his hazel eyes and would sneak passing glances at his arms, his chest, and how pretty his face was for a man. She was happy she had let Sebastian talk her into eating with this sexy man tonight.

"We've talked enough about me and Jake. How long are you here for?" Summer asked, now trying to change the subject from Ethan's last comment.

❧

"I'm down for a week. I'll go back next Thursday. My best friend from Valdosta is letting me use the house I'm staying in because he thinks I need a vacation," Ethan replied, and this time *he* was rolling *his* eyes.

"Oh, really? Is your job stressful or something?" Summer asked.

"It's really not too bad, I don't think. I enjoy it tremendously, but I think it's just the fact that I haven't had a vacation since my divorce," Ethan answered. As soon as he had said that he thought how surprised he was that he went ahead and shared that bit of information with Summer just as he had with Michael and Janine. What was that all about? he wondered. He barely knew Summer, but for some strange reason, he felt comfortable sharing that with her.

"Have you been divorced long? If you prefer not to say, it's okay," Summer asked.

"No, it's fine. I've been divorced a little over three years now. I started and manage a private hedge fund in Valdosta, and getting it off the ground and established has taken a lot of time the last several years. "What about you? How long have you been divorced? If you don't mind my asking, that is," Ethan questioned, wanting to know Summer's divorced status, also.

"Oh, it's alright. I've been divorced for five years," she responded without elaborating further. Ethan didn't press the issue, and their conversation then drifted back to chit chat until their meal was done and Vladimir brought the check to the table. "Let me get my part, Ethan," Summer offered eagerly. Ethan could see Summer wanted to pay her share. He assumed that she must be independent and didn't want him to feel obligated to pick up the check.

"Nonsense. You had dinner with me, and I'd like to get the check. The scintillating conversation with a beautiful woman was well worth it," Ethan added with a smile and a genuineness in his compliment to her.

"Thank you, Ethan. That's sweet of you," Summer replied. Ethan could instantly see a subtle red glow on her cheeks from blushing ever so slightly. Ethan paid for dinner, and they stood and left their table and the restaurant.

Chapter Eight

⁕————••◉••————⁕

AS ETHAN AND Summer stood outside the restaurant, they both were thinking they didn't want the night to end just yet. Each enjoyed the other's company, and they had both gone quite some time without good conversation with someone single from the opposite sex. "Would you like to walk around town and look at the houses? These gas streetlights are so interesting and light the way so well," Ethan asked hopefully.

"Yes, that would be nice. I have a little time before I need to get back to Jake," Summer replied.

"Great!" Ethan said, with excitement in his voice. "Let's take a walk, shall we?" he offered, extending his arm ahead of him with a gentle wave as he spoke.

They began walking slowly down the streets with the gas street lamps flickering brightly against the darkness of the night. The evening air was cool and the sounds of children laughing and playing could be heard in the distance as well as the occasional sounds of adults outside talking in many of the fenced courtyards the homes had in Rosemary Beach. The adults' conversations would fade in and out as they passed each home. The sky was clear and filled with stars everywhere they looked. The night was simply perfect, and Ethan decided the company was, too.

"Summer, what kind of work are you in, if you don't mind my asking?" Ethan probed.

"Oh, I don't care if you ask me that. I'm an event planner in Thomasville.

I try to only plan events locally for things like weddings, birthday parties, anniversaries, and stuff like that. But, to make ends meet, I also advertise and handle events in other places close by, like Valdosta, Albany, and Tallahassee, and on rare occasions here in Rosemary Beach. I love what I do, and being my own boss works so well with Jake and allowing me to make all of his school activities," Summer replied. Ethan observed her smiling brightly as she spoke about Jake.

"That's awesome. It's great you enjoy what you do, and that it allows you to attend all of his school activities, so that seems like a perfect fit. I know being there for him has to be important to you, and you have to like that flexibility self-employment provides," Ethan replied with a true sense of understanding and caring.

"The flexibility is wonderful, and you're right; it's important to him and me to go to his events. So you don't have any children?" Summer asked.

"No, unfortunately, I don't. I had always wanted one or two, but my ex-wife didn't. She stayed wrapped up in church and volunteer organization activities and just never seemed to want to put that on hold long enough to start a family," Ethan replied. Ethan could not hide the disappointment in his voice and facial expression as he was speaking.

"It sounds like your ex was a little on the selfish side, just like mine," Summer replied laughingly. Ethan could tell she was trying to lighten up the conversation.

"Well, you're right on the money there," Ethan said, laughing loudly. "I guess you still see your ex a lot since you have Jake together, don't you?" asked Ethan, curious about how often she saw her ex-husband.

"He has Jake every other weekend for now. He's so wrapped up in his own life with his work, his hobbies, and his girlfriend of the week that he doesn't make a lot of time for Jake," she replied. Ethan sensed the hurt and disappointment for her son and his lack of a real father in her voice.

"That's a shame. No offense, but a boy needs his father in his life, too. While I don't have kids, I did have a dad, and he spent a lot of time with me. In reflection I'm so glad he did, and I'm grateful for it. He made me a better man today because of it," Ethan added, proud of his father and his involvement in his life.

❧

They continued talking and laughing and connecting on so many topics. They had made a complete circle of the town, and by now the two of them had made their way back to the town square near where they started the walk. Summer glanced down at her watch. It was ten-thirty and the time had just flown by, she thought. "Well, I guess I better head back before Jake gets home," Summer said reluctantly.

Just then they were interrupted by a cellphone's ringing. It was Summer's. "Excuse me, Ethan," she said apologetically. "Hey, baby. What's up?" Summer asked her son, Jake.

"Hey, Mom. I'm here at Chad's house, and he asked me to spend the night. Can I, Mom? Please, please, please?" It was apparent to Summer that Jake was pleading because he desperately wanted more time to play X-box tonight and in the morning.

"I don't know, baby. What do Chad's parents have to say about this?" Summer questioned hesitantly.

"They said it's fine with them. It's their idea," Jake added hopefully. Summer could hear Chad's mother, whom she had met earlier, in the background yelling to Summer that it was okay if Jake stayed. He hadn't been any trouble, and they would love for him to spend the night, she heard Chad's mother call out. Summer had a good feeling about Chad's parents and about Jake's staying with them.

"Okay, that will be fine, but listen to me I want you home tomorrow morning by nine o'clock sharp. You got it?" Summer said to Jake with the concern of a mother who meant business and didn't want her son to wear out his welcome.

"Yeah! Okay, Mom, no problemo! Bye!" With that, Jake hung up.

∽

"Well, it looks like Jake is spending the night with his friend," Summer told Ethan with, to him, what seemed to be a mixture of sadness and happiness. The evening might not be over just yet after all, he hoped.

"Are you going to be alright with his spending the night with his friend tonight?" Ethan asked intently.

"Yeah, I think so. He was excited about it, and he'll be fine, but I'll miss him," Summer replied.

"I bet you will," Ethan added, sympathizing with her situation. "Since you have some time on your hands now, how about we stroll back down to Edward's and have one last glass of wine for the night? I'd like to talk with you some more, if you're up for it?" Ethan asked, hoping so much she would say yes.

"Sure! I'd like that, too," Summer said smiling brightly.

As they strolled down to Edward's, Ethan stole glances at her and reflected on the evening so far. The conversation between them had flowed so effortlessly, he thought. She was so easy to talk to, and he felt like he could talk about anything with her, yet they had just met. What was that all about? he questioned, and he could hardly take his eyes off her. Those trusting eyes . . . then there was the flowing brown hair, that sexy figure tastefully displayed in her red sun dress, and those thick, full lips glistening with lipstick. Red was a great color on her, he thought.

✧

For Summer's part, she was just as satisfied with the evening so far. She could not keep her eyes off Ethan either. She was enjoying a relaxing conversation with the most handsome man she'd ever met. He seemed sincere, laid back, genuine, and confident. He was just amazing, she thought.

They had now arrived at Edward's, and after securing a table for two on the sidewalk, Summer watched Ethan seat her, then himself. He's such a gentleman, too, she thought. A young blonde haired woman soon appeared to take their order. "What can I get for you tonight?" the waitress asked.

"I think I'll have a Beringer chardonnay, please," Summer chimed in.

"I'll have the same thing," Ethan said and Summer noticed him smile and nod approvingly at her for such a great selection. The waitress smiled, then left to get their wine. "I'd just like to say I've really enjoyed your company so far tonight. I know it wasn't something we planned, but I feel like it's been great," Ethan said. Summer was flattered by Ethan's boldness.

"I've enjoyed it, too, Ethan. It's been fun," Summer replied, smiling happily.

"Can I ask you a personal question?" Ethan ventured.

"Sure, as long as it isn't *too* personal," she playfully replied.

"How is it that a beautiful woman with a great career and a great son has gone five years without being swept away by Prince Charming?" Ethan asked. Summer noticed him changing the tone to a more serious one.

"Oh, that's easy. I haven't found Prince Charming, and to be honest, I haven't looked too hard. All of the men I've been out with, regardless of their age, have been so into themselves and only had a superficial interest in me. And they had little or no interest in Jake," Summer bluntly but politely replied to him.

"I see. I can't imagine a man not wanting to know all about you or your son, that's for sure," Ethan calmly responded.

"That's sweet, Ethan. Thank you. Can I ask you a personal question?" Summer added with a cautious and soft tone.

"That seems fair; go ahead," he replied.

"Alright. How does a handsome hedge fund manager who's polite, genuine, and a great conversationalist go three years without being snatched up by a sexy young woman?" Summer asked, wanting so much to know but hoping Ethan wouldn't be upset by the question.

"I guess I haven't been looking too hard, either. It's taken so much of my time to get the hedge fund established and off the ground that I'm only just now even able to think about dating," added Ethan.

The two continued to talk and enjoy their wine until their waitress informed them it was past closing time, and they apologized, but needed to close for the night. "I'm getting the wine this time," Summer insisted.

"Are you sure? I really don't mind," Ethan countered.

"No, it's the least I can do," she said happily. With that, Summer paid their check, and they began walking back up the paver-clad incline toward the town square.

✍

They each checked their phone for any messages and noticed it was eleven-thirty. "I guess I should be getting home. It's a good walk back to my flat," she said.

Sensing anxiety in her voice and wanting to be a gentleman and spend more time with her, Ethan offered, "I can walk you back, if you like. I'd feel better about your safety, and it's no trouble. I really don't mind."

"That would be nice if it isn't too much trouble?" she asked Ethan.

"It's no trouble at all," he said, smiling and gesturing ahead. The walk went by too quickly for him, just as the entire evening had. They arrived at Summer's flat and ascended the stairs to the front door.

Ethan was now facing her. He gazed into those deep brown eyes and was mesmerized once again and couldn't speak. There was silence between them. Ethan felt compelled to kiss her. He had just met her, and it wasn't even a planned date, but as he looked into her eyes, he felt he was supposed to kiss those full and inviting red lips.

He couldn't explain why, but he just had to kiss her. He would just have to chance her being offended and slapping him. Ethan felt like her eyes and lips were inviting him to kiss her. He promptly closed what little space there was between them and placed both hands gently on either side of her face. He then leaned in and softly kissed those wonderful lips.

He started by gently kissing both lips, then moving up slightly to kiss the upper, then lower lip, gently sucking on each as he moved to the other. His passion for her instantly started to build. Ethan then began gently French kissing Summer and rhythmically moved his tongue in unison with hers. She's a great kisser, he thought as his tongue weaved against hers, pausing briefly every minute or so just to take a breath. Their tongues glided gently together and stimulated even more passion inside him.

After what seemed like only a couple of minutes, Ethan paused and glanced at his watch. They had been kissing for fifteen minutes straight. What happened to the time? he wondered. He had become completely immersed in the pleasure and passion of the moment.

He paused to catch his breath and recover from the dizzy feeling he had. It seemed like to Ethan that Summer was just as dizzy as he was.

Summer offered, "Um, would you like to come in for one last glass of chardonnay?"

"Yes, that would be great!" Ethan responded, still a little short of breath from kissing her so intently.

They moved inside her flat, and he observed Summer offer, "I'll pour each of us a glass. It's not Beringer, so I hope it's okay?"

Ethan then replied, "I'm sure it will be fine. I haven't had too many bad glasses of chardonnay, you know?" He laughed as he made the comment.

Summer couldn't help but laugh, too, and added, "I know what you mean."

∽

They both made their way into the kitchen. Summer felt Ethan was staring at her intently. She looked up from pouring the wine and could see Ethan's eyes begging to kiss her. After she poured the wine, she watched Ethan ease over to her and this time place his arms on her hips and began kissing her again, now pressing his aroused body tightly against hers. Summer then pressed her voluptuous breasts against his rock hard chest. Their tongues moved together as one, just like two bodies writhing in unison in bed in the throes of passion.

She then gave in to the moment, enjoyed the kissing tremendously, and stood in the kitchen in a passionate embrace while the world and time itself seemed to stand still. She wasn't thinking about anything. Her mind was completely blank and fully engaged in feeling the pleasure coursing through her body.

They continued their kissing and paused only long enough to breathe. There they stood in the kitchen, with their sexy bodies pressed together, making out like horny teenagers with all the energy they had.

Summer could feel herself becoming immersed in the pleasure Ethan was giving her and quickly paused to take look away and take a sip of wine and cool down. She was afraid of what might happen next. She hoped Ethan would take her cue to cool down, which he did. She saw him then look down at his watch. It was now one o'clock.

"I guess we kind of got into kissing, didn't we? It's one o'clock already," Ethan questioned.

Summer was astonished so much time had flown by, and she could see that Ethan seemed just as surprised.

"Oh, wow! Yeah, I guess we did get a little carried away," Summer added.

"As much as I would like to stay and continue this, I know it's late, and you have your son coming home early in the morning. I've got to walk back to my house, too. I think I'm going to call it a night," Ethan said reluctantly.

"That's true. I hate we have to stop, too, but I do need a little sleep before Jake comes rolling in first thing this morning," Summer replied with her bright shining smile.

She walked Ethan to the front door, and just before he opened it to leave, she watched him turn and give her one last passionate kiss, then said, "I really enjoyed tonight, Summer. If you'd like, maybe I could call you and see if we can arrange to see each other more before we both leave?" Ethan asked.

"I'd like that very much, Ethan; here's my number. Feel free to call whenever," Summer eagerly offered after writing her number on a sticky note and handing it to him.

"Okay, I'll definitely do that. Here's my business card, and it has my cell number on it. That way you'll know it's me when I call or text. Goodnight, Summer Davis, and sweet dreams," Ethan told her. Summer sensed his voice was full of caring and sincerity.

"Goodnight, Ethan. I had a wonderful time," Summer replied, and with that, she closed her door. She then ran over to a nearby window and watched Ethan disappear into the night as he headed home.

As each of them lay in bed that night they felt that they had been swept into something they had totally no control over, and that thought didn't bother either of them. In fact, they both welcomed the idea of having met someone that captivated them so strongly. They both could not wait to see the other and continue what started so unexpectedly that night.

Chapter Nine

ETHAN WOKE THE next morning around nine. Having gone to bed late last night and combining that with the wine, he had slept later than usual. He wasn't hung over, but was still dragging from not sleeping quite as long as normal. Ethan followed his routine and ate breakfast, then was off to the gym.

During his workout, and on the drive back home, his thoughts kept returning to last night with Summer. He now had a name to go with that beautiful face, and he actually met her. He had an amazing time with her last night. She was so easy to talk to, she was beautiful, and she seemed genuine.

He could look at Summer and only Summer when he was with her; then there was what happened in her flat. Ethan's passion had taken over, and he kissed her as he had never kissed a woman before. He didn't plan it; it just happened.

Until seeing her two nights ago, he had no interest in even going on a date with a woman, much less spending all evening with one, then making out with her. Was he falling for her? How did she have such an almost magical power over him? Why did her beauty arouse him so greatly when so many others had not? Was Summer thinking about him this morning? Did she really enjoy their evening as much as he did? Once again the questions bombarded him, just as American B52 bombers carpet bombed the German landscape during World War II.

Once he arrived back home from the gym, he showered, then went straight to work on the earnings reports. He wanted to be done with them by one o'clock so that he could call Summer and hopefully see her again that day.

∽

"Mom, I'm home!" Jake yelled as he came barging into their flat at nine a.m. sharp. Summer heard him but wasn't awake enough yet to respond. Jake yelled once more. "Mom, Mom, I'm home, and I'm on time!"

Summer was just now barely awake with sleep still covering her eyes. She couldn't help but laugh, though, at Jake's last comment. "I'm in the bedroom, baby," Summer muttered in a groggy, half-asleep voice.

Just then Jake came charging through her bedroom door like a bull chasing a matador and jumped into her bed. "Did you hear me? I made it on time, Mom. Did ya notice?" Jake eagerly questioned her.

"Yes, I did. I'm so proud of you for being punctual, baby. How was your night and morning with Chad?" she asked curiously.

"It was great! He wants me to play with him some again today, too!" Jake said, Summer could hear his voice brimming with excitement.

"Well, we'll see about that, baby. We're on vacation together, so I *do* want you to spend some of it with me, young man," she said, hoping to shame him to want to be with her most of the day.

"Aw, Mom, we spend time together all the time. I just like playing with Chad while we're down here, that's all," Jake replied.

"Like I said, we'll see about that later," Summer remarked in a tone that meant it was time to leave the subject for now.

As Jake went into the living area and started watching television, Summer began the process of showering and getting ready. While she was getting ready, she couldn't stop thinking about Ethan and last night. She wondered for a second if it was just a dream, but then remembered the way he kissed her and how vivid the experience was, and she knew it was real. It *did* happen. She daydreamed about Ethan's body, his quiet confidence, his interest in her and Jake's life, his being such a gentleman, and, of course, those eyes. How could she forget them after they begged to be kissed by her?

Summer still wasn't sure how it all happened, but she was glad it did. She was almost giddy from the night with Ethan. I hope he calls me today, she thought. I can't wait to see him again and have him kiss me passionately again, she daydreamed hopefully. She wanted to have him squeeze her tightly in his arms once more and kiss her like she's the only woman in the world, just as he had done the previous night.

✍

It was almost one o'clock in the afternoon, and Ethan had finished combing through and making notes on the last of the earnings reports he wanted to review that day. The morning had been productive, and he felt like all of the companies were potential investment candidates. After setting down his legal pad, Ethan realized he hadn't followed up with Greta in a couple of days. He had gotten sidetracked by the Rosemary Beach aura and scenery, and, of course, by Summer. He decided to check in with her.

After dialing Greta she promptly picked up and answered. "Hello, Mr. Phillips. How is the vacation going?"

Ethan responded, "Hey, Greta. The vacation is going wonderfully. I'm sorry I haven't been in touch the last couple of days. I hope you haven't needed me for anything?" Ethan questioned, with concern in his voice.

"No, sir, it's been pretty quiet here since you left. Mr. Francesco had word sent to all the investors about moving the meeting, so that's taken care of. Also, since the meeting is being moved, I've held off on proceeding with the investor packet until you return," Greta went on to say in her typical business-as-usual, professional manner.

After her comments, Ethan realized he hadn't checked on Willie, either. What a terrible friend I am, he worried. He decided he would need to give him a call soon. His thoughts now returned to Greta, and he replied, "Okay, that sounds good. If you need me for anything just give me a call. I've gone through ten of the potential new companies to invest in and made some notes. I should have my notes finalized by the time I leave here, and you can type them after I get back."

Greta replied, "Yes, sir. I will call you if I need you. Enjoy yourself. Goodbye, Mr. Phillips."

Ethan then countered, "Thanks, Greta. Goodbye."

Once he enjoyed a quick lunch, Ethan couldn't wait any longer to give Summer a call. He strolled onto the balcony, and just as he was about to dial her number, he looked out onto the Western Green and saw a young couple entangled in an argument. While he was too far away to hear what they were saying, it was obvious they were extremely agitated with each other, and their yelling was unmistakable. They were speed walking back to wherever they were staying and fussing as they walked.

In an instant Ethan's mind flashed back to that horrible day he discovered Emma having her affair and the anger and argument it triggered. He relived the entire moment from coming home that day to storming off in tears. The picture of Emma and what he caught her doing was now brought back vividly from the far reaches of his mind, thanks to the arguing couple. This image of Emma almost made him sick to his stomach. His tone had immediately flipped from one of expectancy of seeing Summer again to one of sadness. A thick and heavy cloak of pain and hurt curled around his mind and body.

To try and cope with the pain, his logical, rational mind assumed control of his thoughts and reminded him of his pledge to never, ever trust another woman. Doing so, he reasoned, would protect him from heartache, hurt, and disappointment again. What am I doing? Ethan thought. I just met this woman, and already I'm infatuated with her and starting to fall for her.

That's just a recipe for disaster, and I need to just leave her alone, Ethan continued thinking. She'll just end up cheating on me and ripping my heart out. I've just been lonely and let myself get carried away with how beautiful she is, Ethan continued to muse.

He had now come full circle and decided to just leave Summer alone today. He felt like there was no point in risking being hurt again. He had fun last night, but that was simply where it had to end, Ethan concluded. He put his cellphone back down, loaded his cooler, and headed to the beach to relax and attempt to get Summer Davis off his mind.

Summer and Jake had enjoyed a fun-filled day of bike riding, bocce ball, and swimming at the pool. They had also managed to squeeze in a visit to the Sugar Shack for an ice cream cone. It was almost six o'clock in the evening now, and Summer was exhausted, even though, to her disappointment, young Jake was still full of energy. She had crashed on the couch to rest and watch a little television while Jake had gone to Chad's house to continue playing.

As she lay on the couch, she found herself in a state of confusion and disappointment. Why had she not heard from Ethan today? Did he not have a good time? Was he just not that into me? Summer wondered. After he left last night she would have bet every dollar she had that Ethan would have called today and long before now, but she hadn't received a call or text from him, and she was very disappointed she hadn't.

She worked through in her mind all the possibilities as to why he hadn't contacted her. He might have gotten tied up with his work today. He might have had a family emergency to attend to. He might be sick from the meal last night. Summer found herself rationalizing several explanations for why Ethan hadn't called.

Though all of these possibilities were plausible, it didn't change the fact that she hadn't heard from this man who had mesmerized her in just one evening. The exhaustion from the day spent with Jake now overtook her, and she drifted off to sleep on the couch to enjoy a much deserved nap.

❦

Ethan stayed on the beach all afternoon and had consumed several glasses of wine in the process. Though he tried, he was unable to use alcohol to erase Summer from his mind. He couldn't avoid reliving the wonderful evening they had the night before. A large part of him wanted to call her that very moment and arrange another date, but his logical, rational mind just wouldn't yield and let that happen.

After returning from the beach, he had showered and decided to stay in tonight and snack. He didn't feel like getting dressed and going to eat. He was completely drained from the sun and wine and wanted to eat a light dinner and go to bed early. He ate and watched an action movie on television, then crawled into bed. The last thought that ran through his mind before he drifted off to sleep was of Summer and what she was doing at that very moment, yet memories of his painful past wouldn't allow him to call her.

The next morning Ethan woke refreshed from the full night's sleep. Today he opted not to go to the gym, but instead to sweat out the wine from the previous day by running a few miles on the beach. Running wasn't his favorite cardio exercise, but he needed a change of pace. He decided the beautiful beach would provide a nice distraction to allow him to complete the run.

As he hit full stride on the sand, his thoughts inevitably came back to Summer. *I wish I knew she was different and wouldn't let me down*, Ethan contemplated as he ran. If she could only be trusted, he felt like she would be a wonderful woman to get to know better. She had so many good qualities and was so easy to talk to, he continued thinking.

Ethan continued his run and his obsession with thinking about Summer until he was finished and back at the Western Green. After he made his way into the house, he looked over at the bar in the kitchen and saw his cellphone. Ethan was so conflicted with his feelings for her. His logical mind was pressing him to play it safe, avoid her altogether, and prevent any hurt or disappointment she might bring.

His heart, however, craved to see Summer again. His heart and even his soul yearned for both her and the connection she brought. She had touched him so deeply in an instant, and as much as he wanted to, he couldn't drink this feeling away or simply ignore it.

After spending the entire morning caught up in this struggle in his mind of two diametrically opposed forces, he decided to pick up his phone and call her. It seemed his heart had prevailed in his inner conflict, and he chose to take a chance that she was everything he hoped she was and completely different from his ex-wife. As he picked up his cellphone to call her, the phone began ringing. The name Summer Davis flashed on his cellphone screen.

∽

Summer had slept like a rock the previous night, despite her evening nap. Jake had completely worn her out the previous day with all of his energy and activities. She had managed to corral Jake from Chad's house by eleven, and the two of them had slept the next morning until almost nine. She had prepared breakfast for them, then read the morning newspaper.

Jake had scarfed down his breakfast and retreated to his room to play X-box. Summer knew that Jake just loved to ride a bicycle and would undoubtedly want to ride today. She was also keenly aware that he thoroughly enjoyed beating her on one or beating her at anything, for that matter.

After she finished reading the newspaper and catching up on current events, she poured herself her final cup of coffee for the day and went out onto their balcony to enjoy it. As she sat on the balcony, she could only wonder what was going on with Ethan and why he hadn't called. In her mind it just didn't make sense that he hadn't called already. She felt like he was just as into her as she was with him. He seemed so sincere when he said he would call, and how could she possibly forget how he kissed her? She felt like Ethan was making love to her with his tongue, and his intensity and passion for her were unmistakable. The more she thought of him, the more she wanted to see him.

After about an hour of daydreaming about Ethan and their night together, she could take it no more. She came back inside, threw caution to the wind, picked up her phone and Ethan's business card, and gave him a call.

⌇

Ethan was in shock as he gazed at his ringing cell phone. It was just too weird that she called at the exact moment he was about to call her. Finally, after four rings, Ethan snapped out of his trance and answered. "Hey, Summer. It's good to hear from you."

Summer replied, "Hey, Ethan. I hope I didn't catch you at a bad time."

Ethan was now smiling from hearing her voice and said, "No, it's fine. I was just taking it easy after a morning run on the beach. How've you been?"

"I'm doing better today. Jake talked me into riding bikes, bocce ball, and several other things yesterday. He wore me out, but thanks to a nap yesterday and a good night's sleep, I'm back to normal. Well, at least as close to normal as I can get," Summer replied, chuckling as she made the last comment.

Ethan laughed too, and he said, "Wow, it sounds like you did have a busy day yesterday. Jake keeps you young, I guess."

Summer responded, "Yeah, that's one way of looking at it, I suppose." They continued to chat for another ten minutes about each of their activities the previous day until Summer suggested, "Listen, Jake and I are going to eat dinner later, and I was wondering if you wanted to join us. My treat."

Ethan found himself flattered that Summer had not only called him, but had also invited him to dinner. He reasoned she must have at least a passing interest in him to go to that trouble. Fighting off the grip his logical mind had over him, he then replied, "Sure. That would be great! What time are you thinking?"

"Wonderful! I'm not sure just yet on the time. Why don't I give you a call later this afternoon when I have a better idea?" she asked.

"Sure, that'll be fine. I'm going to the beach to relax for the afternoon, but I'll have my cellphone on me. Just give me a call when you see what you have going tonight," Ethan replied, clearly not offended that Summer didn't have all the details worked out. Ethan assumed that young Jake likely kept her schedule unpredictable.

"Okay, sounds like a plan. Talk to you later, Ethan. Goodbye," Summer responded, winding down the phone call so she could get back to Jake.

"Goodbye," he countered, and they each hung up.

Ethan spent the afternoon on the beach alternating between relaxing under the umbrella and occasionally taking brief dips in the cool Gulf of Mexico waters. The water was still chilly in May, but was tolerable after the initial shock had worn off after being in it for a few minutes. Again today Ethan didn't see Michael and Janine. No doubt they had other plans, most likely with their daughter, he decided. He had brought along his cooler again, so he enjoyed a little wine along with the sun and surf.

Time moved by quickly for Ethan, but his thoughts were still obsessed with Summer. He hoped they would have dinner tonight, and he couldn't wait to meet Jake. He sounded like such a neat kid to Ethan. As badly as he was trying, he couldn't get her out of his mind. She seemed so perfect to him. Everything about her entranced him. She was beautiful, smart, witty, humble, and most of all she seemed so true and genuine.

Having finished his supply of wine, he looked at his watch and saw it was almost six o'clock. Ethan had been bronzed even further from the afternoon Florida sun. He decided to call it a day and head back to his house to clean up for an evening meal and wait to hear from Summer.

"Jake, slow down! I'm not riding any faster!" Summer called out, exasperated with her son's pace.

"C'mon, Mom, you can do it! Last one to the beach is a rotten egg!" Jake yelled back. Summer could tell he was taunting her to try and outrun him on her bike.

"No way, Jose! I'm done riding for today. We've been biking for over three hours again, and I'm exhausted! There's no telling how many miles we've covered," Summer yelled to Jake as she was on the verge of complete exhaustion and was dying for a bottle of water and a couch to crash on. She had let Jake get the better of her again, it seemed.

"Aw, Mom, you're no fun! You're just scared I'll beat you!" Jake added.

Summer knew it was Jake's one last attempt to trick her into racing to the beach and extending his bike riding time. But, she was not taking the bait she decided.

"You'd definitely beat me in my condition. You've just about killed me today!" she replied, admitting defeat. They pedaled their way off 30A and back into their neighborhood. They reached their flat and parked their bikes in the bike rack. Their flat overlooked the St. Augustine Green common area, and as they pulled up, they both could see several boys playing kick ball on the lush grass.

"Jake, Jake! Where you been, man?" Chad yelled as Summer watched him sprint over to her and Jake.

"I've been racing my mom and beating her riding bikes. What ya doing?" Jake asked Chad while smiling brightly and gloating about his bicycle performance.

"We're playing kick ball right now. Hey, my Mom and Dad want to take us to eat hot dogs tonight and see a movie. Can ya come?" Chad asked with to Summer what seemed like almost an air of desperation. Summer could tell from his eyes and tone that he had missed his buddy Jake today and wanted to make up for lost time tonight.

"Chad, that's a lot on your parents again tonight. Are you sure it's okay with them?" Summer asked, concerned Chad might be freelancing on establishing their evening plans.

"It's fine, Ms. Davis. My Mom told me to ask Jake as soon as I saw you!" Chad told them.

"Let me talk with your mom first, alright?" Summer asked Chad hesitantly.

"Sure, she's right over there!" Chad replied enthusiastically.

Summer went over and discussed the evening plans with Chad's mother. Her name was Delores White, and her husband was named David, and they were from Louisiana. Delores had confirmed what Chad said and let Summer know how well behaved Jake was and how good he was for Chad. According to Delores Jake always exhibited good manners and would always listen to either she or David when they asked him to do something. He was a positive influence on Chad, and both Delores and David liked Jake, too.

Satisfied he wouldn't be a burden to them, Summer decided to let him go with them. Delores also asked if Jake could spend the night, and Summer agreed reluctantly, after some lobbying by Chad and Jake in front of Delores.

She had not yet mentioned Ethan to Jake, but had planned on doing so as they were getting ready for dinner. She had thought if she made it seem like inviting Ethan was a last minute thing and not a big deal that he wouldn't read too much into meeting him.

Well, Jake won't be with me again tonight and won't get to meet Ethan, but at least I'll have a handsome man to keep me company, she mused happily. With that thought she picked up her cellphone and called Ethan.

"Hello?" Ethan answered.

"Hey, Ethan. This is Summer. How's your afternoon been?" she asked, anxious to hear his reply.

"Hey, there! It's been great! I've been down at the beach most of the afternoon. I just got back to the house about twenty minutes ago, and was getting ready to shower," Ethan replied. "How was your afternoon with Jake? Did he wear you out again today?" he questioned, laughing as he did so.

"Well, he did just about wear me completely out, that's for sure. We biked for over three hours again, and my leg muscles are on fire," she responded with fatigue in her voice.

"Wow, it sounds like you had a great workout. So are you and Jake still up for dinner tonight?" Ethan offered. Summer could feel the expectation come through in his voice. It made her happy that Ethan was excited about meeting Jake.

"I'd like to see you, but I'm not sure I'm up to fighting the dinner crowd tonight. Jake has ditched me for Chad again, unfortunately, so he won't be joining us," Summer replied sadly as she was disappointed she wouldn't eat with Jake once again tonight.

"I'm sorry you don't have Jake. I was looking forward to meeting him, and I know you were hoping to spend more time with him tonight. The sun took a lot out of me today, so I'm a little tired, too. Why don't I just grill us something here at my house tonight?" Ethan asked Summer.

"That would be great, actually," she responded with excitement.

"Awesome! Why don't I drive over and pick you up at eight?" he asked.

"Sure, I'll be ready then. What do I need to bring?" she asked curiously.

"Your beauty and your great personality are all you'll need to bring tonight," Ethan answered. She knew he was attempting to flatter her and it was working.

Summer blushed slightly at the sound of his words and replied, "I don't know about that, Ethan, but I'll be ready at eight."

"Okay, see you then," Ethan replied.

Summer thought that Ethan seemed as happy and excited as she was about going on another date. She hoped that was the case and wished for another great night together.

Chapter Ten

ETHAN SCRAMBLED AROUND his house moving between getting dressed for his evening with Summer, rummaging through the refrigerator and pantry to see what food and cooking supplies were on hand, and making a list of what he needed to pick up from the grocery store.

After he managed to get all three tasks finished, he drove to Publix, the closest supermarket he knew of, and bought some fresh shrimp to grill and plump Idaho potatoes for baking, along with fresh broccoli and zucchini. For dessert he was serving his favorite, and he hoped Summer's, too, chocolate cake.

Ethan returned from the grocery store just in time to get everything out of the car, into the house, and ready to cook. Before he left to pick up Summer, he quickly surveyed the kitchen for anything he might have missed. Uh oh! He thought, what about wine? He looked in the wine rack and saw there were still two stocked bottles of chardonnay which would be enough for tonight. Satisfied he had everything he needed, Ethan made the short drive to get Summer.

❦

Summer had been extremely busy, also. While she was getting bathed and dressed, she also managed to get a bag packed for Jake to spend the night once again with Chad. A mother has to be able to multi-task, Summer thought to herself. Once Jake was all set and ready to go, she escorted him to the White's flat. As she dropped her son off, she briefly chatted with Delores just to make sure it wouldn't be an imposition for Jake to stay with them once again.

"Don't worry about a thing, Summer." Delores said with the utmost confidence. "Jake is an absolute dream to watch over, and he and Chad have such a good time. Jake is a great influence because he's so well behaved," she added with a beaming smile.

"Well, he better be!" Summer added, laughing.

"Oh, trust me; he is. Have a great night, and don't worry about Jake a bit," Delores added as she walked in to their flat to begin herding the family and Jake to go eat.

"Okay, thanks again!" Summer yelled into the closing door of the condo, hoping Delores would hear her.

Summer then rushed back to her flat to finish getting ready. All she needed now was the right outfit, she decided. Decisions, decisions, she thought. After going through her closet for the third time, she settled on a bright yellow sundress which was one of her favorites. Her lightly tanned olive skin complemented the dress well, she felt. Summer added her makeup and a few light sprays of perfume, and she couldn't help but feel she was dressed to impress the man who dominated her thoughts now.

*

Ethan pulled up in front of Summer's flat precisely at eight o'clock. He parked, quickly ascended the stairs, and rang the doorbell. As Summer opened the door, he was hypnotized by the stunning brown-haired, brown-eyed beauty in the form-fitting yellow dress. Could she get any prettier? he thought. He was in astonishment once again at her beauty.

"Hello, Summer. You look stunning again tonight," Ethan told her with a bright, beaming smile as he gave her a gentle hug hello and a kiss on the cheek.

"Thank you, Ethan. You're too sweet. You look handsome yourself," she replied, matching Ethan's smile.

"Well, I pale in comparison to you, but thanks, anyway," he replied humbly.

*

As they descended the stairs and he opened the car door for Summer, she found herself sneaking glances at him. The bright orange polo shirt he was wearing fit snugly against his bulging chest and biceps, and the khaki shorts he was wearing subtly revealed his powerful legs and perfectly round butt. He's so damn sexy, she thought as she entered the car for the short drive to Ethan's house.

After arriving at Ethan's house and going inside, Ethan called out as he made his way to the grill on the deck, "Make yourself at home and feel free to look around. I'm going to get the grill fired up, then get the other food started." The grill was large enough to cook for a small army, but he told her he would only use a small section of it that night.

Summer meandered through the house and admired how well and tastefully decorated it was. Even without already knowing it wasn't Ethan's own house, she could clearly tell the décor didn't match him. It was tastefully done, but didn't fit this mystery hunk who had dropped into her life.

❧

Ethan had the grill going in short order, and as he came back in, he offered with a smile, "Would you like a glass of wine? I have chardonnay and chardonnay."

"Well, I hate to break our tradition, so let's go with the chardonnay," Summer replied with a hearty laugh and a wink at Ethan.

Ethan was compelled to laugh and flirt back. "Perfect choice, madam. Let me get the wine for the pretty lady in yellow." He poured the wine, and as he handed Summer her glass, he asked, "So what do you think of the place? It's not quite how I would have decorated it, but it's nice and a great place to stay for free."

"I like it. I could tell it wasn't you, but it's beautiful, nonetheless," Summer replied with a smile.

"It seems you already know me so well," Ethan replied, grinning, and began working on the vegetables. As he rotated between grilling outdoors and cooking in the kitchen, he and Summer talked about how beautiful the weather in Rosemary Beach was that week, how nice the people were there, Summer's adventure that day with Jake, the stresses a job brings, and just life in general.

Soon Ethan was finished cooking. He pulled the shrimp from the grill, and she helped him set the round glass outdoor table with silverware and the freshly prepared meal.

After they sat down and before they began eating, Summer suggested, "Would you mind if I said a quick prayer to bless the food?"

Ethan was a little surprised by her offer, but it pleased him, nevertheless. He had grown up active as a youth in a Baptist church, but in the two years before his divorce and the three after it, he had allowed his faith and church attendance to wane. He would still attend on a more or less consistent basis, but nowhere nearly as regularly as he did in the years before that.

"Please, that would be nice," Ethan said with a smile and look of contentment. He observed Summer bless the food, and they began eating what he hoped would be a delicious meal.

❧

The evening weather on the deck was perfect once again. The soothing sounds of the ocean's waves cascading against the shore, the cool gentle Gulf of Mexico breeze, and the sounds of the activity in town and on the green provided the perfect backdrop.

As the two of them ate, they continued to learn more about each other, more about who each person really was. They discussed their hobbies, with Summer expounding on her love of reading, fashion, fitness, health and beauty, bicycling, home decorating, and, of course, event planning. Ethan talked about his love of investing, fitness, baseball, watching professional and college football, fishing, reading, and music.

In addition, they delved into more intimate topics like their views on politics, religious beliefs, and their own values and morals. While some of their hobbies and interests were different, when it came to the core beliefs and ideas on what many consider the most critical; like religion, values, and morals, their thoughts were almost identical.

❧

"You continue to amaze me, Summer. I've never met a woman with such different interests from me, yet someone who shares, almost exactly, my beliefs on what I call 'the essentials,'" Ethan added, unable to contain a smile.

"I know, right! It's kind of scary, isn't it?" Summer replied earnestly.

"Yeah, I guess it is, to be honest. But scary in a good way," Ethan went on, clearly pleased they agreed on these things. As they finished eating, he

68

got up and began putting away the dishes, and Ethan observed Summer didn't hesitate to jump right in and help him. In just a matter of minutes, they had the dishwasher loaded and all the leftovers wrapped and in the refrigerator. Now it's time to really relax a little, Ethan mused.

They had each finished their initial glass of wine during dinner, and Ethan offered, "Can I get you another glass of chardonnay?"

"Well, if you're going to twist my arm, I guess you can go ahead and pour me another one," she added, chuckling loudly.

Ethan laughed heartily at her comment, as he really connected with her sense of humor. "Works for me. I think I'll join you in another glass myself," Ethan chimed back, smiling as he spoke. "Shall we make our way out on the deck again? I wouldn't want to waste any part of yet another perfect night," he asked politely, hoping Summer would agree.

"Sure! That would be great," she replied. Her eagerness to go back on the deck was easily observed by Ethan.

As they stood on the deck overlooking the wide expanse of water, now cloaked in darkness, they absorbed their outdoor setting and enjoyed it fully. Ethan gazed upward and pointed out to Summer the too numerous to count bright and shining stars overhead. He noted Orion's belt, a favorite of his. He also directed her attention to the flicker of lights in the condos nearby where friends and family were no doubt eating and connecting with each other.

"This is just so relaxing," Summer said contently.

"I know; isn't it, though?" Ethan replied in complete agreement and paused to continue enjoying this perfect moment and their beautiful surroundings.

❧

As they admired the beauty and quiet in front of them, Summer gently asked Ethan something that had been on her mind since they met. "Ethan, can I ask you a personal question?" Summer questioned gently.

"No, you've already used up your one personal question, remember?" Ethan quipped back with a huge grin. "Just kidding. Go ahead and ask."

"You really haven't dated anyone since your divorce, not even one date here and there?" Summer asked curiously.

"No, I really haven't. Like we talked about before, I've been extremely busy getting the fund performance where I wanted it, and I've just not encountered a woman compelling enough to make me even consider it . . . until I met you," Ethan told her. As Summer gazed at him she saw in his eyes the pure truth in his statement.

Summer was almost speechless at the thought that *she* could be compelling to such a beautiful, sexy man. All she could manage to respond with was, "I see. Thank you for telling me that," as she looked away.

After a brief pause Ethan looked at her and countered, "Can I ask you a personal question?"

"No, sir, one is your limit, too," Summer joked as she beamed a smile back, now recovered from his previous compliment to her. "Go ahead; turnabout's fair play, I guess," she added politely, still with a smile.

"Thanks. Are you having as great a time together as I am, and do our conversations feel as natural to you as they do to me?" Ethan asked intently.

Summer had already been thinking the exact same thing earlier and told him, "Yes. It seems like we've known each other for years, yet we've just met. The conversations just seem so easy with us, don't they?" Summer replied. She looked deeply into Ethan's eyes as they stood together on the deck.

⌖

Ethan found himself looking back into those deep brown, trusting eyes. They drew him in like a lamb to the slaughter. He was utterly defenseless against them. Now fully under their spell, he was pulled in and moved close to her and eased his hands around her waist, pulling her tightly against him. He then began to passionately kiss her.

Just like their previous interlude, his tongue and hers rhythmically and gently rubbed against one another. They kissed for what seemed like five minutes between each breath. They paused only long enough to replenish their bodies with oxygen and for Ethan to occasionally alternate between kissing and gently sucking on her upper and lower lips.

He continued kissing her deeply, each kiss being that much deeper, each time more intense. The passion began flaming inside both of them. Ethan, unable to prevent himself from becoming aroused, pressed his lower torso firmly against Summer's lower body. He then gently eased his hands up from her waist and pulled her even closer to him so she could feel every part of him, then he used his hands to gently rub and massage her back as he continued kissing her.

Ethan was now totally immersed in the moment. He felt like Summer was equally caught up in it as well. He had nothing on his mind but enjoying the pleasure that now permeated his body. The passion was so strong for Ethan and unlike any he had experienced with a woman, even Emma. It took every bit of his concentration and self-control to not, at that very moment, rip all of her clothes off and ravage her on the deck.

As he continued to kiss her, the passion continued to build for him, and almost as if beyond his control, he eased his hands from around her back and slid them gently against Summer's full and supple breasts. He rubbed them gently, only pausing long enough to give special attention to her nipples, which were now at full attention and bulging through her bra and dress.

ᕦ

Summer was overwhelmed with desire for Ethan and didn't pull her lower body away when he pressed himself against her. She was also unable to prevent her passion from triggering blood pulsating through her breasts and lower body as Ethan rubbed and pressed against her. She could feel his size and firmness through her dress and his pants and could only imagine what it would feel like inside her.

As Ethan massaged her breasts, she couldn't stop him. It felt too good, and he seemed so perfect to her in every way. She was powerless and only hoped he would exercise restraint tonight because she knew she would willingly give in to him if he didn't.

The moment for her was the epitome of perfection. The deck, the ocean, the breeze, the strong connection between the two of them. All of it just right, she thought.

They continued their passionate kissing and touching each other for another ten minutes. Suddenly, their romantic embrace was interrupted by a phone's ringing. It was once again Summer's cellphone.

She abruptly stopped kissing Ethan and apologetically offered, "I'm sorry, Ethan. Let me get that. It might be Jake needing me for something."

"It's fine. Please go ahead and take it. Things were getting pretty hot and heavy, anyway," Ethan replied with a gentle smile.

"Thanks, and yes, it was getting pretty hot," she said, catching her breath and smiling back. "Hello?" Summer answered, not recognizing the number.

"Mom, my stomach hurts," Jake weakly said in reply.

"What happened? Do you need me to come get you?" Summer asked, now concerned and giving him her complete attention.

"Yes, ma'am. I need you, Mom," Jake replied, with his need for his mother in a time of anguish and pain obvious to her in his voice.

"Okay, baby. Stay right there, and I'll be there in just a minute," Summer replied, trying her best to hide her panic and concern.

"Um . . . okay," Jake offered weakly, then hung up.

⋙

"What's the matter? Is Jake alright?" Ethan questioned nervously and was now worried himself about the boy after overhearing the conversation.

"I don't know, but I'm afraid I do need to leave. I hope you can understand," Summer responded as she hurriedly gathered her purse.

"Of course, I do. I'll get my keys and drive you back to your flat right now," Ethan replied with obvious concern for Jake. With that, they jumped into his SUV and he drove quickly to Summer's flat.

As she hurriedly turned to get out, Ethan saw her lean over and give him a gentle kiss goodnight. "Thank you for everything. I really enjoyed tonight, and I'm sorry I had to cut it short," she told him.

"Please don't apologize, Summer. Your son's health and well-being are more important. There will be other nights for us," Ethan replied with confidence and a true desire to see her more in the future.

"Thank you for understanding. You're sweet. Goodnight," and with that comment Ethan watched Summer turn and disappear up the stairs.

It seemed to Ethan that fate or God or something else had once again intervened in their life. This time it was to interrupt them and their passionate evening.

⋙

Summer made it to Jake, got him back to their flat, and after talking with him realized he just had a stomach ache from eating too much cake and ice

72

cream after a dinner consisting entirely of hot dogs. Still, though, she wasn't upset with him, was glad to be there for him, and thrilled he was okay.

Later on that evening, as Ethan and Summer each lay in their beds, they couldn't resist replaying in their minds the chemistry and passion that flamed up between them like a raging forest fire being fanned by the unrelenting Santa Anna winds. Each person was left wanting the other that much more and eager to have another date to continue what they had started.

Chapter Eleven

E THAN WOKE TO the bright Florida sun around eight-thirty the next morning. It was Sunday and time for Ethan to review a few more earnings reports. His progress this week had been exceptional, even for him, as he only had two companies left to review. Ethan ate a light breakfast, then began to pore over his company research. He made quick work of it, and in just under two hours was finished and ready to work out.

He then drove up to the gym and did his usual chest and arm Sunday routine. He returned home tired, but refreshed at the same time and glad he had exercised. He opened the refrigerator, grabbed a glass of water, and sat on the couch to watch a little television and recover from his productive morning.

As he gazed out toward the deck, his mind wandered back to last night out there with Summer. The raw passion he felt for her was just as real now as it was last night. Ethan also remembered the wonderful dinner they had on the deck, the great conversation, flowing as it always did, and her beauty both inside and out. What a great vacation so far, he thought, and he owed it all to Willie.

"Willie . . . oh, crap!" Ethan called out to himself. He still hadn't thought to call and check on him even after the call with Greta reminded him to do so. Some best friend I am, Ethan thought, feeling guilty at having forgotten about his best friend. Surely Ann would have called if he had taken a turn for the worse, he rationalized to himself. Ethan had to call and check on the man responsible for this memorable week, he decided.

Ethan quickly found his phone and called Willie, hoping that he would answer. After three rings he heard, "Well, hello, there Captain! I thought you had run away and left the country," Willie answered, laughing loudly at his own comment, as was his way.

"Hey, Willie. No, I'm still here at Rosemary Beach. I'm so sorry I haven't called already to check on you. I hope you're not mad with me," Ethan asked sheepishly.

"Of course not, Captain. You know me better than that! I've been doing just fine. Ann got me home yesterday, so now I'm just taking it easy and driving her crazy by having her do everything for me." Willie added, chuckling as he said it.

"So you're home then? That's great news. You sound great, just like your jolly old self," Ethan chimed back, this time chuckling as *he* spoke.

"I'm doing good, alright. Doc Johannsen says I should be up and about in another week. The bad news is I'm not going to be healed up in time to go on our Hawaii trip. It seems I'll do anything to get out of flying somewhere," Willie added, billowing out another hearty laugh in the process.

"Yeah, it sounds like you pulled out all the stops for that," Ethan replied.

"So, Captain, have you found 'the one' yet?" Willie asked, now with a more serious tone.

"No, I haven't. I have met someone, though, who seems nice," Ethan responded.

"I see now. That's great! I'm glad you met someone. Is she pretty?" Willie asked. Ethan instantly noticed the fact that he had piqued Willie's interest in Summer.

"Yes, Willie, she's very pretty. The weather here has been perfect, too. The sun shines every day, and the temperature has been mild, in the low eighties." Ethan went on trying to quickly change the subject away from Summer.

"That's great, Captain. The weather down there usually is dang near perfect this time of year. You had any good food?" Willie asked. Ethan was grateful Willie had taken his cue to leave discussing Summer.

"I sure have. Everywhere I've been so far has been exceptional. I owe you a big favor for getting me down here, Willie. I mean that," Ethan replied in a more serious tone and making a point to genuinely thank his friend for his generosity.

"Aw, you're welcome. You don't owe me anything. After all the money you've made me the last several years, it's the least I can do. Besides, you needed to get away, cut loose, and get a little crazy," Willie responded, laughing loudly once again. "Well, Captain, Ann tells me it's time to eat and rest now. I think she's enjoying bossing me around a little too much in my condition," Willie continued jokingly.

"Okay, I'll let you go. I'm so glad you're doing better. I'll check on you in a couple of days, if that's alright with you," Ethan offered, hoping Willie would agree so he could check on his friend again and speak with him.

"Sure, but don't break a leg calling me. Enjoy yourself and have a good time. Oh, and Ethan, she *is* 'the one'; trust me. Goodbye, Captain!" Willie added as he hung up the phone.

Ethan felt so confused now. Why is Willie hung up on this 'the one' nonsense? he questioned. He must still be on a lot of pain medication, Ethan decided.

⌁

Summer had enjoyed a nice relaxing morning. She had gotten up about nine, when Jake did. Jake was feeling much better today, and the two of them enjoyed a pleasant breakfast together. Summer had prepared scrambled eggs and bacon for the two of them, along with orange juice. It was a breakfast they both enjoyed, especially when on vacation.

"So, Mom, where were you last night when I called? The lights weren't on in the house when we got back from supper," Jake asked.

Summer sensed Jake's curiosity in his question and was caught completely off guard initially, and it took her a few seconds to decide how to respond. She didn't want to lie to her son. She never had. He was mature for his age, and she was always honest with him.

Summer thought for a moment and decided it was best to just go ahead and lay Ethan out there to see what Jake's response would be. If Jake didn't like the idea of Ethan, or of Ethan, specifically, she needed to go ahead and know now rather than after she became more attached to him.

"Honey, I was with a new friend last night. A man-friend," Summer said cautiously, eagerly reading Jake's expression as she spoke.

"Was it a *date*, mom?" Jake asked excitedly. Summer noticed him raising his eyebrows up and down rapidly for a few seconds and smiling brightly as he spoke.

"Yes, honey, it was," she replied, now smiling herself at Jake's facial expression and reply. "Does it bother you that Mom went on a date?" Summer continued, asking Jake anxiously.

"No way, Mom. It's awesome! Does he like baseball and X-box?" Jake asked in excitement.

"I know he likes baseball, but I don't know about X-box," Summer replied, hoping Ethan's love of baseball would give him enough points with Jake for a meeting.

"Cool, Mom. When's he gonna come over and play ball with us?" Jake asked. To Summer's surprise, it seemed to her that Jake was genuinely excited at the idea of a man who liked what he did and might actually play with him.

"Um, I don't know, baby. He might be too old now to actually play baseball. You want to meet him?" Summer asked, still stunned at Jake's response. She always thought Jake would resent anyone she dated because it wasn't his dad. It never crossed her mind that Jake might actually want a man in his life who would willingly take up time with him.

She knew that time was something his real dad never gave him much of. For that reason and many others, Jake had never met anyone Summer went out with. Summer was now aggravated at herself for not seeing sooner the possibility that Jake might actually want a man in her life.

"Yeah, Mom! Are ya kidding?" Jake chimed back, full of excitement. Summer could see in his expression that Jake was incredulous she would even ask such a question.

"Well, okay then, baby. We'll work on that," she replied, now hoping Ethan would feel likewise about actually meeting Jake.

Ethan had finished a healthy lunch consisting of a turkey sandwich and pineapples. It was a lunch he ate often. He would have loved a hamburger and fries, but all those calories would be impossible to recover from, he thought. His mind veered back once again to Summer. He so wanted to see her again, and he really did want to meet Jake.

Based on all Summer had told him, Jake seemed like a great kid. He pushed back the logical, rational side of his brain and decided it was his turn to give her a call and see if they couldn't all enjoy the afternoon together.

As Jake and Summer were sitting on the couch, her cellphone began ringing. She glanced quickly at the number and saw it was Ethan. She became excited that he had called and quickly picked up her phone and answered, "Hello?"

"Hey, Summer. It's Ethan. How's Jake feeling today? I've been worried about him," Ethan asked.

"Oh, hey, Ethan. Jake's doing fine. It turns out it was just a stomach ache, so nothing serious. He's much better today," she replied, with relief in her voice that Jake was going to be alright.

As she began talking with Ethan, she saw Jake out of the corner of her eye with a mischievous grin, whispering where she could hear, "Ewww, Ethan. Mom is talking to *Ethan*, her *boyfriend*."

Summer couldn't resist a chuckle and rolled her eyes. She then whispered to Jake to stop clowning, which only served to spur him on even more. "Mom is talking to her *boyfriend*," Jake continued.

"Stop it," Summer whispered back with a slight smile.

"Ask him if he can come over and play baseball with us," Jake asked excitedly and still in a whisper.

"Shush! I'm on the phone," Summer replied, still half kidding. She then got up off the couch and stepped onto the deck to finish the call in private.

"I'm glad he's doing better. Say, I was going to see if you and Jake wanted to do something together this afternoon? It's a beautiful day, and I thought we could find something to do like ride bikes, go the beach, go to the pool, or do pretty much anything outside. What do you think?" Ethan asked cautiously.

"How do you feel about baseball today? Jake wants to play with me and some of his buddies, and you could tag along if you wanted. If not, I completely understand," Summer asked, knowing it was asking a lot to play baseball in the afternoon sun with a bunch of kids he didn't know running around like wild men.

"Oh, yeah. That sounds like a lot of fun. Let me get changed and ready to play. What time do I need to be there?" Ethan asked with excitement in his voice.

"Just come on whenever you get ready, and we'll go from there," Summer replied.

"Okay, sounds good. See you in about thirty minutes," Ethan chimed back with excitement and hung up.

Chapter Twelve

BOUT THIRTY MINUTES later, Ethan drove up and parked at Summer's flat. He glanced to his left and saw about a dozen boys scurrying around and playing on another of Rosemary Beach's large green areas. It was the St. Augustine Green, according to the sign, and looked to him like just the right size for a game. Ethan hadn't noticed it before when he had been to Summer's flat. This must be where we're going to play, he thought, as he made his way up to her flat and knocked on the door.

"I've got it, Mom!" Jake yelled, as if his mother was fifty yards away. Suddenly the door sprang open, and there Ethan was face-to-face with the boy he felt like he already knew.

He observed Jake was tall for a twelve year old, and he had light brown hair and bright green eyes. Ethan saw that Jake's eyes glimmered as he looked at him expectantly. Ethan could easily see from his frame that he was going to be an athlete. He had the look of a boy who played a lot of sports, and Ethan knew he did from his conversations with Summer.

Ethan also observed that Jake had an innocence to his appearance, not uncommon in children his age. They were still accepting of most everyone as the prejudices, mistreatments, disappointments, and struggles of this world hadn't affected them yet as they seemed to do to so many adults, Ethan felt.

"Hey, Mr. Ethan!" Jake said with a bright smile. "Mom says you're going to play ball with us today. Is that right?" Jake continued, not wasting any time with formalities.

"Well, hello, young man," Ethan replied, smiling back and matching young Jake's enthusiasm. "Yes, I'm going to play today, if that's okay with you?" he asked politely, already knowing what the answer was.

"Yeah, it's gonna be fun!" Jake said in continued excitement.

"Alright, Jake, let Mr. Ethan come in the house and get out of the sun," Summer called from the back of the flat as Ethan watched her make her way to the door.

"I'm going down to pick teams with the guys, and you're on my team, Mr. Ethan!" Jake yelled, not giving Ethan any say in the matter as Ethan watched him fly down the stairs to join his friends.

⊰

"I'm sorry about his manners today, Ethan. He's just so excited you're playing with them. I guess because his real father doesn't do things like that with him," Summer offered with disappointment shrouding her words and facial expression. The fact that Craig Johnson, her ex-husband, had disappointed her was something she could heal and recover from, but the fact that he hurt Jake by not taking time with him was difficult for her to handle sometimes. She had talked with Craig many times about his involvement in Jake's life, but never got anywhere.

"I'm excited, too. I hope these guys don't wear me out too bad today. I'm used to some cardio, but these old bones haven't trained for baseball," Ethan replied. She sensed Ethan was trying to bring her out of her negative thoughts.

"I'm sure you'll be fine," she responded, now smiling brightly back at Ethan.

"Shall we head down?" Ethan asked as he bowed and motioned his arm toward the front door.

"Yes, let's go," Summer replied as she picked up a small cooler, and they went down to the green.

As they walked onto the grassy area, it was chaos. There were eleven boys, all screaming and talking at one time. Somehow, though, in all the confusion they managed to get the teams picked and decided who would be home team and how many innings they were playing.

"C'mon, Mr. Ethan! It's time to play!" a voice yelled from the green.

Summer observed Ethan turn to see it was Jake and wave and smile back.

She knew he was acknowledging Jake and letting him know he was headed that way.

"I think I'm being paged," Ethan said, chuckling.

"You are, for sure. Get out there and show me what you've got," Summer replied, keenly interested in watching Ethan run and move around with that gorgeous body of his.

"Aren't you playing, too?" Ethan asked her and Summer noticed him with a puzzled look.

"Heavens, no! I included that little tidbit when I asked you, hoping it might get you off the fence if you were undecided about playing," Summer replied with a wry smile and a wink.

"Very clever, my dear, very clever. I owe you one." Ethan smiled wryly back at Summer and trotted onto the field.

As he jogged away, Summer thought what a wonderful man, to take time on his vacation playing with a boy he's never met. Ethan was different . . . special, she decided, and she settled in on a nearby shaded bench to watch the game. The game was to be whiffle ball instead of baseball, due to the size of the field.

∽

"Mr. Ethan, you play right field, and I'm playing short stop. Chad's in center and can help you get any balls you miss," Jake called out to him.

"Okay." Ethan called back with a laugh. He could sense that Jake didn't think he would be a very good outfielder.

There were six kids on one team and five kids and Ethan on the other. The game and time went by quickly that afternoon. Ethan surprised all the boys, and Summer, too, on the first ball hit to him. He sprinted back behind him after a long fly ball and caught it with both hands in full stride. He made two more plays like that, this time moving to either side of his position. Ethan had impressed all the boys, especially Jake, with these catches.

After those plays not many of the boys dared to hit the ball his way for fear of making an out. Ethan had proven himself and earned their respect. He had played baseball in high school and had been a gifted athlete. He hadn't been inclined to pursue college baseball, but he would have played somewhere if he had chosen to; however, Ethan had no regrets about his decision not to play.

Even now at his age, his body flowed when he played, and he made playing outfield look so easy. When Ethan would bat, he would hit the whiffle ball
high and long each time and usually ended up reaching second or third base.

⤷

He was good, Summer thought, really good. Ethan moved on the field like
he was in his twenties, she thought, and she couldn't help but wonder if he
moved in other ways like a man in his twenties. Maybe one day I'll find out,
she thought hopefully.

The day just seemed perfect as she watched her son, as happy as could be,
and gazed at the gorgeous man she just met playing the pivotal role in seeing
that happen.

⤷

The game had moved along to the seventh and final inning. Jake had reached
second base, and there were two outs. Ethan and Jake's team had managed to
tie the game two batters ago. Ethan was up to bat, and the game now rested
on his shoulders. Ethan knew a hit would most assuredly win the game.

"C'mon, Mr. Ethan! Get a hit! Hit it hard!" Jake called to Ethan from
second base.

No pressure or anything, Ethan thought. That's all I need is to lose
the game for Jake today. What a great first impression, he lamented. Ethan
stepped to the plate and focused intently on the pitcher and the ball.

By now the boys knew he could hit it a mile so all the outfielders were
playing well back, too far now to get it over their heads. I can drop it in just
over the infielders, Ethan thought, and Jake could easily score.

The pitcher started his windup and threw the first pitch, which Ethan
fouled off to the right, out of play. He had swung the bat easier that time to
try and drop the ball just behind the infielders, but none of the outfielders on
the other team picked up on what he was doing yet. They kept their positions
deep in the outfield. Two strikes left, he thought.

The pitcher readied and threw in the second pitch. Ethan swung a little
faster this time and slapped the whiffle ball toward right field. The second
baseman jumped up, but it was just high enough, and the line drive glanced
off his fingers and careened into the outfield. Jake had taken off on the sound

of the bat, just as any true baseball player would do with two outs. Jake was running at top speed and rounded third base, headed toward home.

⊸

Summer jumped up off the bench and began jumping up and down, yelling, "Run, baby, run!" She saw that the boys in the outfield were caught off guard and ran in to get to the ball. Just as one of them picked it up, she looked in at home plate to see Jake cross home plate with the winning run.

"We won! We won!" she yelled excitedly and looked in at home plate and saw Jake holding up his arms in victory and jumping up and down.

⊸

After rounding first Ethan looked back in at home plate to see pandemonium and a gang of boys surrounding Jake, cheering and yelling, "We won! We won!"

He hadn't let Jake down after all, Ethan thought. He had won the game for Jake's team, and that pleased Ethan greatly. He then glanced over to Summer, and her eyes met his. He saw she had the most excited, happy look on her face. He watched as Summer smiled at him and whispered, "Good job," and offered two thumbs up.

Ethan just stood in the field for what seemed like ten minutes and watched the celebration. The boys were so happy and so was Summer, which thrilled him.

Suddenly, he saw Jake sprint out from the pile of boys toward him, yelling, "We did it, Mr. Ethan! We did it!" As Jake reached Ethan, he reached up and gave him a high five.

"We sure did, Jake! Great game!" Ethan said.

"Thanks!" Jake yelled and returned to the chaotic group of boys.

⊸

Summer, seeing all this, now made her way over to Ethan. "You've made a friend today, I think," she offered with a smile.

"I think you're right. I'm glad I didn't make the last out. My name would probably be Mudd, then," Ethan replied smiling.

"No, he was thrilled just to have you play with him. Thank you," Summer replied with a caring smile and gently squeezed Ethan's hand.

"You're welcome. It was fun," Ethan countered and she felt him squeeze her hand in return.

After a few more minutes of celebrating, Summer called out to Jake, "Okay, baby. We need to go. I could use a snack."

"Okay, Mom. Gimme just a second," Jake yelled back.

⁓

Ethan observed Summer turn to him and say "Jake and I have a tradition on Sundays here in Rosemary Beach, where we have Mexican, then go to a movie, so we'll have to cool off, then get ready in an hour or two. But, if you'd like, you could join us for a quick ice cream?"

"Sure, that would be great. I'm ready for a snack," Ethan replied enthusiastically as he began gulping from a water bottle he had pulled from Summer's cooler.

"I hope you don't mind my being with Jake tonight, but it's our little Sunday tradition here," she asked Ethan cautiously.

"No, that's no problem. Traditions are important, and you two will have a great time," Ethan replied. "I'm just thrilled Jake wanted me to come play today. I wasn't sure what he would think about me when we met," Ethan continued, with concern in his voice that Jake might be jealous of him or resent him.

"Thanks for understanding, Ethan. It means a lot. Oh, and he definitely likes you if he asked you to play. He must have just had a feeling that you were a good guy, and he's right." she replied. He noticed her beaming those beautiful smiling lips and perfect teeth at him as she spoke which captivated him yet again.

⁓

The three of them then walked over to the Sugar Shack and enjoyed an ice cream under the covered area in front of the shop. They all replayed the game play-by-play and reveled in the victory. Jake was still excited and happy about the win and talked rapidly and full of facial expressions, wild hand and arm movements, and laughter. Summer and Ethan chimed in when they could, and they spent about an hour there eating their ice cream and talking.

⁓

"Well, baby. I guess we need to head on back. It's Sunday night in Rosemary

Beach, and you know what that means, Mexican restaurant and a movie," Summer said, smiling happily at Jake.

"Yep, that's right, Mom. This ice cream was good, but I'm still hungry," Jake added.

"Yes, you two better start getting ready and get to the Mexican restaurant. If it's like the other restaurants I've been to here, it will fill up quickly," Ethan said.

"Yeah, it takes me and little man here a while to get ready. Thank you for spending the afternoon with us. We had fun. I hope you did," Summer mentioned. It seemed to Ethan that Summer was genuinely satisfied at how well the first meeting with her son had gone.

"Yeah, Mr. Ethan. This was fun! You gotta be on my team again!" Jake offered. Ethan was thrilled with Jake's excitement and sensed that Jake really wanted him to help win another game soon.

"That sounds like a plan!" Ethan replied, flattered that he was being accepted by Jake.

"I can call you when we get back, if you like?" Summer volunteered to Ethan.

"That would be great. I'll listen out for you," Ethan replied with a smile.

As she left, with Jake already ahead of her, Ethan watched as she turned to him and blew him a quick kiss. He then looked to make sure Jake was still unaware and blew her a kiss in return. As he walked back to his house, Ethan could only replay the afternoon and think how well all three of them meshed. He so hoped Summer felt the same way.

Chapter Thirteen

FTER RETURNING HOME from the game and ice cream, Ethan jumped into the shower to clean up and cool down from the day's game. He determined he had held up pretty well playing with twelve-year-olds and wasn't the worse for wear. The cool shower water was refreshing to him.

As he showered, his mind drifted to Summer and Jake. The afternoon had gone about as well as it could, he decided, and it had been fun. Ethan hoped Jake and Summer would enjoy their movie night tonight. He finished his shower, then decided to watch a little baseball on television.

He watched the last five innings of the Braves game and was now hungry again and ready for dinner. He was still tired and didn't feel like fighting the crowds, so he re-heated the leftovers from dinner with Summer the night before. There had been enough food left for two or three people to eat again. He made his plate and settled in front of the television to catch up on the day's news.

The evening passed along surprisingly quickly for Ethan, even though he was alone. He ate and took a short walk down to the beach, then walked around town. It seemed the more he was here, the more he didn't want to leave. It was just so easy to relax in Rosemary Beach. He had also managed to wander in and out of all the shops in town again, but found nothing else he wanted to buy.

Ethan then returned a quick phone call to Greta. She had needed to confirm a date for a conference call, and he had done so in short order. With darkness setting in, Ethan decided to relax a little before bed.

❧

The La Cocina Mexican restaurant had been packed, but Summer and Jake had gotten there just before the crowd and were able to avoid a long wait. The food had been delicious, as usual, and Summer had thoroughly enjoyed Jake. She watched him stay perched on cloud nine the whole night from the win and replayed it over and over with her. It thrilled her so to see him happy and excited about anything. Jake and Ethan had definitely hit it off, she thought, even better than she could have hoped.

At La Cocina they each had their usual; fish tacos, and once they finished, they made their way to the theatre. Jake had been wanting to watch the latest animated movie that was out, so that was the movie they chose. It was hilarious, and the two of them laughed through most of it. They shared many qualities, and one was their sense of humor.

After the movie finished, they left and drove back toward their flat. After a long silence during the ride and out of the blue, Jake said, "Mom?"

Summer then replied, "Yes, baby."

"I like Mr. Ethan. He's nice. Will we see him after we go back home?" Jake asked. Summer noticed that Jake now appeared to have a serious, sincere, and concerned tone he hadn't had all day.

"I don't know, baby. Do you want to see him again?" Summer replied, hiding the excitement inside her at the possibility that Jake actually *wanted* to see Ethan again. She could barely contain herself because she wanted to see much more of Ethan herself.

"Yeah, Mom. He's fun, and he's a good baseball player, too," Jake responded, now smiling.

"We'll see if we can make that happen," she calmly replied. She saw Jake smile at her comment. She then watched him turn to look and daydream out his window. He was quiet for the remainder of the ride home, and Summer could only imagine what was running through that little mind of his.

❧

Ethan was enjoying the beautiful evening on the outdoor deck with a glass of chardonnay. It wasn't the same without Summer, he thought, but it was relaxing, nevertheless. His mind was preoccupied with the goddess in his life now. He gazed into the darkness as he thought about her hair, her lips, those mesmerizing eyes, and that incredibly sexy body. He thought how beautiful and sexy she must be naked.

His mind drifted further to what he might be doing with her if she was here naked and how enjoyable and magical that would be. He imagined she could move as well as she kissed and was a woman of many talents. Just then his fantasy was interrupted by his cellphone. It was Summer. That's weird, he thought.

"Hey, Summer," Ethan casually greeted her.

"Hey. What are you doing tonight?" Summer asked curiously.

"Well, I'm sitting here on the deck enjoying a glass of chardonnay before bed and wishing you were here to join me. Did y'all have a good time?" he asked, curious about their evening.

"You're sweet. Yes, we had a great time, and Jake talked about the game the whole night, I think. He couldn't stop talking about your game-winning hit," Summer said, chuckling as she spoke.

"I'm glad y'all had fun and glad Jake enjoyed the game. It was fun for me, too," Ethan replied, with a tone he hoped would make it obvious to Summer that he meant every word.

"Listen, tomorrow is our last full day here, and I was wondering if I would see you?" she asked.

"Of course! I had planned on it," Ethan said with excitement. "I was thinking maybe we might give Restaurant Paradis another try. It was great the first time, and I just love the atmosphere. But if it's too much of a good thing we can go somewhere else," Ethan offered, hoping she would want to return. There was such an air of romance in that place, and he wanted to experience it one more time with Summer.

"Sure, that would be great! I love it, too, and I'm craving their snapper," Summer replied and he sensed her excitement.

"Great! I'll plan on picking you up at seven-fifteen so we can make a seven-thirty reservation," Ethan politely suggested.

"Works for me. See you then," Summer chimed back.

"Sounds good. Good night." With that, Ethan hung up. He couldn't wait for their date tomorrow. He was already falling for Summer and in such a short amount of time.

❧

As for Summer, she felt exactly the same. She had been so hopeful that Ethan would agree to their date. Most all of her idle thoughts now seemed to revolve around him. She relived their dates, his time spent with Jake, and his gorgeous appearance. She would also daydream about his body and how incredibly sexy he must be naked. With these pleasing thoughts, Summer drifted off to sleep anticipating her next meeting with Ethan Phillips.

The next day for Summer was relaxing. She and Jake had ridden bikes for a while, swam at the pool closest to them, played a game of bocce ball on the green, and enjoyed a nice lunch at a bistro in nearby Seacrest Beach. Jake had asked her during the afternoon if he could spend their last night in Rosemary Beach with Chad, and she had agreed.

Summer could tell Chad wanted Jake to come back that night since he left early with his stomach ache the night before last. So, the evening was all set up for Ethan and Summer to have one final night together. A night to remember, she hoped.

❧

Sunday was also relaxing for Ethan. He had worked out, enjoyed more time at the beach, taken a dip in the pool at his house, then to round out the afternoon, he unwound with a glass of wine on his deck.

After enjoying his wine, Ethan showered and was just about ready for their date. All he had left to do was decide what to wear. He wanted to look really good tonight. Looking through the clothes he brought, he settled on a pale blue polo shirt and a pair of light tan khaki shorts. He had received many compliments on the shirt because it complimented his eyes so well.

He then got dressed and sprinkled on a little cologne and was out the door shortly after seven. It was just enough time to make it to get Summer, he thought.

❧

Summer had gotten Jake over to Delores and Dave's flat and had been rushed to shower and dress, but was almost done. She quickly finished getting dressed and was applying the final touches to her makeup and hair. She, too, wanted to dress to impress tonight.

She decided to pull out yet another sundress, but this time one that was slightly more form-fitting and cut lower in the front. It was a bright peach color, and it looked like the dress was made for her against her curved, tanned body. It complemented her figure and her skin tone perfectly. She was dressed to kill, Summer decided.

❧

Ethan pulled up at seven-fifteen sharp and soon knocked at her door. The door opened, and Ethan felt his heart skip a beat once more at the mere sight of her. He was stunned at how sexy she looked.

"Uh, hey, Ethan!" Summer spoke first, greeting Ethan.

"Hey, Summer! You look absolutely gorgeous tonight!" he replied, unable to take his eyes off her.

"Thanks. You're too sweet. You look handsome tonight, yourself. Are we ready to go?" Summer asked.

"Yes we are. I don't know about you, but I'm starving," Ethan responded, still unable to stop looking at her face, her every curve, her lips, her eyes, and her hair. She was beyond beautiful tonight, he thought.

"I'm pretty hungry, myself. I'm excited about going back to Restaurant Paradis," Summer offered. It seemed to Ethan that she was also enthusiastic about returning to the place where they met.

❧

The couple then drove to the restaurant and were seated promptly. Sebastian was off tonight, so she didn't get to see her good friend this time. It's just as well, she thought; she knew he would give her a hard time about having another date with the same man he introduced her to. He would undoubtedly try to take all the credit for it, she imagined.

They ordered and began to talk until their food arrived. Summer was spellbound by Ethan tonight.

"I enjoyed the game yesterday with Jake. I wasn't sure how well I would hold up or how sore I would be today, but I'm fine," Ethan said smiling. Summer could sense that Ethan was pleased he'd been able to run around with twelve-year-olds for the afternoon without an injury or a great deal of soreness.

"That was a lot of fun. Jake enjoyed it, too, and I loved watching you move around out there. You're good," Summer replied with a smile.

"I don't know about that, but thanks," he replied. Summer then observed that Ethan seemed to blush slightly with her endorsement of his athletic ability.

Their food soon arrived, and they ate. Ethan had the rib eye steak this time, and Summer had the snapper she had been craving. Their food was delicious once again, and they continued discussing both the previous day and what each did earlier in the day. The waiter returned from taking their plates and asked if they wanted any dessert. Vladimir was also off tonight, so they had a different waiter.

"Are you feeling up for sharing a slice of chocolate cake?" Ethan asked hopefully.

"I'm game if you are," she replied, and with that they ordered, then shared the cake.

"This cake is a lot better than the one I had for us the other night," Ethan said, almost appearing to Summer to apologize for the quality of the cake he bought that day.

"This one is really good, but so was the one you had," Summer said, smiling and attempting to affirm Ethan's cake selection the other night.

They finished their cake and soon left the restaurant and were standing out front. "I was wondering if you'd like to walk around and look at the homes again, then maybe finish the evening with some wine at my house," Ethan asked expectantly.

"That's just what I was thinking," Summer replied happily, and they resumed their evening together.

⸺

They strolled once again down the romantically lit streets of Rosemary Beach, taking in the breeze, the stars, and the sounds of residents enjoying their courtyards and porches, and they thoroughly enjoyed each other's company. They also ventured off the streets down the numerous wooden footpaths that dissected the streets and homes in town.

As Ethan and Summer walked, they soaked in this special time with each other. They both cherished the time they spent together. After walking through town under the beautiful starlit night, they made their way to Ethan's house. They had spent most of their time during their walk discussing their families and the lives they each had growing up. They shared personal stories from their childhood and talked about high school heartthrobs, their college days, and their dreams of the future.

As the conversation continued, their bond was forming like freshly poured cement, quietly curing with each passing moment and binding them together more and more as each minute passed.

They entered Ethan's house and made their way into the kitchen.

∽

"Will chardonnay be okay again tonight?" Ethan asked, not wanting to bore her if she preferred something else.

"Yes, it *is* my favorite, ya know," Summer replied with a smile. As Ethan poured the wine, he gazed at her beauty. She looked so damn sexy tonight, he thought. Summer had looked that way to him from the very first night he saw her, but tonight she was off the charts, and she was so easy to talk to and easy to connect with. He had never met a woman like her, and he wanted to see more of her, Ethan continued thinking.

∽

Summer was also watching Ethan. She was spellbound by that body of his, his strong and handsome face, those piercing eyes, and the depth that he had. He genuinely enjoyed talking with her, listening to her, and learning about her and Jake's life. Where in the world did this man come from? she thought.

"How's the wine tonight?" Ethan asked. She knew he was curious about what she thought of the brand he selected.

"It's perfect. Is it one you had here, or did you get it somewhere else?" Summer asked.

"It was already here, but the label and where it was made seemed different, so I thought I'd give it a try. I'm glad you like it," Ethan added.

They continued their conversation standing in the kitchen with Summer talking about what events she had waiting to plan when she got back and Ethan talking about the companies he was looking at for his hedge fund and how that process worked. Before they knew it, their wine glasses were empty.

∽

"Can I pour you another glass?" Ethan asked politely.

"I'll have another, if you will," Summer said and smiled back with a devilish grin.

"As you say, 'twist my arm,'" Ethan replied, laughing out loud, and Summer did likewise.

She joined him at the wet bar, and after pouring her glass and handing it to her, their eyes locked onto each other yet again. They were both in a trance with each other's beauty. Without even thinking, Ethan put his glass down, and in the blink of an eye, he wrapped his arms around her and began French kissing her passionately.

Just as he had kissed her before, Ethan used his tongue as a man uses his body to please a woman. Their tongues were tangled together and rubbing vigorously against each other, and after each breath the next kiss was more passionate and deeper than the one before.

As he was kissing her, he took his hands from around her back and slid them up her waist to her voluptuous breasts and began massaging both of them, along with her nipples, gently and rhythmically. He didn't know why he had been so bold, except that his passion was burning inside him now, and the pleasure he was feeling controlled his body.

The passion in Ethan was coming to a boil. It had been over three years since he had been with Emma, and even then, it wasn't nearly this intense. Summer was so much more beautiful and more connected to him and interested in him, Ethan thought. He continued to kiss her and fondle her breasts, then in an instant, his passion was unleashed.

He effortlessly unzipped the back of Summer's dress and slid it off her shoulders. In the blink of an eye it was on the floor, and Ethan was kissing her all the while.

❧

Summer had taken her hands and placed them on Ethan's full and rock-hard chest, then rubbed his chiseled physique. She moved from there to gently rub his now erect nipples. His body was so hard, she thought. Summer couldn't help herself either, then, likewise, she gave in to her desire. It had been over a year for her, and even then, that was with a man riddled with addiction issues. Richard Williams, Summer's ex-boyfriend, was nowhere near the man Ethan was, she thought.

Summer reached down, untucked Ethan's shirt, and pulled it quickly over his head. She then stared at his gorgeous rock-hard chest and torso. Unable to control herself now, she unbuttoned and unzipped his pants and dropped them and his boxers to his ankles. She gazed down at his lower torso and saw his size and how hard he was. She couldn't wait to feel that inside her, she thought.

∽

Ethan was now fully in the moment. He reached down and quickly took off his sandals, and watched Summer reach down and slide off her heels.

Ethan couldn't control any part of his body. His mind was flushed with passion and desire, and these feelings took him over completely. He slid his hand between her legs and inside her panties until he found her pleasure center. He then gently rubbed it from side to side.

∽

With Ethan's touch Summer rolled her head back in pleasure and moaned approvingly. Her juice began flowing like a river over his fingers and onto her panties. Summer, overtaken by pleasure and desire herself, then took her hand, slid it onto Ethan's manhood, and began gently stroking him. It was so big and hard, she thought, and without thinking, she pulled his hand away from her and went down on him and began bobbing her head up and down and sucking gently.

∽

Ethan's eyes rolled back into his head, and he moaned with total pleasure and whispered, "Oh, yes, baby. Yes." He could take it no more, and Ethan abruptly pulled Summer up off him and pulled her down onto the kitchen floor. Laying her on her back, he moved on top of her and quickly slipped himself into her. As he did, he could see Summer gasp at the sudden sensation and size inside her.

Ethan began thrusting in and out of her, slowly at first, but then allowing the pleasure to drive him into her harder, faster, and deeper with each thrust. He soon was pumping so hard that her body was inching across the kitchen floor with each push. The pleasure from being inside her was intense and fueling his motion. He then called out in ecstasy, "Yes Summer. Yes. Yes."

After thrusting her clear across the kitchen floor, Ethan pulled out of her and began kissing and licking her full, round breasts. She was a model, he thought, perfect in every way. He then moved down her stomach kissing and licking her as he went until he reached her pleasure point, and Ethan began licking and sucking on it briskly.

⚶

Summer was unable to control herself and her thoughts. Her mind was blank and full of pleasure and wanting more and more of it from Ethan as quickly as he could give it. He felt so good inside her she thought.

She took a few breaths after he pulled out of her. She watched Ethan work his way down her body with those sexy lips of this. Suddenly, he found her pleasure point and began using his tongue on it in a circular motion. She felt him then follow that by licking it up and down rapidly. When Ethan began doing that, she arched her back, her breathing picked up, and her groans grew deeper and louder. She knew he had complete control over her now as Ethan continued vigorously licking and rubbing her pleasure center.

The pleasure in Summer was building and building, growing stronger with each pass of his tongue, and she could feel her orgasm coming. She couldn't hold it back if she wanted; it was too powerful and unstoppable.

Ethan continued pleasing her with his tongue until she erupted into a loud scream of "Oh God! Yes Ethan! Yes, baby, yes! Her body then began shaking all over with pleasure, as if she was being electrocuted, her juice flowing out of control. She had a vise grip on Ethan's hair as her orgasm pulsated through her body. She then finished with passionate groans and a scream of "Oh, my God, baby! Yes! I love you!"

With her orgasm passing, Summer lay there for a moment, allowing her breathing and heartbeat to return to something close to normal. She was limp after the most intense orgasm of her life. She laid there in Ethan's arms enjoying the moment for another few minutes, and after catching her breath and recovering, she then looked at Ethan and could see he was still hard. She then said to him, "Go sit in that chair."

She watched as Ethan matched her gaze into his eyes, got up off the kitchen floor, went to the kitchen table, and sat in a chair with his legs apart and his manhood at full attention. Summer got up and walked seductively over to him, gazing at him intently. She then placed her hands gently on his shoulders as she got on top of him. She slid her body down onto him and began grinding rapidly up and down over his manhood.

Ethan was so big she almost couldn't handle him on top, she thought, but she kept moving up and down with each of them gazing into the other's eyes and occasionally kissing passionately. She began riding him harder and faster. He felt so good and was the sexiest man alive she thought.

She noticed his body then tense considerably which let her know his orgasm was rushing forward, then after kissing him once more, Summer pulled back as she was riding him and looked deep into those hazel-green eyes of Ethan's and whispered seductively to him, "C'mon, baby. Give it to me. Give it to me. You know you want to."

≫

Ethan was overcome with pleasure. Summer had been sliding up and down on him so easily from her juice flowing wildly he thought. He could feel her grinding her G-spot against his manhood with each stroke. Everything about her was so incredibly sexy and he didn't know how long he could hold back his brewing orgasm.

Just then, Ethan heard her sexy, seductive words. The words pushed him over the edge, and he began exploding into her with relentless bursts of passion. He continued his violent explosions into her for what seemed like ten minutes.

With each powerful release Ethan yelled "Summer", and after the final one could only mutter, "I love you, too."

≫

They both now sat motionless in the chair, as they were completely drained. They kissed gently and rubbed their hands over each other's body. Ethan offered, "I'm exhausted. Let's just sit here for a minute and rest."

They sat in the chair together, with her still on top of him, and they laid their heads on each other's shoulders after the most intense lovemaking either had ever experienced. They both began thinking about how wonderful the other was, how much of a fit they were, how perfect this night and this moment were. As they were thinking, their bodies gave in to the exhaustion and the wine, and they drifted off to sleep.

Chapter Fourteen

─•●•─

THE SOUND OF the ice maker's dispensing cubes woke Ethan from his slumber. He had always been a light sleeper, and this night was no exception. It took him a moment to realize where he was and how he ended up there. Summer was fast asleep on top of him. He now had a crick in his neck, and his lower back was beginning to ache from sitting in the hard kitchen chair for so long. He looked at the clock on the stove, and it was two o'clock in the morning. Wow, he thought, they had been sleeping here a while.

Ethan knew he needed to get both of them into bed to sleep more comfortably. He eased Summer up, and she woke slightly as she rose. Ethan then stood, took her in his arms, and carried her back to the bedroom with her head against his chest and her arms draped around his neck. He laid her down gently in the bed and slid the covers out from under her, then pulled them back over her beautiful, voluptuous body. Ethan then made his way around to his side of the bed and climbed in, and they both drifted off to sleep once again.

The next morning Ethan woke up quickly, with his heart beating ninety miles per hour as his alarm was blaring its morning wake-up call. He reached over, turned it off, and noticed the time was seven-thirty a.m. Summer was now stirring, too, as the loud alarm could wake the dead, Ethan decided. He needed to find a more gentle alarm each morning, he thought. Ethan rolled over to Summer, who was now awake and lying on her side, facing him.

"Good morning," Summer said, smiling happily.

"Good morning, sunshine," Ethan replied, then leaned over and gently began kissing her lips briefly and affectionately.

"That was some night, huh?" she offered. Ethan could almost see a gleam in her eye as she smiled and spoke.

"Yeah, it was incredible," he replied, satisfied with all that happened.

"You were very good last night," Summer said. Ethan saw that she was still unable to stop smiling.

"Thanks. You were amazing yourself," Ethan responded, also smiling.

He noticed her then ease over to him, lay her head on his chest, and Ethan slid his left leg between her legs as she lay across him. How perfect she fit against his body, he thought, almost as if she was made by God to be there. He was so relaxed, happy, and content at that moment.

⤮

Summer laid in Ethan's arms, enjoying the moment for about thirty minutes, then Ethan asked, "So what time do you check out today?"

"Oh, shoot! I forgot about that . . . and Jake!" Summer said with excitement in her voice. She thought quickly and realized she had told Jake she would pick him up from Chad's house at ten, so she was okay on time and didn't need to rush home. She wanted to extend her time with this wonderful man as long as possible.

"We check out at eleven, and I need to get Jake at ten. I've also got to do some packing and get dressed. But as long as I'm back at the flat by nine, I should be okay," she mentioned, now more relaxed that she did have a little time and didn't need to fly out the door.

"That's good. I'm glad you can stay a little longer," Ethan said as he eased out of bed. "I think I'm going to jump into the shower and get cleaned up before I need to take you back," he said smiling. Summer noticed Ethan appeared to have a smile of contentment. "Before you guys get out of here, if you want, I could treat you and Jake to a late breakfast at the Summer Kitchen Café across the street," Ethan offered.

She was flattered Ethan would want to see both her and Jake before they left and spend more time with them on their last day at Rosemary Beach. "Sure, that would be great," Summer replied. "Jake will like that, too," she added.

"Perfect," Ethan said. Summer saw him grinning widely as he got up and made his way into the bathroom.

As he walked naked in front of her, she was prompted to daydream back to last night and what Ethan did to her with that sexy body of his, and she thought how satisfying it would be to have him do that to her again. She then began to picture how sexy he must look in the shower with the water cascading over his firm, naked body, and with that thought, she got up out of bed and went to see if Ethan needed any help in the shower.

❧

Ethan was busily washing his hair and body to get ready to take Summer home. He was replaying the evening in his mind and thinking about how perfect it had been. They had each said they loved the other last night, he thought, but she hadn't mentioned it this morning, so he decided not to, either. She might not even remember she said it, he mused to himself.

Just then, he saw Summer through the glass shower door and heard her say, "Ethan, I wanted to see if you needed help with anything."

Ethan was thrilled she would want to join him in the shower. He then opened the door to see Summer's naked body and said, "I'm sure I can come up with something." With that comment, he pulled her into the shower with him.

Ethan drew her close and began French kissing her wildly. He paused to look at her tight, well-curved body and became aroused just as strongly as he had with her the previous night. He then felt Summer reach down and begin to gently stroke him, sliding her hand up and down slowly. The pleasure from her touch began permeating his body.

While she was stroking him, Ethan slid his hand between her legs and began gently rubbing her pleasure point. He started by rubbing it slowly, then gradually began massaging it faster.

As he pleased her, he saw Summer throw her head back and began moaning with pleasure. It looked like to Ethan that the pleasure was coursing through every vain in her body. He continued pleasuring her for a few minutes, then Ethan stopped and grabbed her, turned her around to face the shower wall, and from behind, he slid into her.

Ethan heard Summer again gasp with his size and the pleasure he sensed she was feeling. Ethan, placing his hands on her hips for leverage, then began moving in and out of her, slowly at first, then increasing the speed of his hips with each thrust into her.

Summer was bent over slightly and had her hands against the shower wall, and by now Ethan heard her moaning loudly and calling out, "Oh, Ethan. . . . Oh, Ethan . . . that feels so good. Please don't stop!"

Ethan, as he was making love to her, he then slid his hands around to Summer's breasts and began massaging them, then gently rubbing her nipples as he continued to thrust vigorously in and out of her. He was fully consumed with pleasure and continued to give himself to her as he would grind his manhood inside her with each thrust.

By now, the steam from the hot shower filled the bathroom like a thick London fog. Their two naked bodies ravaging each other were barely visible. He continued pleasing her a little longer until he noticed Summer stop and turn around to face him. He instantly knew that she must want him to now take her from the front, which he soon did.

As Ethan eased down, then slid into her again, he took his arms, quickly slid them under Summer's legs, picked her up and used his body to pin her against the tiled shower wall. He kept his arms there and used his hands to grab her firm butt. Ethan then resumed thrusting rhythmically into her with his hips.

He gazed into her eyes while he continued to let the pleasure rule his mind and body. Ethan then took his eyes off hers, moved his head down, and began licking and sucking on her breasts before locking in on her left breast and rapidly licking her nipple as he continued giving himself to her.

The flood of sensation was now too intense for Summer, and she could feel her orgasm surging inside. The pleasure of Ethan grinding inside her and stimulating her G-spot was almost more than she could take. Her juice was gushing out over Ethan's manhood. Her orgasm was an unrelenting force and within seconds it erupted and assumed control of her body. It began to make her shake and quiver as she climaxed, with Ethan still driving himself into her. The wave of pleasure and convulsions jolted her lower torso and it caused her to scream out, "Ethan . . . Ethan . . . Oh, God, Ethan!"

Her intense orgasm lasted for thirty seconds with her body constantly quivering the entire time. After the sensations had subsided, Summer felt her body begin to relax as Ethan now pulled out of her. Ethan had just rocked her world once again, she thought.

Wanting to make sure Ethan came, too, Summer then went down on him and began moving her head rapidly up and down on his manhood, sucking on him vigorously. She looked up to see Ethan roll his head back and call out in ecstasy "Summer, baby . . . yes . . . yes . . . oh, that feels so good!"

✍

Summer brought Ethan on the verge of orgasm in no time. She knew just how to use her mouth and tongue, Ethan thought. He could feel her using her mouth to pull his orgasm out of him and he did not want to stop her. The pleasure induced endorphins coursed through his body from the ecstasy he was receiving.

Her mouth and tongue were overpowering and just before he reached his climax, he called out to Summer, "I'm coming, baby" to give her fair warning what was about to happen.

Ethan looked down to see Summer heed his warning. She quickly pulled off him and began stroking him rapidly with her hand, and right before he came, he noticed her position her breasts in just the right path.

Suddenly, Ethan came, spraying himself all over Summer's breasts as Summer looked on with pleasure at getting him off and having him come on her. Ethan's orgasm lasted fifteen incredible seconds as his passion gushed onto her full, round, firm breasts. Then his body went limp when he was spent. He could barely move and felt completely drained.

Summer, having finished him, stood, and they joined together in each other's arms and began kissing softly, cherishing another passionate moment between them.

"That has to be the best shower I've ever had," Ethan said, completely relaxed from their second incredible lovemaking session.

"Yeah, that's my kind of shower, alright," Summer replied, smiling back at him. They then kissed each other gently, turned, and finished showering. "You go ahead and finish getting ready, and I'll wait on you," Summer offered courteously.

"Okay, thanks. I'll hurry so we get you home by nine," he said, flashing a smile back at her. Ethan quickly made a pass at combing his hair, brushed his teeth, then threw on a pair of shorts and a polo shirt and was ready to take her home.

"If you're ready I can go ahead and take you back," Ethan offered gently.

"Yeah, it's about that time, I guess," Summer replied. Ethan observed sadness in her voice at having to leave Rosemary Beach.

❧

They made their way to Ethan's car and drove to her flat. As she was about to get out, she looked over at Ethan, smiled, and leaned over to him for a kiss. Ethan leaned in likewise, and they kissed gently for a few seconds. "Thank you for a great evening and morning," Summer said, beaming with satisfaction.

"You're welcome. It was incredible," he replied, smiling also.

"I guess I'll just meet you at the Summer Kitchen Café at eleven-fifteen? That'll give me time to get checked out and get to the restaurant," Summer suggested.

"Sure, that's fine with me. I'll probably get there a little early and make sure we have a table for three," Ethan replied.

Summer exited the car, picked up Jake, and began the dreaded task of packing their clothes and getting the flat organized before checking out.

Chapter Fifteen

Ethan Made The short walk up to the Summer Kitchen Café at eleven a.m. and promptly secured a table for three outside near the street, which had a great view of The Pearl hotel and all the businesses on Main Street. He was thrilled the weather was perfect again this morning. He was looking forward to one last meal with Summer and Jake.

❧

Summer had miraculously been able to get dressed and pack both her clothes and Jake's and leave the condo ready to be cleaned and avoid any additional fees. She had been able to do all of this and finish before eleven, which gave her plenty of time to check out.

Summer then checked out and found a parking space along Main Street. She and Jake got out and Jake instantly saw Ethan seated down the street at one of the outside tables. Summer felt Jake was genuinely excited he was going to see Ethan again and eat breakfast with him before they left Rosemary Beach.

Once Jake spotted Ethan, he waved and called out, "Mr. Ethan! Mr. Ethan! Hey!"

❧

Ethan instantly turned, smiling at hearing his name, and stood as he watched Jake run toward him at full speed. As Jake arrived after sprinting down the street, Ethan continued to smile and greeted him, saying, "Hey there, Jake! Man, you sure were fast coming down the street."

Jake replied, "Thanks! I'm pretty fast. It sure was fun winning yesterday, huh?"

Ethan felt like he had impressed Jake by commenting on his speed. Ethan replied, continuing to smile at Jake as he observed Summer now arrive at their table, "It sure was. You and I make a pretty good team, don't we?"

"Yes, sir. We sure do," Jake said enthusiastically, with a large grin.

Summer then chimed in, "I see you two are re-living the game yesterday." Ethan could see that she was beaming from ear to ear as she spoke.

"Yes, we were. When you win the game with a walk-off hit it's too memorable not to relive. Here, have a seat and we can take a look at the menu," Ethan offered as he moved around and pulled out her chair.

After they were all seated and had looked over the menu, their waiter came and took their drink orders, then asked if they were ready to order. "Does everyone know what they want, or do we need a minute?" Ethan asked politely.

"I know what I want! Scrambled eggs, bacon, and some toast. And a glass of chocolate milk, please," Jake called out first. It seemed to Ethan that young Jake was starving this morning, and he guessed it was because he hadn't eaten anything yet.

"I think I'd like the same, with orange juice," Summer politely replied to the waiter.

"I think let's make that three of those, except I'd like hash browns, too, and orange juice to drink, also," Ethan said.

"Very good. I'll get this in right away," the waiter politely replied, then went back inside to place the order.

While they waited, Ethan and Jake dominated the conversation. "Did you play baseball when you were a kid, Mr. Ethan?" Jake asked.

"I sure did. I started playing from the age of five and played all the way through high school. It was my favorite sport," Ethan replied, happy that Jake was interested in his baseball past.

"Cool! What position did you play?" Jake questioned.

"All the way from first grade through high school I was a shortstop, so I played there mostly, but I did pitch a little in high school. I wasn't all that good at pitching, though," Ethan responded.

"Did you ever make all-stars?" Jake continued questioning intently.

Ethan felt that Jake was probing the skill level of his mom's new friend and his new teammate.

"I did, actually. I made it pretty much every year until I started high school ball, then I made All-Region three years," Ethan added with satisfaction in his words and expression that he had been an accomplished player, at least through high school.

"Awesome! You were good," Jake smiled and responded.

"What about you, Jake? Have you made all-stars, and do you play short-stop on your baseball team, too?" Ethan asked, now turning the conversation to learn more about Jake's skill level.

"Yes, sir. I've made all-stars the last three years. I just play shortstop," Jake replied proudly.

"Very good. You know, they say the person who plays shortstop is the best athlete on the team," Ethan replied, hoping Jake would catch on to the compliment.

"Really? That means I'm the best, huh?" Jake called out. Ethan could see the gleam in Jake's eye, and he knew Jake had indeed understood his compliment.

"I think it does," Ethan replied with a smile.

⌒

"I think you two could talk baseball all day," Summer said, trying to jump into the conversation.

"Oh, I'm sorry. I guess we did get a little caught up in it, didn't we? We didn't mean to ignore you," Ethan replied apologetically.

"Yeah, Mom, we haven't forgot about ya," Jake added.

"Oh, it's okay. I'm only teasing you two. I'm glad y'all are getting along so well," Summer replied, pleased that her son and this new man in her life were hitting it off so wonderfully. It was just that effortless with her and Ethan, which pleased her greatly.

"So, are you guys headed back to Thomasville right after we eat?" Ethan asked.

"I'm afraid so. I need to get little man here back by six today so that he can stay with his dad for a few days. We'll probably stop in Tallahassee on the way back, though, and shop in the mall a little while," she replied with disappointment in her voice. She was saddened to be leaving Rosemary Beach and

Ethan and sad she had to leave Jake with his dad, knowing he wasn't going to give him the attention he wanted or needed.

"Can we go by the toy store and get me a new Lego set for Dad's house? Please! Please!" Jake asked. Summer could see he was making his case for a new set to build with while he stayed with his dad.

"We'll see, young man. It depends on how well you behave between now and then and on how bad the traffic is today," Summer replied, casting a slight smile at Jake. Their conversation had allowed time to pass quickly.

The food soon arrived, and they all began eating. It was quiet while they ate, as they were all famished since none of them had anything for breakfast.

❦

As Ethan was eating, he was compelled to glance at Summer and admire her beauty once more and to replay in his mind the amazing night and morning they had with each other. She was just perfect, he thought. She was so pretty, yet so easy to talk to and fit together so well with him.

Their conversations flowed so effortlessly from their first meeting, he felt. There were no long, awkward pauses nor uncomfortable moments. He had been comfortable with her from the very first meeting; and how could he not think about the amazing sex with her? She had pleased him like no woman ever had before.

❦

Summer was thinking the exact same thing while they were eating. She would secretly gaze at this gorgeous man. He was so down to earth, so easy to talk to, so genuine and caring, so eager to listen to what she had to say. Their conversations were easy and covered all ranges of topics.

He also took a genuine interest in her son and in spending time with him. This was something even Jake's own father did very little of. Ethan seemed to enjoy it, too, which made it even more special to her. Finally, he had the most amazing body she had ever seen, and he could move every part of it like no man she had ever known. It was as if he could read her mind and know exactly how to please her. It was almost as if God had made Ethan just for her, she decided.

After they finished eating their meal, Ethan and Jake continued talking baseball, and occasionally, Summer was able to jump in and join the conversation, too. The check came, Ethan paid it, and they finished up their conversation before Summer and Jake had to leave.

"Thank you for breakfast, Ethan. I could have gotten it," she offered, gratefully.

"No, I invited you guys to eat, so I had planned on paying the whole time. It was my pleasure and worth it to get to see you two before you left today," Ethan replied, smiling happily at both Summer and Jake.

"Thanks, Mr. Ethan. It was good," Jake offered politely.

"You're welcome, Jake. I'm glad you liked it," responded Ethan.

"I hate we have to go so soon, but if we don't leave now, we won't have time to stop in Tallahassee and make it to his dad's by six and deal with the traffic today," Summer said with a somber tone from having to leave Ethan.

"And go to the toy store, Mom!" Jake chimed in loudly.

"Yes, the toy store, too," she answered with a wry smile at her little man.

"Well, it's okay; I understand. These early checkouts are no fun at all. It seems like you don't get to enjoy the day at all before you have to leave," Ethan replied.

Summer sensed genuine understanding in his voice and replied, "I know. Right? It's such a rush to get ready and leave, and it gives you no time to relax on the last day," she added.

"Mom, can I go look in Gigi's Toy Store before we go?" Jake asked hopefully.

"Baby, we have to leave soon," Summer answered.

"Please, Mom, please! Just five minutes!" Jake lobbied. Summer knew that Jake was once again trying to persuade her with his pleading.

"Alright, five minutes. You go ahead and walk up there, and I'll drive down and get you, so look for my car, okay?" Summer replied with that serious 'do it or else' look only a mother gives a child.

"Sure thing, Mom!" Jake said happily and took off running up Main Street toward Gigi's at full speed. Summer knew Jake all too well and could easily see he was trying to impress Ethan with his speed once again.

"The things a mother does for a child," she said with a sigh.

"He's a good kid, and he really does listen to you, so I don't think you'll have any trouble getting him to leave," Ethan said.

"Yeah, he really is well behaved most of the time, which is why I try to let him do things like this when I can," Summer replied with an element of pride in her young son evident in her voice.

❧

Ethan had been ogling at her once again and admiring all the wonderful qualities Summer possessed. He didn't want her or Jake to leave. He wished they could stay with him until Thursday when he had to leave. He just had to tell her what a great time he had with her. He didn't know why, but he just felt compelled to tell her his thoughts, which had been so unusual for him, especially with a woman. Until meeting Summer, he had no problem keeping his thoughts internalized.

"Listen, I just want to say I've had a wonderful time with you this week. Last night and this morning were unbelievable, but more than that, I've just enjoyed being with you and talking with you and getting to know you and Jake. I hope we can continue that after we resume our lives back in Georgia," Ethan offered, with true feeling and genuineness in his words, tone, and expression.

❧

Summer wanted to do a 'happy dance' at hearing these words but contained herself. She felt likewise and told Ethan, "I'm glad to hear you say that. I've had a great time getting to know you too and so has Jake. It was God, fate, luck, or all of the above that caused us to meet, and it's been a great week for us, too. I'd love to see you again, and I know Jake feels the same way. Well, I better go get Jake.

❧

They walked up almost to the top of Main Street and climbed into Summer's SUV. After she started her car, Ethan couldn't resist kissing those beautiful lips one last time and quickly reached across to her, gently pulled her face to his and began kissing her. There were probably fifty people gawking at them, Ethan thought, but he didn't care. This kiss from Ethan was no different than the others he shared with Summer. It was rhythmic, intense, and passionate. The kiss only lasted a minute or so, but for him, time froze.

When they finished, Ethan pulled away and said, "I'm sorry I just jumped you like that, but those lips of yours looked too inviting. Plus, I didn't want you to get out of here without a kiss goodbye."

"I'm glad you kissed me. It was nice. I was hoping to get a goodbye kiss from you," she replied, smiling brightly.

Summer then pulled her SUV out and made the short drive down in front of Gigi's, and there was Jake, ready and waiting. Ethan hopped out of the front seat and held the door open for Jake to get in. He then closed the door behind Jake and watched as Summer let down the passenger side window.

"Y'all be careful going home, okay? Do you mind texting me or calling me when you get home so I know you made it there safely?" Ethan asked wanting to know for sure they made the trip home without incident.

"Sure, I can do that," Summer answered. Ethan observed her smiling widely as she spoke.

"Great. Goodbye, Jake! Goodbye, Summer!" Ethan replied, waving and smiling happily.

"Goodbye, Mr. Ethan!" Jake said loudly.

"Goodbye, Ethan," Summer added. Ethan saw her give him a wink that Jake couldn't see. With that, these two people who had been so much a part of his life the last few days pulled away, rounded the corner, and were gone. Ethan was now alone again in Rosemary Beach.

Chapter Sixteen

ETHAN NOW FELT isolated and completely alone. Until he met Summer, he had welcomed the solitude and escape of Rosemary Beach, but now, after having had a brief, whirlwind romance with her, he was feeling a kind of separation anxiety from her. Why was he feeling this way about a woman he just met? Was it the sex that he was going to miss with her? Was it his new little buddy Jake? Was he just lonely now after spending so much time with her the last few days? As usual, the questions were zooming through Ethan's mind much too quickly to answer.

As he took his time and processed it all, he decided it wasn't any of those things. It was something so much more. It was something deeper than he had ever experienced. He was in love, but it was a deeper love than he had ever felt. He had told Summer he loved her in the heat of passion, and he meant it. She had said the same to him and actually said it first.

Since then Ethan figured that because Summer never said anything else about it that she hadn't really meant it. Maybe she was just caught up in the heat of the moment, he wondered, but Ethan also realized he didn't really know since he hadn't asked her.

Regardless of *her* feelings, Ethan was now coming to grips with the fact that he was indeed in love. He already missed the interesting conversations with her, the walks through the neighborhood at night, the meals they shared together, the glasses of wine they enjoyed, and, of course, her unequaled beauty and ability to rock his world, sexually; and he missed young Jake.

Ethan enjoyed their game and talking with him. The connection with Summer and Jake had been brief so far, but with Summer especially, it had been more powerful than anything he'd experienced before.

He was convinced he *had* to be in love. There was no other explanation for his feelings. How had it happened so fast? Why had he fallen for her? Was it fate or something else that brought them together that night at Restaurant Paradis? Would these feelings really last, or was it just infatuation, instead? Was it just a summer fling? Did she feel even remotely the same? Again, there were more questions bombarding his mind.

He did know that Summer wanted to see him more in the future. She had said that to him before she left. She had at least a passing interest in him, or she wouldn't have wanted to pursue seeing him in the future. He would just have to wait and see where his relationship went with her, if anywhere.

Ethan's pleasant thoughts about Summer were then suddenly invaded by ghosts from his past. He had loved Emma, too, or at least thought he did, Ethan pondered. Look at what happened to me when I fell in love with Emma, Ethan mused. I thought we'd be together forever, and she betrayed me in such a terrible, horrible way. I thought Emma was perfect for me, just like I now do with Summer, Ethan continued thinking. Does she have a boyfriend back in Thomasville whom Jake just didn't know about yet? Ethan wondered.

Ethan's mind then drifted further to a more sobering memory. Ethan had told himself he would never, ever be hurt again and that if he couldn't trust Emma, he could never and would never trust another woman. He knew he could count on his abilities as a hedge fund manager. He felt his talents weren't an emotion, but rather a reality and a skill and would never let him down. Ethan had spent the last three years honing that skill further, relying on his logical, rational mind to drive his actions.

The result was the last three years he had enjoyed tremendous financial success, and he didn't have to be concerned with affairs of the heart. Ethan didn't have to worry about being betrayed or let down by a woman. He could count on himself alone and his skills and abilities. He knew what he could do, and it was solid, dependable, and reliable. There was no element of risk in his life the last three years, he reasoned. Ethan knew in his heart his current career was his calling, and he was excellent at it.

After all, could Summer really be any different from Emma? Wouldn't she end up betraying him and hurting him just as Emma had? Maybe she was just after money or security. Maybe she was just using me for sex, he continued contemplating.

Ethan had geared his life, his mind and his emotions to not allowing love back into his heart. After three years of this mindset, he had convinced himself that he had successfully trained his mind and emotions to be impervious to its reaches, but Summer had broken through his defenses so easily and quickly, which disturbed Ethan and left him very, very conflicted.

Ethan, now exhausted from bouncing around in his mind all of these thoughts about Summer, had decided to just relax for a while and escape from thinking about Summer and love. He looked over the remaining wine selection at his house and determined he was completely out of chardonnay. The other wines looked good enough, but were not appealing to him today. Ethan decided only a chardonnay would do, so he walked up to The Cowgirl Kitchen to rummage through their wine selection.

Once inside, he quickly found one of the chardonnays that he and Summer had shared. The owner of the house must have purchased it here, he thought. Ethan bought two bottles of the wine and left the store. He then headed back to his house to drink one of them.

As he left The Cowgirl Kitchen, Ethan heard a voice yelling from behind him, "Hey, kid! Kid! Ethan!" Upon hearing his name, Ethan turned around to see Michael, the friend he met on the beach that first day. Michael was walking quickly toward him, and this time, without his wife Janine. What a relief, Ethan thought, hoping that would mean no personal questions today. He was just not in the mood.

As Michael finally reached him, Ethan said, "Hey, Michael. Where's Janine today?"

"Hey, kid. I wasn't sure I'd get your attention since you were walking away from me so fast. Janine is at the house getting packed for us to head back to New York," Michael replied. Ethan could tell he was winded from the brisk walk to catch up with him.

"I see. So y'all are headed out today, then?" Ethan asked.

"Yeah, I need to get on back for my investor meeting in New York. I didn't get a chance to tell you the other day on the beach, but I'm an investor in a large hedge fund in New York," Michael replied.

"What a coincidence! I think I mentioned I manage a small hedge fund for some investors in Valdosta," Ethan replied.

"I did remember that, Ethan, which is why I had hoped to see you again before we left," Michael replied.

"Has your fund done well?" Ethan asked curiously.

"You know, our fund has done really well. The guy running it has been able to generate a fifteen percent return on investment each year for the last ten years, so we've been pleased," Michael responded. Ethan sensed that Michael was brimming with pride at how well the fund and his investment had fared under this manager.

"Well, a fifteen percent return is certainly something to be proud of. He obviously does his homework and has a knack for selecting the best companies and industries to invest in," Ethan added, wanting to be supportive of Michael's opinion of the fund.

Ethan, however, knew his fund had been able to generate a return of over twenty percent per year since it started. His fund had been operating ten years also, and he would stack his performance up against anyone, he thought.

"Yeah, he's thorough, alright. Listen, I'm glad I saw you today. I wanted to tell you if you're ever up in New York, please look me up, and you can stay with us while you're there. I'll give you a tour of Wall Street. Since you're in the industry, I think you'd love it," Michael offered.

"That's nice of you, Michael. If I'm ever up there, I'll definitely call you, and when you find yourself in Valdosta again, please let me know so we can get together and talk investing," Ethan offered in return.

"Sure, will do, kid. I've gotta run. Tell Karl I said hello, if you don't mind," Michael asked politely.

"I sure will. I'll probably see him next week and will tell him for you. Have a safe trip home," Ethan replied.

"See ya, kid. Bye," Michael called out as Ethan watched him begin walking away just as quickly as he arrived. Ethan felt he was clearly a man on a mission. It was nice to see him again, Ethan thought, and he then turned and proceeded back to his house.

∽

The drive home for Summer was entertaining, as usual. She could always count on Jake for plenty of conversation and kidding around. They talked all the way to Tallahassee, and now, after finishing their shopping, they were on the remaining drive home to Thomasville. Jake had picked up his I-pod and began playing games, so Summer had time alone with her thoughts.

She missed Ethan terribly already. She found herself longing for conversation with him, eating with him, taking walks with him, enjoying wine with him, staring at his handsome face and rock-hard body, kissing him, and so much more. He was so kind and considerate of both her and Jake. He had such a kind spirit, she thought, and the passion that man had was unbelievable, nothing like she had ever seen nor experienced.

Summer couldn't help but think, too, that there was so much more to this man. She couldn't wait to experience what that was with him. She wondered what he was doing at that very moment. Was he thinking of her? Was he thinking of someone else? Did he really mean it when he told her he loved her? Summer knew she did. She couldn't believe she said it, but for her, it was real. She had fallen so quickly for him. Everything about Ethan and their relationship thus far had been so effortless, she thought.

How could she not think about how effortless it had been between him and Jake? He was so good with Jake, and the two of them had hit it off better than she could have possibly dreamed. They genuinely seemed to enjoy each other and connect in an unseen way, from their very first meeting. They both enjoyed baseball, but she felt it was deeper than that with the two of them. Summer knew Jake would tolerate Ethan if he knew his mother liked him, but he actually enjoyed seeing and being with Ethan. It was obvious to Summer in Jake's eyes when he talked about Ethan.

Summer found herself in awe of everything about Ethan. She couldn't help but wonder, was their meeting simply fate, chance, or a coincidence? Summer was a woman of deep faith in God and knew better and didn't believe in such things. She knew in her heart it was divine intervention that caused her to meet Ethan Phillips. That was the only explanation she would accept. Ethan seemed too perfect for her and for Jake for the meeting to just be some strange twist of fate or act of random chance.

Suddenly, her thoughts were interrupted by an anxious comment from Jake, saying, "Hey, Mom, are we almost home? I have to go to the bathroom."

Summer quickly replied, "Yes, baby. We're about ten minutes away, so just hold on."

"Okay, but hurry," Jake nervously answered.

The drive from Tallahassee had gone so quickly, Summer thought, thanks to her daydreaming about Ethan. Shortly, they pulled into their driveway and were back home. Jake sprang out of the car like a jack in the box and into the house to go to the bathroom. Time to return to reality, Summer thought and was sad to do so, especially without the amazing new man in her life.

Chapter Seventeen

SUMMER WAS HOME, and she turned her attention to unloading the car. She only had about thirty minutes to spare before she had to get Jake over to his dad's house for the next four days. He normally didn't get this much time with Jake, especially during the work week, but insisted on it to make up for the vacation week the boy had spent with Summer. She knew he was just being difficult and cared more about inconveniencing her than spending time with Jake.

Just then, she remembered she had told Ethan she would let him know when she got home. Summer thought it was nice to now have a man in her life that cared for her well-being and safety. She pulled out her phone and typed him a quick text so he wouldn't worry. It said, *Hey Ethan! I just wanted to let you know we made it home safe and sound. I hope you have had a great day! Talk soon. Summer.*

With the text sent, she could move ahead with emptying the car. She wouldn't have time to get everything unpacked, but she could at least get all the beach supplies out of her car before taking Jake. Thankfully, she had thought ahead and already packed Jake's bag for him to take to his dad's.

Jake came back to the door after having safely made it to the bathroom and asked, "Mom, can I have a snack?"

"No, sir," she replied. "Your daddy is taking you out to eat when you get there, and you're not going to spoil your dinner," she continued.

"Aw, Mom, please!" Jake pleaded. Summer knew he was simply angling for a snack in the event that supper with his dad didn't meet his expectations.

"No, sir," Summer reiterated. "Go look in your room and make sure there aren't any toys or games you want to take with you to your daddy's," she advised Jake, knowing all too well he was prone to forgetting something.

"Okay," Jake replied sadly and Summer watched him slump to his room to take a look around.

⌘

Ethan had spent the afternoon on the beautiful white sandy beach. The temperature had been ideal yet again, and he had soaked in plenty of sunshine. His complexion was gradually getting darker with each day's exposure to the sun. He had also sipped on some refreshments from his cooler on the beach, and he had taken a few brief dips in the cool gulf waters. It had been a great afternoon. The only thing missing was Summer and Jake, he thought.

With it nearing six o'clock, Ethan was drained and tired from his refreshments and his afternoon on the beach. He walked back into his house and was about to wash off the sun, salt, and lotion from the afternoon when suddenly he heard his cellphone chime. It was his text message alert. He walked to the table and saw there was a text from Summer. Ethan read it and was relieved to know she and Jake had made it home safely.

Based on what she had said, he knew it would be late in the afternoon before she made it, so he had not been worried about her just yet. Ethan was glad she and Jake were home safe, but he missed her. How nice it would be to be able to eat dinner with her again tonight, he contemplated, as he prepared to shower.

⌘

"Jake? C'mon, baby, it's time to go. We don't want to be late to your daddy's," Summer yelled through the house to get Jake's attention.

"Coming, Mom!" Jake yelled from his room in the back corner of their house. Summer watched him come rambling through the rooms, jogging lightly and making a game of dodging the furniture as he made his way to the carport door.

"Do you have all the toys you need?" Summer asked.

"I'm good, Mom. I've got a lot of stuff over there already, and I've got the Lego set you just got me," he replied.

"Alright, if you say so. You just remember that I'm not running over there if you forgot anything, okay?" Summer warned. She had made numerous trips to Craig's house during Jake's time with him, and her patience had finally run out. Jake was getting old enough now to be more responsible, she thought, so now she would only remind him before he left to make sure he had everything he needed. Summer knew that Jake had responded well though, as he usually did, and since that time she was pleased he hadn't asked her to bring him anything.

Craig lived about twenty minutes from Summer's house, so it was a short drive. It was too close for comfort for her. She would be satisfied if she never saw the man again, but she knew they had a child together. She had to tolerate Craig and communicate with him at least until Jake made it through college.

The drive to Craig's went by quickly, and Jake had been quiet and absorbed in his I-pod game. "I want you to behave for your daddy, okay, baby?" Summer reminded Jake nicely.

"I know, Mom. I know," he responded. Summer sensed Jake's exasperation at being reminded yet again to behave.

They arrived at Craig's house, and she pulled up in the driveway and parked. Craig wasn't outside and was no doubt self-absorbed in something inside the house or in the back yard, Summer thought. She was just fine with not having to see him, and she watched as Jake got his things and got out of the car.

"Goodbye, baby. I'm going to miss you! I had fun this week," Summer cheerfully told him and meant every word of it.

"Bye, Mom. I had fun, too! Love you!" Jake called out. Summer watched him run to Craig's garage door.

"I love you, too, baby," Summer called back as she leaned out the car window. She then pulled out and made the short drive back to her house. After she returned to her house and resumed unpacking, she could only wonder what that wonderful man Ethan Phillips was doing right now. Summer knew one thing; she already missed him terribly.

෴

Ethan had the shower water running, and it had just reached his ideal temperature. As he entered, he flashed back to his and Summer's smoking hot encounter in there. He would never be able to see that shower the same way again, Ethan decided. Ethan quickly showered, then when he finished, he exited and finished getting dressed.

While getting dressed, his thoughts turned to dinner. What do I want to eat tonight? Ethan pondered. Do I want anything here in Rosemary Beach? Do I want something different? These questions ricocheted around in his mind briefly, then he decided he wanted something totally different tonight.

Ethan got into his car and drove to Panama City Beach to see what kind of restaurant he could find. As he was entering Panama City Beach on Back Beach Road, he came to Pier Park. It was a large, sprawling shopping complex complete with restaurants and retail shops for almost every person's taste. Ethan decided he would pull in there and see what he could find. As he was easing around through one of the cozy streets, a sign for a Five Guys Burgers caught his eye.

He loved Five Guys Burgers, but seldom ate there because doing so would totally derail his diet. He was on vacation, Ethan decided, and gave in to his desire for fast food. He pulled in and ate a hamburger and fries and thoroughly enjoyed it. It was so good, and he wished he had his metabolism from his teenage years so he could eat it more often. The sun had drained Ethan that afternoon, and after having eaten, he was feeling sleepy. He decided to head straight back to the house and just relax a little, then turn in early.

During the drive back to the house and now, as he lounged on his deck, Ethan had continued to think of Summer and all of her amazing qualities and their brief time together. She was just so perfect, it seemed to Ethan. Ethan decided he genuinely missed her today. Their conversations were amazing, and time flew by when they were together. Their sexual chemistry was explosive, he thought, like fire and gasoline mixed together.

Ethan also wondered if Summer was thinking about him. Darkness had now set in, and it was a little after nine o'clock on Tuesday. Maybe I should give her a call and say hello, Ethan questioned.

⸙

Summer unpacked hers and Jake's suitcases and was now knee-deep in laundry. It's amazing how much laundry two people can generate in just one week, she mused. While the washing machine and dryer were working steadily, Summer was enjoying a little television on her spacious pale yellow couch.

The couch was comfortable and fit nicely in her large great room. In fact, the entire home was spacious. It was just over twenty-three hundred square feet, and it was located in a gated community on the north side of Thomasville called Martha's Plantation.

Summer had chosen the subdivision because it was gated and because it was occupied by families. There was a real sense of safety and community there. The common areas were well landscaped, and the streets were all paved and lit well at night. The subdivision was convenient to town, and the residents often had gatherings in the community pavilion.

It was just a neat place to live for both her and Jake, she felt. Summer's house was tastefully done on the outside, with sections of hand-laid stone, and the rest of the house was trimmed in wood siding that was a pale yellow in color.

Summer had been unable to think of much else except Ethan since she returned home from dropping off Jake. In fact, she had been so caught up with being at Rosemary Beach and meeting and spending those magical moments with Ethan that she had completely forgotten about updating her daily diary.

Until the evening she met Ethan it had been a daily ritual for her to write down her thoughts and experiences each day; however, she had been consumed by the whirlwind known as Ethan Phillips, and since that night the diary had completely slipped her mind.

Now curled up on her couch with a glass of chardonnay, she began cataloguing those wonderful last few days in her life. Summer wrote at a furious pace as her thoughts came racing through her mind faster than she could write. Her words and thoughts just flowed onto the pages and, before she knew it, two hours had passed by.

She soon finalized the last entry for today, then suddenly, she was startled by her cellphone's blaring out its usual ring. She then looked over and saw it was Ethan, and she smiled happily. That's crazy, he's calling just as I'm writing about him, she thought.

❧

"Hello?" Summer said as she picked up the phone.

"Well, hello there, Ms. Davis," Ethan replied with a wry smile. "Did I call you at a bad time?" he asked.

"No, Mr. Phillips, you didn't. I was just sitting here on my couch watching a little television and enjoying a glass of wine," Summer replied. Ethan observed that she was cleverly matching his exaggerated formality.

"Very nice. I'm here on the deck outside doing the same thing. Let me guess you're enjoying a glass of chardonnay, right?" Ethan asked, hoping his gut hadn't failed him.

"Very good; you're correct. I'm sure the view and weather are perfect on your deck, aren't they?" Summer asked.

"Yeah, it feels great out here, and it's almost perfect. I'm just missing one thing tonight," Ethan offered with his voice trailing off as he finished his sentence.

"What's missing?" she asked expectantly.

"I'm missing a certain brown-haired, brown-eyed girl tonight, or the evening would be perfect," Ethan quickly replied with his flirtatious tone oozing through the phone.

She replied, "You're sweet. It would certainly be nice to be there with you, alright."

"Did you get unpacked and get Jake to his dad's this evening?" he asked, interested in how her day had progressed once she returned home.

"I sure did. Jake wasn't thrilled to go, as you might imagine, but that went good, and I have my last two loads of laundry in the washer and dryer," Summer responded. Ethan could tell from her happy tone that she was satisfied with her accomplishments that evening.

"That's great! Do you have a lot of events to catch up on after being off for a week?" Ethan asked intently.

"I do have some catching up to do, but not too much. I have a wedding not this coming weekend, but next, that I'm working on. Most of the work will come next week, I think," Summer responded.

The two continued to talk, with each inquiring about what the other's week would be like, how great a time each of them had with each other, and how quickly their time together passed by at Rosemary Beach. Before they knew it, they had been talking for forty-five minutes.

As they talked, Ethan wanted to ask her so badly if she wanted to drive back down Wednesday afternoon and stay with him his final evening. He wasn't sure, though, if she would think he was crazy or being too forward to ask such a thing. Was it too much trouble for her? Would she be offended? Would she think he was expecting sex, which he wasn't? The questions again overran Ethan's mind.

He knew though that he simply wanted her company. Finally, after juggling all the questions around in his head as he was talking with this fabulous woman, Ethan decided to put all of his money on red and just go for it and ask her. Summer was special to him. He loved being with her, and he had to ask.

"Listen, Summer, I know this might be a lot to ask, but I wanted to see if you might want to drive back down tomorrow afternoon and spend the afternoon and evening with me on my last night here? I'd like to see you again, but if it's too much, I'll totally understand, given the distance involved," Ethan asked hopefully.

๑

Summer was so flattered he had asked her to come back down. She could hardly contain her excitement as he asked her. She had butterflies in her stomach now and felt the happiness she was feeling rushing rapidly throughout her body.

Gaining her breath and composure, she responded, "That would be great, Ethan. Let me see what I have tomorrow afternoon to do for this wedding. If I don't have much pressing and could leave here by one or so in the afternoon, then I think I'd be able to come. I think it's only like a three-hour drive from here."

๑

Ethan was now ecstatic himself. While Summer didn't definitely agree to come, it did sound like she wanted to and was going to try. He began to feel *his* stomach now fluttering with excitement, too, at seeing this beautiful woman again.

"Okay, yeah, that makes sense. I'd love for you to come down if you can. I can cook here, or we could eat out close by here in town. The weather is supposed to be perfect all week, so that shouldn't be an issue. I could even meet you halfway, and we could ride the rest of the way together, if you wanted," Ethan replied, with excitement in his voice.

"Alright, why don't I just either text or call you around lunch tomorrow and let you know what I think I can do," she offered hopefully.

"Sure, that will be great! I'll just listen out for you tomorrow then. I better let you get back to your laundry so you aren't up all night doing it. I hope you have a great night and great day tomorrow, Summer," he replied, with his excitement still obvious in his voice.

"That sounds good! I'll be in touch tomorrow. Enjoy the beach tomorrow, Ethan. Bye!" Summer replied happily.

"Goodbye, Summer," Ethan replied as he hung up.

They both were again on cloud nine with the thought of being together one more night at romantic Rosemary Beach. They each wondered if their passion would erupt again in that special place, and both hoped so badly that it would. Their passions were burning for each other like a cauldron of hot lava and there was little that could extinguish it.

Chapter Eighteen

SUMMER RELAXED ON her couch for another hour that evening enjoying her wine, thinking about Ethan and hoping her schedule would allow her to see him again tomorrow. The past week had been so special, she thought. She would no doubt look back and read about it in her diary one day and see it was the beginning of something great, she dreamed.

The next morning was busy, but productive for Summer. She was able to respond to all her emails and also return phone calls to the vendors who called about the upcoming wedding. She also talked with new callers wanting to arrange meetings with her to get quotes for their upcoming events.

She was almost to the point of needing an assistant, as her reputation was now growing with each satisfied customer. It was nearly eleven in the morning, and she decided to check in on her parents and see how they were doing. She hadn't talked to them since she went to Rosemary Beach, and she felt guilty and wanted to see how they were.

Summer's parents were both in their late seventies. They were quite the couple and loved each other tremendously, but it wasn't obvious. Her father, Mark Davis, was a retired real estate broker. He was tall at 6'3" and had always been considered handsome. His hair was now solid gray, and his bright blue eyes contrasted with his hair sharply. He had made a small fortune selling homes and land in Thomasville and Tallahassee in the eighties and nineties and had been able to retire relatively young at the age of fifty-five.

The early part of his retirement he had maintained his same professional manner, for the most part, that he had during his working years, but his wife, Sharon, had suffered a mild stroke when they both had just turned sixty-five. Since then, the toll from looking after Sharon and himself and from maintaining their house and farm in the country had changed him.

Now, he had evolved into someone less concerned with his appearance and what people thought about what he said or did. He basically did what he wanted and what was convenient. He also said what he wanted and could care less what anyone thought about it.

In addition, he had developed an affinity for bourbon, which he used every day to cope with the stresses in his life and with his now increasing pain in both of his knees. He had been active all his life and, as a result, the cartilage in those knees was gradually giving way and causing him pain.

Her mother, Sharon, had been a beautiful woman all her life until the stroke. She was still pretty, but the effects of the stroke on her wrinkles and body were unmistakable. She still had light brown hair, thanks to her hairdresser. Her brown eyes were still as pretty as ever, and it was clear to anyone who met her that she had given Summer her eyes. She had a quick wit and temper, and her temper had gotten progressively worse since the stroke.

Her patience was now almost nonexistent. The stroke she suffered had limited the use of her left arm and left leg, which meant she was unable to drive or see about much around the house. She was also able to cook very little. Most all of that responsibility fell now to Mark or to their maid that came three days a week.

To the casual observer, Mark and Sharon would appear to stay in a constant state of argument, but the reality was that was just how they communicated, usually. It had worked for them for over fifty years of marriage. They loved each other now more than ever, and Summer knew that. They lived only a few miles from her home.

Summer arrived at their house and promptly went in the back door, unannounced, as she always did. As she opened the door and entered the kitchen, Mark was bent over in front of her emptying trash from under the kitchen sink.

Mark had developed a habit of making "homemade" outfits, and today, unfortunately for Summer, he had chosen to wear one of his creations. He had on a yellow T-shirt with the sleeves cut out and gray jogging pants that he had cut the legs out of. While bent over the trash can, these "shorts" were too loose and sagged down in the back, revealing almost half of his white butt to Summer. It wasn't a pretty sight to a daughter, and she could only roll her eyes and say, "Hey, Daddy."

It had become a family tradition for the Davises that every holiday Mark would invariably show all of his derriere, or at least part of it, to the family. It usually happened after a few glasses of bourbon when he was bending over taking out the garbage or getting pots and pans out of the kitchen cabinets. It had become a standing joke between Summer and her brother. It seemed to Summer that Mark could care less that he showed his butt to anyone.

Summer watched him stand upon hearing her voice, turn around, and say with a beaming smile, "Hey, there, Sunshine! How's my baby today? I've missed ya!"

"I've missed you, too, Daddy. How've you been?" Summer asked.

"I've been about the same, child. I've been busy seeing about the old ball and chain in there in the living room," Mark said lightly and with a chuckle. Summer could tell by his quiet voice and expression that he hoped Sharon didn't hear him.

"I heard that, you jackass! If I have to come in there, you won't like it!" Sharon called out. Summer knew she had unbelievable hearing, which landed Mark in trouble constantly. "Are you talking to yourself again?" Sharon continued.

"No, Sunshine is here, and I'm talking to her, thank you very much. You can go back to sleep now," Mark called back to Sharon as he laughed and smiled at Summer, quietly, of course. Summer was well aware that he enjoyed aggravating Sharon. Summer also knew that Sharon drew a great deal of satisfaction from drilling Mark.

"How was the beach, Sunshine?" Mark eagerly asked Summer.

"It was fun, Daddy. Jake and I had a really good time. We just got all wrapped up in Rosemary Beach. You know how it is there," she replied.

"Yes, honey, I do. Me and your Momma had some good times there. How's my little buddy?" Mark asked.

"Jake is doing just fine, Daddy. He had a great time and hated to leave. He's at Craig's now for a few days," Summer continued with sadness again overtaking her expression as she mentioned Jake's staying with Craig.

∽

About this time her mother had managed to work her way into the room. "Hey, honey. I'm here now, no thanks to El Lardo," Sharon blurted out. Mark could tell she was clearly aggravated with him, as was usually the case. She and Mark weren't arguing, but they had a different way of communicating with one another.

"I'm glad you could join us, Sharon," Mark offered with a devilish grin flashed at Summer. He couldn't resist taking jabs at Sharon, too. He knew walking was slow for her, and if she really needed his help, she would ask him. He, of course, would be there for her as he always was. After all, he loved her deeply.

Just then, Mark turned and made his way across the kitchen, too, and as he did, he tripped over his shoelace and almost fell.

"Are you okay, Daddy?" Summer called out excitedly.

"Yes, honey, I'm fine," Mark replied.

Sharon then callously chimed in, "I know one thing. A person with two good legs who can't walk across the kitchen without tripping like you doesn't deserve to have 'em."

∽

Mark, knowing Sharon was just aggravating him for his smart comment, ignored Sharon's statement and asked Summer hopefully, "You going to stay with us for lunch, honey?"

"Thanks, Daddy. I'm probably going to go grab something downtown though. What are you having?" Summer questioned.

"Well, child, I'm boiling some hot dogs, and they're almost done. I'm about to pour in some rice right quick, too," Mark replied, clearly happy with himself for his innovation at finding a way to cook two separate items simultaneously in the same boiler. Mark enjoyed finding odd ways to cook things together that didn't belong, in the interest of saving time. It was something usually no one else but he could stomach eating.

"Um, no thanks, Daddy," Summer replied. Mark couldn't miss the queasy expression on Summer's face.

⁓

With that comment she and her mother made their way into the den to talk.

"Nobody in their right mind wants to eat a hot dog with rice, Mark," Summer heard Sharon call out as she walked into the den with her. "Only a fool would do that!" Sharon continued.

"How was your trip, honey?" Sharon asked Summer. Summer perceived that her mother was anxious to know how the vacation went.

"It was good, Momma. Jake and I had a blast, and I actually met a guy from Valdosta, believe it or not," Summer offered, with her face glowing as she began talking about Ethan.

"What? That's great! I've been praying you would find a decent man. Lord knows you deserve one after living with that fool you were married to," Sharon replied. Summer knew that her mother had a painfully obvious distaste and resentment for Craig Johnson. She also knew that neither she nor Mark cared much for him after the way he treated her.

"Aw, Momma. That's in the past, so let's just let it go. The guy's name is Ethan, and he met Jake, too, and they hit it off really well. We both hit it off with him. It was surreal how well it went with him and how well he and Jake connected," she replied, trying to get her mom away from talking about Craig.

"That's good, honey. I'm so glad. I hope it's gonna work out for you two. So what's he like?" Sharon asked.

"Thanks, Momma, me, too! He's tall with brown hair and hazel-green eyes, and he's athletic and strong. He's so easy to talk to, and he seems to enjoy me as much as I do him. We can talk for hours without stopping and don't seem to get tired of each other's company. I've never been with anyone like him, Momma," Summer elaborated, smiling brightly the whole time.

"Wow! It seems like you two really meshed, huh? Just take it slow, honey, and enjoy the journey with him," Sharon replied. Summer cringed because she felt like her mom was once again giving advice. Summer knew she probably wouldn't heed it either as she rarely had listened to her mother.

"I will, Momma," Summer replied, knowing it was way too late to take it slow. She had already had two fantastic sexual escapades with Ethan and couldn't wait for more. "So, how's your week been?" Summer asked, trying to get her Momma away from giving advice.

"It's been fine. We had some excitement, though, honey. Your Daddy went into town yesterday to get groceries, and somebody came and knocked at the door. They just kept knocking and knocking so I finally had to call the sheriff to come out here. He looked around and couldn't find anyone, then asked if he could come inside for some coffee, so I let him. We talked for a while, and he just bragged on how well I kept the house, and I couldn't thank him enough," Sharon replied.

By this time Mark, who had overheard all of their conversation, as he usually did, was making his way into the den. Once he was in the den, Summer watched him as he stood behind Sharon and quietly shook his head *no* side to side and mouthed the words, *she's at it again* to Summer and smiled as he said it. Summer smirked just a little after understanding what he said.

For some unknown reason, since Sharon had her stroke she would on occasion make up a tale about something that never happened. She would go into great detail about what supposedly occurred, and it took Summer and Mark a while to realize she was making it all up. Sharon would tell the stories after she had been alone without Mark for more than an hour or two. Summer and Mark would laugh about these stories with each other now that they knew Sharon was making them up, probably because she was lonely and had an impaired mind as a result of her stroke.

"Whoa, Momma! That's scary! It's a good thing you thought to call the sheriff and they came out, huh?" Summer replied sympathetically.

"It sure is! I'm fine, no thanks to El Lardo! He just went off and left me here, and my being a stroke victim!" Sharon responded. Summer could see the indignation on Sharon's face as she spoke.

"Aw, you're too mean for anyone to mess with, Sharon," Mark chimed in. Summer noticed him winking at her as he spoke.

Now trying to change the subject and prevent more arguing, Summer said, "I wanted to let you know I may run back down to Rosemary Beach this afternoon to see Ethan. In case you need me, I'll have my cellphone. Jake is going to be with his daddy through Thursday, so he's taken care of."

"Ethan is his name, huh, child?" Mark asked, raising his eyebrows up and down rapidly like W.C. Fields as he asked her. "Don't fall for that boy, honey. He's probably just after your money," Mark added.

"Oh, Daddy, stop!" Summer replied with frustration. Summer did not appreciate her dad providing his unsolicited opinion.

"Yeah, you leave her alone, Mark. You don't know any better than to leave a stroke victim by themselves, so you shouldn't be giving anybody advice," Sharon fired back at Mark.

Summer watched Mark chuckle at Sharon's comment and quip back with a smile, "Aw, you won't remember this conversation tomorrow anyway, honey."

Summer by now had become exhausted from her parents' constant arguing. When she spent much time with her parents doing so always made her feel this way. While the way they communicated both stressed her out and wore her out, it clearly had worked for Mark and Sharon for fifty years and continued to do so. She was ready to get back to work and get caught up so she could go see her handsome, sexy man in Rosemary Beach.

"Alright, you two lovebirds, I'm going to head on to my office. Call me if you need me. Bye; love you!" Summer offered as she walked out and headed to her office.

"Bye, honey. Be careful and see you soon. We love you!" Mark called out for both him and Sharon as Summer walked to her car and left.

Chapter Nineteen

TUESDAY WAS PASSING fairly quickly for Ethan. He had settled back in to his "pre-Summer" routine of exercising, working some, and hanging out at the beach. His routine helped the time pass, but he knew part of the reason it passed so easily was that he would hopefully see Summer later on that day. The expectation of seeing her again excited him greatly. He missed her immensely already. Ethan couldn't wait to see her again, talk to her again, kiss her again, hold her again, and make passionate love to her again.

He had received a brief text from Summer at lunch that read, *Hey Ethan. Looks like I'm going to be able to come down. I'm leaving here at two. Looking forward to seeing you! Bye!* Ethan had replied how happy he was that she was coming and reminded her to be careful on the drive. He was ecstatic to have her coming back down to be with him.

Ethan wanted to have something special for Summer when she walked into his house again. He knew from one of their long conversations that she loved sunflowers, so after finishing his lunch, he decided to find her some. He needed to buy some groceries for tonight anyway, so he would go to the supermarket first, then look for some flowers before coming home.

He thought he would surprise Summer by cooking for her again tonight. She seemed to enjoy it before, and it was more relaxing for them to talk and connect, Ethan felt.

Ethan finished getting dressed and drove to Publix to find all the ingredients to prepare a meal to impress the beautiful lady in his life now. As Ethan was walking in the automatic door at Publix, he was stunned. The first thing he saw as he went in the door are the numerous bright bouquets of sunflowers to his right. What? That's really weird, he thought. I don't remember seeing those when I was here before. He was happy to have found them here and quickly gathered three or four of the small bouquets and resumed his shopping.

He worked his way through the supermarket quickly. He had settled on a more traditional South Georgia meal for tonight. He had become homesick for his traditional cuisine and hoped Summer would feel likewise and not be upset they weren't going out to eat again. If not, Ethan decided, he had made a reservation at Edward's as a backup.

Ethan was going to grill some chicken and also have fresh cut green beans, field peas, bread, and salad, with chardonnay to drink, and no meal would be complete for him and Summer without a dessert. Chocolate cake was a big hit before, so Ethan found a few individual slices in the bakery section, and his list was now complete. All that remained was to prepare everything tonight and hope it would be edible.

∾

Summer found the drive back to Rosemary Beach to be extremely long this time. She knew it felt that way because she was so anxious to be back there and because she couldn't wait to see Ethan again. She was so excited that he had asked her to come back and visit before he left.

Summer was also grateful that her work hadn't prevented her from making the trip. It was unusual for her to have been gone for a solid week and not have to be running around like a chicken with its head cut off, trying to play catch up from being gone. It was meant for her to see Ethan again that day, she decided.

She found herself daydreaming about him again as she drove. Summer contemplated the passion this man had for her and how well he could express it. She also thought about how genuine, sincere, caring, and sweet he was. Why couldn't she have met this man twenty years ago? she wondered. She then thought if she had, then Jake wouldn't be here. She wouldn't trade him for anything, and her faith always told her everything happened for a reason.

She knew in her heart this was the man truly meant for her. She had only just met him, but it was a strong, powerful feeling inside that was as certain to her as the rising sun. Her dreaming was suddenly interrupted by a car honking its horn at her from behind.

She snapped out of her trance and realized she had arrived at Rosemary Beach and been daydreaming at the traffic light leading into there. She quickly regrouped at the green light and went ahead down 30A into Barrett Square. She was back, and she drew contentment from the fact that Ethan was waiting for her.

⤧

Ethan had finished getting showered and dressed and was now quickly surveying the house to make sure everything was in order. The sunflowers were perched neatly in the kitchen on the bar. He had found a vase in one of the cabinets in the house to put them in. The grill was ready to start when they were hungry and so was the rest of the food. Suddenly, as he looked around one more time, he heard the doorbell ring. It's Summer, he thought.

Ethan dashed over to the door and opened it, and there she was, in all her beautiful splendor. She had a bright blue sundress draped around that perfect figure of hers. It was clinging tightly to her gorgeous body. In the front the dress was cut low and revealed more than enough of those voluptuous and perfect breasts to ignite his imagination, he thought. Ethan instantly began to remember what those breasts looked, felt, and tasted like. He snapped out of his brief daydream.

"Hey, Summer! You're right on time. I'm so glad you could come," he said with excitement as he stepped over and gave those perfect lips a gentle kiss hello.

"Hey! I'm glad to be here. It's good to see you again, especially here. Thank you for inviting me," she replied. Ethan observed obvious excitement in her words.

"Oh, you're welcome. I've been looking forward to seeing you. I know you must be worn out from that drive. Come in and relax while I take care of your bag. Can I pour you a glass of chardonnay to unwind with?" Ethan offered, wanting to be the perfect host.

"Yes, that would be great!" Summer replied.

As Ethan poured their wine he watched Summer as she glided around the room, familiarizing herself with the house once again. He pondered how beautiful she was, how sweet she was, and how perfect she seemed for him.

"This is our favorite chardonnay. I bought another bottle or two since we liked it so much," he mentioned as he turned to place the bottle back into the wine cooler.

❧

Summer turned when he spoke and walked to the kitchen bar where the poured glasses were. "What pretty sunflowers! Were these here before?" she said, admiring them, but not remembering having seen them in the house before.

"Thanks. No, I just bought them today. I remembered your saying you liked them, so I thought I would have some here to welcome you," Ethan said, smiling. Summer observed from his reaction that he drew satisfaction from pleasing and impressing her.

"No way! You remembered that? I'm impressed, Ethan. Thank you!" Summer replied and was floored at his memory and caught off guard at his thoughtfulness.

The two of them then sat in the living room, enjoyed their wine, and caught up with each other on the happenings in their lives that last two days. Ethan was interested in Summer's work and what she had left to do this week.

Summer, for her part, was also interested in what Ethan's week was going to look like once he left tomorrow. The time passed quickly once again for them, and before they knew it, the afternoon had slipped away, and it was now seven.

"Would you mind a change of plans and we eat in tonight?" Ethan asked.

Summer was starving and said excitedly, "Yes that would be perfect."

"I've also made a reservation at Edward's tonight just in case" Ethan continued.

Ethan had thought of everything once again, Summer thought. She indicated she was tired from the drive and eating in would be perfect. Ethan then went to work preparing their meal for the night.

Summer was thrilled to eat in and pleased with Ethan's choice of cuisine again tonight. She helped him prepare everything they would eat. They even cooked well together, she thought.

❧

Dinner turned out to be excellent once again, and they both had eaten too much. The chocolate cake they had for dessert, they decided, had nearly put them over the edge. They both wanted to have the cleaning out of the way, so as soon as they finished eating, they quickly cleaned the kitchen up. It was now time to enjoy each other, and they refilled their wine glasses and retired to the deck to continue talking.

Their conversation on the deck covered a wide range of topics, as was typical with these two. They spent time walking down memory lane, reflecting once again on their childhoods, their parents, their siblings, and how different the world was then.

Summer and Ethan also spent a great deal of time talking about their faith. Summer's was much stronger than Ethan's at this point in their lives, but it was obvious to her that Ethan's had been equally strong at one point. They both shared the same Baptist faith, and she listened to Ethan mention that he had allowed his faith to wane the last few years. They each also told funny stories about their parents and interesting experiences they had encountered with them.

⁓

The sun had set, and now darkness covered Rosemary Beach like a thick blanket. The sky was replete with glittering stars. Many of the surrounding homes were dark, and it seemed like to Summer that everyone must be eating out tonight.

"I have an idea," Summer said with excitement. "Why don't we turn off all our lights and see how well we can see all the stars tonight since it's so dark," she added, wanting to enjoy an evening under the stars with the handsome man she was with.

"That's a great idea! If you'll pour us another glass of wine and turn down all the lights, I'll find something for us to lie on the deck with," Ethan replied.

"Great. Sounds like a plan!" Summer said and made her way into the kitchen to refill their glasses, then made the rounds turning off lights except for those she knew Ethan was using.

⁓

Ethan rummaged through closets looking for anything that would be comfortable to sit or lie on to watch the stars and talk. The deck was gorgeous, but was hard as a rock, and he knew they would need something under them to be able to stay out there and enjoy the evening. All he could find were a couple of thick blankets, so he grabbed those as well as two pillows from his bedroom.

He made his way outside and began setting up their nest to watch the night sky. "This is all I could find. Hopefully it will make it comfortable enough for us to stay out here a little while, at least," he offered apologetically. Ethan was slightly disgusted that he hadn't been able to find anything more suitable.

☙

"Don't worry about it. This will do just fine, I'm sure," Summer replied with kindness and support to let him know what he found was just fine with her. She spread the blankets and pillows and lay down to enjoy their wine, the stars, and more conversation. As she lay there, the wine had served to relax her and bring her guard down. Summer now felt at ease, asking something she had wondered about since that first magical night they spent together.

"Ethan, can I ask you a question?" Summer asked quietly, now shifting their conversation to a serious tone.

"Of course you can," he replied.

"Did you really mean it when you told me you loved me, or were you just caught up in the moment and said it because I did?" Summer asked, wanting to know the answer so badly yet at the same time fearing his reply.

"I did say it in the heat of the moment, as you did, Summer, but I meant every word of it. I still don't understand how I can fall in love with someone so quickly, but I did, and I have. I can't explain it," Ethan replied. Summer could feel genuineness and sincerity filling each word as he spoke. "What about you? Did you mean it, or was it just the moment?" he asked quietly.

"I definitely meant it. I'm like you. I can't explain it, but my feelings are real. My being apart from you briefly has only strengthened my feelings for you," Summer replied lovingly.

"I'm so glad to hear you say that," he said and she noticed him smile back at her.

☙

Ethan then gently eased in and began kissing her softly. He felt her kiss him in return. Suddenly, their passions erupted as they had before. Ethan placed his hands on the sides of Summer's face and began French kissing her passionately. Their tongues were soon again in rhythm like two naked bodies woven together making passionate love.

Ethan couldn't help himself and gently laid Summer down on their homemade bed, and as he continued to kiss her, he eased his right hand down and gently began rubbing her firm, voluptuous breasts. He took his time over the nipples and gently stroked them to make sure they were fully aroused.

He then eased his hand down to Summer's right thigh and slid his hand up under her dress. He soon found her G-string panties and quickly slid his index and middle finger inside them to pleasure her. As he gently began massaging her pleasure point, he could feel her juice flowing and covering his fingers and her panties which filled him with passion for her.

Suddenly, Ethan stopped, sat up, and began gently taking off his shirt first, and then sliding off his pants and his underwear. He then saw Summer, taking his cue, sit up and unzip her dress and slide it off, then quickly take off her bra and panties. What little light that was around allowed Ethan the opportunity to gaze briefly at her perfect body. He was in awe once again of how sexy Summer was.

Ethan moved on top of Summer, then gently slid inside her. He then eased onto his knees, took her legs, and raised them perpendicular to the floor and straight up into the air. He then had her wrap her ankles around the back of his neck and rest her legs against his chest and torso.

As Ethan stroked inside her, he put his hands under her butt, and used his hands, neck, and upper body to lift her off the ground slightly. He continued stroking in and out of her, only now this new position allowed his manhood to rub thoroughly against her G-spot with each thrust. He began stroking faster and faster now, and he heard her moan loudly with pleasure. He watched as she took her hands and placed them over her head and against the wall of the house undoubtedly to hold herself as his forceful thrusts pushed her against the wall.

✄

Summer had never felt anything like this before and never had sex in this position. Pleasure ruled her body as Ethan was inside her. She was loving it. Her G-spot was being massaged constantly with Ethan's manhood and was driving her wild and making her juices flow like a torrential rain. She was in ecstasy and called passionately out to Ethan, "Don't stop, don't stop, baby. Please don't stop."

⁓

Ethan continued to thrust in and out of Summer robustly with his rock hard manhood. As Ethan continued to please her, he heard her groans grow louder, and then she began screaming, "Oh, Ethan, oh Ethan, give it to me. I'm almost there."

He began to thrust into her even harder and faster to ensure an unleashing of her orgasm. He then felt her begin twitching wildly and knew she must now be giving into wave after wave of her orgasm. He continued to thrust and watch as Summer arched her back and called out, "Oh yes . . . yes . . . yes!" He heard her moaning loudly with pleasure, calling his name for another ten or fifteen seconds. He continued to thrust vigorously in and out of her until her body became limp. He also sensed her breathing was slowing but was still rapid and shallow, like she was running a marathon.

Ethan pulled out of her and looked down on her, smiling at having pleased her so well. He saw Summer gaze back at him and whisper, "That was unbelievable, Ethan. I can't see straight."

Ethan then lay down beside her as Summer tried to catch her breath and recover from being worked over by this gorgeous man. He observed her turn on her side toward him and begin kissing him. He felt her begin rubbing his chest and arms. Ethan then saw her looking down to see he was still fully erect.

Summer then said, "I don't think we need to let that go to waste."

Ethan smiled back at her and said, "I was hoping you'd say that." Ethan then got up, sat in one of the deck chairs, and motioned Summer over to him. "I just love it when you do me in a chair," Ethan whispered. "This time I want you to face away from me while you ride me," Ethan said seductively.

⁓

"Okay," Summer whispered back, came to the chair, and eased herself onto him with her back facing Ethan. Ethan had his legs together, and she was straddling him now and began riding him, slowly at first, then much more briskly. She placed her hands on each of the chair's armrests for extra support as she rode him.

138

Summer felt Ethan's hands massaging her buoyant breasts, and then begin fondling her nipples as her breasts bobbed up and down with each thrust onto him. Summer then eased up off him slightly as she rode him, then began sliding up and down on him violently.

⊰

Ethan was overwhelmed and couldn't concentrate on Summer's nipples any longer. He dropped his hands onto her hips and laid his head back as he felt his orgasm approaching. He was in ecstasy with this gorgeous woman with the sexiest body on Earth riding on top of him. They pleasure she induced throughout his body was at critical mass and he couldn't contain it any longer.

⊰

She could tell that Ethan was close to climaxing. His body was tensing and his hands had a vise grip on her hips as she rhythmically rode him. As she was gliding up and down on him, Summer looked over her shoulder and whispered, "Come inside me, Ethan, come inside me, baby."

Summer continued to gaze at him seductively as her words then catapulted him into orgasm, and she felt him explode inside her, calling out "Summer . . . Summer . . . Oh, baby . . . Yes . . . Yes!" As he was releasing his passion into her, she kept looking over her shoulder at him and riding him just as fast to make sure he gave her all of his orgasm. She wanted to feel all of it inside her.

Finally, after she saw Ethan was spent, she stopped riding him. She leaned back against his chest, Ethan wrapped his arms around her, and they embraced each other. Summer and Ethan sat together, feeling wonderful and amazed at what they just experienced together. Ethan then mustered the strength to say, "Wow! Each time is more amazing than the last."

Summer then replied, "Yeah, I know what you mean. I think you blew my head off that time."

"That was intense, very intense. You're amazing, just amazing," Ethan whispered with sincerity.

"Thank you. I don't think I can move," Summer replied with exhaustion in her voice.

"Let's see if we can move enough to lie back down on the deck at least, okay?" Ethan offered gently.

139

"I think I can manage that," Summer replied.

❦

They then lay back down on the blankets and snuggled with each other under the stars. Each was now completely drained, and complete relaxation and a state of euphoria consumed them. They drifted off to sleep. They didn't bother to cover up; they were too exhausted, and if any of the neighbors managed to sneak a peek at them, well then more power to them, they decided. There on the deck they slept naked and in each other's arms under the beautiful, star-filled sky, and neither had ever slept so well.

Chapter Twenty

*T*HE NEXT MORNING Ethan was first to be awakened by the rising morning sun. It took him a minute to figure out where he was, then he looked at Summer and saw her still resting comfortably. She was so beautiful, even early in the morning. He could just sit here and stare at her for hours, he thought. He almost had to pinch himself to remind him last night wasn't a fantasy, but rather was very real and very powerful.

This new woman in his life was unlike any he had ever known, and now, in this moment, he knew more than ever he was totally and completely in love with her. He didn't understand it, but it was too powerful to deny.

Ethan gently eased out from under her so as not to wake her and went to the bathroom. When he came back into the kitchen he glanced at the clock and saw it was eight o'clock. They must have been sleeping for over nine hours, he thought, because he knew it hadn't been a late night for them. Ethan wasn't a coffee drinker, but he knew Summer was. He proceeded to stumble through the process of making her some coffee for her to enjoy when she woke.

As the coffee began brewing, the aroma covered the house and drifted throughout. Its fragrance was enough to bring Summer out of her slumber, and Ethan notice her wrap one of the sheets around herself and step into the kitchen following the smell of coffee.

"Good morning, sunshine," Ethan said to her smiling.

"Well, good morning, sir," she replied with an equally large smile. "You were unbelievable last night," she said, smiling brightly and raising her eyebrows as she spoke. Ethan sensed complete satisfaction from her with their interlude the previous night.

"You were pretty amazing yourself," Ethan replied, smiling as if he had just won the lottery.

"So you drink coffee?" Summer asked him curiously.

"No, I don't, but I knew you did. So, I'm attempting to make you some. I hope it'll be good," Ethan added, almost apologetically.

"You're too sweet to me. Thank you," Summer replied.

The coffee finished brewing, and Ethan proceeded to pour Summer a cup. He watched Summer take the cup and gladly began to drink it. Ethan grabbed a Diet Coke from the refrigerator and began drinking that. "So, would you like some breakfast?" Ethan asked hopefully to Summer, as he was starving.

"I would, but I'm going to make it for you. It's the least I can do after what you did to me last night," she replied with a flirtatious grin. "You go relax a little while I whip up some scrambled eggs and bacon," Summer added.

"Yes, ma'am. I'm not arguing with that. Thanks for cooking breakfast. I'm sure it'll be great," he replied, happy Summer would do such a thing for him. He was not used to such treatment from someone he cared about. Ethan sat at the kitchen table while she cooked breakfast.

They then talked again about their families and also re-lived their sexual escapade last night. Fortunately, whoever had stocked the house before Ethan arrived had thought to have bacon and eggs. Summer's bacon and eggs were delicious, and they ate all she cooked, then talked a while longer.

As they finished their conversation, they both helped clean up the kitchen, and it was finished in no time. By now it was after nine o'clock, and Ethan suggested, "Well, would you like to shower first?"

"Oh, no, that's okay, Ethan. You go ahead, and I can go after you," Summer replied politely.

"No, ladies first. I insist," he continued with a smile as he spoke.

"Alright, I guess I can go ahead. It'll probably take me longer, anyway," Summer responded. She then had her shower and began getting ready.

While Ethan was showering, Summer was standing at the bathroom mirror, but still only in her towel. She was hoping Ethan might take advantage of her again before they left and didn't want to get dressed any sooner than she had to.

She looked on in anticipation as Ethan finished his shower, opened the door, and stepped out to dry off. Summer was able to see him, *all* of him, through the mirror as she was getting ready. Now she really hoped he would take her, as she found herself wanting him badly once again. She looked him over like a cheetah would a wildebeest it's about to chase down and devour.

∽

Ethan finished drying off, wrapped his towel around his waist, and moved into the lavatory to join Summer. He came up behind her, wrapped his arms around her, kissed her gently on the cheek, and said, "I'm glad you were able to come back down yesterday. As strange as it may sound, I missed you."

Summer smiled brightly and replied, "I missed you, too, and I'm so glad I was able to make it."

∽

She then turned to face him and they began kissing passionately. Summer pressed her body against his and began gently rubbing her hands all over Ethan's firm chest and arms. She took her hands and gently dropped his towel to the floor.

She watched Ethan undo hers and join his on the tile. She then dropped to her knees and began using her mouth to pleasure Ethan. She gently slid her lips up and down on his manhood, hoping to fill Ethan with pleasure.

∽

Her touch is irresistible, Ethan thought, as he was fully aroused as she worked her magic on him. Ethan looked down and watched her work and grabbed her behind the head and guided her up and down. Damn, she's good at that, he thought. Finally, he couldn't take it any longer. He just had to have her at that moment.

Ethan quickly pulled her off him and led her to the bed in the master bedroom. He kissed her passionately once again for a minute or so, then quickly turned her around and bent her over the bed. Summer had her hands on the bed as she bent over, then Ethan quickly entered her from behind.

He heard Summer begin moaning almost as soon as he was inside her. It was obvious to him from her reaction that she loved it when he took control of her and made her do what he wanted.

Ethan had his hands now around her hips, and he was using them for leverage. He began thrusting hard in and out of her with their bodies slapping together loudly and rhythmically with each stroke. Ethan felt Summer's juice now pouring out over him and he knew her body was once again saturated with pleasure. Ethan could feel her so much more in this position, and within only a matter of minutes of thrusting wildly into her from behind, he could feel his orgasm about to be unleashed. As it neared, he called out in ecstasy, "Oh, Summer, Summer, oh, God, Summer!"

Ethan looked up to see Summer had turned her head slightly and, looking over her shoulder, seductively said, "Give it to me, Ethan, give it to me. Don't stop!"

Instantly her words triggered Ethan's orgasm and he erupted it into Summer, calling out, "Oh, Summer! Yes, baby, yes!" as his passion throbbed into her. It felt so good climaxing inside her, he thought. He gave Summer every bit of his orgasm as she kept whispering, "That's it. Give it to me, baby, all of it."

After thirty seconds or so of unleashing his passion into her, Ethan then pulled out of her. He raised Summer back up and kissed her gently. "That felt good, huh?" she asked with a smile.

"You have no idea," Ethan replied, still a little short of breath. He hugged her tightly and kissed her gently for a few minutes before he pulled back, looked at her, and said, "Your turn."

Ethan led Summer over to the wall nearest the bed and used his body to pin her against it. He took his right hand, eased it between her legs, and gently began massaging her pleasure point. As Ethan began, he could hear Summer instantly start groaning with satisfaction. He continued to fondle her, then eased his head down onto her right breast and began licking and sucking it gently.

He then started using his tongue to gently lick Summer's nipple. At first he began licking it slowly, but then more rapidly to match the pace of his fondling, doing both in unison.

❧

A wave of pleasure now coursed through Summer's body and mind. Her only focus was on how good this stud made her feel. She watched him move to her left breast and resume licking that nipple rapidly as he continued to stroke her in perfect rhythm. Summer's juice was flowing everywhere and dripping down her leg. She was engulfed with pleasure. Summer had her head leaned back against the wall with her eyes closed and continued to moan and occasionally utter, "Ethan, oh, Ethan, Ethan."

Summer sensed Ethan wanting to send her over the top as he stopped fondling her, got down on his knees in front of her, and began licking her pleasure point rapidly. Summer grabbed Ethan's hair with both hands as she could feel her orgasm building. She had a death grip on his hair and was using his head like a steering wheel to maximize her pleasure. He was so good at this, she thought. "Here it comes, Ethan, here it comes baby," she called out.

Ethan began fondling her with his tongue even faster, then the orgasm overtook her. "Oh, God! Ethan! Oh, God, baby! Yes! Yes!" Summer screamed as the electrical current from her powerful orgasm surged through her body, seeming to stimulate every muscle at one time. Each of her lower torso muscles convulsed wildly and uncontrollably. Her back arched and became rigid from the pleasure driving through her body. She continued her vise grip on Ethan's hair, calling out "Yes, Ethan! Yes, baby, yes!" and screamed with pleasure until she was done. Her orgasm must have lasted at least thirty seconds or more.

Once it was over, she let go of Ethan's hair and slumped against the wall, totally exhausted from what this man had done to her once more. She was unable to move.

⤚

Ethan led her to the bed to lie down and recover. She laid in his arms for about five minutes before she could speak. "That was just incredible," Summer muttered.

"I'm glad you liked it. It was the least I could do for you after what you did to me," Ethan replied with a devilish grin.

"Well, if nothing else, we know how to get each other off, huh?" Summer asked as she chuckled.

"Most definitely! We have that part down pat, I think," Ethan responded, laughing.

They lay there about ten minutes longer in silence, enjoying each other and the moment. Ethan glanced at the clock and saw it was almost ten now. "Well, I guess we need to finish getting dressed so we can be out of here by eleven, don't we?" he proposed.

"Oh shoot! Yes, we do," Summer agreed, and they got up and finished getting dressed. She helped Ethan get the house ready to leave while he finished getting ready and loaded both of their cars.

Ethan suggested they have another late breakfast at the Summer Kitchen Café. They were both famished from their sexual romps, and they each devoured their breakfast. After they finished and he settled the bill, they made their way out to their cars before the long drive home.

"Thank you for another great time," Summer said with a beaming smile.

"You're welcome. I had a blast. I hope I can see you again soon once we get back to Georgia?" Ethan asked hopefully.

"I'm counting on it!" Summer replied happily.

"Great!" Ethan replied with satisfaction.

"I guess we need to head back now," Summer offered reluctantly.

"Yeah, I guess so. You can lead, and I'll follow you back to Thomasville, then head on to Valdosta from there, if that works," Ethan asked, wanting to make sure she made it back safely.

"Sure, I'd feel safer if you did that, if it's not too much trouble," Summer asked.

"It's no trouble at all, and I want to do it," he replied, then leaned in to kiss this special woman goodbye.

❧

They each got into their respective cars and made the drive back home. True to his word, Ethan followed her to Thomasville, and then drove home to Valdosta from there. They both could only think of the other as they drove and thought how nice it would have been to be riding back together and talking the whole way home. Perhaps the next time they came to Rosemary Beach that would be possible, they thought.

Chapter Twenty-One

ONCE ETHAN RETURNED to Valdosta, he quickly settled back in to his routine. He was able to get all of his notes and thoughts summarized, then conducted the investor meeting with everything going well.

He had resumed his workout regimen and was eating well again, also. He had allowed himself to drift on his food and beverage choices while at the beach, but he decided it had been vacation, which in his mind amounted to a free pass on maintaining his diet. Besides, it was well worth it all to have allowed him to experience all he had with Summer, he felt.

Ethan had also taken the time to visit Willie the day after he returned. He spent most of the afternoon at Willie's home catching him up on his trip and on Summer. Willie had soaked up every word of their conversation and was thrilled Ethan had a wonderful time and relaxed. He was also overjoyed that Ethan had indeed found someone special there as he knew Ethan would.

❧

Summer had jumped right back in to her event planning and taking care of Jake. She had also resumed writing each day in her diary. The diary gave her a way to unwind each day, vent on bad days, and relive the fond memories on the good days. She was also excited to have Jake back on a regular schedule, which meant that she had him with her most of the time now.

Each of their schedules had been extremely busy since returning from

Rosemary Beach, and they hadn't been able to see each other yet; however, Ethan did call Summer every other night to talk and catch up on her life and she on his. She would usually talk for an hour or two with him unless he or she had something pressing going on in their lives. Talking on the phone wasn't the same as seeing each other, but it was the best they could do at the moment, she decided.

Summer had been busy preparing for her wedding event, and it had come and gone without a hitch, which had been a tremendous relief. Before she knew it, two weeks had gone by without seeing Ethan, and it seemed like an eternity to her. Hopefully that was about to change soon, she wished.

꿎

Late one Wednesday evening, it was time for Ethan to call Summer, so he dialed her number, as usual. "Hey, handsome!" she greeted Ethan as she answered her cellphone.

"Hey, sexy! How are you doing tonight?" he flirted back.

"I'm doing fine. I just finished going over homework with Jake, and he's taking his shower and getting ready for bed. What are you up to tonight?" she asked Ethan curiously.

"Well, I've just poured myself my evening chardonnay, and I'm winding down for the night. After we get off the phone I'll probably head on to bed. My five-thirty a.m. workout will come all too soon in the morning," he replied with disgust clear in his voice at having to rise so early to work out, but with his work schedule for the hedge fund, he knew it was the only way he could consistently get a workout in each day.

They continued to chat with each other about how their day went. Summer shared that she had another even larger wedding coming in three weeks and a small birthday party next weekend. Ethan mentioned he was knee deep in company analysis and making investment decisions for the fund. He also told her that he would spend a good bit of his time talking with his investors who would call to ask him about a company or his ideas about a certain investment strategy.

It was now almost eleven and time for each of them to go to bed when Ethan decided to ask before hanging up, "So, I was wondering if we could go on a date Friday night?"

"I'd love to, Ethan! I found out tonight that Jake is supposed to spend the night with his dad then and see some of his cousins on that side of the family who are in town for the weekend," Summer replied.

"Great! I can drive down to Thomasville and take you to dinner and a movie, if that works for you," he asked hopefully.

"Sure, that would be great. I'd love that. What time are you thinking?" Summer questioned. Ethan seemed to notice distinct excitement in her voice making it clear to him that she indeed wanted to see him again.

"How about I pick you up at six-thirty? That way we'll have time to eat and make a movie," Ethan offered, wanting to ensure they had time for both.

"Sure! That sounds like a plan," she replied.

"Awesome! I'll plan on seeing you then. I think I'm going to turn in tonight. I've enjoyed talking to you and can't wait to see you Friday," Ethan said.

"Okay. I'm excited, too. I'll see you then. Bye," Summer replied as she hung up the phone.

"Good night, Summer," he replied. He then settled in bed for the night with anticipation of seeing Summer Friday.

Ethan had productive days both Thursday and Friday. As was typical for him, he was always thrilled when Friday arrived and the week ended. For Ethan, the weekends provided a welcomed respite from phone calls from investors as they were busy enjoying their own families. He finished up reviewing his fund's performance for the day, then was showered and dressed in thirty minutes. He headed out the door of his cabin at five forty-five to drive to Thomasville.

⚬

Summer had spent Friday on the phone, for the most part. The upcoming wedding she was planning in Albany was going to be her largest event ever. It seemed there were conference calls with vendors almost daily, then she had the bride and her family making changes practically every other day, which posed its own set of challenges.

Still, it was going to be a large payday for her. If she did a good job, she knew the referrals she would get from all those attending would be enough to put her on the "A" list of wedding planners in Albany. She had finished the last of her phone calls and was back at home. She quickly got dressed and was ready early for her handsome new man to pick her up. She was so excited to see Ethan and spend the evening with him.

✍

The drive for Ethan went quickly. The location of the farm worked out wonderfully with seeing Summer because it placed him that much closer to Thomasville. He could easily make the trip in less than forty-five minutes with no traffic. The directions she had provided were spot on, and he went straight to Martha's Plantation, punched in the gate code Summer gave him, and he was soon in her driveway.

As Ethan pulled up he instantly fell in love with her house. It was just the right size for her and Jake, he thought, and he absolutely loved stone on a house. He exited his SUV and walked to her door dressed in his typical summer wear, a polo shirt with khaki shorts and sandals. He had chosen a white shirt for this date, hoping that might be just a touch cooler since the South Georgia sun and heat were in full swing. He knocked, and Summer opened the door dressed beautifully once again. She, too, was in her typical summer wear with a bright red and white sun dress.

"Hey, sexy. You look stunning tonight," Ethan offered, flashing those beautiful teeth and that killer smile at her.

"Thank you. You look handsome tonight yourself," Summer replied, matching his smile with a beautiful one of her own.

"Are you ready to eat?" he asked politely.

"Yes, I'm starving! I could eat my arm off! Let's go, if you're ready. I can give you a tour of the house later," she replied.

He was famished, himself, as he had only snacked lightly during the afternoon. He then seated Summer in his SUV, and they were off on what he hoped was another special evening.

Ethan had done some research on restaurants in Thomasville and had come across several that would have done nicely for his dinner with Summer. The Plaza Restaurant, however, seemed particularly appropriate to him, and he was sold on the menu when he reviewed it online. He had surprised her with where they were eating, and he noticed that she seemed to love his choice.

They each decided to have shrimp scampi and chardonnay, of course, and they both enjoyed their meal and conversation immensely. They spent their time talking about their work and what was pressing, and Ethan wanted an update on Jake and what he was doing. He mentioned to Summer that he hoped they could all three get together soon and do something. She agreed that would be fun.

They finished their meal and headed to the movies. Summer had wanted to see a new love story from her favorite author, and Ethan had agreed to watch it with her. He didn't care what he was doing with her; just being with her was enough for him.

The movie lasted about an hour and a half, and as they were leaving, even Summer reluctantly admitted it was only slightly more interesting than watching paint dry. You win some; you lose some, he decided, and drew great satisfaction in that he wouldn't watch it again.

As they left the theatre, Summer offered for them to return to her house for the remainder of the evening, and Ethan agreed. He wanted a tour of her house and to spend some quiet time with his brown-eyed beauty.

Once back at her house, she gave Ethan a complete tour, and he was impressed. Most of the house had a beach theme, which he thought was most appropriate for Summer. Once she finished showing Ethan around, she offered, "Well, that's my house, such as it is. I was thinking since the weather is nice tonight with the breeze, maybe we could walk around my neighborhood for a while?"

"Yeah, that would be great. Maybe we could take a glass of chardonnay for the trip?" Ethan asked with a devilish little grin.

"I think that can be arranged, sir. We'll just have to take it in these plastic cups so none of my neighbors become suspicious and turn me in to the police," Summer replied, smiling with her own devilish grin.

"Works for me. There's nothing like a redneck wine glass, is there?" Ethan asked as he laughed out loud with a deep, billowing laugh.

"Very true. Okay, let's go walk a bit," Summer said as she chuckled, too.

They made their way through the subdivision with the conversation dominated by Summer, giving Ethan the story on all her neighbors. She indicated it was basically a family-oriented subdivision and an overall nice place to live. She told him that most of the people she had met there were cordial and friendly.

They had made the circle through most of the subdivision when they came upon the event pavilion and swimming pool for the subdivision. The pool was above average in size, and the pavilion was large enough to accommodate a hundred people or more. Both structures were just the right size for neighborhood events, Summer mentioned.

❧

As they walked up to the fence surrounding the pool, Ethan continued to sneak glances at Summer. Her dress was again form fitting, and gazing at her breasts fueled his imagination. As they came up and leaned on the fence surrounding the pool, Ethan was looking over at her with an intense *I want you now* look and said, "You know, I've never been skinny dipping. Have you?"

❧

Upon seeing his stare and hearing Ethan's question, she knew exactly what he had on his mind. She thought it would be a great idea, but was worried about getting caught. "I have, but it's been a long time. We'd probably get busted if we tried it," Summer said reluctantly.

"I don't know, it's pretty dark around the pool since the only security light is way over there. Why don't we go back to your house for a little while and let everyone go to bed, then come take a dip?" Ethan asked. She saw he was still maintaining that same look of intensity at her. Summer was mesmerized by it and also couldn't wait to see his naked body again and have him do whatever he wanted to her.

"Oh, why not. Probably half the adults in here have done it already, anyway," Summer replied, chuckling to herself.

"I'm sure they have," Ethan agreed, so they returned to her house and enjoyed another glass of chardonnay, perhaps to help work up enough courage to go to the pool and test their luck, Summer thought.

❧

After about an hour they eased down to the pool, not talking at all so as to not draw attention to themselves. They looked around, and for the most part, the neighbors appeared to be in bed. There were few houses nearby that had interior lights on. The gate to the pool was locked, but Ethan easily climbed over the fence, then found a chair and placed it on Summer's side of the fence for her to stand on to scale the fence.

Ethan then grabbed Summer by the waist as she was standing in the chair and hoisted her inside the pool area with him. They made their way quietly to the pool. They looked around one more time for nosy neighbors before taking off their clothes and hiding them in the shadows.

The water in the pool was relatively warm now, thanks to the early South Georgia summer. The pool had depths of three feet, four feet, and five feet to accommodate both children and adults. Ethan and Summer slipped into the pool and came together in the four-foot section of the pool, hugged, and began kissing almost immediately. Ethan then took his right hand and began stroking her full breasts and firm nipples. She has a perfect body, he thought, as he rubbed her.

They then began kissing wildly, almost like two savages in the jungle who had been without sex for too many years to count. It was almost primal the way they kissed each other at that moment. They hadn't seen each other or been together in a few weeks, but it seemed like a lifetime to Ethan. He had the feeling that Summer felt the same way.

Ethan then took his right hand, grabbed Summer's hair on the back of her head, and pulled her head back slightly as he used his tongue to dominate hers as they kissed. It was almost as if he were trying to use his tongue to subdue and hold her down like he had done before with his body. He watched as Summer seemed to give into him readily.

They continued to kiss wildly for few minutes before Summer felt Ethan then let go of her hair and move his hand between her legs. She felt him massaging her pleasure point just as vigorously as he kissed her. He can do whatever he wants to me, she thought. Being naked and vulnerable in the pool as Ethan had his way with her turned Summer on even more. Her juice began gushing uncontrollably into the warm pool water and the water's surface cascaded gently against her round, buoyant breasts.

"That feels so good," Summer whispered seductively to him.

"I'm glad. I'm just getting started with you," Ethan whispered back. Summer knew he had the confidence of a man who was going to take a woman and please her in a way she had never felt.

Summer, flushed with desire at this point, managed to look down at Ethan's waist and saw his manhood at full attention. She took her hand, eased it down onto him, and began stroking him and matching Ethan's intensity. She watched him roll his head back now as he gave in to the pleasure she was giving him.

∽

Summer stroking him in the water served as a lubricant to Ethan and felt even more pleasurable than normal. He could stand it no more and took Summer and led her into the middle of the five-foot section of the pool. "Put your arms around my neck and take your legs and wrap them around my back," Ethan ordered her with an intense look in his eyes he hoped she would see and figure out meant she better hang on for dear life.

"Okay," Summer replied and did as he asked, then slid down onto his manhood. They each groaned with pleasure as their bodies became one. Ethan then grabbed her shoulders with both hands and began thrusting his lower torso rapidly in and out of her, using his hands draped over her shoulders for leverage. The water and its buoyancy properties served to make Summer's already modest body even lighter, which allowed Ethan to work that much harder to please her. His violent and rapid thrusting was now making small waves in the pool and splashing water, too.

∽

As he was taking her, Summer groaned with pleasure at what he was doing to her and had an occasional whisper of "Ethan, oh, Ethan." She was bobbing up and down from each of his powerful thrusts like a buoy marker in rough seas. She was in ecstasy at this moment and loving every minute of it. She could only groan as he was giving her all she could handle.

∽

The pleasure and the moment quickly became too much for both of them, and they couldn't hold it back any longer. Their orgasms had been charging forward and were too powerful to contain. They were both now about to give into the unrelenting force inside them.

Summer then whispered to Ethan, "I'm almost there. Don't stop, please don't stop, baby."

Breathing rapidly now to give his body enough oxygen to continue, Ethan replied, "I'm almost there, too. I'm about to explode inside you, and you can't stop me."

❧

When Summer heard his dominating words, it ignited her orgasm, and a wave of pleasure washed over every inch of her body. Her muscles began to spasm violently from the intensity of her orgasm. Her body was now flailing as if someone had thrown a running hair dryer into the pool. As the orgasm controlled her body, she began to scream into the night, "Yes, Ethan! Yes, Ethan! Yes!"

❧

Just as Summer was uttering those words, Ethan's pleasure reached its breaking point, too, and he exploded violently inside her. As his manhood pulsated wave upon wave of passion inside her, he called out into the darkness, "Yes, Summer! Yes! Yes, baby, yes!"

His orgasm continued another fifteen or twenty seconds before the wave of passion and pleasure gave way to satisfaction and exhaustion. He could hardly move and it seemed to him that Summer couldn't either. They managed to ease over to the steps of the pool and lie in the shallow water in each other's arms to try and recover.

After about ten minutes, Ethan snapped out of his pleasure-induced stupor to quickly glance around for neighbors. They had hardly managed to be quiet in the heat of battle, he thought. Thankfully, as he looked around, he didn't see anyone. Hopefully, everyone was asleep or had their television volume up and didn't hear them, he thought. "I guess we probably should get back to your house," he offered, but was reluctant to leave their comfortable spot.

"Yeah, I guess so. I could stay here all night, but we better get out of here before we get busted and they run me out of here on a rail," Summer replied.

They then dried off quickly, scaled the fence, and made it safely back to her house. Ethan was exhausted from their intense encounter and observed Summer was also. When they were back inside her house, they took off their clothes and went straight to bed, sleeping soundly in each other's arms. As they drifted off to sleep, Ethan thought what another incredible night it had been.

Chapter Twenty-Two

THE TWO SLEPT like statues the entire night, resting comfortably in each other's arms. Ethan woke first the next morning, around seven. He felt great from having slept so well. He didn't want to leave Summer, but he needed to get back to his cabin to prepare for a rare Saturday conference call with his investors later that morning. As he got dressed, he observed Summer slowly begin to wake up and open her eyes and say, smiling, "Good morning, handsome."

"Good morning, sexy," he greeted her in return with a large smile.

"Why are you getting dressed?" she asked. Ethan couldn't miss the look of disappointment Summer had.

"I have a conference call with my investors this morning, starting at ten. I need to get on back and prepare a little first. We normally do them on Monday, but a few of them are leaving on business this Monday and wanted to do it today. I'm sorry I have to leave you so soon. I'd love to stay here in bed with you all morning. I enjoy being with you," Ethan replied with a now softer, kinder smile.

❧

Summer was touched by his comment and said as she continued to smile, "I feel exactly the same."

She then leaned up from her bed, gave him a soft, gentle kiss goodbye, and said, "I love you."

"I love you to Summer," Ethan smiled brightly.

Summer's heart skipped a beat as she heard these words from Ethan. She was ecstatic and wanted to jump up and do another "happy dance" but contained her enthusiasm. "I just love hearing you say that," she replied, also continuing to smile.

∾

Ethan was also delighted to hear those words from this woman who had touched him so deeply. His stomach now felt like butterflies had just hatched from a cocoon and begun flying wildly inside it. He, too, managed to keep his enthusiasm in check and responded, "I'm glad to hear that. I don't want to leave you, but I must. Duty calls."

"I know you have to go, but I wish you could stay the day. I do have a huge wedding coming in two weeks, though, and I still have a ton of work to do on it. Jake will be rolling in here in an hour or two, anyway. Hopefully we can see each other again soon," she replied. Ethan noticed the unmistakable warmth and sincerity in Summer's words.

"Yeah, maybe one day we'll both strike it rich, and we can just retire and live a life of luxury together," Ethan responded, now laughing at the thought of this dream actually managing to come true.

"Maybe so, but don't laugh, Ethan. You never know. . . ." Summer replied. Ethan sensed a more serious tone now, Summer's voice trailed off at the end of her comment.

"We'll see. I'm going to head on now. Thanks for another great evening," he replied, smiling widely again, and he leaned in and gave her one more kiss goodbye.

"Alright. Goodbye, and be careful. I love you," she responded. It seemed to Ethan that she was speaking with true sincerity.

"I love you, too. Goodbye," Ethan said as he smiled and headed out of her room and back to his cabin in Valdosta.

∾

The weekend and the first part of the next week went by quickly for each of them. Ethan had been really busy with his hedge fund, as he and the investors had interviewed and admitted two new investors into the group from Valdosta. Anytime a new investor came in, Ethan and Greta had to put in several long days to provide all required information to the potential investors, answer the myriad of questions, and consult with the existing investors. He also had to research and make sure he complied with all regulatory requirements to assure his fund didn't run afoul of any requirements of the Security and Exchange Commission.

❧

Summer had been equally busy. The large wedding she had coming up in Albany was taking more time than any of her previous events. It was stressful and time-consuming, and she hoped it was going to provide the future payoff she was anticipating. She had also been busy with Jake and his homework, baseball games, and church activities.

Summer and Ethan hadn't been able to spend any more alone time together, but they had managed to talk on the phone each night now. She, Jake, and Ethan had managed to meet and have dinner a few nights in Thomasville though.

❧

Jake continued to be enamored with Ethan. Ethan had been able to catch the last few innings of two of Jake's baseball games before eating that week, which totally thrilled Jake. Jake's dad lived in Thomasville and was his father, yet he only managed to take time to make a few of his games each season.

❧

Ethan and Summer made the most of whatever time they could spend together, and each night they talked on the phone it was usually for a couple of hours. They continued to talk about anything and everything, including their feelings for each other, how much they missed each other, and how they longed to spend time with each other again soon. The situation wasn't ideal, but was better than no contact at all, they both had decided.

They were on one of their nightly phone calls to work in another date night Wednesday night. Each had a full day of work, but they felt like it was their best shot at seeing each other over the next week or so. Summer had offered to make the drive to Valdosta this time and indicated she wanted to see Ethan's cabin and land.

❧

Ethan was thrilled to have Summer coming to his house and thought it would be a nice change of pace for them. He had set to work making sure his place would be spotless by the time Summer visited Wednesday night. He decided to try his hand at grilling for them again and was preparing filets on the grill, as well as grilled vegetable kabobs, baked potatoes, and, of course, chocolate cake and chardonnay.

Ethan had finished his work for the day and had also received a surprise phone call from Michael Fredericks, the hedge fund investor he had met at Rosemary Beach before meeting Summer. Michael had called to say hello and wanted to let Ethan know he had called Dr. Karl Johannsen to catch up with him. He informed Ethan they had talked at length about him. Michael said that Dr. Johannsen had sung the praises of Ethan and his hedge fund managing abilities and the performance of the fund.

Ethan was shocked that Dr. Johannsen showered so much praise on him. Ethan felt like Dr. Johannsen was a difficult man to impress about anything, so this was a huge compliment. Michael told Ethan that several of his fellow investors were wanting to diversify some of their earnings and excess cash with a new hedge fund and manager.

Michael went on to say that after Dr. Johannsen's glowing review of Ethan and his providing some investment return data, Michael and his fellow investors decided to see if Ethan would be interested in being added to their short list of managers to interview. Michael asked Ethan if he would come up for a few days to interview with them. Ethan was flattered and told Michael he wanted to think it over tonight and call him in the morning, and Michael agreed.

Even with all of the activity that day, Ethan had managed to shower and shave well before Summer would arrive at seven. He had decided to don his typical attire of a polo shirt, khaki shorts, and sandals. His choice of color for the shirt today was red, which like many colors complimented his dark skin tone well. Ethan put a great deal of thought into his clothes any time he saw Summer. He was dressed and had everything ready to begin grilling as soon as she arrived. He couldn't wait to see her. He had the excitement of a child on Christmas morning.

❦

Summer had another stressful day Wednesday. She had endured several such days lately and was beginning to question whether planning weddings was even worth it. It was such a stressful time for the bride and groom and their families.

In addition, they invariably took much of that stress out on the planner. The money was substantial, and she needed the weddings to get her business off the ground. Today, however, it just seemed like the stress she had to endure wasn't worth the money.

She had managed to get home in time to shower quickly and get dressed in a rush, which she hated. Summer chose a Tiffany blue sundress and flats to wear to Ethan's cabin. She already had the directions. Also, based on what he had said she was expecting him to be waiting for her at the highway near the entrance so he could lead her in to his farm. She was excited to see Ethan again and to see the home of this wonderful man who now had her heart.

Summer left Thomasville and made the short drive down State Road 84 and soon arrived at Ethan's driveway. He was there waiting, as promised, and she followed his escort into his secluded cabin for what she hoped was another romantic night. She observed that Ethan's driveway was long and winding. She followed him for about five minutes before the thick planted pine trees and undergrowth opened up to reveal a quaint cabin.

Summer was instantly impressed and drawn in by the cabin. The exterior was cedar log siding with a hunter green metal roof. The cabin was tastefully landscaped with lava rock flower beds consisting of several local varieties of shrubs as well as Japanese maple trees strategically spread around the house to contrast the lower height of the shrubs. The lawn wasn't large, but was neatly manicured.

She parked beside Ethan in the gravel parking area on the side of the cabin. From there she could see the rear of the structure and the spacious wood deck and outdoor fireplace.

᠅

"Good evening," Ethan said with his enthusiasm at seeing her and having her here at his cabin obvious. She looked gorgeous, as always, he thought. Her full brown hair was curled and perfect, her beautiful brown eyes were drawing him in, and those thick, full sexy lips glowing with lip gloss were begging him to kiss them. Ethan then came over and quickly kissed them softly before she could reply.

༄

Summer was mesmerized with Ethan's home and was again in awe of his appearance, too. He was just so handsome and muscular, and those intoxicating hazel eyes were beaming at her as bright as any star in the night. She enjoyed his brief but passionate kiss as a feeling of warmth covered her entire body.

"Hey! I love your place," she replied, smiling and flashing those perfect white teeth of hers, having quickly recovered from his kiss.

"Thank you. It's not much, but its home. Follow me, and I'll take you inside," Ethan offered as he gestured with his left hand for her to walk ahead of him.

Summer followed Ethan inside the front door, and she was greeted by a spacious great room with a cathedral ceiling and a stone fireplace. She saw that the room was large enough to hold two couches, a recliner, and a sitting chair. She then gazed at the hand-laid stone comprising the large fireplace that went from floor to ceiling and served as the focal piece of the great room. The average size kitchen and small dining area joined the great room in an open floor plan. The kitchen was divided from the great room by a spacious bar with a granite countertop and wooden stools.

She observed the great room and kitchen floors throughout were flagstone and had been covered with a sealant that served to give the floor a glossy shine. She also noticed a large bathroom that was tastefully decorated and had a rustic elegance. Finally, she encountered a master bedroom that was spacious and had its own separate entrance to the master bath. The master bedroom and other bedrooms had pine flooring and walls, and all of the bathrooms had the flagstone, along with pine walls.

Summer was impressed with Ethan's house and even more so after he revealed he had made most all of the interior décor decisions himself. Finally, she was escorted onto the wooden deck in the back that ran the length of the rear of the house. It had a large outdoor fireplace in one corner of the deck and a large hot tub in the other corner. The deck overlooked a small lawn in the back that soon yielded to the thick pine forest that surrounded the entire cabin.

"I just love it, Ethan. It's cozy and warm, and I love all of your décor.

How long have you been here?" Summer asked, impressed by all that she had seen.

"I've been here about three years. I bought the land and built the house right after my divorce was finalized, and I've been here since. I just love the privacy, and you can see I've made the dining room area my office, so I work here as much as possible. I also have a small office in a professional district in town where my administrative assistant works, but I'm only there when I need to be, which is mainly for meetings," Ethan replied, and it was obvious to Summer he was proud of his home and enjoyed spending time there.

"I don't blame you for staying here as much as possible. I would, too," she added.

❦

Summer looked beautiful, as always Ethan felt. Her sundress flattered her gorgeous body just as everything else he'd seen her wear. "Can I pour you a glass of chardonnay to unwind before dinner?" Ethan asked, wanting to be the consummate host.

"Yes, that would be awesome," Summer replied. Ethan observed her flash yet another beaming smile.

Ethan then went to the kitchen and prepared the glasses for them both. As he was pouring the glasses, he looked over his shoulder and said with his flirty smile, "By the way, you look gorgeous tonight. I love the dress."

Ethan observed Summer blush slightly as she replied, "Thanks. You look sexy yourself."

Ethan went to work grilling dinner, and he and Summer chatted away on their happenings that day. Ethan had shared with her the details of his phone call with Michael, and she thought it was a wonderful opportunity and that he should visit New York. He told her that he had just about decided that's what he wanted to do, but did want her thoughts first.

He listened intently to Summer say it couldn't hurt anything to take a free trip to New York and see what they have to say, and Ethan agreed. He was happy that she was so supportive, but he had come to learn that was just one of her many good qualities.

Ethan finished grilling fairly quickly since he had the grill warm and ready when Summer arrived. They ate dinner on the deck as the weather had gotten a little cooler with the sun beginning to set. They enjoyed the meal and serene surroundings immensely. After they finished eating they had another glass of wine, then decided to move back inside as the mosquitoes had begun their summer evening ritual of taking over the yard as the sun was fading fast in the west.

As they entered the cabin, Ethan asked, "So, would you like a piece of chocolate cake? No meal of ours would be complete without it, right?"

Summer then smiled and answered, "Yes, that would be great, actually. But I just need a small piece." He then cut the cake and served her and himself. It was just the right size to top off the meal, he decided.

They consumed the cake in no time, then Ethan got up from the couch where they had been seated, eating, and put their plates away. "Can I get you another glass of wine?" Ethan asked as he was eager to please this woman he was totally in love with.

"Of course, but only if you're joining me," she replied with a flirty smile. Ethan saw her wink at him as the wine had begun to affect Summer, even with eating a meal.

"Yes, I will. It would be a crime to allow a beautiful lady to drink alone," Ethan flirted back and smiled. Ethan saw Summer blush again at his flattery, knowing all too well he meant every word of it.

They took their wine glasses and began walking slowly around the great room, continuing to talk. Summer seemed to be truly captivated by his rustic cabin décor and impressed Ethan had been able to execute it himself, he thought.

As they walked around the room he would take peeks at the white and blue sundress Summer wore. It hung tightly to her voluptuous body and the "V" created in the front of the dress revealed the top and sides of her magnificent breasts. Just the mere sight of part of her breasts fueled his passion for her. He found himself having to hold back from simply taking her right then. She was so incredibly sexy, he thought.

Summer then spoke and served to distract his thoughts at least for the moment. "I'm so impressed you decorated this yourself. It must have taken a lot of time," she offered.

"Thanks. It did take a little time, but I had a rough idea of what I wanted, which made the process easier," Ethan responded. They continued to tour the house and talk. Ethan enjoyed simply being with her so much.

He finished giving Summer the nickel tour of the cabin and talking about all of his furnishings and paintings. By now, darkness had overtaken the daylight completely, and a quiet calm surrounded the cabin. The silence was only occasionally interrupted by the gentle chirping of crickets and the occasional rant of bullfrogs from the river in the distance. He saw Summer gazing at the fireplace and comment, "It's a shame the weather is so warm, or we could build a fire and enjoy the fireplace."

"Yeah, I know. It would be romantic, wouldn't it?" Ethan replied, now longing for it to be winter at this moment. He had a crazy thought come over him, which he shared with Summer. "I have an idea, but you'd probably think it's stupid," he offered sheepishly, fearing she might laugh at his "brilliant" plan.

"No, silly, I would never do that. What is it?" she asked with curiosity, smiling the whole time.

"Well, I was thinking I might turn the thermostat down low and drop the temperature in the cabin down several degrees. We could then kill the lights and enjoy a fire inside. Is that crazy?" Ethan asked, almost reluctant to have offered such a wild idea.

"Oooh, yes, Ethan! That's a great idea! Can we do it?" Summer asked, seeming to him to almost bounce with excitement.

"Sure, I'll turn down the thermostat now, and we can finish enjoying our glass of wine. When we're done I can start the fire," Ethan replied with a proud smile for having come up with something so bold, yet something Summer seemed to love.

He turned down the thermostat and neatly arranged the cushions on the floor in front of the fireplace. He also had some fresh strawberries and whipped cream that he brought out for the two of them to enjoy with their wine in front of the fire. After about an hour of the cabin's air conditioner working at a feverish pace, it managed to cool the cabin significantly. They both now had a chill, so Ethan built the fire.

He then made the rounds assuring all of the lights were turned off, then reached into his hall closet, found two thick blankets, and laid them on the floor in front of the fire to make an even more comfortable nest for them to sit on. They then took a seat on the floor in front of the hearth with their glasses of wine, strawberries, and whipped cream.

As they talked and sipped on their wine, they began feeding each other strawberries gently. They would take turns dipping the berries in the whipped cream, then gently holding them up to the other's mouth to take gentle bites of the delicious fruit. The wine, the fire, the strawberries, and the moment itself soon overpowered both of them. They leaned in and began gently kissing each other. Their bodies were silhouetted perfectly by the bright flames of the now roaring fire.

While still kissing each other, they put their wine glasses down and Ethan moved the strawberries from between them. Ethan was burning with desire for Summer and eased his left hand around her back and began gently unzipping her dress. He felt Summer slide her right hand down between his tan legs and find his manhood. He then felt her begin gently stroking the hard bulge in his pants. "It's getting a little warm in here. Why don't we lose these clothes?" he asked Summer seductively as he looked at her once again with those *I want you now* eyes.

He noticed her trance from gazing at his eyes and she could only reply, "Okay."

They then stood and finished undressing, with all of their clothes dropping to the floor. They moved close against one another. They were kissing each other intensely at this point, with Ethan completely controlled by his passion and driving his tongue as deep as he could into Summer's mouth. Their tongues were now rubbing together furiously, and if they had been two sticks of wood, they would have started a raging conflagration.

Ethan paused, locked onto Summer's eyes, and told her, "Get on top of me and ride me and make me come inside you."

Summer, still in his trance, did just what he said and climbed on top of his body, which was now lying on the blankets directly in front of the fire. She then slid herself down gently onto his fully erect manhood. She moaned as he entered her, then she began gently sliding up and down on him as she straddled him with her knees on the floor on either side of him.

"Oh God, Ethan. You're so hard, and you feel so good," she called out in pleasure.

"You feel good, too, baby," he whispered seductively to her.

Summer now increased her thrusting on top of him. She got into a passionate, rhythmic stroke on him as she flung her head back with that full, flowing brown hair flying wildly behind her head as she rode him like a bull rider does a rampaging bull. She couldn't resist calling out, "Yes, Ethan, yes. I love you, baby."

⁖

Ethan was in awe of her sexy body straddling him. He looked at her slender, tight body and her full, round breasts moving up and down on top of him and couldn't take his eyes off her. The light from the fire made her body glow with an orange hue and allowed him to see every inch of her. She was gorgeous, the sexiest woman he'd ever seen. "I love you, too. Give it to me, baby; ride me hard," he replied, locking eyes with her again and keeping her under his spell.

⁖

Summer then began riding him even faster. She worked his manhood inside her so it rubbed her G-spot with each powerful stroke, and the pleasure engulfed her body and mind. As she used his manhood so perfectly, she began to moan even louder with each thrust on him. Ethan used his hands and reached up and began gently stroking her already aroused nipples. The additional pleasure served only to thrust Summer deeper under his control and further into pleasure.

After a few minutes she felt his right hand between her legs massaging her pleasure point as she rode him even harder now. As she felt Ethan stroke her, she moaned louder and louder. She continued to work his manhood inside her for another two or three minutes before Ethan told her, "C'mon, baby, give it to me now. You know you want to."

The passion and ecstasy she was consumed with reached a crescendo. Within just a few seconds of his uttering these words, a giant wave of orgasm pulsated violently through Summer's body, making her scream out wildly with pleasure. "Oh, God, Ethan! Oh, yes, baby, yes!"

Her body was now out of control with violent muscle spasms, and Ethan whispered, "That's it, baby, that's it." The powerful orgasm short circuited her brain and all she was thinking about was getting as much pleasure from Ethan as fast as she could. Summer continued to ride him and call out his name just a few moments longer before she had to stop; the pleasure was just too much for her to continue. She couldn't take it anymore and was about to pass out.

❧

After she stopped riding him Ethan reached up and grabbed her arms, and in one swift move eased her down on the cushions on her back. He then moved on top of her without even pulling out of her. He then began thrusting vigorously in and out of her. His orgasm began rapidly building momentum with each dominating thrust into Summer. It was building powerfully like pent up steam in a superheated boiler right before it's unleashed.

He then heard Summer whisper seductively into his ear, "Come in me, Ethan. Come in me now. I want all of it, baby." She knew exactly what to say to drive him over the edge, he thought.

Her words were so seductive and triggered an almost instant explosion into her, and he groaned loudly with pleasure as he gave himself to her. He managed to utter, "Oh Summer, Summer. I love you," as his passion surged into her with waves of throbbing pleasure. Within a few moments, his orgasm had vanished just as quickly as it started.

They were both weak and exhausted. Neither could talk as they were out of breath and in a state of total relaxation and contentment. Their bodies were blanketed with pleasure.

Ethan moved off her and lay on his back on the cushions. Summer then put her head on his chest as she lay on her side, tight against him, with Ethan's left leg eased between her legs. It was their usual sleeping position, and sleep came very easily that night.

Chapter Twenty-Three

THE NEXT MORNING it was Summer's turn to leave early. She had awakened first this time, gotten up off the floor, and gone to the bathroom. She then decided to start some coffee brewing.

❧

The rich aroma of the brewing coffee soon woke Ethan. Ethan did enjoy the smell of it brewing in his house now because he knew it meant Summer was there. He had purchased a coffee maker just for her. As he got up he said, "I guess you have to be the one to get an early start today, huh?"

❧

Summer, with a sad look, replied with exasperation, "I'm sorry, but yes. This wedding I'm doing is driving me crazy. I've got to meet with the bride and her crazy parents again today."

She could feel the anxiety and sympathy in Ethan's voice as he offered, "I'm sorry. I know from all you said it's been stressful for you. But who knows, if you nail this wedding, it may just be what you need to have your business take off, ya know."

She listened intently as always to what Ethan said and nodded in agreement, saying, "Yeah, I hope so. That's my plan, anyway."

By now, the coffee was brewed, and she enjoyed a cup as she took time to make breakfast again for the two of them. They talked more about their upcoming day as they ate together. Their connection to each other only grew each time they were with each other.

After they finished eating and cleaning up, Summer said with a chuckle, "Well, Ethan, I hate to eat and run, but I've got to get out of here and meet with the bride from hell."

She watched Ethan laugh and reply, "Well, I hope it's not that bad. Good luck today. It sounds like you're going to need it."

"Thank you, I'm sure I will. Oh, good luck today on your phone call with Michael. You're going to New York and visit, right?" she questioned, raising her eyebrows and nodding yes.

"Yes, I am. It can't hurt anything. I suppose with the wedding and all you wouldn't be able to go with me?" Ethan asked reluctantly.

"I'm afraid not. I would love, love to go to New York with you, but I just can't spare the time right now," Summer replied with a look of true sadness and disappointment.

"I hate you can't go, too, but we'll get up there together one day, maybe," Ethan offered hopefully.

"I hope so. Okay, handsome, I have to leave now. Thank you for a wonderful night. You were totally amazing again," Summer said with a giddy smile.

"You're welcome. It *was* amazing and so were you. I can't wait to see you again," Ethan replied, smiling brightly at her.

"I'll talk to you tonight, okay?" Summer offered as she headed toward the front door.

"Sounds good, and please be careful. I love you," Ethan replied. Summer noticed that he was staring deeply into her eyes as he spoke to her.

"I love you, too," she replied as she matched his intense stare, then kissed him briefly but tenderly and reluctantly headed back to Thomasville.

Ethan took the rest of the morning to work out and make his routine morning phone call to Greta to see what was on the agenda today. He only had a few phone calls to make that day. The morning had sailed by, and it was almost lunch. He decided to give Michael a quick call to set up the New York trip.

"Hello, this is Michael. How can I help you?" offered Michael professionally as he answered his phone.

"Hello, Michael. This is Ethan Phillips. How are you?" Ethan replied.

"I'm great, kid. It's so good to hear from you. I was going to call you if I didn't hear from you soon. What do you think about coming up to visit with us?" Michael asked. It seemed to Ethan that Michael's voice was full of excitement and hope that he would agree to come.

"I've thought it over and decided I'd like to come visit and talk. New York is a long way from Valdosta, but I can't resist the opportunity to at least listen to your proposal and let your fellow investors see what they think of me," Ethan responded with excitement in his own voice at having such a great opportunity.

"That's fantastic news, kid! Listen, I know it's short notice, but we would love to have you here tomorrow to tour our offices and Wall Street and to meet the other investors. It's difficult to get all of them together very often, and tomorrow is one of the few days we can do that. You could then stay Friday night and Saturday night, and Janine and I can give you a tour of the Big Apple. Janine would love to see you again, as would I," Michael offered.

"I don't have much planned tomorrow, but I don't know if I can get a flight up there today or not on such short notice," Ethan replied hesitantly.

"We had thought about that and were going to fly our Lear jet down today and pick you up around four. We could have you back in New York and up here at my condo by sunset tonight. Would that work for you?" Michael asked.

Ethan was shocked and then thought for a moment. This really could be the big time if it worked out. How nice it would be to fly in a private jet anywhere he needed to travel to. He really wished Summer could have gone now. "Yes, I can be packed and ready at the Valdosta airport by four," Ethan replied with excitement.

"Great, I'll plan on seeing you tonight then. I'd pack a nice suit for tomorrow and dinner tomorrow night, then casual clothes for the rest of the weekend. I look forward to seeing you. Goodbye, Ethan," Michael said hurriedly, as it was obvious to Ethan that Michael needed to get off the phone.

"Sounds good, Michael. Thank you, and I'll see you tonight. Goodbye," Ethan replied and hung up.

Ethan immediately resumed work on his to-do list for the day so he could make his flight. After he finished his phone calls and as he was packing and getting ready to go, he called Greta and let her know he had to make an unexpected trip to New York, but he would be back on Sunday. He also let her know that he would have his phone and access to email if she needed him.

Ethan knew he also needed to let Summer know how the call went, but she was knee deep in wedding planning by now, he surmised. He opted to just send her a text and let her know how the call went and that he was headed to New York. He also told her he would try to call that night if possible. Before he knew it, three-thirty had come, and it was time to leave. He already had the car packed, and he locked up the cabin and drove to the airport.

As Ethan pulled up to the airport, he could instantly see the Lear jet on the tarmac. It was too large not to notice and not an everyday sight at the Valdosta airport. It was a brilliant white, and the bright South Georgia sun gleamed off it.

When he walked in the terminal the pilots were there waiting for him and took his bags to load onto the plane. They immediately escorted him out to the plane and got him on board. The captain offered apologetically, "Sorry for the rush, Mr. Phillips. Mr. Fredericks has us on a tight schedule today, and we don't want to be late getting you back to New York."

"Oh, that's fine. I don't mind, and to be honest I'm anxious to get there myself," Ethan replied with a courteous smile.

"That's good. Go ahead and buckle up, and we'll be taking off shortly. The ride will be a tad bumpy until we rise above this South Georgia heat, but it should be pretty smooth after that," the pilot mentioned to him.

"Great. I'm all for smooth, uneventful flights," Ethan replied, smiling as he buckled his seat belt and prepared for takeoff.

The flight to New York proved to be smooth with no major bumps along the way, which suited Ethan just fine. He tolerated flying when he had to, but didn't enjoy it very much. He was always glad to land.

They landed at La Guardia airport on one of the smaller runways for private aircraft, and Michael had a limousine waiting for Ethan just outside the terminal. Ethan was escorted from the tarmac through the terminal and into the car by Peter Williams, his personal liaison for the day.

Peter was tall and thin with light gray hair, bright blue eyes and was dressed impeccably in a black Armani suit. As they left the airport, Peter offered in a professional New York accent, "Welcome to New York, Mr. Phillips. We're headed to Mr. Fredericks' Manhattan condo for you to have dinner," Peter informed him.

"Very good, Peter. That sounds great," Ethan politely replied. On the drive to the condo Peter served as Ethan's personal tour guide informing him of each significant landmark along the way. It was obvious to Ethan that Peter knew New York well and that this was his job each day. Ethan felt he did it flawlessly, and his demeanor and personality suited him well for the position.

They had arrived at Michael's condo, and as they got out of the car, Peter gathered Ethan's luggage from the trunk to escort him to the condo. Like most people visiting Manhattan for the first time, Ethan couldn't avoid looking up in awe at all the skyscrapers surrounding him. He knew he must look like a child in a toy store marveling at all that surrounded him, but he was compelled to admire the buildings.

After briefly gawking at the skyscrapers he entered Michael's building. Within a few minutes they were up the elevator and in Michael's condominium by dusk, just as Michael had promised.

As Ethan shook Michael's hand and entered his condo, he smiled and Michael asked, "Hello, Ethan. How was your flight and drive over?"

Ethan smiled in return and replied, "The flight was smooth, which was just fine with me. The drive over was nice, too. Peter does a good job."

Ethan could see that Michael was pleased the trip up for him had been a good one, and he smiled contently and said, "I'm so glad. I wanted you to have a great experience coming up. I'm happy you enjoyed the ride with Peter, too. He does an excellent job and pays attention to every detail."

Just then Ethan heard a voice screaming from the rear of the condo and moving toward him quickly. "Hey, sweetie! How are you?" It was Janine, with her Texas twang and bubbly personality, as always. Before Ethan could respond she came over to him, reached around, and gave him a big hug.

Ethan felt compelled to be polite and hugged Janine in return even though he barely knew her. "You look so handsome, just like I remember you," Janine said, smiling brightly.

Ethan blushed and replied, "Thanks, Janine. It's good to see you, too."

Janine was friendly, and he enjoyed talking with her up to a point. Ethan knew that she would be the type of person to get on his nerves after a while because she did tend to pry into one's personal life. As expected, Janine asked "So, have you found anybody yet?"

Ethan thought for a moment. He knew he had found someone special, but he wasn't about to tell Janine. The questions would go on all night, so he decided a little white lie would save him a mountain of questions and he politely replied with a smile, "No, not yet. Maybe one day I'll find her."

"Just keep searchin' sweetie. If you stay up here long lookin' like that, the ladies will be all over you," Janine said, smiling and winking back at Ethan.

Ethan, Michael, and Janine talked for about thirty minutes. Since it was late when he arrived, Michael had decided Ethan would probably want to relax from the flight, so they had dinner prepared in the condo by their personal chef.

After Ethan changed into more comfortable clothes, they ate dinner and enjoyed talking in the spacious living room with a balcony that overlooked Central Park. Michael and Janine's condo was gorgeous and elegantly decorated in high end contemporary Manhattan style. It was obvious to Ethan that Michael had done well for himself and Janine and that they, or someone they hired, had an excellent eye for decor.

For another hour they continued to talk and catch up, and after finishing their second glass of wine for the evening, Ethan was now feeling extremely tired and sleepy. "I don't want to be rude, but I think I may turn in for the night, if that's okay," Ethan asked politely.

"Sure, kid, that's no problem. We have a busy day tomorrow, and I'm going to bed soon myself so I'll be ready. Let me know if you need anything," Michael offered and showed Ethan to his room. It was apparent to Ethan that Michael had entertained a great deal and knew exactly how to treat a guest.

After Michael left, Ethan shut his bedroom door and changed into his sleeping attire. Had Summer been with him he would have no doubt slept naked, he thought. Summer was on his mind once again.

As he lay in bed thinking of her, he finally had an opportunity to check if she had replied to his text earlier. He saw her reply, *Wow! That's great Ethan! Please be careful on your trip and call me tonight if you have time. I love you!* Ethan could only smile upon reading it. It was nice to have someone so special in his life who obviously cared about him as much as he did about her, Ethan thought.

He wanted to talk with her, but the flight had worn him out so he decided to send her a brief good night text instead. *Hey, Summer! I'm here in New York at Michael's condo. The trip went great, but I'm exhausted from the flight so I'm just texting you right before bed. I hope your day went good with the bride and her parents. I wish you were here! I will call tomorrow. Good night and I love you, too!*

Within a minute or so he received Summer's reply. *Hey! I'm glad you're safe and no worries on just texting me. It went really good with the bride today . . . yay! I hope you have a great day tomorrow and can't wait to hear all about it. Good night and I love you, too!* Now having heard from the special woman in his life, Ethan almost instantly gave in to his exhaustion and drifted off to sleep.

Morning came early the next day, but Ethan was well rested and had slept like a baby. Michael had a busy day planned with most of it involving Ethan meeting his fellow investors and being interviewed by them. They would then follow that up with a tour of Wall Street in the afternoon, then drinks with all of the investors that night. The drinks would be a more informal opportunity for the investors and Ethan to get to know each other better and feel each other out.

Ethan was up and dressed impeccably in his dark gray three-piece suit. Michael had arranged for their chef to have breakfast ready, so Michael joined Ethan at the table. Janine was still sleeping, Michael said with a chuckle. They ate quickly, then headed out to Michael's building to start their hectic day.

Michael's office was located in the famous Trump Tower. It was a fabulous building to see in person, and Ethan was in awe. He would love to have time to take a tour of it one day, he thought. Equally impressive was the interior and Michael's office. It was located on the 28th floor and was exquisitely decorated with artwork, vases and luxurious contemporary furniture. It was a posh professional office space and had a wonderful view, Ethan felt.

Michael escorted Ethan into a large conference room with a massive wooden mahogany table and eleven gentlemen seated around it in black leather high-back office chairs. A chair was reserved for Ethan at the head of the table. All of the men instantly rose when Ethan entered the room, and Michael led Ethan around the room making introductions. They exchanged introductions and pleasantries for about fifteen minutes before Michael called the meeting to order.

As Ethan sat down, he was facing twelve men. It was clear to him that these were men who had all been successful in life. It was a situation anyone could have been uncomfortable or nervous in, but not Ethan Phillips. He was confident in his investment knowledge and his ability to manage money.

Besides, he knew he had nothing to be stressed about. He already had a successful fund in Valdosta that was giving him a comfortable lifestyle. He was going to just relax and be himself and see what they thought of him and likewise what he thought about them. He had nothing to lose, he determined.

The morning flew by for Ethan. For most of the meeting each man in the room asked Ethan several standard questions they had prepared for all of the candidates they interviewed. The men were all keenly interested in his investment philosophy and particularly in how he determined which companies, stocks, or other investments he chose to invest a fund's money into. Ethan patiently answered all of each man's questions and did so with full disclosure of how he chose to invest other people's money and how he preferred to interact with his investors.

Some of the questions were personal in nature, but mainly focused on whether Ethan would be willing to live in New York on a permanent basis and be able to adjust to living in a large city. He had assumed living in New York would be a requirement when he decided to interview, and he told them for the right opportunity, he would move there.

In the back of Ethan's mind he had thought that if he did well up here, Summer and Jake might want to join him. If not, he might make enough money to fly home to Valdosta on weekends to see them or to fly them up to New York. It wouldn't be a great long-term strategy, but for now, he knew they would continue to see each other about the same amount of time as they did now, given their busy schedules.

The final investor had finished asking his last question, and Ethan had answered it and all the previous questions professionally with his elegant Southern drawl. Michael then stood and said, "Ethan, it's almost lunch time, and I'd like to thank you so much for patiently answering all of our questions and for making the trip to New York on such short notice. Many of these men have busy schedules, and today was the only day for them to meet. We appreciate your willingness to come and talk with us. Gentlemen, if there aren't any more questions, then please excuse Ethan and myself. We have lunch planned, then a tour of Wall Street this afternoon. Remember, drinks and socializing tonight at Daniel at seven."

Ethan then stood, said goodbye to all the investors, and followed Michael out of the conference room and office.

Ethan and Michael were having lunch at an upscale bistro in Michael's building. As soon as they were off the elevator and Ethan saw the sign Pierre's Bistro, he chuckled to himself.

During one of his and Summer's long conversations, she had told the story about her dad having lunch one day at a 'bristo' and how wonderful it was. He was so sure of himself when he told the story and called it a 'bristo' that she didn't have the heart to tell him any different. She and Ethan had since shared many laughs about it, and they now referred to bistros as 'bristos' any time they saw or heard of one.

Now, he was really starting to think about Summer and how badly he wished she were here. Just then his thoughts were interrupted when Michael asked, "Is a table by a window okay with you?"

Ethan instantly snapped out of his daydream and said, "Sure. That will be great. I'd love a nice view."

They sat and talked, and each enjoyed a delicious lunch. Michael spent most of the lunch quizzing Ethan about what he thought of everyone and the questions they asked. Ethan was honest and said that he had enjoyed the meeting. He offered that it was a bit long, but given what they shared about the amount of money they were each putting at risk, it was understandable.

Ethan felt compelled to ask Michael his thoughts on how the meeting went. Michael replied, "I think you handled yourself quite well. With the other two men we interviewed, at some point at least one of our guys would sense some weakness, move in for the kill, and grill them to trip them up. They didn't do that with you, which means they either weren't interested in you at all or were very interested in you and impressed. However, knowing them all like I do, I would have to say they're interested in you."

"Well, that's good. I was just being myself and being honest because that's all I know how to do with people, especially people I'm investing money for," Ethan replied with his typical transparent sincerity.

"I know, and I think they picked up on that right away," Michael offered.

They finished talking, Michael paid the check, and they left the restaurant for the afternoon tour of Wall Street.

The tour that afternoon went just as quickly as the morning meeting. Michael was the consummate host and led Ethan all around Wall Street. He even got Ethan access to the trading floor of the New York Stock Exchange and arranged for him to meet and talk briefly with actual traders on the floor. This was a treat for Ethan because all of his trading had been done with the computer, and it was nice to meet the people 'down in the trenches' trading each day.

It was a madhouse on the floor, though, with all the activity, people, and noise. Ethan wondered how any of the men and women managed to live until age fifty because of all the stress they must be under down there each day. All of the traders he talked with were nice and gave him what little time they had to answer questions.

⋘

They finished their tour with Michael's arranging for Ethan to have a bird's-eye view of the ringing of the closing bell of the New York Stock Exchange. It was a rare honor in the investing world to have the privilege to ring the bell, and as the bell finished ringing, Michael leaned over and said with a smile, "You know, if you come up here and do as well as you have in Valdosta, that will be you ringing the bell one day soon."

"I don't know about that," Ethan replied, smiling and chuckling slightly. With that, Michael led Ethan back to his condo for the remainder of the afternoon to unwind and relax before dinner.

⋘

The down time was nice for Ethan. It allowed him to check his voice mail and emails and to also send a quick text to Summer to give her an update on the day. After catching up on all of his voice mails and emails, he and Michael enjoyed a glass of chardonnay just before leaving. Michael had his limousine take him, Ethan, and Janine on the short trip to Daniel for dinner.

The restaurant was classy and elegant with both its tasteful contemporary décor and neo-classical architecture. It was apparent to Ethan that this was a place frequented by the movers and shakers of New York. Michael had arranged for their party to use a few of the elegant sofas in the bar to unwind and get to know each other more intimately. Afterward he, Ethan, and Janine would enjoy dinner in The Skybox which was perched above the main dining room and provided a spectacular view of the restaurant.

They had arrived at the bar at seven on the dot. All of the other investors were already there with their wives. Ethan instantly thought of Summer upon seeing the investors' wives. He once again wished she were there to share this experience with him.

Ethan watched Janine immediately begin to work the room with her bubbly personality, striking up conversations with all the investors and spouses. It was clear to Ethan she was the designated hospitality host, and it was a role she seemed to relish playing.

Ethan made the rounds, too, talking with each man and his wife. They all came from varied backgrounds, and none were from Georgia. Ethan, however, equipped with his good looks and charm, intricate investment knowledge, and incomparable social skills, was at complete ease with everyone there. He enjoyed meeting people from different backgrounds, and he always tried to learn at least one new thing from each person he met.

He would occasionally catch some of the investors' wives staring at him, but it had no effect on him. He was used to having women stare at him, and he was flattered, but his heart belonged to Summer now. There was no one who could change that, he thought.

Ethan spent his time learning about each person and who they really were. They also learned a great deal about Ethan and his personal life. They each learned what the other enjoyed doing and what their careers had allowed them to enjoy in life and what their families were like. They also began to develop an understanding of each other's personalities, which would be important, to Ethan especially. He was adept at quickly determining someone's personality type, then figuring out how to communicate best with that person.

After two hours had passed of socializing, Michael now called everyone together. He was the leader of this group of men. "Okay, listen, guys and gals. Ethan, Janine, and I have a nine o'clock reservation in The Skybox so we're going to excuse ourselves. Please stay as long as you like and thanks for coming. Good night." The maître d then escorted Ethan, Michael, and Janine to The Skybox and seated them.

"What do you think of Daniel?" Michael asked Ethan curiously.

"It's nice. Thank you for bringing me here and for everything thus far. I've enjoyed it and meeting everyone. It was nice tonight to get to know them and their families better. It's important to have a good understanding of who all of my investors really are as people and to understand their personalities. It helps me so much when communicating with them," Ethan replied gratefully for the opportunity to interview in New York.

"I'm glad to hear you say that, kid, because I think that's critical to being an elite fund manager. I've always said great communication skills are a cornerstone of most successful people in the world," Michael said.

"And being a hunk doesn't hurt a thing, does it, sweetie?" Janine chimed in, now joining the conversation after being engrossed in the menu.

Ethan laughed and said, "I don't think I'm a hunk, but thanks anyway, Janine."

"Trust me, sweetie, you definitely are. Did you see the way those wives were lookin' you over? I think a couple of them would have thrown you into a closet and jumped you right then if they had half a chance. Lord knows I've heard a few of them have been known to 'put their hand in the cookie jar,' if you know what I mean," Janine replied. Ethan noticed her wink with last comment.

Undoubtedly, she had heard rumors of some of the wives' exploits, Ethan thought. He observed Michael appearing irritated with Janine sharing gossip and say, "Janine, now you know that's only rumor! Don't spread something you don't know is true, especially with someone we're interviewing."

"Oh, it's fine, baby. Me and Ethan are tight, aren't we, sweetie?" Janine replied with another wink. Ethan could see Janine was now tipsy on top of her outgoing personality. After Michael looked back at the menu Ethan saw Janine gain his attention and mouth to him, "Stay away from the investors' wives. Most of them are whores."

It took all of Ethan's restraint not to burst out laughing, but he knew doing so would probably only irritate Michael further. Ethan didn't want to distract from the wonderful evening, so he managed to contain his laughter and simply smile at Janine and mouth okay after her comment. The wine had taken its toll on Janine, and he saw that she was freely sharing things she knew or thought she knew. Ethan thought it was great and was entertained by her that night.

Michael quickly changed the subject back to the fund. He and Ethan talked over dinner about what Michael had in mind for the fund and what his expectations and goals were. He also shared a rough idea of the total amount to be invested and the typical fund manager fee they paid to someone. Based on this information, Ethan was quickly able to rough out in his head that he would easily make four times what he did currently in Valdosta.

They continued to talk as they ate, and after having a small dessert and one final glass of wine, they decided it was time to head home. In less than thirty minutes, they were back inside Michael's condo.

Ethan was exhausted and excused himself for the evening by saying, "I've had a great day. Thanks again for everything. I'm going to head on to bed, if that's okay?"

"That's fine, kid. See you in the morning," Michael responded with a smile. Ethan then quickly was in bed and took a moment to text Summer and tell her he missed her and good night and that he would fill her in soon. He couldn't wait to return to Valdosta and see her and catch her up on his trip.

Even though he had only been in New York barely two days, he was already homesick for Summer and South Georgia. The trip so far had been a wonderful opportunity whether he was offered the job or not, but Ethan was chomping at the bit to get home, see Summer, then tell her about everything that happened.

The next morning, which was Saturday, saw Ethan up early at seven. He showered, got dressed, then made his way into the living room. He watched television for about thirty minutes before Michael appeared from his bedroom. They greeted each other, then Michael called in the chef to prepare breakfast. The chef prepared a bacon, egg, and cheese omelet, toast, hash browns, and orange juice for them. The two men sat down and enjoyed breakfast together.

"Well, when are you thinking you want to go back, kid? I can arrange for you to take in a baseball game this afternoon if you like, or have Peter give you a tour of the city," Michael offered. Ethan felt like Michael wanted to make sure he was entertained and fully enjoyed his visit to New York.

"Actually, if it's okay with you, I was going to just take it easy here this morning, then see if maybe I could fly out after lunch," Ethan asked, almost reluctantly.

"Oh sure, that's no problem. You're welcome to stay with us all weekend, though. We have plenty to keep you entertained," Michael replied, smiling now.

"I don't doubt that at all, but I do have more new investors coming into my fund, and I have a great deal of paperwork and filing to get done by Monday. I hope you understand," Ethan asked.

"Yes, sir, I do. That's no problem. I've got to make a few calls myself, but I can be back here at one to take you to the airport, okay?" Michael asked.

"That would be just fine. I'll see you then," Ethan replied, smiling and standing as Michael left. Ethan did have several hours' worth of work to do to admit the new investors, but his main reason for wanting to return home was Summer. He missed her so much.

Ethan lounged around the condo, watched television, and texted Summer to catch her up on what he'd been doing. He had received a text from her that said she had been busy herself and couldn't wait to talk with him after he returned to Valdosta. He also took thirty minutes to pack his luggage, then double check his guest room and bathroom to make sure he didn't leave anything behind. Time passed quickly, and before he knew it, lunch had come and gone, and it was one o'clock. In walked Michael at one o'clock, on time, as always.

"Are you ready, kid?" Michael asked.

"Yes, I am. Lead the way," Ethan replied.

They talked in the limousine all the way to the airport. Michael was quizzing Ethan, trying to determine what he thought of the opportunity and his willingness to come. Ethan was smart, though, and kept his intentions and inner thoughts close to the vest. He wouldn't know completely what he wanted to do until he had an actual offer and the opportunity to get Summer's insight. They pulled up to the terminal, and Michael escorted Ethan to the tarmac.

"Well, kid, have a safe flight home. I'll be in touch next week to give you our thoughts and to get yours, if that works," Michael asked cautiously.

"Yes, I'd like that. If you could make it Tuesday or later that would be perfect for me and allow me to get past admitting these new investors," Ethan asked in return, hoping his timeline wouldn't be a problem.

"No problem. We have a couple guys to follow up with via telephone on Monday, so that will work just fine. Take care," Michael offered as he smiled, shook Ethan's hand, then turned and left.

"Goodbye, Michael, and thanks for everything," Ethan replied.

Ethan observed Michael walk hurriedly away, throw up a hand to wave, and said loudly, "You're welcome, kid, you're welcome."

Ethan boarded the plane and began the long flight back home. He couldn't wait to return to his cabin, and hopefully, he'd soon see the woman he loved and be able to share this experience with her and gain her insight.

Chapter Twenty-Four

SUMMER'S FRIDAY HAD been extremely busy. She had three conference calls with vendors on the wedding she was planning and also had to have another 'emergency' call with the bride-to-be. Summer thought if she ever made it through this wedding, she would never plan another one. She was only kidding, but planning this particular wedding had been more stressful than all of the others combined. She had decided it was that way solely because of the bride and her family, however.

Summer had determined in the future she needed to do a better job screening new clients instead of just accepting any and every event opportunity that came along. She decided that by doing so, it might mean less money, but her stress level and quality of life would be immensely better.

She had just finished the last of her phone calls right at three o'clock and would be leaving the office soon. Just then, her front door opened, and she heard the alarm chime gently to let her know someone was up front. She walked toward the lobby, rounded the corner, and was totally shocked.

Summer was floored to see Richard Williams standing there and she was caught completely off guard. She almost fainted from the shock. Richard was the man she dated before Ethan. He was tall at six feet three inches and had black hair, bright blue eyes, and an athletic frame, but she never knew him to work out daily, which translated into a few extra pounds around his mid-section. He had a great smile and was a handsome man but not striking to the eye. Summer and Richard had dated for nine months and had broken up a year before she met Ethan.

Richard was a good man who had treated her well and had a great job in Thomasville as a real estate agent, but he had injured his back in an automobile accident while they were dating. His recovery had taken three long months, and during that time, he had been prescribed pain medication to help him cope with the intense pain in his lower back.

Once Richard had recovered from the accident, he had continued to take the pain medicine and had developed a habit of taking it, along with several glasses of wine each day. His addiction started small at first, like most do, but grew into a terrible problem for him, and eventually every day Summer would see him after work he would be high on pain medication and alcohol. She had tried several times to convince Richard to get help, but he had refused.

He and Summer had been in love and were growing close before his addiction took over his life and forced Summer to end the relationship. She was not able to handle a relationship with a drunken drug addict. Richard was not himself when under the influence and would be very loud and verbose.

When Richard drank excessively, he became wild and hyper. He was very difficult to control and would often say very embarrassing things both to Summer and to people they knew as well as total strangers when they were in public. He also became distant with Summer and avoided conversation with her, and his main focus seemed to be staying high and being the life of the party.

She had kept Richard from meeting Jake for fear of what Jake might think of her dating someone, and she also feared Jake might sabotage the relationship. From Jake's experience with Ethan, she now knew that might not have been the case, but still, she didn't regret keeping Jake from him because of Richard's addictions and behavior.

"Hey, Summer! You look fantastic, sweetie. How've you been?" Richard asked with a flirty smile. He had always called her "sweetie," which made her feel almost like a child, but she had endured it because she knew he meant it in the most affectionate way possible.

"Uh, hey, Richard. I'm doing great. What are you doing here?" Summer asked with the look of utter shock and surprise covering her face and reflected in her voice.

"I wanted to stop by and say hello and catch you up on some good news of mine. I finally took your advice and got some help for the pain meds and alcohol. I just finished going through rehab for six months, and I've been clean the whole time. I wanted to see if I could treat you to dinner one night and catch up. It's the least I could do for you for all I put you through," Richard asked. Summer sensed a look of true sorrow and regret on his face.

"I don't know if that's a good idea, Richard. I'm seeing someone now, and I'm just not sure that's appropriate," Summer replied, still astonished from Richard's surprising her.

"I'd heard you were dating again, but I'd like to just sit down again over dinner and talk and bring you up to speed on where I am. And I'd like to hear what's going on with you. I'll be a gentleman, you know that," Richard added with a smile. Summer could see from his expression that he was hoping she would say yes.

"I don't know, Richard. Let me think about it," Summer responded with a look of total confusion now overtaking her face. She looked down and began to shuffle some papers that were up front and put them in her attaché case, hoping Richard would get the hint she was busy and leave.

"That's fair enough. I'll just follow up with you later then. I'm headed over to the bank now to make a deposit. I have to get back to the office to meet a client in about thirty minutes. Take care, and I'll call you soon. You look great, sweetie," Richard said excitedly as he smiled at her, turned, and hastily walked out the door. Summer decided her life had just gotten a lot more complicated.

✧

Ethan had enjoyed an uneventful flight home and subsequent drive to his cabin. He managed to leave New York just before two, and now it was almost six in the evening on Saturday. He finished unpacking all his clothes from the trip and began doing laundry so he would have plenty to wear for the next few days.

He then contacted Greta at home to let her know he was back in town and to see if she could work some tomorrow afternoon so they could make sure they had all of their required documents in order and filed by lunch Monday. Greta agreed, as always, and they decided to work from one until six Sunday afternoon, and that would give them plenty of time to finish all the paperwork that remained.

Ethan finished his call with Greta, then sat on the couch to enjoy a glass of wine and watch a little television. He needed to catch up on emails that evening and review some of the documents before he and Greta worked tomorrow, but he decided to break for an hour before tackling all of that.

As he sat on the couch, he thought of Summer, so he sent her a quick text to say hi and let her know he would call her that evening. She had texted him back and asked if she could take a rain check on talking on the phone that night. She was going to Jake's last baseball game and was then spearheading a team dinner and swimming party at the YMCA.

She asked Ethan to join them at the party, but with his just getting back and the work he had to do, he just couldn't make it. He was disappointed he couldn't go and apologized for not being able to come, but he felt that she understood.

Ethan resumed watching television and paused occasionally to daydream about Summer as he would look at the fireplace and remember that awesome night. He wished she were here with him at this very moment.

✍

Summer had been in a state of confusion since Friday afternoon. Seeing Richard and having him come in and talk to her at her business had stirred up old feelings. Some of these feelings were good, and some of them were bad, really bad. The bad feelings were also quite painful. She wished he had just left her alone and almost wished he hadn't cleaned himself up and gotten sober.

She had loved Richard and was in love with him when they broke up, but just couldn't take his addiction and what it did to him, to her, and their relationship. She thought at the time she loved Richard in the highest and best possible way, but that was before Ethan.

Her love for Ethan was immeasurable and deeper already than it had ever been with Richard or anyone else she had dated. Still, though, part of her had missed the good times with Richard before the addiction, and she wondered if some of her feelings for Ethan had been caused by her possibly still being on the rebound from Richard.

After all, Ethan was the first man she had more than one date with after

Richard, and their relationship did start quickly, perhaps *too* quickly, Summer thought. They had slept together after knowing each other less than a week, and they had met at one of the most romantic places on earth.

Perhaps her feelings for Ethan were tied more to the amazing sex with him and to the romantic place they met than actually to who he was and true love, Summer wondered. She loved Ethan very much, but couldn't help but feel she should at least hear what Richard had to say. It couldn't hurt to hear him out, and maybe doing so would give her true, complete closure to move on with Ethan.

She felt guilty, extremely guilty, for even considering meeting Richard for dinner now that she and Ethan were dating. She had never in her life cheated or betrayed anyone she dated or married and didn't want to start now. The entire weekend Summer bounced around in her mind the feelings she had for Richard and Ethan.

&

Ethan had finished his work Saturday and met Greta on Sunday. They had a productive afternoon and were able to finish all of the necessary paperwork on the investors. Greta would just need to assure everything was filed Monday morning. He was excited because now he could devote all of his energies on Monday to returning calls to investors and making new calls to potential companies the fund would invest in. He could then determine if their answers satisfied him sufficiently to buy stock in their company.

After he worked out Sunday evening, he sent Summer another text. *Hey! I hope you're having a good weekend. I can't wait to see you and talk again. When do you think we can?*

Summer soon replied to him. *Hey yourself! I can't wait to see you either! Monday is gonna be crazy so maybe Tuesday or Wednesday??* Ethan agreed that would be perfect and looked forward to hearing from her. He couldn't wait to see her again, hold her again, kiss her again, and talk to her again. He missed her so much.

&

Summer had gone to church Sunday with Jake, then they had a wonderful afternoon at the park. Jake was so happy when he was with her and would ask often about Ethan, and she would tell him, "Soon, baby, soon." They had gotten home from the park, eaten supper, and were settling in for the night.

Jake was in his room on his I-pod, and Summer was cleaning up the kitchen when her cellphone rang. She looked at it to see Richard Williams on the screen. She reluctantly decided to pick it up. "Hello?" Summer said rather curtly.

"Hey, sweetie, it's Richard. How you doing today?" Richard asked. Summer felt like he seemed a little too happy.

"I'm good, just cleaning up the kitchen," Summer replied with little emotion and not elaborating at all.

"I see. I know that's not any fun, is it? Hey, listen, sweetie. I wanted to see if we could have an early dinner tomorrow and talk? I have so much I want to tell you and feel like I need to tell you. I owe you such a great debt for being the impetus for getting me into rehab," Richard replied, still full of happiness with his true gratitude to her evident to Summer in his voice.

"Like I told you, Richard, I'm dating someone now, and I'm just not sure that's a good idea or is proper," Summer said, still with little emotion and very matter of fact.

"Listen, sweetie, I know I hurt you in so many ways, but I do owe you a lot and just want a chance to make things right with my sweetie, ya know?" Richard added.

It was obvious to Summer that Richard still had feelings for her. She was flattered he was pursuing her and glad he had gotten clean, but she loved Ethan. However, she was conflicted. After thinking through all of the pros and cons over the weekend, reluctantly she said sternly, "Alright, we can have dinner, but that's all this is. You can tell me what you need to tell me, but don't expect anything more than that."

⤚

"Okay, that's fair enough. I'll just meet you at our favorite place, The Plaza, at five o'clock, if that works," Richard asked expectantly. He wanted to eat there with hopes it would trigger memories for her of the good times they had. Richard still loved Summer deeply and wanted her back very much, especially now that he had heard she was dating someone.

"That's fine. I'll just meet you there. Goodbye, Richard," she blurted back.

"Goodbye, sweetie," Richard said lovingly as he hung up the phone.

After he hung up, Richard decided maybe he still had a chance to win her back after all, and that thought pleased him greatly.

∽

Summer felt extremely guilty after getting off the phone with Richard. She loved Ethan more than she had any other man and wanted to continue seeing him and growing with him, but she had these lingering feelings for Richard that she hoped by meeting with him and talking to him she could finally put to bed and have true closure with him. She could then resume building her life with Ethan.

Summer knew what she was doing wasn't fair to Ethan, and that if he had done the same to her, she would be upset and hurt, but she had decided this was something Ethan didn't need to know about, and after dinner tomorrow she would officially be over Richard, and no harm would have been done. In the end, she rationalized, she was setting herself up to move ahead with Ethan by meeting Richard tomorrow, and the ends would justify the means. Her life would be so much better and richer with Ethan once she had closure with Richard tomorrow, she convinced herself.

∽

Monday was a great day for Ethan. He started the day with another intense workout, then moved right into his phone calls for the day. He was very productive and accomplished all of his goals that day, and in the process he had finalized three new companies to invest in. He had also talked with five of his current investors and brought them up to speed on the new companies and new investors. They were all ecstatic about the new investment opportunities and the returns they would inevitably bring.

Greta had been able to file all of the required documents for the new investors, so now it was just a matter of time before the new investors would be officially admitted into the fund. Ethan hung up from the final phone call of the day, looked at his watch, and saw it was already four o'clock in the afternoon. The day had flown by, he decided. He had been so busy he missed lunch and was in his kitchen at the cabin preparing a snack when his phone rang once again. Ethan looked, and it was Michael Fredericks.

"Hello, Michael," Ethan greeted Michael politely as he answered his phone.

"Hey, kid. How are you today?" Michael asked happily.

"I'm great. It's been a great Monday for me. How about you?" Ethan replied with great satisfaction.

"That's great, kid. I've had a good day, too, that will hopefully get better. I know you wanted me to wait until Tuesday. But with the tight regulatory deadline we're on, I needed to go ahead and call you. I hope that's okay," Michael offered hopefully.

"No, Michael, it's no problem. You've actually called at just the right time," Ethan replied sincerely.

"Great. Listen I won't beat around the bush and keep you long. My investors and I talked, and we voted unanimously to offer you the position to manage our new fund. We're willing to guarantee you compensation of $2 million annually with a bonus structure for any returns above 10%. We also will provide a condo for you to live in near Central Park here in New York, as well as the use of the company jet for up to ten hours per month of flight time for personal trips.

Based on your performance with your fund, we think with bonuses you can easily make over $3 million in the first year. This compensation would be in place for the first year, and then if you perform as we expect, we'll create a long-term compensation and incentive plan for the next five years. How does that sound?" Michael asked.

"Whoa, that's great news and a substantial offer. I'm assuming I could use the flight time for *any* personal trips I wanted up to ten hours a month, right?" Ethan asked, wanting to clarify that point further.

"Yes, that's correct. We put that item in there so you could either fly back to Valdosta to see your family and friends or possibly have them come up to see you. We thought that might help you make the transition to New York easier," Michael replied.

"Okay, yes, that's probably what I would use it for, alright. This is a lot to think about and process. Can I give it some thought and get back with you?" Ethan asked tentatively, hoping he had some time to make such an important decision.

"Sure, we expected that. But we need to have a final answer by tomorrow evening. I know it's a tight timeline, but we have several regulatory deadlines we're up against to get the fund started. We'll have a significant delay if we can't get a decision on a fund manager by end of day tomorrow," Michael added. Ethan felt like Michael was being honest with him and genuinely didn't have a lot of time to work with.

"Okay, I understand. I'll be in touch sometime tomorrow with my answer. Thank you so much for this offer and the opportunity," Ethan responded with excitement and happiness in his voice.

"You're welcome, kid. Don't worry, you'll earn every dime of it, but we know you're the guy and will do great. Talk to you tomorrow. Goodbye," Michael replied, then hung up.

As Ethan got off the phone he was blown away with the offer and the opportunity. What was he going to do? he wondered. He knew who he needed and wanted to talk to before making this decision.

⤜

Summer had a wonderful Monday, also. She made it through one day without the "bride from hell" changing her mind on something or freaking out and having panic attacks. She had completed all her meetings and conference calls on time, which was rare, and she had even had time to enjoy a nice lunch with one of the wedding vendors at Jonah's Restaurant.

Jake was with his Dad for the next three days, and Summer wished Ethan was coming to see her. She missed him so much and wanted to see him, be held in his arms and kissed by him, and just talk with him. He made her feel so special.

All her thinking over the weekend had helped her today to decide that it was indeed true love with Ethan. There was so much about this man and how he made her feel that it just had to be love. Summer was certain now and her love for him was deep in her soul.

She came out of her thoughts, then made one final glance at her appointment book and saw the dinner date with Richard. Suddenly, her mood changed to an ominous one. It was as if a thunderstorm sprang up from nowhere on her horizon and had settled right on top of her. She wondered what in the world she was doing eating with Richard. She felt in her heart she was over him and had previously thought the dinner would bring closure, but now she found herself dreading it and feeling guilty for doing this behind Ethan's back. She wanted to just call Richard and cancel, but decided it was too late now.

Summer determined she would just endure it, get it over with, tell

Richard she had moved on, then get back to building her life with Ethan. She was convinced the dinner would serve to end things with Richard and solidify her feelings for Ethan so the two of them could continue to develop and deepen their relationship.

Summer thought, expectantly, that two hours from now she would be finished with Richard and close a chapter in her life which would allow this new chapter to flourish and bloom. The thought of getting to that point soon gave her the courage and resolve to tolerate Richard for an hour or two.

✵

Ethan was on cloud nine and was running all the possible scenarios in his head for how he and Summer might make their relationship work with his living in New York. He had decided it wasn't an ideal situation, but given how difficult it was for them to see each other much during the week, that maybe the actual time they spend together would be about the same with him in New York. Ethan felt like they could manage it for a while until he saw if he liked the job, then who knows? Maybe Summer would want to come live in New York. Or perhaps, maybe he would tire of the pace and rat race and be ready to return to Valdosta.

It was a lot to think about, and he wondered, too, what to do about his Valdosta fund. He didn't want to leave the fund and his investors. He had developed deep relationships with many of them, especially Willie. It would be hard to turn them over to someone else or shut it down. Ethan wondered if he could just continue to manage the Valdosta fund from New York. He could do much of the work at night and could lean on Greta more to assist him. If he did that, Ethan felt like the Valdosta investors might not be as upset with his moving to New York.

Just then, Ethan thought of Willie. He knew he needed to talk to him and feel him out about moving to New York and continuing to manage the fund. He decided he would call him after he went to Thomasville. He first wanted to surprise the love of his life and obtain her insight on this remarkable opportunity he had just been presented with.

192

Chapter Twenty-Five

SUMMER WAS PREOCCUPIED the whole time she was getting ready to meet with Richard. She was constantly thinking of Ethan. She was aggravated with herself now for doubting her love for him and for even thinking twice about seeing Richard. If nothing else, the impending dinner with Richard had served to cement her feelings for Ethan.

She had spent countless hours over the weekend thinking through her feelings and all she and Ethan had experienced. She knew she loved him now, and she knew she was truly over Richard.

At dinner tonight she was going to make sure Richard Williams knew exactly how she felt about Ethan so he would move on with his life and leave her to be with Ethan. Summer couldn't wait to get this dinner over with. She finished getting ready early and was parked in front of The Plaza waiting on Richard to arrive. He was on time, as usual, and they greeted each other and promptly made their way into the restaurant and found a table.

"Thanks so much for meeting me for dinner, sweetie. I have so much to catch you up on," Richard said. Summer could see he was smiling and seemed to be almost brimming with excitement at having dinner with her.

"You're welcome, Richard. I just don't want you to read too much into this dinner. I care about your wellbeing and happiness, but I'm dating someone else," Summer said firmly, without so much as a hint of a smile.

"Okay, sweetie. Whatever you say is fine with me. Just don't count on my giving up on trying to change your mind," Richard said, smiling widely. Summer then saw him give her a wink of the eye.

∽

Richard then proceeded to apologize to Summer for all he had put her through. The process of going through rehab had made him regret his behavior with her when under the influence. He told her he was genuinely sorry for the hurt he caused her. He also thanked her for all she had done for him during their relationship and expressed his gratitude to her for suggesting he get help for his addiction when they broke up.

He told her that their breakup had forced him to realize what a grip the alcohol and pain medicine had on his life. He was grateful to Summer for the breakup, even though it had been hard for him. He shared that he knew it had to have been awful for her, also.

Richard also went on to discuss how successful his real estate business was now, thanks to his recovery. He now truly appreciated his business and all it allowed him to do. He also appreciated life now and was determined to live it to the fullest, with no regrets. Richard had also reestablished his relationship with God and shared with her his now active religious life, which he said had given him so much peace and direction.

He went on to share with her that he wanted one more chance to make things right with her, and that he was so sorry for the hurt and pain he caused her. He wanted to start over fresh, and he knew this time would be different now that his addiction was controlled and he could truly appreciate both her and life, in general.

Richard was convinced they could make a new start and be happy, perhaps even happier than before they broke up. Finally, he went into great detail about how much he still loved Summer and how strong his feelings were for her.

∽

He was a changed man, and it was obvious to Summer that he had his addiction at bay now. By all appearances, he had changed his life for the better, she thought.

He seemed to Summer like his old self, the man she knew before the pills and alcohol. He was kind again and attentive to her and wanted to meet her needs, also. He was now the man she had fallen in love with, she thought.

Even with Richard's metamorphosis and persuasive and convincing words, her love and feelings for Ethan were unchanged as she listened to him. All that Richard shared with her didn't change how she felt about Ethan or give her any reason she should leave Ethan for Richard. In fact, she was now even more certain than ever of her love for Ethan and him alone.

Summer had listened to all Richard had to say and offered words of encouragement to him throughout the conversation. She did care about him and wanted him to be happy and do well. It was plain and simple to her. She just didn't love Richard Williams anymore. She had moved on physically, mentally, and emotionally, and in the process had found a man who was her perfect match and the man God destined for her.

After Richard finished laying out his case to her, Summer replied, "Richard, I'm happy you've been able to turn your life around. It seems like you have your addictions under control. I'm proud of you for doing that and all the great changes you've made to yourself. I hope you get the best out of life, and I truly hope you find the right person to share that life with. But I've met someone else, like I mentioned before, and I love him very much. He means a great deal to me and is the only man for me. I did once love you and wanted to be married to you, but those feelings have passed."

Summer continued, "I believe every experience in life happens for a reason, and I believe your addiction was supposed to happen to put each of us down new and separate paths. I believe God orchestrated that for both of us. I'm sure He did for me, and I think He did for you, too. I know that may hurt to hear, but I have to be honest with you. I'm sorry, but I'm not prepared to break up with the man I'm in love with for us to try and start over. I love and care about him too much to do that and jeopardize what we have. I hope you can understand that."

Richard was dejected and hurt to hear these words from Summer. Despite what she had told him in their phone conversations, Richard had held out hope that by her agreeing to meet with him and listen to him share his rebirth of sorts, that deep down she still wanted him back. Richard was determined, though, to keep trying to pursue her. He still felt he could win her back, given the opportunity.

"I see. Are you sure, sweetie? I know I surprised you by popping back into your life. It's a shock and a lot to absorb tonight, but maybe we could just try having a few dates and make sure that's what you want. Your feelings for this other guy might change or go away once we went out a few times," Richard offered hopefully.

"That's just not going to happen, Richard. I'm in love, and if you love someone, you don't date someone else behind their back for whatever reason. That's not how I would want to be treated, or you either, for that matter. I'm afraid tonight and this dinner has to be it for us," Summer said. Richard could feel the conviction and firmness in her words.

"Alright, sweetie. I hate to admit it, but that seems clear enough. I still want you back, but I'll respect your decision. I'm disappointed with what you've told me, but I do understand where you're coming from. You can't blame a guy for trying to win back a hottie like you, especially one he's in love with," Richard replied.

"But just remember, if your feelings ever change or it doesn't' work out with this guy, I'll be here for you. I mean that with all my heart," Richard continued with a kind smile.

⌇

Summer chose not to respond to his flirtation. It seemed to her that he was finally beginning to accept how she felt about him and Ethan.

"How about we just finish talking a little more, then call it a night?" Richard added.

"That's fine as long as we're straight on where I'm at with my feelings for you," Summer replied.

"I get it, Summer, I really do," Richard replied smiling. Summer observed that Richard was beginning to accept the fact that she was over him. They then proceeded to finish their meal and briefly catch up on the lives of each of their children.

⌇

Ethan drove quickly over to Thomasville. He couldn't wait to talk with Summer and tell her the exciting news about his job opportunity in New

York. He was a bit nervous, though, because he wasn't completely sure what her reaction would be. In his mind the reality was that the two of them in the short term would continue to see just as much of each other as they already did. Given both of their busy schedules and living in two separate towns, it hadn't been possible for them to see each other even every week.

The perk Michael had thrown into the package of allowing Ethan to use the corporate jet to get back to South Georgia, in Ethan's mind, had suddenly made his working in New York a much more viable possibility. He knew Summer would be an excellent sounding board for his thoughts and ideas and that she was level-headed.

In addition, Ethan knew she loved him. His gut told him she would work with him to make the New York job a reality if that's what he decided. He hoped so badly that his gut was going to be right again this time.

Ethan continued to think as he drove and analyzed the New York job and how he could keep Summer and his Valdosta investors happy. As a result the drive to Thomasville was over in no time. He didn't know where Summer was right now, and he had been so lost in his thoughts that he had completely forgotten to text or call her. He would start looking for her at her house, then go from there.

⁂

Richard and Summer had spent the brief remainder of their dinner finding out how each other's child was doing now and what activities they were into. Summer was glad the dinner had ended on good terms and was so ready to leave and talk to Ethan.

She was about to wish Richard the best and to politely say that it would be best if they didn't meet or talk anymore when Richard asked, "I've been meaning to ask you tonight if I left my tennis racquet at your house. I've looked high and low in my house and can't find it. I'm going to start back playing in a tennis league at the YMCA soon and hoped to use it. I wanted to see if maybe I left it there. I've looked everywhere else."

Summer was caught off guard by the question and stammered, "Um, I'll have to look, Richard. I haven't seen it since we broke up. Are you sure I have it?" Summer asked.

"I don't know if you do or not, but I was going to see. If you remember, I bought it overseas, and it's expensive. I'd like to use it again," Richard replied. Summer could sense that Richard genuinely wanted the racket back.

"Okay, I'll see if I have it. If I do, it'll be in my front closet. I've been cleaning out all of my closets the last few weeks. That one is last on the cleaning list, and I haven't gotten to it yet. I'll look and let you know," Summer offered, wanting both to get rid of it if she did indeed have it and to also end the evening so she could get home and call Ethan.

"I'd like to get it tonight, if I could, sweetie. I have my first group practice tomorrow night. We're going to play a few games with each person in the league and determine how the players are grouped and ranked. Is there any way I could just follow you to your house and you look right quick? It won't take but a second," Richard asked hopefully.

Summer wasn't in the mood to spend any more time with Richard, but if she did have the racquet, she knew she didn't want it. If she did go ahead and look for it tonight, she would be done with Richard for good. She wasn't thrilled about his coming to her house, but decided if it would get him out of her life, she would look for the dumb racquet now and be finished with him. "I have a busy evening left, so you can meet me there. I'll look quickly, then you can be on your way," Summer offered in a matter-of-fact tone.

"Great! Thank you so much! I'll get the racquet and be out of your hair, sweetie," Richard said. Summer noticed he was excited and smiling brightly.

The two of them left the restaurant and drove straight to Summer's house. Summer didn't waste any time getting home. They were soon through the gate and at her house. Summer asked Richard to wait in the foyer while she quickly rummaged through her closet. She was beginning to think this was just a wild goose chase and a ploy by Richard to spend more time with her, when under a box of old photos, she found the racquet. "Here it is. I found it," Summer called out.

"That's wonderful, sweetie! Thank you for looking and for finding it," Richard replied excitedly.

"You're welcome. I didn't remember it being there. I need to run now and call Jake," Summer said anxiously as she opened the front door and let Richard out under the front porch. She needed an excuse to make sure Richard would leave right away.

⤮

Ethan had made his way to Summer's home, despite the unusually heavy traffic. He had decided there must be an event in town that night or something else going on to have everyone on the road. The traffic had held him up about fifteen minutes longer than usual getting to her house. He was so hoping Summer was there so he could talk to her. He needed her now and couldn't wait to surprise her and tell her about the new job offer. Ethan felt like she would be excited for him and would have some words of wisdom.

He couldn't wait to hold her and kiss her and just gaze at her beauty. He wasn't sure if her gate code was the same or not, but he tried it, and sure enough, it was. He wandered through the subdivision and made his way around the final bend to her house. Finally he was almost there and hoped so much the woman he loved was there, too.

⅋

Richard turned to leave Summer's house, but just before he did, he made one final but unusual request of her. "Listen, Summer, I appreciate your having dinner with me tonight. I wish you felt differently about us, but I understand and realize my opportunity has now unfortunately passed. I know it's a lot to ask, but I'd like at least one final good memory of you and us. Is there any way you could give me one final kiss goodbye? I promise I will leave right after that, and I promise not to contact you anymore. You're right; that's not the right thing to do if you're in a relationship," Richard offered solemnly.

The drive to Summer's house had allowed Richard to replay in his mind all Summer had said. There was no wavering nor doubt in her words. He knew she was over him, and it stung, but he knew he had to accept it.

⅋

It was clear now to Summer her message had gotten through to Richard now as he had acknowledged the two of them were done. She wasn't happy about being asked to kiss him, though. "Richard, I'm glad you understand where I'm at. I just don't think a kiss is a good idea at all. There isn't anything that will change my mind about who I'm dating and how I feel. I think it's best if we just shake hands and part ways," she replied curtly, now ready more than ever for Richard to leave.

"I know it's a lot to ask, Summer, but please, just a kiss. Let me just have that to remember you by. I'm not trying to change your mind, honest. After all, one last kiss is all I'll have going forward," Richard said.

Summer observed the sadness in his face and voice. She could tell Richard was sincere. Reluctantly, she decided to give in one final time to get him out of her life forever. "Okay, one kiss, then you leave. No exceptions," Summer said sternly. Despite her feelings for Ethan, she did feel sorry for Richard just a little.

Richard then leaned in, put his arms around Summer, and kissed her. Summer gently put her hands on Richard's arms to push him away if the kiss lasted too long. As they kissed briefly she felt absolutely nothing for Richard. Nothing. She was completely sure now beyond all doubt Ethan Phillips was the only man she loved and wanted in her life.

◈

As Ethan came around the final bend he saw Summer's house, then her car, but oddly, there was also a strange car parked behind hers. It must be one of her friends, he thought. Ethan now had a clear view of the house and driveway and noticed there were two people standing on the front porch. The were two people kissing, then he realized what he was witnessing . . . Summer and another man.

Ethan parked the car and now felt sick to his stomach. He had an unusual feeling come over him. It was as if someone took a ten-inch dagger, plunged it into his back, and twisted it while simultaneously and violently punching him in the stomach repeatedly.

He was shell shocked and could barely move. He didn't want to get out of the car. He wanted to crank up his car and take off. It took all of his strength, courage, and resolve to just open the car door and stand up to hear whatever bullshit explanation Summer Davis had for him, he thought.

◈

As Richard and Summer were finishing the brief goodbye kiss, she abruptly stopped and pulled away from Richard when she was startled by an approaching car. She didn't like to kiss in public for all the world to see. As she looked to see who was coming, she gasped when she realized it was Ethan's SUV.

Oh, no! Summer thought. She hoped he hadn't seen them kissing; however, she had a sinking feeling that Ethan had seen their embrace. A heavy, dark cloak of guilt and anxiousness surrounded her. She was now terrified she might have just jeopardized her relationship with Ethan.

Finally, after a pause while she was trying to get a few thoughts together, Summer pushed Richard to the side and dashed across the lawn to the front of Ethan's car. Overcome with emotion now at what she knew he had just seen and what she had done, she then frantically blurted out with tears now streaming down both sides of her face, "Ethan! Please let me explain! I promise it's not what you think! I promise!"

She watched Ethan come around to the front of his car, stop, and yell back with a look of both intense anger and disappointment, "What the hell do you *mean*, it's not what I think? You're kissing another man, right? What is it supposed to look like then, huh? Do you think I'm a fool?"

Summer didn't know which question to answer, and now sobbing loudly and crying even more intensely, she called back passionately, "It was just a huge mistake, Ethan! We aren't dating or anything, I promise! Please believe me! I would never hurt you, baby! Just please give me a few minutes to explain what happened. I promise I still love you, and I'm not seeing him or dating him or anything."

Ethan was unmoved by her words and still had the same look of seething anger and bitter disappointment. "You're damn right it was a mistake, my mistake! But I'm gonna fix that right now! We're finished, Summer! It's over! That fool on the steps can have you! I'm not about to date or consider marrying a cheater! I'm done, and I'm out!" Ethan replied, shouting his words in anger the whole time he spoke.

Ethan found himself so furious and hurt at what he witnessed. He was also bitterly disappointed in Summer beyond words. He would have never in a million years believed Summer Davis would cheat on him. He had trusted her, and that was his mistake, just as it had been with Emma, he determined.

There wasn't any argument she could produce to Ethan at this moment that could explain what he saw her doing. She was kissing another man, and who does that if you're in love with someone else? Ethan wondered. He felt like if she really, truly loved him, she wouldn't have done that or even put herself in that situation. Ethan was so frustrated and disgusted with her he had to get out of there, fast.

❧

"Please, baby, please! Just give me ten minutes to explain all of this! I promise I haven't cheated on you! He's my ex-boyfriend, and I told him we were through and that I love you! I swear that's the truth!" Summer shouted back at him through her intense crying and tears. She could barely get the words out she was crying so hard.

❧

Ethan turned around, and as he was getting into his car, he yelled, "Kissing your ex-boyfriend? That's even worse! I can't believe I was stupid enough to ever trust you! I thought you were different, Summer! I thought you really loved me and would always be there for me. And to think I was dumb enough to come down here to confide in you. How stupid could I have been! You're just a lying, cheating slut like Emma was."

Ethan got in his car, slammed the door, and cranked it up. He squealed the tires as he sped off from her house like a bat out of hell.

❧

Summer was left standing alone on her lawn, in a state of total shock, with her head in her hands and crying uncontrollably. She wondered if she should go after him or call him. She desperately wanted to try to explain everything to him. Now completely distraught, Summer turned to get inside and realized Richard was still on the front porch. He had seen and heard everything, which only made the whole scene worse for Summer

Summer watched Richard offer sheepishly, "Summer, I'm, uh, sorry. Is there anything I can do or get you?"

Summer then glared at him sternly and between sobs said, "No! You've done quite enough tonight, I think. Get out of my life!" With that comment she quickly ascended her two front steps and was inside, slamming her front door loudly behind her.

Summer sat on her couch and fully gave in to the emotion of the moment. She fell to the floor in a ball, bursting out loudly into tears with the most intense crying she had ever experienced. Tears were pouring wildly down her face, and she couldn't help but cry out as they did. "No, Ethan! No, no, no! Please come back! Please come back, baby!" She was devastated at what she had just done to Ethan and their relationship. She had hurt deeply a man she loved like no other she had ever known.

That thought was almost more than she could bear. She couldn't believe she had been so foolish to believe a date behind Ethan's back wouldn't have any consequences to it, and on top of the date, she had been dumb enough to kiss Richard, she thought. Even if it all was innocent and only a way to prove her feelings for Ethan, she now realized it was a huge mistake and had cost her the man she loved so much. As she continued to cry uncontrollably, she wondered what in the world to do next and if she would ever have Ethan back in her life again.

Ethan hurriedly pulled out of Summer's subdivision and in the blink of an eye was back on Highway 84 headed back to his cabin. He was completely lost in his thoughts the whole ride home. Unlike before with Emma, the tears and sadness weren't in control of him now.

This time Ethan was angry; very angry. He was angry at himself for allowing his emotions to take over his logical, rational mind. He was angry he had trusted another woman again with his heart. He was angry that he had been stupid enough to believe whatever Summer told him. He was angry that he had fallen in love again, and most of all, he was angry at himself for breaking a promise. It was a promise to never, ever allow himself to be hurt by a woman again.

Instantly, the vivid memory of that awful day with Emma that had been seared into his brain rose again. Ethan was simply devastated. He had truly, truly loved Summer, more so than even the love he had felt for Emma. He had given her the very best of himself and put her first in his life. He had shown her love like he had never done for any other woman. Even though their romance had been brief, it had been more powerful and deeper than any relationship he had ever experienced.

Ethan thought her feelings were identical, but after the events today, he was convinced that was a lie or a ruse for some plan Summer had for him. Ethan had believed she was the woman God had created just for him and was his one, true, once-in-a-lifetime love. She seemed perfect, like an angel, but Ethan now decided all women were alike. Given enough time, they all only use, hurt, and lie to you. In summary, Ethan felt at that moment women will always let you down.

Ethan also felt let down and hurt by God. He wondered why He would give him the woman intended for him only to have her stab him in the back and hurt him so deeply. It was cruel for God to do that to someone He loved, Ethan thought.

Ethan began to question his faith, too. His faith hadn't been ideal the last five years or so, but he had prayed regularly and read the Bible some. He also had attended church on a somewhat consistent basis. He loved both Jesus and God and had since he was a boy.

Ethan, in this moment, just couldn't understand why God would let him be hurt so badly again, especially after the devastation Emma wreaked on him. He wondered what had he done to deserve such a fate and why a God of love would do this to him.

As he neared his cabin, he decided that a life without love would also be a life without the hurt, lies, and disappointment, and such a life for his future seemed like a wonderful idea now. Maybe, too, he needed a break from God for a while. It seemed like God had turned His back on him, and Ethan decided things couldn't get any worse, anyway. He pulled up at the cabin and drew a tiny bit of solace at how his life would be different from now on. He was determined to keep women and God out of it.

He glanced down at his phone as he got out of his SUV and saw he had ten missed calls and five voice mails from Summer. It's too damn late and too damn bad, Ethan thought. She can go to hell for cheating on me and hurting me, he thought to himself. The only ray of hope he could see at this moment was that there would be no Summer, nor any other woman, for that matter, and no God. It would be just him and him alone, and that thought seemed so inviting and comforting, like the best idea he'd ever had.

He couldn't wait to move to New York now and build his new life by himself and leave behind those who let him down. He knew he could count on himself and his abilities and didn't need to rely on others so they could just hurt him later. Ethan was now firmly committed that no one else was getting close enough to him to hurt him or let him down again, and no one was changing his mind this time, no one!

Chapter Twenty-Six

Two years later . . .

THE NEXT TWO years had been eventful for Ethan Phillips. He had blossomed and excelled at managing the new hedge fund for Michael and the other investors in New York. He breezed through the first year of managing the fund, generating a 25% return on investment. All of the investors were only too happy to lock Ethan in with a lucrative, long-term management contract after one year had passed.

Ethan was now making more money than he could possibly ever spend. His management fees alone for the fund amounted to over $2 million per year, and his bonus had added another $3 million plus annually. Ethan had upgraded from the condo Michael's group had provided initially and leased a luxurious two bedroom condo with a gorgeous view of Central Park and the city. He had chosen to lease versus buy because even with all his financial success, he wasn't sure how long he would remain in New York.

With all the money pouring in to Ethan's bank account, he had to seek ways to invest the sizable portion that he didn't need for his lifestyle. Approximately one year earlier Ethan had decided to purchase the home in Rosemary Beach that he and Summer shared together. Willie had informed Ethan that the home was being sold during one of their weekly phone calls.

Ethan had convinced himself that he was purchasing the home strictly for its return potential. While he had no intention of ever reuniting with

Summer, Ethan felt like the home would be an excellent investment opportunity given how nice the area was. Perhaps one day when his wounds had healed, he might be able to enjoy spending time living or vacationing there. If all else failed he was certain the home would only appreciate in value, and one day he could sell it for a substantial profit.

There wasn't much in this world now Ethan wanted that he couldn't afford to buy. While that feeling had given him great satisfaction, he still wasn't truly happy.

He hadn't spoken to Summer since that fateful day in Thomasville. For weeks and months after that day, he had received texts and phone calls from her, apologizing and begging him for a chance for them to get together and talk and work things out, but Ethan had refused to call or text her back. Even now, he was still so angry with her and hurt by what he had seen her do that day. Thankfully, also about a year ago the phone calls and texts stopped, which had allowed him a chance to try and hide Summer and their romance in the darkest corners of his mind.

Ethan stayed close to his good friend, Willie Francesco. Before he committed to accepting the job with Michael, he and Willie had met and had a long conversation. Willie, as usual, was there for Ethan and assured him that both he and the Valdosta investors were willing to try letting Ethan continue managing the Valdosta fund from New York. Willie had also attempted then and on several subsequent occasions to convince Ethan to meet with Summer or at the very least have a telephone conversation with her. Willie told Ethan if nothing else, it would bring him closure.

Ethan, however, wouldn't hear of it. He was done with her and was moving on, he shared with Willie. As for the other Valdosta investors, they knew they would be hard-pressed to find a better manager than Ethan, and at the same time, they were loyal to him for all the money he had made them in the past.

The Valdosta investors and Ethan substituted video conferencing for their face-to-face meetings, and Ethan had generated even higher returns for them after coming to New York. The wealth of resources, information, and people Michael and the other investors provided made Ethan even better at managing their hedge fund.

In addition, Ethan had hired an assistant for Greta, which had allowed her to take more of the workload off him. Both the Valdosta and New York investors were extremely satisfied with the job Ethan Phillips was doing for them.

As for his cabin and farm, Ethan had hired Greta to check on it and clean it occasionally. He also told her she was welcome to stay there when she wanted, so that the appliances continued to be used on a regular basis. Ethan paid Greta generously for the time she spent keeping the home up while he was in New York. Ethan had left for New York two days after he and Summer broke up. He packed up and attempted to quickly leave behind both Summer and any memory of her.

He hadn't returned to Valdosta since leaving and had no plans on ever returning. He wanted no reminder of the betrayal and hurt he'd been caused while living there, yet he was unable to just simply sell the cabin and farm, just as he was unable to sell the home he had purchased in Rosemary Beach the previous year.

Despite all the negative feelings he still harbored toward Summer, he couldn't bring himself to let go of the real estate connected with her. He believed since they were out of sight, they would remain out of mind. He thought he would eventually sell both at some point in the future.

Summer Davis had endured a difficult and eventful two years since Ethan left. She still carried tremendous guilt for hurting Ethan and causing their break up. She regretted it so much, yet there was nothing she could do about it since Ethan wouldn't communicate with her. She had been to his home numerous times, but she found the gate locked to prevent her from entering no doubt, she felt.

After they broke up she had initially either texted or called Ethan each day; however, as time passed, the texts and phone calls moved from daily, to once a week, then to once a month, and finally stopped altogether. Summer had told herself she would give Ethan one year to come around and respond to her and see what happened.

One year came and went, and there wasn't so much as a peep from Ethan. She had reluctantly accepted defeat and moved on with her life. Her wedding planning business had boomed, though, despite her personal turmoil. She now had three assistants to help with planning and implementing her events, and she would soon need to add a fourth. Like Ethan, she too enjoyed tremendous financial success over these two years, but wasn't truly happy.

After Summer had given up on Ethan ever contacting her, she had decided to resume seeing Richard. Once he found out Summer and Ethan had broken up, Richard had pursued Summer relentlessly. Summer had decided that Richard would be someone nice to have dinner with occasionally, and they began only sharing dinner together, initially. Richard remained totally in love with her and treated her well. He was managing his addictions and lived his life now with purpose, focus, and meaning.

Over time, Summer's love for Richard was rekindled, albeit not nearly as deeply and powerfully as what she experienced with Ethan, but she decided Ethan was gone now, and there was no point hanging on to the past and waiting for him to return. She and Richard eventually started dating steadily, and their relationship became quite serious.

In fact, on their one year anniversary of resuming their relationship, Richard proposed to Summer, and she said yes. She loved Richard, and he was good to her. She had decided perhaps Richard was the man God truly intended for her and not Ethan. In her mind she wasn't settling for Richard because she knew she was attractive and could easily find other suitors.

Richard adored Summer and treated her like a queen. His love for her was infectious. She had committed to marry him and was fully prepared to do so, but in her diary she continued to write about Ethan. She was still not over this man and his powerful effect on her, and perhaps she never would be Summer thought.

Summer would barely go a week without at least one entry about this captivating man from her past. This mysterious man and the whirlwind romance they experienced just simply would not fade from her mind. She could stop thinking about him for brief periods of time, but that would only last a few days at most.

In fact, she started watching CNBC after Ethan left for New York, hoping to catch some mention of him. She knew he would do well and felt like he would be on television one day being recognized for his investing ability. Even today she continued to watch the channel, hoping to get a glimpse of the wonderful man from her past. In her mind, Summer had given up on Ethan Phillips and moved on, but her heart was a totally different story.

❧

It was eight-thirty a.m. on a Monday, and Ethan had begun his morning ritual of working out. He then headed into the office for a full day of managing the hedge fund. Michael had some vacant office space on the floor he was already leasing, and he worked out a deal with Ethan to set up his office and small staff there. As Ethan was sitting at his desk reviewing news before the market opened, his cell phone rang, and it was Michael. "Good morning, kid! How are ya today?" Michael asked with excitement.

"Good morning, Michael. I'm doing pretty well, for a Monday," Ethan replied, laughing slightly.

"I hear ya, kid. Listen, I just got a call from CNBC, and they want to interview you tomorrow. You're evidently all the buzz on Wall Street, and they want to get your insight on where you think the market is headed the remainder of this year. I told them I thought you would say yes, but I needed to double check. What do ya think, kid?" Michael asked hopefully.

"Yes, I'll definitely do that! Are you kidding? I'd have to be crazy not to accept an invitation to be on CNBC. What segment do they want me on?" Ethan asked, full of excitement.

"They'd like you on tomorrow during the Power Lunch segment. They indicated you would probably be on around twelve-thirty," Michael added. Ethan sensed the continued excitement still in Michael's voice.

"That's great! I love that segment, and I can't wait! I'm so excited!" Ethan blurted out over the phone. He was elated to be invited to be on the Power Lunch segment.

"Great, kid. I'll let them know you're in, and someone from CNBC will contact you and set up the details."

After hanging up with Michael, Ethan turned up the volume on the television in his office so he could hear what was being said on CNBC. He couldn't wait to hear them announce he was going to be on Power Lunch. Ethan thought now that he had finally arrived in New York. He didn't have to wait long because before lunch Monday CNBC was already advertising Ethan Phillips being interviewed on Power Lunch the next day. They had even included his picture from the hedge fund's website.

Ethan was thrilled at this moment, at least on a professional level, and he knew who he needed to share his good news with. He picked up his cell-phone and called Willie.

"Well, hello there, Captain! How's the best fund manager in the good ole U.S. of A. doing these days?" Willie asked, followed by his usual bellowing laugh.

"Hey, Willie! I'm not all that, but I'm doing great! I have some news for you. I'm going to be on CNBC on Power Lunch tomorrow. Isn't that great?" Ethan asked, almost shouting into the phone. He was brimming with excitement and anticipation, which he couldn't contain.

"What? Are you serious? That's the best damn thing I've heard in a while! I'm proud of ya!" Willie shouted back through the phone.

It was evident to Ethan that Willie was just as excited as he was about the interview. "Thanks. I owe it all to you. I wouldn't be here if you hadn't taken a chance on me years ago to manage money for you. Then, on top of that, you brought in more investors, too. I couldn't have done it without you," Ethan replied, now with a softer tone, and as he finished his thought, he found himself having to fight back becoming emotional over the magnitude of what Willie had done for him and the friendship they had built.

"Nonsense, Captain. You're there because you got what it takes! You could sell ice to an Eskimo, and on top of that, you can back up what you promise. You're a special man, Captain, and I'm glad the rest of the world is about to see it. Lord knows if anyone deserves a day in the sun, it's you," Willie countered, also in a softer tone and now with no laughter.

"Thanks, Willie. You're the best friend a man could ever hope to have. I've got to run now, but I'll be on sometime between twelve and one, so you and Ann check it out," Ethan offered.

"Oh trust me, Captain. I'll have to stop chasing Ann around the house long enough to catch your segment, but I wouldn't miss it for the world. Take care," Willie said affectionately, then they each resumed their day.

✍

Summer's Monday morning had been productive. She had been forced to secure a larger office to accommodate her ever-expanding staff and client base. She spent each Monday morning reviewing upcoming events with all of her staff in a group meeting. Due to the increased level of business, these meetings usually took most of the morning for them to thoroughly discuss each event and plan action items for the week for them.

It was nearing lunch time, and Summer and her staff had finally finished reviewing the week's to-do list. Summer exited, then moved to her office to catch up on voice mails and emails before a marketing meeting she had at three. She had a television in her office that she kept on most of the time, primarily because she just worked better if there was noise in the room.

Oddly, she chose to keep the channel on CNBC each day. She still hoped one day she might hear about Ethan's exploits, and she thought that if he did indeed do as well as she expected that he would surely be mentioned on CNBC at some point. She was no financial expert, but she knew that anyone famous and/or successful on Wall Street usually landed on the network at some point.

It was now almost twelve-thirty, and Summer had thus far worked through lunch and was about to take a break when a commercial caught her attention. They were announcing that Ethan Phillips would be on Power Lunch tomorrow, and as she looked up at the television, her breath was taken away. They had a picture of Ethan on the screen along with his name and the name of the fund he managed.

Summer was instantly mesmerized by his picture. The intensity and passion in those hazel eyes blazed through the television screen to her. She thought back to their romance at Rosemary Beach and all the passion and love they experienced.

Over the last year she had convinced herself she had finally put Ethan behind her, but that was before seeing a picture of him. He looked as sexy as ever with that beautiful face and engaging smile of his. Summer made a note on her phone to catch the Power Lunch episode tomorrow. She was full of excitement now at being able to see Ethan, even if it was only on television and even if he had long since forgotten about her.

Summer couldn't contain herself and knew who she had to call, her friend, Sebastian. After her breakup with Ethan, Summer had spent a great deal of time confiding in Sebastian about all that happened with Ethan, her feelings for him, and what she should do about them. She had also worked with him on a wedding for a couple who were good friends of his, which had given the two of them even more time to talk and allowed Summer to confide in Sebastian even further.

She felt Sebastian had been understanding of her feelings and what happened, but like a true friend, he didn't automatically take her side on an issue. He was quick to give a differing view point if he felt strongly about it, but he was always tactful and not mean-spirited.

Summer was convinced he thought the world of her, and she knew he wanted so much to help her and be there for her. She also remembered he told her that he wanted her and Ethan to reunite at some point because he felt strongly that they were meant for each other.

After recovering from seeing Ethan on television, Summer picked up her cellphone and called Sebastian.

❦

"Well, hello there, darling! How's my favorite boo?" Sebastian asked, full of excitement to hear from his close friend.

"You're too funny, Sebastian! Hey, I'm doing pretty good. How's everything with you?" Summer asked in return.

"Everything's just fabulous, darling. Work has been the best it's ever been, and Eric and I are planning a trip to New York soon to see the Broadway musical *Wicked*. Isn't that amazing?" Sebastian always had a dream of him and Eric seeing the musical one day.

"That's great! I'm so happy for you two. I know you've wanted to see it for quite a while," Summer offered. She seemed to Sebastian to be genuinely excited and happy for their opportunity to see New York.

"Yes, honey, it's a dream come true. So what do I owe the pleasure of hearing from you, darling?" Sebastian asked.

"I was watching TV here in my office today and had the channel on CNBC, and up pops a picture of Ethan! He's going to be on there tomorrow. Can you believe that?" Summer asked. It appeared to Sebastian that Summer was brimming with the most excitement he had felt from her since she dated Ethan.

"Oh, my! I bet he's just as delicious-looking as ever, isn't he, honey?" Sebastian asked, now equally excited for Summer. From all of their long talks over the past two years, he knew that even though Summer was engaged to Richard, she was still very much in love with Ethan.

"He looks pretty good, I guess," she replied.

"Listen, boo, you can't play that here! I know how you feel about him,"

Sebastian said in a more direct, but non-threatening tone. He knew she was only trying to appear uninterested in Ethan.

"I just can't hide anything from you, Sebastian. Yes, he looks really good. He looks gorgeous, actually. I couldn't help but stare at his picture and think about all we did," Summer replied. He noticed that her voice now sounded like a school girl gripped by puppy love.

"Boo, you know you're still in love with that man. You've got to meet up with him and settle everything before you marry Richard. You can't marry that man until you talk to Ethan and get closure. It's not fair to you or Richard," Sebastian replied firmly, but his concern for Summer and her happiness was still evident in his voice.

"I know, I know. I've tried. He just wouldn't ever talk to me or communicate with me at all. I keep praying about it but so far no breakthroughs," Summer replied. Sebastian knew she had long been exasperated that Ethan wouldn't even talk or text her after two years had passed.

∽

Summer had decided that it wasn't just the hurt she had caused Ethan, but also that he must have been hurt badly by his ex-wife. She based that on his comment about her being like Emma right before he sped off that day they broke up. The two hurts combined had caused him to withdraw completely and push her out of his life for good, she determined.

"Just keep prayed up, boo! A breakthrough is coming. Ya know, you could always go with Eric and me to see *Wicked* in New York, and you could look him up and try to settle this soap opera, honey," Sebastian said. Summer could hear a light chuckle at the end of his comment.

"No, I just can't make myself stalk him in New York and show up at his door. I'd hate to go all that way and spend all that money, then Ethan wouldn't even see me, or worse yet, see him with another woman," Summer replied with her fear of more hurt and rejection evident as well as her desire not to resurrect the terrible guilt she still carried for what she did to the man she truly loved.

"Maybe it's just me, boo, but I wouldn't give up on a man I was totally in love with without even seeing him and talking to him one last time, especially if I was about to marry another man. Think about it. Ethan rocked your world, honey, both physically and emotionally, and if it were me, and if a man that gorgeous did that to me, I'd be on him like white on rice, honey," Sebastian stated. Summer knew he was trying to persuade her to not just give up and walk away.

"You're probably right, Sebastian, but I just can't do that, at least not right now," Summer responded with a firm tone.

"You won't ever be happy with Richard unless you resolve this. Just think about it, please, darling," Sebastian asked hopefully.

"Okay, I'll think about it. Listen, I've kept you too long, and I've got a phone call to make for an upcoming party. Thanks for listening, and thanks for the advice. Even though I don't always agree with you, I know you have my best interests at heart," Summer replied caringly and appreciatively to her best friend.

"Awe, you're so sweet to me, boo. I'll talk to you later and update you on our trip to New York. Bye bye, darling," Sebastian said with excitement as they each hung up.

∽

Ethan spent all of his available time on Monday researching and modeling forecasts of economic trends over the next twelve months. He reviewed all the major sectors and companies his hedge fund was invested in so that he could talk intelligently and effectively about his fund and the next twelve months. He wanted to be prepared, and he was almost as intense at preparing for this interview as he had been dating Summer . . . almost.

On Monday evening as Ethan was lying in bed trying to go to sleep before one of his most significant professional achievements, his mind for some unknown reason to him thought of Summer. Ethan thought how much he hoped Summer might see him on television and decide to catch the next flight out to New York and surprise him. He had thought how nice it would be for her to be waiting in his condo when he arrived tomorrow afternoon. He imagined how passionate their reunion would be and how special it would be.

Just as suddenly as the daydream began, it was interrupted with his logical, rational mind overriding his thoughts to never forget what Summer did to him, never forget his promise to himself to never, ever trust a woman again, and to never allow himself to be hurt again.

His rational and logical mind wouldn't allow those feelings for Summer back in, and these thoughts quickly rushed in to drown out Summer Davis every time they surfaced. As he was just about to fall asleep, once again Ethan had chosen the logical, rational thoughts over his heart, just as he had the last two years.

Once again he pushed Summer back into the furthest recesses of his mind. If only she would stay there, he thought. His logical mind was his comfortable place, and he was unwilling to leave it again after all the pain and hurt he had endured.

Tuesday morning came, and Ethan prepared his thoughts, reviewed his economic trends, and memorized his hedge fund's performance and holdings data. Once twelve-thirty rolled around, Ethan was ready and excited about the opportunity.

During the segment the host asked Ethan about his hedge fund background, then a few brief questions about his fund's performance. He then asked Ethan to expound on the major sectors and companies his fund was currently invested in and why those would excel in this market environment over the next year. Ethan answered each question flawlessly and was persuasive with his opinions on the market and his fund's holdings.

The host and co-host seemed mesmerized by him and were thoroughly engrossed in his ideas and rationale. He then wrapped up the segment with his economic outlook for the next twelve months, and the interview was over.

Ethan then thought, all of that preparation and it was over in five minutes. The episode flew by for him, but he had enjoyed it tremendously. He felt like he conveyed all of the viewpoints and data he had hoped to. He was pleased with how well he did. Just then his phone rang.

"Ethan, it's Michael. Listen, great job, kid! Everyone I've talked to so far is raving about your performance. You were credible and came across trustworthy and honest. Listen, let's celebrate tonight at my house. I'm going to have a small party for you. Be there at eight, okay?" Michael asked. Ethan sensed Michael was full of pride from the interview and wanted to celebrate.

"That sounds great! I'll be there," Ethan replied happily as he hung up and returned to his work for the afternoon of managing his now famous hedge fund. Late that afternoon he had also received a congratulatory phone call from Willie. All of the Valdosta investors had gathered at Willie's house to watch Ethan's segment. Willie had shared with Ethan all of the fellow investors' congratulations and continued support. Ethan had a very, very good day, he decided.

⌁

Summer had spent Tuesday morning primarily on the phone. She had a large retirement dinner this Friday night, and it was her primary project for the week given its size and importance in the Thomasville community. She wanted to make sure it went perfectly, and she knew the only way to assure that happened was for her to handle the majority of the details herself.

She had set a reminder on her phone, though, to make sure she tuned in to CNBC to watch Ethan's interview. Her fiancé, Richard, had called around eleven to make lunch plans with her, but Summer told him she had too much work to do and was going to work through lunch. There was a large amount of truth in her statement to Richard, but the reality was she didn't want to miss this one chance to see Ethan.

As twelve-thirty arrived, Summer was glued to her television, and upon seeing Ethan on air, she was instantly under his spell again. She locked into those beautiful eyes and smile and found her eyes roaming all across the screen staring at his body. It looked like he had been working out even more, and she could only imagine all the muscles and bulges he must have now. She remembered how gorgeous he looked naked, especially when he was lying beside her and holding her in his arms.

As the interview ended, Summer felt cheated that it only lasted five minutes. In her mind that wasn't nearly long enough to look at Ethan and fantasize about him. For about ten minutes after the interview, she daydreamed about him. She remembered all they shared and the incredibly strong feelings she still had for him.

Finally, she pulled herself out of her daydream and returned to reality. Ethan was gone and wasn't going to ever even talk with her again. She had made a poor decision to kiss Richard, and Ethan had seen that. She would always have trouble forgiving herself for doing that. Even now, if he did come back to her, Summer knew once Ethan found out she was engaged to Richard that would only cement his anger and disdain for her.

She knew she was wasting her time daydreaming about Ethan and hoping he would come back, but inside her heart she simply couldn't give him up. She couldn't explain it, but he just wouldn't leave her heart. Late that evening before she went to bed, Summer continued her daily ritual of writing in her diary. She spent over an hour recounting, then documenting all she experienced with Ethan Phillips and documenting the interview she watched and the feelings she still harbored for him.

༒

Ethan arrived at Michael's home at eight o'clock on the nose. As he entered, he was swarmed by guests coming up to him to congratulate him and talk with him. It seemed Michael had made this a large party on Ethan's behalf. Ethan wasn't much for basking in the spotlight, but he decided he would just enjoy the night.

"Hey, kid, come over here," Michael called out and Ethan noticed he was on the other side of the room.

Ethan made his way through all the handshakes and pats on the back and said graciously, "Hey, Michael. This is a great party. Thank you!"

"It's no problem, kid. You deserve it, and besides, it gives me a chance to throw a party and have some drinks," Michael replied, full of excitement. "Listen, kid, my buddy from Victoria's Secret is here, and he brought a couple of models with him tonight while they're in town for a photo shoot. Why don't you go introduce yourself? I think they're eager to meet ya," Michael said with a smile and a wink.

"I don't know, Michael. I told you just a little about my last breakup, and I'm just enjoying the single life right now," Ethan replied with sadness in his voice.

"Listen, I know, kid, but just talk with them for a little at least, since you're the guest of honor, okay? I'd consider it a personal favor," Michael replied. Ethan could see Michael's smile and the gleam in his eye.

"Okay, I won't be rude and make you look bad," Ethan replied, then worked his way over to the models. Ethan then spent the remainder of the night talking with the models and all the other party guests who came up to him to congratulate him on his performance and wish him luck. The two models couldn't take their eyes off Ethan and followed him everywhere, but Ethan was simply not interested.

Every time he saw a beautiful woman it only made him think of Summer and Rosemary Beach. As a result he tried his best to avoid women without being rude so that these feelings for Summer wouldn't keep surfacing.

The night had flown by, and it was now almost midnight. Ethan had mingled and spoken to everyone. It seemed that all those in attendance thought he had done an outstanding job, and this was going to be the first of many, many interviews on television for the striking hedge fund manager, everyone told him. Ethan thanked them all for a lovely evening and went to find Michael to tell him good night and thanks.

As Ethan was almost to the front door, he spotted Michael and said, "Listen, Michael, this was a great party and thanks so much for having me and honoring me. I've got a long day tomorrow, so I think I'm going to head home. Thanks again . . . for everything."

"Aw, you're welcome, kid. Listen, you deserve it, and I'm glad you enjoyed yourself tonight. Go on home and get some rest, and we'll start all over again tomorrow," Michael replied with a smile and hearty laugh.

"Yeah, you're right about that. See you tomorrow," Ethan replied as he headed out the door.

Ethan made the short trip from Michael's house to his condo. As soon as he arrived home, he changed into sleeping shorts and shirt and poured a glass of chardonnay. He then slipped out on his balcony to reflect and relax before bed. As he gazed over the brightly lit skyline of New York and all the hustle and bustle that went with it, he could only feel unfulfilled and disappointed.

Here he stood on what was one of the most significant achievements of his life and he had enjoyed both tonight and earlier today essentially alone. Sure, Willie, the Valdosta investors, Michael, the New York investors, and all the well-wishers were there, but he didn't have that special someone in his life to share this milestone with. He didn't have the woman who had captivated his heart, mind, and body, he thought.

Ethan was on the top of the mountain professionally, and most certainly financially. After all, he was making more money than he ever had in his career. It was so much money he couldn't come close to spending it all if he tried, and he had just been watched all across the United States on a well-respected television program.

He had all of this financial and career success, yet, as he sat on his balcony tonight, he was so alone and unhappy. He had been so much happier with Summer in his life, he felt. He knew he could be happy with her even if they were dirt poor.

Why had she betrayed me? he continued thinking. How could she say all those things to me, then be in the arms of another man, kissing him behind my back? he wondered. She said she loved me and looked at me like I was the only man in the world, yet I'm not enough for her. How is that possible? he asked himself.

By now the wine from the evening had taken a toll on Ethan. He was still so confused by what Summer had done and wanted to know why so badly, yet his pride wouldn't allow him to reach out to her to find out. She made the mistake, and she was in the wrong, he thought.

The only way he would ever talk with her is if she walked into his living room in New York and apologized to him face to face. Even then, Ethan wasn't sure he could move past it, but in his mind, it was the least she could do. She owed him that much, he felt. Weary from thinking of Summer, he surrendered to the wine and exhaustion and decided to go to bed.

As he lay down, he wished he could enjoy this moment more, but it was just not possible. His life was empty, despite all of his professional accomplishments. He still had an open wound from what Summer had done to him, yet he refused to do anything about it. Hopefully, in the morning all of these memories and feelings for Summer will pass, Ethan wished, as he lay in his soft, comfortable bed. With that, his fatigue engulfed him, and he faded off to sleep and abandoned his thoughts of Summer Davis, at least for a while.

Chapter Twenty-Seven

ETHAN SPENT THE next week basking in his performance on CNBC. As it turned out, he was quite a hit with both the viewers and with his colleagues. It seemed CNBC was so impressed with him they were even considering making him a regular contributor on the network. Ethan was completely caught by surprise at his instant popularity on the show and with his fellow colleagues. He was humble by nature and never considered himself to be a "big deal," but that was exactly what he became after the television appearance.

He began another extremely busy workweek with his usual morning review of business news and researching potential new companies for the hedge fund. He was interrupted by a knock at his office door, which was already open. His administrative assistant didn't usually arrive until shortly before nine a.m., and it was just now eight.

Michael, however, would often either drop by and talk or call Ethan a few days a week in the morning before the market opened. It was the ideal time for both of them to talk before they became too busy to come up for air. In the process of talking so much and seeing each other almost daily, they were beginning to form a strong friendship, and they had enormous respect for each other.

"Hey there, kid! How's the morning treating you so far?" Michael asked. Ethan could see he was smiling from ear to ear and brimming with energy and excitement which was not uncommon.

"Good morning. I'm doing well. I'm just doing some research on a few companies I have my eye on for the fund," Ethan replied, smiling. He was always glad to see and speak to Michael.

"Listen, I've got some more good news, for you mainly, and also for our fund. Guess what it is," Michael asked. To Ethan, he looked like one child trying to convince another to guess what prize he was holding behind his back.

"I have no idea. Um, you've found a new big shot investor?" Ethan asked hopefully.

"No, sir, not yet, but with your popularity I'm sure that's not too far around the bend. I was contacted today by a couple of my friends about interviewing you. One is John Cranston, who's the lead writer for *Money Magazine*, and the other is Fred McShay, a writer for *Forbes*. They both want to interview you and write a story about you and our fund. Isn't that great?" Michael asked. Ethan noticed Michael was still full of excitement and he appeared to be smiling like a Cheshire cat.

"Wow! That's awesome! They *both* want to interview me? What an opportunity. What did you say?" Ethan asked hopefully.

"As usual, I said I would need to talk with you first, but that I thought you would be willing to do both interviews. Was I right?" asked Michael.

"Of course you were! There's no way I'm turning that down. I can't wait. When are they wanting to do the interviews?" Ethan asked hopefully, now sitting on the edge of his office chair as he was talking.

"They know you're busy, so they want to do it about this time of morning. *Money Magazine* is free tomorrow morning, and *Forbes* is free on Thursday. So I tell them yes?" asked Michael. Ethan almost laughed from seeing Michael raise his eyebrows up and down rapidly and smiling as he did so.

"Of course you do. I'm there!" Ethan shouted back with excitement. The significance of the interviews was now sinking in with him.

"Great! I'll set each of them up to be here at seven-thirty each morning. I've gotta run, kid. The stock market is calling. I'll check with you later," Michael called out. Ethan watched him as he began quickly walking out of his office and onto his day ahead.

Ethan slumped back in his office chair and slowly spun around to gaze out of his full-length office window at the New York skyline. As he thought, he began to get nervous realizing he needed to be prepared for the interviews.

He knew what his next few nights would look like because he didn't want to show up for either interview unprepared.

Over the next few days Ethan prepared, then breezed through both interviews. Ethan felt both John Cranston and Fred McShay proved to be easy to talk with and asked insightful and thought-provoking questions. Ethan felt he established a good rapport with both men and thoroughly enjoyed the interviews.

❦

Michael had called after each interview for a report. Based on his conversations with Ethan and the feedback John and Fred had initially given him, Michael told Ethan that he genuinely felt like the articles would be well received.

Both Michael and Ethan resumed their hectic Wall Street lives the next three weeks. The fund continued to do exceptionally well, and all of the investors continued to be thrilled with Ethan's management of the fund. Michael now had potential investors constantly calling to attempt to enter the fund. However, the original group of investors had decided to cap the number of investors at twelve, the same number the fund began with.

❦

Late one evening around nine o'clock Ethan had a phone call from Fred McShay at *Forbes*. Fred asked Ethan if they had his permission to put a picture of him on the cover. Ethan was almost speechless initially, but recovered and gladly said yes. To his complete surprise John Cranston called the next day and requested to do the very same thing with their next issue.

Someone could have blown Ethan over with a feather after both phone calls. Ethan happily agreed to both requests, and the only person who was as excited as Ethan was Michael. He walked around Wall Street like a kid who had received every toy he asked Santa for at Christmas.

Both magazines were for the May issue and were placed in circulation nationwide by the last week of April. Michael surprised no one by wanting to have yet another celebration party when both issues came out, and he did exactly that. For this party Michael spared no expense and rented the restaurant Daniel for this affair. He invited all of the investors and their wives as well as all of his high profile colleagues on Wall Street.

The party was a truly grand event, and Ethan, Michael, and everyone who attended enjoyed it thoroughly. The food was exquisite, and the alcohol had flowed like a river that night. Everyone had a great time, and as usually was the case at any event he attended, Ethan had spent much of his time trying to get away from the numerous women in attendance who were trying to monopolize his time and vying for his attention.

At just before midnight Ethan had enjoyed about all of the festivities he could handle and made his way to the door. He looked up and saw Michael from across the restaurant and mouthed to him *thank you* and indicated he was headed home.

He saw Michael smile back at him with wild eyes from one too many glasses of wine, raise his eyebrows and mouth back *okay kid* and gave him two thumbs up. Ethan smiled brightly and made his way out the door.

A few weeks had also passed for Summer and she found herself at the grocery store, which had become her Thursday evening ritual. Young Jake usually spent Thursdays with his dad, so it was a perfect opportunity to buy all of their groceries unimpeded from questions and requests from him. Richard had agreed to join her, and they had separated in the store to implement a divide and conquer strategy with the grocery list.

Summer had made it about halfway through the store and came up to the magazine section. She continued to walk on by, as she knew she already had subscriptions for three magazines at home that she was behind on reading. Just as she was almost past the magazine section, a large photo on the cover of *Forbes* magazine immediately caught her eye. She stopped and reached for the magazine, with her eyes glued to it and her mouth wide open. "Holy shit. It's Ethan," Summer whispered to herself.

It was rare for her to curse, but she was stunned and completely surprised to see him on the cover. She could only stand there and gaze at his picture, roaming her eyes all over it, soaking in Ethan's sexy photograph. She would definitely be purchasing this magazine and reading it tonight, she thought. She couldn't wait to get home and read all about Ethan.

As she was standing there mesmerized by Ethan's picture on the cover, a voice called out from beside her. "Summer. Summer. Hey. Summer," Richard said. She felt him touch her on the shoulder to snap her out of her trance.

"Oh, hey, dear. Sorry, I was um, caught up in reading these headlines. I think I may get this and read a few of the articles." Summer said nervously as she quickly threw the magazine into her buggy.

"*Forbes*? Since when do you care anything about financial magazines?" Richard asked. Summer noticed a perplexed look on his face.

"Well. I do have that Roth IRA I started a few years ago, and I've been meaning to start a college fund for Jake, too," Summer responded, quickly trying to divert any possibility of Richard's realizing she was staring at the picture, not the headlines.

"Whatever, sweetie. You know I don't trust those Wall Street guys. They're all just a bunch of greedy thieves in my book. Real estate is the place to be," Richard offered. Summer was relieved he casually walked off and continued shopping. She could tell that he had clearly not picked up on her staring at Ethan's picture and obviously didn't remember Ethan. She hoped Richard had forgotten Ethan from the day of their argument two years ago, and it seemed he had. She just had to have this magazine and read all about the man who was still in her heart.

Later that evening Summer returned home with Richard and put up all of her groceries. She and Richard talked for a while about each other's day. It was almost ten o'clock in the evening, and Summer knew she had an early day tomorrow to begin setup for a rehearsal dinner Friday. She asked Richard if he minded seeing himself out while she went on to bed. Richard had gladly agreed, as always, and would do most anything, it seemed to Summer, to make her happy.

After Richard left, she made her nest in her bed, turned on the bedside lamp, and began reading about Ethan. She read the entire article three times back to back. It seemed she just couldn't get enough information on the life of this man who had rocked her world.

She had combed through the article for any mention of a woman in Ethan's life and found none. There was no mention of a woman anywhere. The article only briefly talked about Ethan's personal life, and the rest of the article covered his investment approach, fund performance, and economic outlook.

Oh, well, why am I even concerned about what he's doing? Summer thought. He's probably sleeping with a different model every night. I'm sure they're throwing themselves at him left and right. Besides, he's long since forgotten about me and written me off. I'm sure I'm out of sight and completely out of his mind by now, Summer reasoned, and it was just as well, she decided.

She knew she was engaged to and committed to marry Richard now. They had set a wedding date of June 29th, less than two months away. Richard had been there for Summer and loved her dearly, and she loved Richard in return, but she knew she needed to resolve things with Ethan and get closure with him so she could try to move on with her life.

As she laid down the magazine and got comfortable under the covers, she knew she needed to talk with Ethan. She was still fearful of seeing him and having to admit her mistake and that it was all over. Just before she drifted off to sleep, Summer said her nightly prayer, and in closing, she asked God to help her resolve the situation with Ethan according to His plan.

❧

Ethan had arrived home late from a long day at the office, but he was in no mood to sleep. He was alone, as usual, and he had found a way to cope with being alone so much of the time. In a strange way being alone gave him peace.

After Summer, he had made the decision to take the easy way out and shut out any woman who tried to be anything more than a colleague with him. While this approach had left him lonely at times, it was safe. It had meant no more heartache, no more disappointment, no more lies, and no more betrayal. It was a tradeoff Ethan had convinced himself was worthwhile.

As was his habit late in the evening, Ethan poured himself a glass of chardonnay and made his way onto his balcony overlooking Central Park. He hoped this glass of wine would make sleep come easily tonight. As he leaned on his balcony rail sipping his chardonnay, he wondered what Summer Davis was doing right now, at this exact moment. It would have been so wonderful to enjoy the evening with her and all of his recent success, Ethan thought. He wished he would just stop thinking about her, but Summer wouldn't vacate his mind. He could keep her blocked out for days at a time, but at times like this, he always thought of her.

Ethan decided he wasn't going to let the woman who betrayed him occupy any more of his thoughts that night. After all, she was probably long over him and married by now, likely to that loser he caught her kissing in Thomasville, he decided. She's not ever coming up here to apologize, and I'm never returning to Valdosta or Thomasville, so what's the point in wasting any more time on her? Ethan thought as he made his way to bed for the night. His logical, rational mind prevailed yet again.

Wednesday morning came early for Ethan due to his late night working. Shortly after arriving in his office at seven a.m., Ethan was startled as his cell phone rang and interrupted the silence in his office. Not surprisingly, it was Michael.

"Good morning, kid! How's it going?" Michael asked enthusiastically. Even early in the morning Ethan noticed that Michael was in his typical good humor. Ethan had rarely seen him down or upset since he met him.

"Good morning. I'm doing great! I was up here until nine and went home and had a little wine before bed, and that's about it," Ethan replied full of energy himself.

I know what you mean, kid. I worked late myself," Michael added.

After a brief pause Michael continued, "Listen, I know this is super short notice, but a *very* good friend of mine has two tickets to the Broadway musical *Wicked* this Friday, and he gave them to me as a personal favor. He thinks he's doing something wonderful for me by giving them to me, and I don't have the heart to turn him down. I can't stand musicals, and I was wondering if you would do me a huge favor and go in my place," Michael asked. Ethan picked up on a pleading tone that bordered on begging coming from Michael.

"Oh, I don't know, Michael. I've always wanted to see a Broadway musical, but I'm not sure that's what I had in mind," Ethan replied, not at all interested in the offer.

"Please, Ethan, I'd consider it a tremendous personal favor and will make it up to you, I promise. You wouldn't have to bring anyone, and I think it only lasts like two hours. You can then tell me about it in case my friend asks me how I liked it," Michael offered laughingly.

"Oh, okay, I'll do it. What time is it?" Ethan asked, chuckling to himself at Michael's comment. He knew Michael would indeed make it up to him, and even if he didn't, Ethan figured it was the least he could do for the man who had brought him to New York and given him the opportunity to secure all of his recognition and money.

"It's at seven o'clock. I'll send someone by with the tickets today. Thanks a bunch, kid, gotta go! Bye," Michael called out as he hung up and was off to the rat race on Wall Street. Ethan resigned himself to the fact that he would just have to endure the musical that evening and "take one for the team." In his mind he knew that was going to be the best case scenario for the evening.

✌

The next couple of days breezed by for Summer. Summer had begun her Friday early at seven o'clock by beginning the setup for a large rehearsal dinner for the wedding she was handling on Saturday. The wedding was going to be in Thomasville and held at the First Baptist Church there. The rehearsal dinner was being held at The Plaza Restaurant. Summer had taken responsibility for a majority of the setup herself since this was a large wedding for a prominent family in Thomasville, and she wanted everything to be perfect.

As she was loading decorations into her car to take to the restaurant, she received a text message. She looked down and saw it was from Sebastian, and it read, *"Hey, boo! Check us out!"* It included a picture of him and Eric in front of the Statue of Liberty with big cheesy smiles. Summer immediately laughed out loud at the picture. They looked so happy to be there. She sent a text back telling them to have a great time in the Big Apple and enjoy the musical, and she then resumed her work for the day.

✌

Ethan had a smooth Friday. There had been little news to move the market that day, and he had spent most of his time reviewing three new companies for the New York hedge fund. He also had a few brief phone calls with a couple of the investors in the Valdosta fund, and that was the extent of his day.

He had managed to get home and relax with a glass of chardonnay before getting dressed to go see the musical Michael had roped him into. Ethan hoped the musical wasn't too terribly long and was at least somewhat entertaining. He knew it was about the Wizard of Oz, but that was about all the knowledge he had of *Wicked*.

Ethan was dressed in his black tuxedo and arrived at the musical just in time to find his seat before it began. This was the first Broadway musical or musical, period, he had ever attended. It was clearly not his type of entertainment, but the event did manage to keep him interested and entertained the entire evening. In fact, it had kept him interested enough that he hadn't even checked the time during the performance.

As the closing number finished and the curtain dropped, he looked down at his watch to see that it was almost ten o'clock. Wow, he thought, it's been three hours. As everyone began standing up to leave, Ethan quickly did the same and attempted to make his way out as fast as possible to get home before midnight.

As Ethan made his way into the lobby, he looked to his left and saw a tall man with a bald head and a black beard staring at him. Ethan thought that the man looked familiar. I've seen him somewhere; I just know it, he said to himself.

Ethan dismissed the thought and continued to make his way through the lobby toward the door when he heard a man from behind him call out, "Ethan! Ethan! Ethan Phillips!" Ethan turned around to see that same bald headed man walking briskly toward him, moving in and out of the crowd of people in the lobby. The man's height worked to his advantage because it allowed him to keep his eye on Ethan and where he was the entire time as Ethan watched him fight his way through the crowd to reach him.

Finally the man made it through the sea of humanity and reached Ethan, now short of breath, and said, "Ethan . . . I thought that was you. I'm sure you don't remember me, but I'm Sebastian. I was the maître d at Restaurant Paradis in Rosemary Beach the night you met Summer. She may have told you, but I already knew her then and arranged for her to sit with you. She and I were friends then and have continued to be good friends since."

"Well, hello, Sebastian. I don't think Summer ever mentioned that to me. I knew I recognized you when I came out of the theatre into the lobby, but I couldn't place where I'd seen you before. What in the world are you doing in New York?" Ethan asked in amazement that he had run into Sebastian again, and in New York, of all places.

"Well, my partner, Eric, and I have been dying to see *Wicked,* so we saved up to come see it, and here we are," Sebastian said. Ethan saw him smiling and noticed he seemed quite proud that he had finally made it to New York.

Just as he finished his comment another man walked up beside him. Ethan hadn't met him before. Ethan observed he was much shorter than Sebastian and was rather unremarkable to the eye, with sandy blond hair and an unusually large nose. "This is my partner, Eric Francis. Eric, this is Ethan Phillips, Summer's ex-boyfriend," Sebastian offered as Ethan watched him motion toward him.

"Oh yeah, I remember her talking about you. Nice to meet you," Eric said. Ethan noticed that Eric seemed to have a dryer personality than Sebastian.

"Nice to meet you, Eric. So, how is Summer these days?" Ethan asked Sebastian curiously.

"She's doing okay, and her business has blossomed. She's all the rage now in Thomasville," Sebastian replied.

"Well, that's good. I knew she would do well," Ethan replied blandly and with a hint of sadness in his eyes.

⊷

Seizing on the opportunity he believed Ethan had given him by asking about Summer, Sebastian quickly added, "Listen, I'd like to sit down with you for a few minutes and catch you up on her if you have some time." He had wanted for a long time to reach out to Ethan and be a mediator and try to get him back together with Summer. He just knew in his heart that Ethan and Summer were made for each other, and he couldn't stand by and watch them give up on their relationship.

In fact, in the back of his mind that was one reason he wanted to come to see the musical in New York. He had so hoped he might run into Ethan, and lo and behold, that was exactly what happened.

Ethan then responded, "I appreciate the offer, Sebastian, but I don't think so. I've moved on, and I'm sure Summer has, too. I just don't see what benefit there is from opening old wounds. I hope you understand."

"I do, Ethan, but I wish you would reconsider. I'm sure you'd be interested in what I have to tell you about her," Sebastian replied, almost with an air of desperation. Here he was in front of the man he knew Summer needed to talk with, and he could sense the opportunity vanishing for him to talk with Ethan and connect them.

"I promise I won't take much of your time. I'd appreciate it if you could give me thirty minutes. That's all of your time I need," Sebastian continued, pleading now.

"I'm sorry, but I think it's best for the past to remain in the past. Summer made a choice, and she has to live with it, and besides, I've moved on. You can tell her I said hello, but that's the extent of what I have to say. I don't mean to be rude, Sebastian, but it's just not something I'm willing to do. I hope you can respect that," Ethan responded curtly. Sebastian saw the obvious lingering hurt in his voice and expression.

"Okay, I understand. I hate we couldn't have just a few minutes to talk. I'll pass along your hello, Ethan. It was good to see you and best of luck. If you change your mind, here's my card," Sebastian replied somberly as he handed Ethan his business card, then turned and slumped away with Eric close by his side.

As he walked away all Sebastian could think about was that he came so close to bridging the gulf between Summer and Ethan, and he had failed. He had let his best friend Summer down. He was dejected and disappointed as he and Eric made the walk back to their hotel.

⁂

Ethan was also in a somber mood on his walk back to his condo. His pride and hurt feelings wouldn't allow him to talk about Summer with Sebastian. In addition, seeing Sebastian served to bring up memories of her. They were great memories of Rosemary Beach and their passions, but they were inevitably followed by the memory of that awful day in Thomasville. He trudged his way home deep in thought, and after arriving, he quickly downed a few glasses of wine and a sleeping pill to attempt to rid Summer from his mind so he could sleep.

Saturday morning Ethan woke up around ten. It was highly unusual for him to sleep that late, but the sleeping pill mixed with the wine had knocked him out for all of the night and most of the morning. Once Ethan was up, he ate a quick breakfast, then had his shower.

As he stood in the shower with his palms against the wall in front of him, the warm water cascaded gently over his head and down his body. The shower was so warm and soothing, and he could feel the effects of the heavy sleep washing down the drain with the water. The steam from the hot water had created a dense fog in the bathroom.

Ethan re-lived the encounter with Sebastian the previous night. He thought it so odd that he would see him here in New York. He was the last person he expected to bump into, especially at a Broadway musical, of all places. Now he hoped that Sebastian hadn't thought he was rude with his decision not to talk with him about Summer. At that moment that was his feeling about reviving any memories of her. Ethan had thought it best to just leave them in the past, but as he continued to think and let the hot water wash over him, he realized that the memories of Summer were constantly being revived.

As much as he hated to admit it, he had numerous experiences and conversations since he came to New York that reminded him of her. In fact, on the two most accomplished nights of his professional career, he thought of Summer and even, for a moment, wished they were together again to share them.

The more he thought of the encounter last night with Sebastian and about Summer, he realized she wasn't erased from his mind and probably never would be, especially if he didn't talk or meet with her and try to bring closure to their relationship, but it seemed the more he considered talking with her, the more his pride, deep hurt, and pain swelled inside him to snuff out that idea.

After about thirty minutes of this mental tug-of-war, he pulled himself out of it and finished his shower. As he was drying off his chiseled granite frame, he knew he needed an escape today, and he knew exactly where that was located.

Since he was a boy, and especially since he arrived in New York, he had always wanted to visit the toy store FAO Schwarz. It was a place he'd seen in a movie on television as a child, and it had captivated his imagination. It seemed like a place where Christmas was kept year 'round, and he absolutely loved Christmas. He finished getting ready and ventured out to find his place of escape.

Ethan arrived at the toy store, and as he entered, he was greeted warmly by a tall, elderly gray-headed man dressed as a toy soldier. He was the doorman for the toy store and was a signature of the business. Upon entering the store, Ethan was filled with wonder as he walked and gazed around the store.

Instantly, he felt as if he'd been transported back in time and was once again that little boy with a fascination with toys, expectantly waiting on Christmas. The store was everything he had imagined it would be. There were toys everywhere. Giant stuffed animals, life-size doll houses, numerous assortments of candy, and a giant train winding its way through the store on tracks overhead. All of these things were there for him to see. Ethan was filled with awe and amazement. He thought, what a happy place to be, and he was so glad he had come.

As he continued his slow stroll through the store, he knew there was one thing he had to see there, the giant piano. He had always wanted to see the piano and step onto it and attempt to play.

When he walked up to the piano there was strangely no one dancing on it and attempting to play. Ethan looked around the store with a guilty look like he was about to steal something. He wanted to hop up on it and play but was apprehensive about what the other customers might say. He thought for a moment and decided to just go for it and play. He had always wanted to do this, and he wasn't going to let the fact that he was thirty years late getting here stop him.

Ethan stood with both feet on one of the keys, then began timidly, at first, hopping from one key to the next. He had never had any piano lessons, and it showed instantly with the tune he tried to play.

After hopping around on several of the keys, just enjoying the fun of it, he decided to play the only tune he knew how. He walked over to the left edge of the piano, then with both feet, jumped onto the first key, then quickly hopped with both feet to each succeeding key, and as he did so, he was smiling and singing do, re, mi, fa, sol, la, ti, do. He then jumped off the keyboard after landing on the final key of his tune.

As he landed, he was caught by surprise by hearing small applause behind him. He turned and saw a familiar tall, bald-headed man with blue eyes and a neatly groomed black beard. It was Sebastian, and he and Eric were smiling brightly and calling out, "Bravo, honey, bravo!"

Upon seeing them, Ethan could feel his complexion turn beet red with embarrassment at having someone he knew see him on the piano. He quickly tried to brush off his embarrassment, took a bow, smiled, then walked over to Sebastian and Eric.

"I didn't know you were a piano player, Ethan, darling," Sebastian said, continuing to smile.

"I didn't, either," Ethan quipped back with a small smile. Ethan, for the second day in a row, was talking to Sebastian in a place where he never thought he would see him. In fact, Ethan never expected to see Sebastian again after leaving Rosemary Beach. He had considered him to be just one of those many fleeting people a person meets once in their life.

"I see you're a kid at heart, just like me and Eric," Sebastian replied.

"Yeah, I guess I am. I've always wanted to come here and do that, so here I am. Y'all aren't headed back to Florida yet?" Ethan asked curiously.

"No, but we are tomorrow. We just had to take in some of these fabulous sites while we were here. I don't suppose you've changed your mind about chatting with me? Thirty minutes, I promise," Sebastian said, continuing to smile and raising both eyebrows slightly.

Ethan blurted out almost without thinking, "Oh, what the hell. Why not. I need some closure."

"Wonderful, just wonderful," Sebastian called out, smiling and clapping his hands together. "There's a chic little coffee shop just around the corner we can go to for a little privacy. Eric will just hang out here while we talk, won't you, Eric, darling?" Sebastian continued.

"Um, yeah, I guess so," Eric replied. Ethan sensed Eric's disgust at being left behind.

"Alright, that's fine. I'm going to find some candy to take with me, and I'll meet you over there in thirty minutes," Ethan replied with little emotion.

"Fabulous, see you there," Sebastian responded exuberantly.

❧

Sebastian was thrilled to have his chance to convince Ethan to talk with Summer before she was married and it was too late. He just knew he could sway him to meet with her if he had a little time to share what he knew. He knew he needed to make the sales pitch of his life to convince Ethan to meet with Summer. Sure of his task, Sebastian was ready to reunite Ethan and Summer.

❧

Ethan felt differently, however, and as he walked over to the candy, he could feel the dark cloud of hurt resurfacing with just the idea of talking about Summer. He wasn't sure exactly why he blurted out that he would meet with Sebastian, but he decided a lot of it was the fact that he was frustrated with continuing to think about her. He hoped that maybe one conversation with Sebastian would silence those thoughts.

Ethan soon left FAO Schwarz and arrived at the coffee shop. He quickly found Sebastian in a corner booth and sat down. They each ordered something to drink, then Sebastian jumped right in to the conversation. "Listen, Ethan, I don't mean to be a pest, and I may be out of line, honey, but I just had to talk with you about Summer. She and I are *very* good friends, and I know she's still goo goo over you. I also know you two are a fabulous couple."

"It's okay, Sebastian. It's been two years since we broke up, so I'm past all of that, and frankly, I'm only talking with you to hopefully put all of that to rest once and for all," Ethan replied, trying his best to conceal the feelings he still had for Summer.

∽

"If you don't mind me being nosey, does that mean you've found someone new?" Sebastian gently probed, wanting to see if he could find out Ethan's relationship status.

"No, I haven't dated anyone since her. I haven't felt like it and don't want to get hurt," Ethan replied bluntly.

"I know what she did to you was wrong as hell, honey, but she's still in love with you," Sebastian replied with a serious tone, hoping that by letting Ethan know how Summer felt that it might sway him to talk with her.

"She still loves me, really? How do you figure that?" questioned Ethan, raising his voice slightly as his Sebastian saw Ethan's eyes light up with the comment.

"Yes, honey, she definitely does. She's about to marry the guy you saw her kiss, and I know her heart isn't in it. It's a total mistake. That's why I jumped at the chance to talk to you," Sebastian said.

∽

Sebastian didn't realize it but he had just dropped a bomb on Ethan revealing that Summer was about to marry Richard. Ethan was enraged. Instantly, all of the hurt, anger, and disappointment from that day in Thomasville flashed back into Ethan's mind and he was infuriated with the thought of her marrying that man. Immediately his frustration boiled over with Sebastian.

"What? She's marrying that loser? Why the hell are you talking to me then? He can have her, as far as I'm concerned! She'll just stab him in the back, like she did me," Ethan fired back without even thinking, with anger in his eyes and his lingering hurt still firmly wrapped around everything he said and evident in his facial expression.

❧

Sebastian remained calm and was mature enough to take Ethan's comments in stride. He knew that if Ethan was still that upset about Summer from what she did to him over two years ago, he must still love her, too. Sebastian was not about to give up now.

Chapter Twenty-Eight

"'M SORRY, HONEY, I should've eased into that part better. I'm just a bull in a china shop when it comes to playing Cupid. Ethan, she is about to marry Richard, but trust me, honey, she truly, truly loves you. Her eyes shine like Elton John's wardrobe when she talks about you! That girl's watched CNBC every day for two years hoping to just see or hear *anything* about you. She watched all of your interview on television, and that's all she could talk about with me the next day. She even put off lunch with her fiancé that day just so she wouldn't miss your performance, honey!" Sebastian elaborated.

He continued, "And she texted me and said she bought the magazines you just made the cover for and read the articles in both of them multiple times. Think about it, she tried for a *year* straight trying to get in touch with you and apologize and get back with you, even when you wouldn't give that child the time of day. She kept all of your texts and voice mails, and she replays those *all* the time. And I haven't even talked about her diary. I know you're all over that, too."

Sebastian further elaborated, "All of that is why I'm here, boo. I can't just sit back and watch my best friend marry another man when she's still totally in love with you after all this time. I love that girl too much, and besides, Ethan, you're the one for her. There's no doubt in my pretty little mind, honey," Sebastian said as he smiled and ended his opening arguments in the case of Summer Davis and Ethan Phillips. Sebastian's passion about what he was saying and his true friendship and love for Summer were made abundantly clear to Ethan during Sebastian's passionate appeal to him.

Ethan had said nothing while Sebastian had talked, and he had just listened and let everything soak in. He was still enraged at the thought of Summer's marrying the man he saw her cheating on him with and kissing. The thought of a woman he loved so totally and completely betraying him and marrying another, to boot, was an almost unbearable thought. Not unlike many men, the pain and hurt manifested itself with anger in Ethan.

Finally, after Sebastian had finished, Ethan resumed his tirade. "You're trying to sit here and tell me she's about to marry the man she cheated on me with, and she's still hung up on me? That just sounds like bullshit, Sebastian. If she didn't love that guy, she wouldn't be about to marry him. I bet she's just hung up on the sex! She was just using me for sex, anyway. No one is forcing Summer to marry him. She's just a damn paramour and can't be happy with one guy and is looking for another cheap thrill! Well, she can just forget it with me! I'm done with her, and you can tell her I said kiss off!"

Ethan's voice had escalated with each passing word, and by the time he was finished, he was nearly yelling. The pain, the hurt, and the betrayal were leaping from every angry word from his mouth.

Sebastian was caught off guard and speechless. He could only manage to stare at Ethan, with his mouth gaping open, during Ethan's rant. He was blindsided by the intensity of the hurt and pain that this man was still carrying after two years. It was painfully obvious to Sebastian that Ethan still loved Summer very deeply and was still hurting equally as deep.

Sebastian observed Ethan stand after finishing his tantrum, and as he did so, Sebastian sprang up quickly from the booth and pleaded soothingly, "Listen, Ethan, I'm sorry. I didn't mean to upset you. Please, please let me finish."

With his toxic vent complete, Ethan's rage began to subside, and he looked Sebastian straight in the eye with an intensity Sebastian had never seen before. He said, while pointing his finger at Sebastian, "It's over. Make sure you tell her *that*." Ethan then turned and stormed out of the coffee shop and headed back to his condo.

⊷

Sebastian slowly slid back down into the booth, lay his head in his hands, and lamented the fact that he had just destroyed what he was trying to save. He was bitterly disappointed that he had failed Summer and Ethan. If only he had chosen his words better and eased into Summer's marriage, he thought.

He then thought what in the world would he tell Summer, and how would he look her in the eye knowing he just ran away the man she totally adores? Sebastian could only sit in the booth by himself and dine on ashes.

⊷

Ethan was able to hail a taxi and make it back to his condo in record time. The whole ride home all he could do was replay over and over in his mind his brief conversation with Sebastian. He was still fuming over learning of Summer's marriage to Richard. It was impossible for him to believe she would marry Richard if she still loved him. To his logical, rational mind that made no sense. She kissed Richard while he and Summer were dating and now was about to marry him. The reality was it was much easier and safer for Ethan to believe that Summer really was in love with Richard all along.

The only thing contradicting all of Ethan's thoughts was what Sebastian told him about her following him and his accomplishments. If she didn't care about him, she wouldn't be following his career so intently. She would have just simply forgotten about him and moved on, he reasoned.

Just then Ethan arrived at the door to his condo and was soon inside, and despite it being only three in the afternoon, he put on some comfortable clothes to stay in for the rest of the day. He grabbed a large bottle of chardonnay from his wine cooler and a glass and climbed into bed to watch television and drink until he passed out. He wanted no more thinking about Summer or Sebastian. Finally, after a few hours and his second bottle of wine, Ethan accomplished his goal and fell soundly asleep.

It was shortly after midnight and Ethan groggily opened his eyes from the coma-like state and alcohol-induced fog he was in. What in the hell is that noise? he thought. He looked to his left to see where all this noise was coming from, and it was his cellphone. He picked it up and looked at the caller ID. Ethan instantly thought he *must* be dreaming. The caller ID said Willie Francesco. Ethan was astonished to see that his good friend was calling him.

He quickly answered the call, and as he said hello, Ethan heard, "Ethan" . . . sniff . . . sniff. "Ethan, is that you?" It wasn't easy to make out the faint voice, but he could definitely tell it was a woman, and after a few seconds Ethan realized it was Willie's wife, Ann.

Once Ethan had this revelation, he called out excitedly, "Ann? Ann? Is that you? Yes, this is Ethan. What's wrong?"

◆

"Ethan, it's Willie," replied Ann, and that was all she could get out before bursting into tears. She began sobbing and crying loudly as her emotions got her.

"Ann, what's happened to Willie? What's wrong? Please tell me," Ethan pleaded with her.

She continued to cry for a few minutes more, then managed to pull herself together.

"Ethan, Willie's had another heart attack, and this one was worse than the one before. I managed to get him here to the hospital quickly. I gave him aspirin like before, but according to Dr. Johannsen, Willie has sustained some significant heart damage and" Ann had to break off her conversation as she began crying and sobbing uncontrollably again. The fear, worry, and anxiety had made a habit of bombarding Ann the last few hours.

◆

Ethan knew very well that she absolutely adored Willie, despite the age difference. He could only imagine that seeing him in his condition must be almost more than she could handle.

"Take your time, Ann. There's no rush; just take your time," Ethan offered in a calm and soothing voice.

Ethan could hear that Ann was attempting to pull herself together once again. She then said, "Ethan, the damage done to Willie's heart is permanent, and he's not likely to receive a transplant due to his age. Things just don't look good. We're praying for a miracle."

Ethan listened to her, then asked with his voice full of worry and concern,

"So if things don't look good, and his heart is badly damaged, and he can't get a transplant, what are they saying anything about how long he has?"

⚜

Ann began sobbing again, but managed to reply, "Well, they say he has. . . ." Just then Ann erupted into crying uncontrollably again. She had tears streaming down both sides of her face like a raging river during a one-hundred-year flood. The thought of what she was about to tell Ethan just didn't seem real to her, and the idea of what she was saying was a terribly painful thought.

"It's okay, Ann, just keep taking your time. I'll stay on as long as we need to," Ethan replied.

Ann had now recovered again, at least for the moment, and resumed, "They say that he has no more than a year, but that, realistically, it's probably just a few months."

⚜

Ethan was utterly speechless. Willie only had *months* to live? Ethan couldn't believe what he was hearing. Willie was too young to die. Suddenly, a dark, ominous, and overpowering veil of sorrow and guilt enveloped Ethan and his thoughts. He couldn't respond. He was in shock, and he now also felt unbelievably guilty for leaving Valdosta and his friend Willie and not returning the past two years.

The thought dominating Ethan's mind was that Willie was going to die before he could make it back to Valdosta to see him and talk with him. Ethan then managed to snap out of his train of thought and ask Ann, "Only months? Is he able to talk at all, like on the phone?"

"No, I'm afraid not, Ethan. He's so weak right now he barely stays awake for more than an hour at the time, and even then he only manages to whisper. He keeps asking for you when he's awake. I just had to call you. I know you're in New York, but I was just hoping and praying that . . ." Ann replied and Ethan noticed her voice trailing off at the end of her sentence.

"You've been hoping and praying I'd come see him," Ethan asked.

"Yes, Ethan, I have. I knew it would probably not be possible for you to get away on short notice, and even if you did, Willie might not......" Ann countered and Ethan listened as she burst into tears again before she could finish the sentence.

"Ann, I'll come! I'll come! The next time Willie wakes up tell him I'm coming. I'll get there as soon as I can. No promises on what time, though. Where are y'all?" Ethan questioned, with his sincerity and gritty determination to get there embodied in his voice.

"Oh, Ethan! Thank you, thank you, thank you! It'll mean so much to us both! He's in room 517 in ICU at South Georgia Medical Center here in Valdosta. I'll make sure the nurses know to bring you back when you get here," Ann replied. Ethan noticed her tone change in an instant to one of hope and happiness.

Ethan felt she was genuinely thrilled he would come from New York to Valdosta on such short notice. "Sounds good, Ann. I better let you go; I have some packing to do. You hang in there, and tell Willie to do the same. I'll see you guys soon, okay?" Ethan replied again in a calm, supporting, and soothing voice.

"Okay, thank you again so much, dear! Be careful getting here. Remember, we love you. We both love you very much. Goodbye," and with that Ann hung up.

Ethan was so flattered and happy to hear Ann utter those last words. Even though they hadn't been married long, Ethan had picked up on the fact that there was a strong and powerful bond between Willie and Ann. He knew they both cared deeply for each other and for him.

The next thought that Ethan had was that he needed to say a prayer for Willie. Ethan wasn't sure that God even remembered him now, given he had turned his back on Him the last two years. He knew his God was one of forgiveness, and he could only trust that forgiveness also applied to him. Ethan then took about five minutes and gave a heartfelt and sincere prayer for Willie's recovery. Next, Ethan shifted his thoughts to finding a way to get back to Valdosta in a hurry.

Ethan wasted no time in getting back to see Willie. Right after he finished his prayer, he called and woke Michael and told him about Willie's condition and that he needed to leave town.

Ethan had previously told Michael that he and Willie were close. He saw how supportive Michael was of his desire to get back when he quickly offered, "Just take the jet back, kid. I'll call the pilots right now and wake them up. If you can give them two hours to take off, they can be ready to go by then," volunteered Michael. Ethan believed Michael was a top shelf guy, and to Ethan that fact came through in every interaction he had with the man.

"That's kind, Michael, but we can go in the morning if we need to," Ethan replied, not wanting to put a huge burden on Michael or the pilots to fly on such short notice.

"Nonsense, kid. I've done it to them before, and trust me, they're always prepared for things like this. They'll be fine, and when they find out why they're flying, they'll be more than happy to help you," Michael said approvingly.

"Well, okay. If you say so. Thank you so much. I don't have the words to express my gratitude," Ethan replied, almost choking up as he finished his sentence. He was deeply touched by Michael's kindness and generosity.

"It's nothing, kid. I'm glad to do it. Be careful going down, and keep me updated on Willie. Good night, kid." and Michael hung up. Ethan immediately turned his attention to packing clothes. He had little time to waste to be packed and at the airport in two hours.

Ethan amazed himself. He was dressed, packed, and at the airport in just over an hour and a half. He didn't know for sure how long he would be in Valdosta, so to be safe, he had packed for several days. He also remembered that he had left a few clothes behind at his house. Thankfully, with his workout regimen, he hadn't gained any weight, and they would all still fit if he needed them, he determined.

The entire flight back to Valdosta early that Sunday morning found Ethan in deep thought. The idea of Willie's dying soon, perhaps even before Ethan could get back to Valdosta, had totally changed his idea of what was important in life. All of his financial and professional success now seemed insignificant and to have come at a heavy price. He had missed out on two years with Willie that he could never get back. Worst of all, Willie was now at death's door, and he would have little time in the future with his best friend.

Also weighing on his mind now was his anger, hurt, and resentment at what Summer had done to him and the fact that he had punished Summer and himself for over two years for betraying him. That hurt now seemed petty and small and paled in comparison to his best friend being at death's door. Ethan began to feel foolish for not responding to Summer at all and even allowing her a chance to explain what happened.

Sebastian's words were also beginning to resonate with him, too. He wondered if Summer might indeed still be in love with him since she was still following him that closely after all that time. For Ethan, like most people, in times of death, or the threat of death he began to focus on what was truly important in life, and that was the people who cared about him.

Suddenly Ethan's thoughts were interrupted by the loud screech of the jet touching down on the runway. He was shaken out of his thoughts of Willie and Summer and knew his priority right now was his best friend and trying to get him well and spend as much time with him as he could. He surmised he couldn't figure out what he needed to do with Summer on a flight from New York to Valdosta.

He would have to save figuring that issue out until he had more time. Right now, he had to get to Willie, and he hoped so desperately he was in time. It was now four thirty a.m., and Ethan was home for the first time in over two years. He couldn't wait to reach Willie.

Ethan grabbed his luggage and was off the plane as soon as it had come to rest and the door was opened. The pilots, with their attention to every detail, as usual, had arranged for Ethan to use one of the courtesy cars at the airport until the next day. Ethan took barely more than five minutes to find the car and get his luggage in it and was speeding off to the hospital. He was driving like a bat out of hell to reach his best friend in time.

He just knew he was going to encounter a policeman along the way, but he decided the Lord was smiling on him, and he was able to speed to the hospital without incident. He parked the car in the parking deck, and in less than ten minutes, he was exiting the elevator at the fifth floor, the ICU floor of the facility.

As Ethan exited the elevator, an overwhelming case of déjà vu came over him. This scene was all too familiar to Willie's last heart episode, only this time, Willie's prognosis was much worse. Ethan then looked to his right, and he and Ann made eye contact simultaneously.

∽

Ann couldn't contain her excitement and screamed out as she came running across the room, "Oh, my God! Ethan, it's you! You're here!"

After reaching Ethan, Ann immediately wrapped her arms around him and gave him a hug as she leaned her head against his broad, firm chest. She was squeezing Ethan as tightly as she possibly could. Ann kept her death grip around Ethan for another minute or two before pulling back, smiling from ear to ear and choking back tears, and said, "I can't believe you got here this quickly! I'm so glad to see you! Willie and I have missed you more than you can possibly know."

"It's good to be here, Ann. It's been way too long," Ethan replied apologetically.

"Yes, son, it has. Willie will be so happy to see you! I left him about two hours ago to rest and just before I left, he whispered, 'Is he here yet, honey?' I told him no and to just relax and get some rest and that you would be here tomorrow. That seemed to appease him because he's been quiet since and hasn't asked again," Ann replied, smiling brightly.

"So how is he?" Ethan asked. Ann could tell he was concerned and worried by the tone of his voice.

"He's stable right now. It's been a stressful evening. We're just taking it hour by hour, praying a lot and enjoying our time with each other," Ann replied, choking back tears as she spoke.

"Yeah, that's the best thing to do. Are you staying here tonight?" Ethan asked.

"They have a vacant hospital room they're letting me stay in tonight. It's down two floors, but it lets me stay close in case Willie needs me. I just haven't felt like leaving him yet," Ann replied.

"That's a great idea to just stay here. I'm glad they're letting you do that," Ethan replied and Ann noticed him nod approvingly.

Just then they were interrupted as the nurse came rushing up to Ethan and Ann. "Mrs. Francesco, Mr. Willie is awake and calling for you and Ethan again. Please tell me this man is Ethan," the nurse asked, almost exasperated as she looked at Ethan.

"Yes, ma'am. I'm Ethan. Can I see him now?" Ethan asked hopefully.

Before the nurse could respond, Ann chimed in, "Yes! That would be great! Go surprise him, and I'll stay here so you can talk," Ann replied, almost giddy now that Ethan was here and about to finally visit with Willie.

"Okay, I won't stay long and tire him out," Ethan said reassuringly as he turned and followed the nurse to room 517 and his best friend.

Chapter Twenty-Nine

ETHAN'S MIND WAS racing as he made the walk through the automatic doors into ICU and down the hallway. He didn't know what to expect from Willie with his condition or what to expect from himself when they saw each other again. Ethan was nervous and excited at the same time. He couldn't wait to see Willie, and he hoped and prayed that somehow Willie would make a miraculous recovery.

Ethan watched as the nurse stopped at the entrance to the room and motioned him to go inside. Ethan knocked gently on the door, then eased into the room like a cat burglar in the night. As he came through the short hallway he looked to his left and his eyes and Willie's met. Willie smiled brightly and whispered weakly, despite his best efforts, "Captain. You made it."

As soon as those words rolled off Willie's tongue Ethan instantly broke down and began sobbing. His tears soon began streaming down both cheeks. His sobbing was so strong he couldn't manage a single word in reply. He tried his best to fight back the tears, but they were unstoppable. All he could muster at that moment was to stand beside Willie with both of his hands around Willie's right hand and cry.

Ethan was completely overcome with emotion. His mind was flooded with guilt and regret for spending the last two years apart from his best friend, and on top of that, Willie's health had deteriorated in the meantime.

Ethan knew he had lost the last two years with Willie. The guilt he was feeling for leaving his friend to pursue fame and fortune was enormous. Ethan continued to look at Willie and cry. He hadn't cried since Emma. He hadn't cried at all with Summer, mainly because he was so furious with himself for falling for her to begin with.

⁂

Willie could see Ethan was overcome with emotion, and with a smile he quietly said, "Easy there, Captain. It's okay. Everything's going to be just fine. I'll do anything to get my good buddy back down to see me, huh?" Willie questioned, with his usual roaring laugh now replaced with a soft chuckle due to his weakened condition.

Ethan was still sobbing, but couldn't help but smile at Willie's remark despite the tears. Willie always tried to make Ethan smile, even under the most difficult and stressful circumstances.

"Um, hey, Willie. I'm sorry I lost it when I came in," Ethan offered apologetically. Willie smiled and watched Ethan wipe away his tears as he spoke.

"Aw, it's okay, Captain. I'm so glad to see you I just can't stand myself. If I wasn't so weak from my old ticker acting up, I would have cried, too," Willie replied, trying to put his best friend at ease for showing his emotions. "Besides, there's nothing wrong with a man crying. I've done it many times when life was unkind to me," Willie said weakly.

"I know, but here you are lying in ICU, and I'm the one breaking down. I need to be strong for you right now," Ethan said sheepishly.

"Shoot, Captain, you're being strong for me just by traveling all the way from New York to see me so quick. I just can't thank you enough. I've missed ya," Willie replied, now almost crying himself. The emotion of seeing and talking with Ethan again was beginning to sink in with him, as was the magnitude of Ethan's commitment and concern for him by dropping everything going on in his life in New York and rushing to his bedside.

"I've missed you, too, Willie. I should have come home long before now. I feel guilty for letting these two years slip by between us, and we won't get them back. And on top of that, I did that mainly because of my breakup with Summer. I shouldn't have let that keep me from coming home to visit my best friend," Ethan said softly. Willie observed sadness and regret on his face and in his voice.

"Shoot, Captain, don't apologize for not coming home. You've been busy starting a new fund and a new career on Wall Street and trying to keep us old farts here in Valdosta happy with our fund, too. That's a lot on anyone's plate. I know you didn't avoid my handsome face and infectious smile on purpose," Willie said, smiling widely, laboring to speak, and continuing to try to inject humor into the situation.

"I know I've been busy, but I just feel like I should have come to see you already. I let all that stuff with Summer keep me from coming home, mainly because I just didn't want to run into her anywhere. I wanted to get away from anything that reminded me of her," Ethan replied.

"Captain, speaking of her, I have to tell you something," Willie said, now with his voice and facial expression changing from his normal jovial one to a serious and somber tone.

"What is it, Willie?" Ethan replied anxiously.

"Well, you remember when I set up that little retreat for you in Rosemary Beach, right?" Willie questioned.

"Sure, Willie, how could I forget it?" Ethan replied, still anxious.

Willie then began the rest of his story by saying, "Two nights before I told you about it here in the hospital and had set that all up, I had a dream about me getting you a nice little getaway at Rosemary Beach. It was odd as hell because I've only been there once myself. And the really weird part was that dream had you meeting the woman of your dreams there. I thought I was getting senile or just plain going crazy or maybe just had some bad sushi that day. I kinda dismissed it until the next day."

Willie continued, "But the next evening after I got home from having drinks at The Landing with you, I got a phone call out of the blue from one my Atlanta buddies who owned the house you bought and stayed in that week. I bet I haven't heard from him in five years. He said he was calling just to see if I or anybody I knew would want to stay in his house at Rosemary Beach for the next week. He apologized for the short notice, but they had some renters back out on them. He said I was the first person he thought of when that happened. He and I go way back, and he owed me a couple favors, you see. You could have blown me over with a feather when he offered the house to me. I immediately said yes because I knew I would let you use it, and the rest is history, I guess."

❦

"Really, that's a strange coincidence," Ethan offered in shock at both Willie's dream and the ensuing phone call he received.

Willie replied, "There are no coincidences, Captain. I think it was God. That's why before you left at The Landing that night I was so interested in your love life. And that's why when I told you to go on the trip that night here in this very hospital that I said you were gonna find the one for you. Lastly, after you got back from your vacation and told me you met someone that's why I told you she was the one. I just knew it in my heart, then had a tremendous peace about her when you told me about your week together after you got back."

"It seemed like she truly was the one until I caught her kissing her ex-boyfriend," Ethan replied with anger and hurt still very much a part of him when it came to speaking or even thinking about Summer.

"Captain, think about it. You didn't even give her a chance to explain. You didn't even *talk* to her at all after that day. I know she was wrong, and Lord knows I know Emma hurt you bad too. But I just think you should have talked to her. I'm not trying to get in your business, Ethan. You know me better than that, I think. I've tried not to really force the issue until now, but I think the silent treatment has gone on long enough. I've seen your face when you talked about her. You lit up like a Christmas tree at night in Rockefeller Center. That kind of person comes along just once in a lifetime. I hated to see you give up on it and until now just didn't feel like it was my place to really hold your feet to the fire. But after my little hiccup with my ticker, I guess it's just given me more insight into how precious and short life is. I don't want you to waste another night by not being with that gal if she makes you that happy." Willie said earnestly.

"I appreciate that, Willie, but I didn't *want* to talk to her. I was just so hurt by her, and it still hurts even today thinking about it all. I don't know why after all that happened to me with Emma that I ended up trusting her, but I just never thought she would hurt me, and she did. After I caught her kissing that man I was so angry at myself for falling for her and letting myself be hurt again, you know," Ethan said sadly.

"Captain, you know you're my best friend, right?" Willie questioned sincerely.

"Of course, I do," Ethan replied.

"You know I love you like a son, right?" Willie again questioned Ethan sincerely.

"Sure, Willie. I love you like a father," Ethan replied.

"Then do a broke down old man a favor and talk to Summer, okay?" Willie asked hopefully.

"That would be hard to do now. I ran into one of her friends in New York, and he told me she's about to be married to the guy I saw her kissing," Ethan said with his voice and facial expression blanketed in hurt and disappointment.

"I'd definitely talk to her then. If I loved a woman like I know you love her, I would have to give her a second chance, or at the very least a chance to explain what happened. You would want that same shot if the shoe was on the other foot. And I wouldn't give up so easily on a gal I loved that much and made me that happy," Willie offered. Ethan could easily see the intensity in Willie's eyes as they were locked onto his.

"Yeah, I guess you're right. I'll think about it, but no promises. Listen, that's enough about my love life or lack thereof. What is Dr. Johannsen saying about your condition?" Ethan asked, now changing the conversation back to Willie and away from Summer and a painful topic of conversation for him. He was more interested in the condition of his best friend and eager to stop talking about Summer.

"Don't tell Ann I know, but Doc Johannsen snuck in here and said my old ticker's seen its better day. I'm probably too old to make the transplant list, so I've just got to take it easy and make the best of it, I guess," Willie said. Ethan sensed Willie was trying to return to his jovial tone and disguise his worry about his condition.

"So what does that mean?" Ethan asked with his eyes now getting large.

"Well, Captain, it means I don't have a long time here on this good old earth. All I can do is take it easy and take some medication they gave me and try to just make it as far as I can. Looks like this old horse isn't too far from going out to pasture," Willie replied. Ethan noticed him smile and chuckle again. Ethan knew he was trying to disguise his nervousness and fear of what's ahead of both him and Ann.

"I'm sorry, Willie, very sorry. Now I *really* hate missing the last two years and not seeing you. I just feel horrible for not being here. I hope you forgive me," Ethan said sadly.

"Aw, don't sweat that, Captain. There's no way you could know this would happen. You've been a busy little bee the last two years, and you've accomplished a lot. You shouldn't have any regret for pursuing your dream, trust me. Just don't let that gal get away in the process, okay? Now *that* would be something to regret," Willie said, smiling happily.

"Okay, Willie, okay. I'll talk to her, I promise," Ethan replied in exasperation, as he knew Willie wasn't going to give up on getting him to talk with Summer.

Ethan watched Willie struggle to take several breaths before he said, "Great, Captain. Thank you. I know you'll be glad you did and you'll make an old man very happy."

Ethan could see on Willie's face that all of their talking had left him fatigued. Ethan knew he was completely exhausted from his conversation with him. He'd been talking with Ethan for almost thirty minutes, significantly longer than he had talked with anyone since he arrived at the hospital. As a result he was now totally spent. Ethan took his weakened condition as a cue and got up to excuse himself and said, "I'm going to let you rest now. Get some sleep, and I'll talk with you later."

Willie's eyes now closed as he gave in to his exhaustion, and as Ethan left, Willie managed to tell him in a whisper, "Bye, Captain," and he drifted off to sleep.

Ethan eased out of Willie's room and stopped in the waiting room, but Ann had already gone to her room to sleep. Sleep, Ethan decided, was something he desperately needed himself, and he immediately headed back to his house to get some rest at a place he hadn't seen in over two years.

✧

Life for Summer had remained as busy as ever. Her business was booming and began occupying more and more of her time each day and even on weekends, despite the staff she had brought on board. Summer knew quite soon she was going to have to begin mentoring one of her staff to be able to take even more responsibility off her so that she could focus on growing and managing the business.

All was good for her, Richard, and Jake right now. The last month she and Richard had spent most of their free time planning the wedding. They had almost all of the arrangements in place and were locked in on their June wedding date. Since it was Summer's expertise to plan weddings, they had not needed to hire a wedding planner, but as a tradeoff, her stress level was much higher since she was handling most of the details for her own event.

She woke up early Saturday morning so she could get showered and dressed and pick up Jake from his dad's. Jake had been with his father the last few days, and she missed him terribly when they were apart for three days at a time. Summer was almost finished getting dressed when she heard her cellphone ringing and vibrating loudly. As she picked up the phone, she saw it was her good friend Sebastian calling her. Summer answered her phone and said, "Hey, Sebastian. You're up early on a Saturday. How was *Wicked?*"

"Honey, it was totally fabulous; do you hear me! Eric and I just loved it! We were both on the edge of our seats the whole time," Sebastian replied. Summer could hear his voice climbing a couple of octaves in excitement talking about the musical.

"That's awesome. I'm so glad y'all enjoyed it. I knew you would have a good time. Was the theater crowded?" Summer asked curiously.

"Listen, boo, we were packed like sardines in that little matchbox theater, but the seats were so plush and soft we didn't mind it a bit. We could have sat another three hours in there and watched *Wicked* again, honey," replied Sebastian. Summer could tell he was still brimming with excitement by the sound of his voice.

"That's too funny," Summer replied, laughing at Sebastian's comment.

"Listen to me now. Guess who Eric and I ran into at the theater?" Sebastian offered excitedly.

"Um, let me see, was it the mayor of New York?" Summer replied, grasping at straws as she had no idea what celebrity they might have run into. She knew Sebastian had a way of accidentally bumping into well know public figures.

"No, honey, better than that," Sebastian replied dryly.

"Well, knowing you, I bet it was Cher, wasn't it?" Summer guessed, now excited herself at the prospect Sebastian might have met her as she was one of her favorite artists.

"No, honey, even better than that," Sebastian replied dryly again.

"I don't know then. I'm out of guesses," Summer said, now tired of this little game Sebastian was playing.

"It was your man, boo," Sebastian replied. She noticed he appeared to be taking on a serious tone now as he spoke.

"What? *My* man? Richard is here in Thomasville, Sebastian. What are you talking about?" Summer replied, totally confused with what he said.

"No, boo, *your man*," Sebastian quipped back and Summer heard his strong emphasis on the last two words he uttered. As soon as he finished speaking, the light bulb went off over Summer's head. She then knew Sebastian was talking about Ethan. He had seen him at the musical, she surmised.

Summer found herself getting excited at the mere thought of hearing about a conversation Sebastian might have had with Ethan. Suddenly it felt as if butterflies were flying wildly inside her stomach. "You saw Ethan, seriously?" Summer replied, almost in disbelief at what she was hearing.

⤦

"I did, boo," Sebastian responded with a serious tone. He had debated whether he would even mention to Summer that he had run into Ethan and had a conversation with him. He knew she would possibly be upset with him for intervening and trying to talk with Ethan about their relationship. He felt extremely guilty about it, but he decided only to tell her about parts of his conversation with Ethan. He just didn't have the nerve to tell her right now that he had blown any chance of getting Ethan to talk to her.

He had elected to just say a prayer for God's will to be done with Ethan and Summer and simply let her know he saw and chatted with Ethan. The ultimate resolution of Ethan and Summer would have to rest in God's hands, Sebastian had decided.

"Well, what did you talk about, silly?" Summer questioned.

"We started by chatting in the lobby after the musical," Sebastian offered, then he shared with her part of the conversation as Summer listened intently. It seemed to him that she was hanging on every word he spoke and soaking up each detail as he talked.

After Sebastian finished laying out the summarized conversation, Summer then chimed in, "So it sounds like he's over me if he doesn't want to meet me or even talk. I guess I did the right thing by moving on with Richard, huh?"

"I don't think he's over you, boo. You should have seen how upset he was when he found out you were getting married. And, honey, on top of that, I know he said he had moved on, but he sure wasn't very convincing to me. Based on what you've said, that man has many talents. But being an actor, he's definitely not. He was wasting his time trying to sell me that line of bull about not wanting to see you again. The man is still hurting, boo, and he's hurting because he still loves you and isn't with you. He's just too damn proud and stubborn to admit it and do anything about it after what happened," Sebastian replied with conviction and absolutely no trace of doubt in his voice.

"I don't know if I believe that, Sebastian. I really don't," Summer replied skeptically.

"Summer, believe me, I know when a man is in love, and trust me, that man still loves you, a lot! He's still hung up on ya, boo!" he said excitedly. He carefully omitted all the specific reasons why he was sure Ethan wasn't over her like some of the excerpts he said during the violent tirade when he found out she was getting married to Richard. Sebastian knew Ethan wouldn't have reacted so strongly if he wasn't still in love with Summer, and he certainly would have begun dating again if he was over her.

Sebastian was sure in mind and heart of everything he was saying. He hoped he could sway Summer to run to New York and see Ethan without having to mention all the details of the coffee shop encounter specifically. He was convinced if she went to New York and explained everything, Ethan would eventually take her back.

"I don't know. It's just hard to believe he wouldn't slam the door in my face if I went to see him. You may be right, but I just don't think I can do it. Besides, I'm about to marry Richard, anyway," Summer replied. Sebastian picked up on an almost defeated tone in Summer's voice.

"That's all the more reason to go see Ethan, honey. If it were me, and I loved that man as much as you do, I'd have to see him face to face and make him *tell* me it's over! I wouldn't settle for sirloin if I could have filet mignon," Sebastian quipped emphatically, trying so hard to get Summer not to settle for a man she did have feelings for when there was a man of her dreams he knew she loved passionately and was the man God intended for her still out there to be had.

Summer sighed and said, "I'll think about it, Sebastian."

"Okay, honey, just think about it. You owe it to Ethan, Richard, and most of all yourself to try and work this out. I gotta go, honey. Eric's about to have a cow to go eat Mexican for lunch. I'll talk to you later. Bye bye, now," Sebastian called out with an air of frustration at being rushed by Eric to finish the call.

❧

After Summer hung up, she sat on her familiar yellow couch and immediately opened her diary to catalogue her phone call with Sebastian and all the feelings brewing inside her at this very moment. She had a plethora of thoughts and feelings she needed to get on paper after her call with her best friend Sebastian.

❧

Ethan made it to his house and got into bed by five o'clock Sunday morning. He was dead tired from lack of sleep and from the stress of Willie's condition. He fell fast asleep as soon as his head hit the pillow, and he slept like a baby until almost three Sunday afternoon. Even the bright South Georgia sunshine had not managed to wake him from his slumber that day. Once Ethan woke up, he decided to wander through the house and check on everything.

In his zombie like state early that morning, he had done nothing else but walk in the door and go straight to bed. As he walked through the house, he saw that everything was exactly like he had left it two long years ago. It was as if time stood still inside the cabin. Even with Greta cleaning the house regularly, he could see everything was still exactly where he left it. Ethan was not surprised, though, because he trusted Greta implicitly and would have expected no less from her.

A strange feeling came over Ethan, though, as he meandered through the cabin. He found himself having flashbacks to times he spent with Summer in each area of the house. When he came into the living room, he thought of the magical night in front of the fireplace. In the kitchen he thought of the dinner they shared and the coffee she made there, and as he looked at each of his paintings and pictures, he reminisced about the tour he gave Summer when she visited for the first time. These were all good memories to Ethan, except for the fact that she had betrayed him.

The thoughts of Summer and their time at the cabin now began to bombard Ethan. As a result, he decided to give up on surveying the cabin and to just get ready so he could go to the hospital and check on Willie again. It was time to get back to reality and spend time with the friend he had abandoned these last two years. He needed to be there for Willie and Ann during this difficult time in their lives.

Chapter Thirty

AFTER SHOWERING AND getting ready, Ethan drove to the hospital to check on Willie and Ann. He felt so much better today after having had some sleep. His mind and body were now functioning normally, and he spent all of the drive drifting between thinking about Willie and Summer.

Ethan was so worried about Willie and what the future held for him and Ann. He didn't know if Willie would be here a year from now, and that thought hurt Ethan greatly. Willie had always been there for him and was the best friend a man could ask for. He hoped and prayed he could just have a few more years with Willie, and this time, he wouldn't be absent.

As for his thoughts of Summer, the advice Willie and Sebastian gave him had started to sink in. He began to feel like perhaps he had been too harsh on Summer. He was coming to grips with the fact that the two men were right. He should have at least let her make her case and tell him what happened. She deserved a chance to tell her side of the story and try to explain, even if she was in the wrong. Ethan knew if the roles were reversed, he would want that exact same chance because of the love he had for her.

Ethan determined that he had been too blinded by the pain, hurt, and betrayal by both Summer and Emma to begin to see that until now. Just then, Ethan pulled up at the hospital, quickly found a parking place, and went straight to ICU.

As Ethan entered the ICU waiting room, to his right he saw Ann talking with Dr. Johannsen. When he saw Ann, he noticed her eyes light up as she smiled brightly, raise her right hand, and wave frantically for Ethan to come over. Ethan smiled, waved in return, and walked over to them.

∽

"Ethan, I'm so glad you're here," Ann shouted as he arrived. "Willie is sitting up in bed today for the first time! His color is so much better, too. Isn't that great news?" Ann asked loudly and full of excitement that the love of her life was doing so much better today.

"That's great! I guess we owe a great debt to Dr. Johannsen here for helping him so much," Ethan replied, smiling at Ann and Dr. Johannsen.

∽

"It's the damnedest thing I've ever seen, Ethan. Last night Willie was tired, couldn't sit up in bed, and could hardly speak louder than a whisper, and today he's totally different. He's sitting up in bed, smiling all the time, has his voice back, and almost seems like he never had the heart attack. It's amazing," Dr. Johannsen told Ethan, almost in disbelief at the recovery he had seen Willie make in the last 24 hours.

∽

"That's incredible, Karl! I've never heard of anything like that! I guess we owe it to the power of prayer. I know I've been praying for him, and Ann definitely has, too. I'm so glad to hear he's better today," Ethan said now, with the same excitement and happiness Ann had.

"I've definitely been praying, Ethan. God is so good! Why don't you go on back to see him," Ann asked, still smiling brightly.

"Yes, Ethan, go on back. I think part of his miraculous improvement has to do with seeing you again, too," Dr. Johannsen added.

"Yes, I totally agree," Ann chimed in.

"I don't know about that, y'all. I do want to see him, though. See y'all later," Ethan replied and smiled and made his way to room 517.

Ethan entered Willie's room, and as advertised, Ann and Karl were right. Willie seemed like a new man. Ethan pulled up a chair and sat down, and the two best friends began to talk, just like old times. They talked briefly about the Valdosta hedge fund and the Valdosta investors, but spent most of their time talking about New York and the hedge fund there.

Ethan noticed that Willie was bombarding him with question after question about New York. They had talked on the phone many times the last two years, but Willie now wanted a face-to-face account of all that had been going on in the life of his best friend.

It seemed to Ethan that Willie couldn't get enough of talking and catching up with him. The nurses even had to bring Ethan dinner when they brought Willie's because the two didn't break stride in talking. Finally, about eight o'clock, Ethan could see that Willie was tiring and needed rest. "I think I'm going to bow out now, Willie, and let you rest. It's been great catching up, though," Ethan said, smiling at his friend.

"Yeah, Captain, the old man is getting a little winded, I guess. I've been just as happy as a fox in the hen house after the dog died sitting here talking with you. Are you coming back tomorrow, or do you need to get back to New York?" Willie questioned.

"Oh, yeah, I'll be back. I'm not going to New York for a few days, I think. I want to make sure we get you home," Ethan replied with a smile and a wink at Willie.

"That's great, Captain. You take care and don't forget to do what you promised me," Willie replied and winked back.

"I gotcha. I won't forget. See you tomorrow," Ethan said as he reached out and gently shook the hand of his best friend. On his way out Ethan stopped and talked with Ann briefly and gave her a summary of his conversation with Willie. He also gave her his thoughts on his condition.

Ethan sensed Ann was elated he had spent that much time with Willie. He knew she must have needed to go home and rest for a while and see about a few things around the house. Ann and Ethan then hugged goodbye, and Ethan left the hospital. He was headed back to the cabin after he stopped to get some much needed food from the grocery store.

❧

Summer had a wonderful Sunday. She and young Jake had ridden bicycles in her neighborhood and had gone swimming at the neighborhood pool. They then spent the late afternoon drawing and painting together in her kitchen. She just adored Jake and savored every minute she spent with him. It seemed to her that Jake seemed to enjoy the time equally as much.

As they were wrapping up their painting session together, Summer glanced at the clock and panicked. They had been having so much fun the afternoon had almost gotten away from them. Summer and Richard had a wedding party to go to that night at the Glen Arven Country Club in Thomasville.

Several of their mutual friends had gotten together and decided to throw the couple a big bash to celebrate their upcoming nuptials. Summer hastily threw some of Jake's clothes into an overnight bag and drove him to her parents and dropped him off. She then returned home to get ready.

On the drive home from her parents' house, her thoughts were of Ethan. Anytime she spent the day with Jake and had a wonderful time, she would recall the vivid memories she had the day of the baseball game in Rosemary Beach. She was still in awe at how quickly and easily Jake had taken to Ethan and likewise how Ethan became enamored with Jake. Their connection was so natural, just as hers had been with Ethan.

Her daydreaming was interrupted as she arrived back home. She pulled into her garage and went inside. She needed to hurry and get ready so they could make the party by seven-thirty, but she now had Ethan Phillips on the brain. She was tired, too, from all the swimming today and trying to keep up with her youthful son.

As she made her way to the bedroom, she decided to take just a few minutes and sit on her bed, relax, and write in her diary. Since her breakup with Ethan, the diary had been the only cure for allowing Summer to cope with the thoughts of Ethan. Once she put all she was feeling and thinking about him on paper, she was then able to move on with her day. It was a way for her to vent her true feelings for this man in a way she couldn't do with any of her friends or family.

While leaned against the pillows on the bed Summer began writing. Her mind flowed with thoughts of Ethan Phillips. She thought of his amazing body, his gorgeous and mesmerizing eyes, his wonderful smile, his infectious laugh, and his warm and caring heart. Summer became engrossed in her thoughts, and today, for some reason, she was writing what seemed like a treatise about Ethan. She had so many vibrant memories running through her mind.

Today she was especially occupied with the amazing sex they had and all of the fun places they had experienced it. She had never had a man make her feel that way before. She could almost imagine him right now on top of her working his magic on her as no other man could.

Summer's mind was engrossed in Ethan and everything about him. She was writing at a furious pace and had completed five pages, front and back, when suddenly she was startled by a sound. It was her doorbell, and instantly her heart sank as she realized it was Richard here to pick her up. Oh crap, Summer thought, and she hastily threw her diary down onto the bed and rushed to answer the door. She then hurriedly threw open the door and saw Richard standing there.

"Well, hey there, sweetie. Are you going for the casual look tonight?" Richard asked with a beaming smile. Summer could tell he was being sarcastic, and she knew he had a difficult time passing up any opportunity to tease her.

"I'm sorry. I came back from taking Jake to swim, then got sidetracked here," Summer offered apologetically. Summer knew she dared not tell her fiancé what, or who for that matter, had gotten her sidetracked this afternoon.

"It's okay, sweetie. We still have time to be fashionably late if you hurry," Richard said caringly. Summer knew he was always accommodating of her and her desires.

"Okay! Make yourself at home, and I'll hurry! I'm so sorry," Summer said frantically as she turned and raced to the back of her house to begin getting ready. Fortunately, she already had her clothes laid out, so it was just a matter of showering, getting dressed, and putting makeup on. She quickly closed the door to the master bathroom and jumped in the shower. All thoughts of Ethan had suddenly been pushed aside as her focus now became getting ready for this party and making it there on time, or as close to on time as possible.

⤙

Richard had gone to the kitchen and found a few cookies to snack on while he waited. He knew even if they arrived on time that the first hour of the party would be drinks and socializing before they actually sat down to eat. Richard was starving and couldn't wait that long, so the cookies would do just fine holding him over until their meal later.

After he finished the cookies he wandered to the back of the house, and while in the hallway, he heard the water to the shower cut off. Summer was done showering, he thought, and he decided to spend the rest of his time waiting in her bedroom. He had always enjoyed waiting within talking distance of Summer when she was getting dressed. He thoroughly adored talking with her.

Richard made his way into the bedroom and had a seat on the edge of her bed. He heard Summer still drying off in the shower when something caught his attention out of the corner of his eye. He saw to his right on the bed lay a bright pink book with handwriting in it. Richard picked up the book, looked it over thoroughly, and noticed the words My Diary on the front cover. I wonder what great things she has to say about me in here, he thought.

He debated not reading the diary and putting it down, but his curiosity got the better of him, and Richard felt compelled to read some of the innermost thoughts of the woman he loved and adored. He flipped back a few pages to the beginning of the last entry dated today and began to read.

⁓

Summer had finished drying off, exited the shower, and quickly put on her robe. She then wasted no time in turning on the hair dryer and beginning the long process of drying her thick, flowing brown mane. Her long hair was such a chore, she thought, but she knew she needed to look her best tonight at the party. It was going to be a grand affair, as there were twelve couples giving the party for her and Richard, and they were friends with all of them.

She hoped she could somehow get ready in time so they wouldn't be late. It just would not look good to be late to their own party, at the Glen Arven Country Club, of all places.

Summer was looking forward to seeing all of her friends tonight, but at the same time, she would be glad when it was over. She hadn't wanted any parties at all before her marriage to Richard. Her ability to truly celebrate and be totally happy had left her after she broke up with Ethan. She had never been able to find happiness in the quite the same way again; however, Summer's friends had insisted on giving her a big party, and she didn't want to say no and hurt their feelings.

As Summer was finishing drying her hair, she noticed the door to the bathroom open slowly. She knew it must be Richard, and she smiled and turned to speak to him. She observed Richard open the door and come into the bathroom as if in a trance, holding a bright pink book in front of him with both hands as he shuffled in the door. Summer immediately saw the book and thought, oh shit! He's seen my diary! She then looked up from the book to Richard's face, and her heart sank.

As she looked at him, she saw a man totally dejected and deflated. It was obvious by looking at his lost and broken expression that he had, at a minimum, read her entry from today. She saw that he had the countenance of a man who had just lost everything he possessed. He looked completely broken to her, and his color seemed to her to be as white as a sheet of paper.

Summer's eyes met Richard's, but saw he could barely speak. He managed to say, "Is all this . . . *true*? Do you feel that way about . . . *him*?"

Summer was in shock herself, simply with the moment. She couldn't believe what she was seeing and that she had left her diary out wide open for him to read. She was never that careless with it. As everything started to sink in, though, Summer found herself angry at Richard for invading her privacy.

Even though she should not have left her diary out in the open, she felt it was still wrong of him to pick it up and read it. It was obvious it was a diary, and he should have known it would contain her innermost thoughts.

Before really thinking, Summer blurted out, "What are you doing reading that? That's my personal diary, and it's private, Richard!"

Summer felt like Richard was unfazed by her remarks as he seemed to look at her with the same heartbroken expression and he sternly repeated, "I said, is all this *true*, and do you feel that way about *him*?"

Summer now found herself in a quandary. If she was honest it might end their engagement and ultimate marriage, and if she said she didn't mean it, she would be not only lying to Richard, but also to herself about her true feelings for Ethan. She thought for a moment, then replied, "Yes, Richard, what I wrote is really how I feel about Ethan. I'm sorry you read it and are hurt by it, but I can't lie to you and say I don't feel that way about him. I love you, Richard, and . . ."

❧

Before Summer could finish her sentence anger assumed control of Richard as he violently threw down the diary to the bathroom floor, turned and stormed toward the front door. As she watched him walk away, without turning around, he angrily yelled, "I'm not going to that damn wedding party with you after reading *that*! Maybe you just need to call Mr. Wonderful and get *him* to go with you!"

Summer was walking briskly behind him and called out to him, "Wait, Richard, please wait! I do love you, and I want. . . ."

Before she could finish that sentence she observed Richard still with his back to her, throw up both of his arms and yell, "I don't want to hear it! You're still in love with *him*. Kiss my ass," then slammed the front door, got into his car, and hastily drove away.

⁊

Summer stammered into her living room in a confused and bewildered trance and sat on the edge of the couch. She was speechless and in shock at what had just happened. In the blink of an eye she had jeopardized her impending marriage with Richard. She couldn't believe she had been so foolish to leave her diary out like that. She was also disappointed in Richard that he had infringed on her privacy and read it. She would never had done such a thing to him, she thought.

The entire moment from Richard's finding the diary forward was so surreal. She couldn't believe it really happened, yet was sure it had. In a strange twist of fate, she found herself quite possibly broken up with Richard at the exact same place she broke up with Ethan, her home and with each man being the cause for the break up with the other.

Strangely enough, however, the more she sat and thought about the possibility of her impending marriage to Richard being over, the more of a sense of peace and serenity came over her. This time she wasn't sitting on the couch crying desperately as she had when she broke up with Ethan. She didn't even feel the need to go running after Richard or call him.

She felt strange at this moment because she did love Richard and had been looking forward to their marriage, but now the prospect of the wedding not coming to pass and the prospect of breaking up with Richard gave her a sense of tranquility.

I should be upset and crying and beside myself, Summer thought, but she didn't have those feelings now. All she felt was . . . relief.

Summer sat on the couch and spent almost ten minutes replaying what happened with Richard, thinking about her feelings and what to do about the party that night. It didn't take much thought on the party for her. She knew she needed to go, even if Richard didn't show up.

It would look horrible if both she and Richard didn't go, and they would be the scourge of high society in Thomasville. If nothing else she could go and just say that Richard became suddenly ill with an acute stomach virus and wasn't able to come.

She also knew it was possible that Richard would still show up, despite what he said, just so none of his friends would be disappointed. Either way, she knew she had to suck it up and make her appearance at the party. She hurried back to the bathroom, and this time, after putting away her diary in its usual hiding place, she resumed getting ready for the party.

Despite all the turmoil and drama at her house, Summer managed to pull herself together and be dressed and at the entrance to Glen Arven Country Club shortly after seven thirty. On her drive over to the club she had fashioned a story about the sudden "illness" that struck Richard. She had even sent Richard a text message letting him know what she was going to say at the party so that they could be on the same page. He had curtly replied "*Ok*" but said nothing else.

Summer put on her best front and pretended to be the expectant bride and managed to convince all the attendees that poor Richard was in bed sick with a stomach virus. Any Hollywood actress would have been proud of her performance that night. Summer smiled and chatted with all the guests, as if none of the events in her bedroom earlier that evening had occurred.

The food at the party was excellent, and she had enjoyed connecting with her friends once again. It was strange, in a way, because despite all the turmoil with Richard earlier, Summer had a good time at the party.

She was still sad that Richard had been hurt, but at the same time she experienced a sense of contentment at the possibility she might not be getting married to him. She loved Richard and did mean it when she told him that, but it was a very different love from what she felt for Ethan.

It was now almost ten-thirty, and Summer had become tired from the party and all the drama of the day. She made her way around to all the hosts and thanked them for the party and a wonderful night. She apologized to all the hosts again for Richard's not being there. She told them she needed to get home to check on him. The hosts all seemed to hate to see her go, but she felt they understood as they exchanged hugs.

Summer exited the country club and was soon in her car in the parking lot. She was about to crank her car and head home and pulled out her phone to check her text messages and voice mail. She saw she had a voicemail from Richard and listened to him say, "As you can see, I didn't come tonight. I'm sorry, but I just can't marry someone who feels that way about another man. I love you, Summer, more than I have anyone in my life, but it's obvious you don't love me, or at least you don't love me like you do Ethan. I can't handle being married to you knowing you feel that way about a man other than me. I'm sorry this is a voicemail, but I just couldn't handle seeing you tonight. I'm headed out of town for a few days to get my head together. We can work out telling everyone when I get back. Bye."

Summer was deeply sorry to have hurt Richard, but even before hearing his voicemail, she had decided that he wouldn't marry her now. She knew the male ego was a powerful and fragile thing to a man, and she had unintentionally destroyed Richard's. She felt like any man worth his salt wouldn't marry a woman after finding out what he did. She just hoped and prayed Richard stayed clean and sober. She didn't want to be what caused him to slip back into his addictions.

Before she started the car, she took a moment to say a small prayer for Richard's well-being and happiness. When he returned and they talked, she would sit down and apologize to him. Hopefully they could part ways in a civil manner, she thought.

Summer then gazed down at her left ring finger at the engagement ring Richard had given her. She gently pulled the ring off and found a safe place for it in her purse until she could get home. She hated their engagement was now over, but she knew in her heart it was ultimately the best thing for both herself and Richard. She didn't need to marry Richard if she was still consumed with Ethan and continued to write about him in her diary. In time, she felt like Richard would realize it was for the best, too, but she hated that he was hurting now because of her.

Summer collected her thoughts and then cranked the car and left the country club. As she was headed home, her mind wandered to Ethan once again. All of her writing about him today had brought him back to the forefront of her mind. Perhaps it was her conversation with Sebastian and just knowing Sebastian had seen him and talked to him. For such a long time Summer had been starving for a conversation of any kind with Ethan, and maybe now that she had heard from him, albeit through Sebastian, that was why she was thinking about him so much today.

As she approached Highway 84 to Valdosta, Summer decided for some unknown reason to turn and head toward Valdosta and drive by the entrance to Ethan's cabin. She had been by there dozens of times the last two years driving back and forth to Valdosta with her business. The gate had always been closed, not that she would have dared go in, anyway. Besides, Summer knew from Sebastian's phone call that Ethan was in New York and was likely never coming back.

She couldn't explain why, but she just wanted to drive by there tonight. She wanted to see the closed gate and something that belonged to him, that would remind her of him and all the wonderful times they shared together. She just felt the need to see with her own eyes *his* place.

Tonight she did not want to stop thinking about him. She wanted to dwell on him and how he made her feel. She knew seeing the entrance to his house would do that for her, and that was precisely where she was headed.

Ethan's evening had been quiet. He had spent about an hour in the grocery store stocking up his cabin for the next several days. He wasn't sure how long he would be there, but with Willie in the condition he was in, he had no plans to leave right away. He would call Michael tomorrow and give him an update on Willie and discuss his expected return date to New York.

As Ethan arrived at the cabin, he had chosen to leave the gate by the road open. It was rare for him to do that, but he fully expected to get back to the cabin and realize he had forgotten something of great necessity from the grocery store. He was sure he would have to make another trip to the grocery store that night, but, to his complete surprise, after he had unpacked all the groceries and put them away, he determined that he had actually done well and gotten everything he needed except for laundry detergent, and that could wait until tomorrow.

It was now approaching eleven o'clock, and Ethan didn't like to leave the entrance to his cabin open. He felt much safer with it closed. He debated taking his truck or his ATV and driving back down to the gate and locking it, but he just simply didn't feel like it. He was worn out from the stress of Willie's condition and visiting him at the hospital. Maybe no one will come in here tonight and try to rob me, he thought. Ethan poured himself a glass of chardonnay and lay down on the couch to relax and watch some television.

As he lay down, though, it was impossible to be in his cabin and not think about his and Summer's magical time together. He couldn't avoid dwelling on how powerful and intense their connection had been. He had all of these vivid memories coming back, and he sat there and relived them. Ethan wondered what Summer was doing right now. He decided she was probably spending it with her fiancé. That would make perfect sense under the circumstances.

He then began to think back to his conversation with Willie in the hospital. It was so unusual for Willie to intervene in his dating life, and the story of how he came to book the house and his revelation that Summer was the one for him were just amazing to Ethan.

As much as Ethan hated to admit it, Willie was exactly right. It was totally unfair to deny Summer a chance to explain what happened. Even though Ethan knew she was completely wrong for what she had done, he also knew he was wrong for not even listening to her explanation. He would have wanted that same chance to explain if the situation were reversed.

A strange and frightening thought now came into Ethan's mind. What if what he saw was a complete misunderstanding of the situation, or worse yet, what if what he thought he saw wasn't actually what happened?

Ethan now became sick to his stomach with the mere possibility that he might have thrown his relationship with Summer away because of a mere misperception. Ethan was also beginning to understand why he had reacted in such knee-jerk fashion. He had never really dealt with the hurt Emma caused him.

He had neatly buried Emma in the back of his mind and declared it over and done with, but he was now discovering that if he didn't face that hurt and resolve it, it would surface again one day in another relationship, if he had one. For the first time since he split up with Summer, he was feeling guilty for not talking with her.

Until his return home, he had considered all of his actions justified because she had been in the wrong and she had hurt him deeply. He had lost no sleep over ignoring her, but now after his talks with Willie and Sebastian, Ethan felt differently. The guilt and regret he was feeling was only growing, and he knew there was no way he would sleep tonight unless he got sopping drunk; however, he didn't want to do that. He knew what he had to do. He had to find Summer and try to talk with her, resolve this conflict, and end this guilt.

Ethan realized she was getting married, and he had no grand illusions of that changing. He just wanted each of them to have the chance to sit down and find closure so both of them could heal. He wasn't going to be able to deal with Willie and this situation with Summer at the same time. Ethan had to find her, wake her up, and talk through this, if she would even give him the time of day at this point. Ethan, now sure of his task, jumped up from the couch and hastily got dressed to leave for Thomasville.

Chapter Thirty-One

ETHAN REALIZED IT was late, but he felt compelled to find Summer and try to talk with her. He had put it off far too long, and he realized now that he needed to have a conversation with her to heal and move forward. He just hoped and prayed that she would allow him the opportunity to talk to her tonight, especially after he had ignored her for over two years. He went to his closet, found a pullover shirt and threw on some khaki shorts.

He took just a minute to straighten his hair, then he was ready to go to Summer's and hopefully talk. He would just text her on the way to Thomasville so that she could meet him somewhere for their chat. He hoped she would agree to come and her fiancé would allow her to come.

It seemed that being back home and in his cabin had filled his mind with all the good things about Summer, and Sebastian and Willie's interventions had helped him see that even though she had hurt him by going out with and kissing Richard that he was wrong for not at least talking with her afterward and resolving the situation. Ethan was also certain now that if he had dealt with the hurt and betrayal from Emma, his reaction would have been much different with Summer.

❧

Summer had thought of Ethan on the entire drive down Highway 84. She was remembering all the great times they had together and how he made her feel inside. Everything about this man had captivated her. He cast a spell on her that she hadn't been able to remove.

She had tried to forget about him. She had even dated, become engaged, and was about to marry Richard with the hope that would break Ethan's grip on her. She had unintentionally ruined her marriage to Richard by accidentally leaving her diary out, but with all the peace she now had in her heart, she realized it truly was for the best. She knew whom she still loved.

Despite his ignoring her for two years and moving to New York to start another life, she still loved him just as much as she did that day they broke up. She loved everything about him. She loved his eyes, his laugh, his gentleness, his compassion, his loving way with her, and of course, she loved his body and the way he moved it.

She knew he wasn't at home tonight and was in New York, but she just wanted to see that familiar gate and cast her eyes on *his* place before she went home. She felt led to do it, like she *must* do it tonight before she would be able to rest.

As she arrived at the entrance, she pulled in off the highway so she could turn around and head back home. When she pulled in to the gate she was astonished to see her headlights revealing it was open. Why is it open? she thought. I've ridden by here dozens of times, and it's *never* been open. Summer now wondered what she should do. She was undecided about whether to go in or not. What if someone is in the house and has borrowed it for the night? she questioned. Summer knew she would look like a fool driving up on them, and there was no way to turn around until she was at the house. She sat at the gate for about five minutes trying to decide what to do.

Finally, she decided she had come this far, so why not go all the way. The worst case was there was someone staying at the house. She could always play the "innocent lost woman who's bad with directions" routine and excuse herself. She forged ahead and made her way down the long, winding drive, and as she neared the house, she could see lights on. Oh crap, she thought, there *is* someone here.

As she pulled closer, though, the only vehicle she saw was a black BMW X-7. It looked like the one Ethan drove, and as she pulled into the parking area beside it, she saw that it was indeed Ethan's car. Could he possibly be here? Summer thought. There's no way he could be because Sebastian just saw him in New York the other night, she reasoned.

She parked the car, turned it off, and sat inside. She peered through her windshield into the back door window of the cabin trying to catch a glimpse of whoever was there. She waited a few minutes, then saw the profile of a man flash by the window. She didn't make out who it was, but then the man reappeared and stared out the window toward her in the parking area.

The parking area wasn't well lit, so her dark colored vehicle was difficult to see. As she stared intently at the man looking out from the widow, her heart seemed to skip a beat as she realized it was *him*! Ethan was here. Oh crap, what am I going to do? Summer thought. She wanted to see him, but didn't want to upset Ethan by having an argument with him.

She continued her deliberation for another few minutes, then decided she just had to see him. If he blessed her out, she decided, she deserved it, but she had to talk to him and see what they could work out. She wished for a quick glass of chardonnay to down right then and settle her nerves and butterflies before she went to the door. Oh, well, here goes nothing, she thought. She took a deep breath and climbed out of her car to face the man she could not get over.

Ethan was about to head out the door and could have sworn he saw lights coming up the driveway. He had looked all around the house and out at the parking area after getting dressed, but couldn't see that anyone was there.

He finally decided he must just be tired and seeing things and grabbed his keys and opened the back door, then couldn't believe who he saw as he stepped outside. "Uh, Summer? Summer, is that you?" Ethan called out, unsure if his eyes were playing tricks on him or not.

"Yes, Ethan, it's me," she replied as she tried to catch her breath from seeing him. "I'm sorry to barge in. I didn't know you were in Valdosta and I umm . . . pulled in out of curiosity, I guess," Summer said sheepishly. She hoped he wouldn't be angry with her for just driving in.

"No, no. It's okay, really," Ethan said and Summer could see he appeared startled and to be having to catch his breath also.

"I guess you were headed somewhere, so I won't keep you," Summer said apologetically.

"Actually, I *was* headed somewhere. I was headed to see you," Ethan said with a small grin as she watched him turn and toss his keys onto the bar in the kitchen.

She felt like doing her happy dance right there in front of him when he said he was coming to see her, but she restrained herself and asked, "What? No way, Ethan. You were coming to see me? Why?"

"I was coming to do something I should have done a long time ago, and that's sit down with you and talk about what happened. I know you're about to get married. Sebastian told me that when he came to New York. You're moving on with someone else, and I guess I found out I need the closure and you probably do, too," Ethan said somberly.

"I've wanted to talk with you, Ethan. I'm so sorry about what I did," Summer offered.

"Listen, since you're here, would you like to come in and get away from these mosquitoes?" Ethan asked hopefully.

"I'd love to," Summer replied.

She watched Ethan motion her in, and she was happy to see the inside of his house was just as she remembered it. It smelled the same and had all the furniture, paintings, pictures, and knickknacks in exactly the same place. She observed Ethan offer her a glass of wine, chardonnay, of course, which she gladly accepted. She needed something to calm her nerves so they could talk, and she felt like Ethan probably did too. Ethan handed her the glass of wine, and she took a healthy drink from her glass, then they sat and resumed their conversation.

"Ethan, let me start. I'm so sorry for what you saw and for hurting you. I made some decisions in poor judgment, and I regret it deeply. Richard approached me, and I agreed to go out with him just to make sure I was really in love with you. I know that doesn't make sense to you, but at the time, it did to me. I hated the whole evening with him, and I agreed to kiss him just to get him to leave. I felt nothing when I kissed him. Nothing. I was completely over him after that date. I know it was wrong, and I'm so very sorry. I should have just trusted how I felt about you. I've hurt you so badly, and it's haunted me for two years," Summer said, crying almost immediately after she had begun talking. Sitting down with Ethan and talking with him had resurfaced all of the pain she experienced from hurting him that fateful day.

⮜⮟

Ethan listened intently as she had talked and was moved by her emotion. It seemed genuine to him. After she paused, Ethan said, "But Summer, you're about to marry this man that you said you were over, and I'm guessing he's pretty much the only guy you dated after me. Now you're engaged and on the verge of marriage. From my standpoint it seems hard to believe you were over him then, but then fell back in love with him now. It seems to me you were never over him at all."

"Well, I don't think I'm on the verge of marriage now," Summer replied through her tears.

"What do you mean?" Ethan asked, surprised.

"Today I was writing in my diary about you, and Richard had come over to pick me up for a wedding party for us. I accidentally left the diary out, and Richard chose to read it. There's no way we're getting married now," Summer said. Ethan noticed her crying beginning to subside.

"How do you know Richard won't marry you?" Ethan asked skeptically.

"I went ahead to the party and told everyone Richard was sick. I didn't want neither of us to show up because that would have been a scandalous thing to do. So I went to the party, and when I got into my car to leave and come home, Richard had left me a voice mail. He said he couldn't marry me now knowing that I felt like I did about you and that he was taking a few days to think. He said when he got back we could sit down and decide how to tell everyone we weren't getting married," Summer replied. Ethan noticed her eyes locked into his eyes the entire time she spoke.

"So how *do* you feel about me?" Ethan asked as he got up to pour himself another glass of chardonnay to ease the pain he was sure her response would bring. Summer got up with him and followed him into the kitchen. Ethan had his back to her pouring the wine. He felt her grab his right arm, and gently pull him around to face her.

He could see Summer begin crying feverishly again as she said, "Ethan, it's always been you. I think about you *every* day. Most of what I've written in my diary since we met is about *you*. I relive everything we did and every conversation we had. I love you so deeply, and you're more a part of me than *any* man ever has been. It's been so painful being without you, and the guilt

I've had has been overwhelming at times. I'm so sorry for hurting you and chasing you away to New York. Please forgive me!"

Ethan could see her tears were flowing like a river as she continued "I made a mistake by going on a date and kissing Richard. I thought it would just confirm my feeling for you, and it did. But it was wrong to do that to you. I'm so very sorry. And tonight after Richard found the diary, all I've felt is a sense of relief our engagement is over. The only man I've thought about since he found the diary is you. I love you, Ethan, with all that I am."

Summer, still crying strongly added "I came over here tonight not expecting to see you, but to just see the gate and let it trigger a wave of good memories of you and us. I didn't want the memories of you to stop tonight. I've cut them off and pushed them to the side since we broke up. But tonight I just wanted and needed the memory of you to wash all over me and my mind."

Her genuineness and deep love for him were now as plain as day to Ethan. Summer's emotion and sincerity touched his heart. He looked directly back into her deep brown eyes and said, "I love you more than I have ever loved anyone. I've never stopped loving you, either."

Ethan's passion then took over his mind and body. He grabbed Summer around the waist, yanked her over against him, and began kissing her passionately. He weaved his tongue inside her mouth almost savagely. As he grabbed her he could feel her put her hands on either side of his face, and he felt her match the intensity of his kisses. He was flooded with endorphins from the intense pleasure he was feeling. He didn't have anything on his mind but perpetuating this burning passion that he had been starving for the past two years.

❧

As Summer was pressed tightly against Ethan, she could feel his fully erect and bulging manhood against her lower torso. She knew she couldn't wait to feel him inside her again. She too was flooded with intense pleasure from Ethan. She wanted him right now.

❧

Ethan was consumed with desire for Summer. He continued to press his tongue against hers, and he wanted to grind his body against hers, too. His passion reached its limit, and while still kissing her, with both hands he violently ripped Summer's dress in the back, then threw it to the floor. With his passion still raging and while still passionately kissing her, he then ripped her bra in the back and threw it to the floor.

Now almost having her completely naked, he decided to finish the job and ripped her panties and threw them to the side. He then paused from kissing her and pulled back to admire the voluptuous breasts and the perfectly curved body he had missed so desperately. He was stalking her before ravaging her.

⁓

Summer took this moment to yank the shirt Ethan was wearing over his head and toss it to the floor. She stared at the ripped and rock-hard chest and arms Ethan had. He was even more sculpted and chiseled than before, she thought. Summer couldn't wait to see the rest of him and reached down and ripped open his shorts and dropped them to the floor.

Finally, she grabbed his underwear with both hands and yanked it to the floor too. She quickly took her hand, and as she resumed kissing him, began stroking his manhood. She would pause from kissing him occasionally to look down and marvel at his size and imagine how good it was going to feel inside her again.

⁓

Ethan was boiling with desire as Summer worked her magic on him, but he knew what he had in mind for her. After a few minutes, he stopped her from stroking him and grabbed her right arm, took her to the back of the couch. He spun her around quickly to face the couch, then pushed her back down so she was leaning on her forearms on the back of the couch.

He then grabbed a handful of her flowing brown hair as he entered her from behind. He began slowly sliding in and out of her, and as he was doing so, he would pull back on her hair to show his dominance.

⁓

Summer's passion was gushing now, and she felt Ethan move in and out of her effortlessly. With each stroke she only drew more pleasure. She could also feel her hair as he pulled on it while stroking in and out of her. She almost passed out from the intense pleasure she was feeling. She would let him do whatever he wanted to her, and she loved Ethan's dominating her and having his way with her. His passion was primal, and she couldn't get enough of it.

She felt him then begin stroking her faster and pulling back on her hair even harder as he did. Summer was groaning loudly and calling out, "Give it to me, baby! I love you, Ethan! Don't stop!"

After a few more minutes of passion, suddenly Summer stopped him and pushed him out of her. She then looked seductively at him and walked around to Ethan's large wooden coffee table. She reached down, and with one swipe, she pushed all the magazines to the floor. She then lay on her back on top of the table and locked onto Ethan's eyes. "You're amazing. Finish me here."

⌘

Ethan was fully into the moment, and the pleasure and passion blocked everything else from his mind. All he cared about was making passionate love to her. Ethan matched the intensity of her stare, and still with the look of the tiger stalking his prey, he stood over her fully aroused and said, "You're amazing, too, baby. I'm gonna finish you, alright."

Ethan got on top of her and slid inside her, and as he did, he used his hands to pin Summer's hands against the table. As Ethan began thrusting in a circular motion inside her, he was pleased he had decided several years ago to opt for the solid wood six-foot heart pine coffee table. At this moment its considerable size and weight was well worth every penny he spent.

Ethan began violently sucking and licking Summer's fully aroused nipples as he continued to grind his manhood inside her in a rhythmic, circular motion. Each time his manhood passed her G-spot, he could see an even greater rush of pleasure on her face. Ethan continued grinding her and holding her down as he did so, then he whispered in her ear, "I'm going to explode in you, and there's nothing you can do to stop me."

"Come on, baby, I want you to. Give it all to me, every drop," Summer whispered back.

On cue, Summer's words drove Ethan over the edge. He began thrusting rapidly in and out of her with all the force he could generate. It was all he could do to hold Summer's arms down enough to keep from pushing her right off the table. The table itself was inching across the floor with each powerful thrust. Summer then took her legs, wrapped them around Ethan's back, and told him, "Oh, Ethan, you feel so good, baby."

Ethan was immersed in pleasure and said, "You're mine now, baby! Give it to me now! You know you want to! Come all over me!" Ethan was stroking feverishly inside her with every ounce of energy that he had in his body. He could hear his body slap loudly against hers each time he would bottom out inside her.

✍

As he was driving himself into her wildly, Summer gazed at the perfect man and his perfect body that was inside her giving her so much pleasure and screwing her brains out. She could feel a powerful orgasm about to erupt, and she yelled, "Oh, God, Ethan, I'm almost there, baby. Please don't stop."

After hearing her words she felt him continue thrusting vigorously in and out of her, and Summer could take it no more, threw her head back, and screamed, "Ohhhh, Ethan! Ethan! Oh, God, Ethan! Ohhhh!" Summer's orgasm was intense, as her body was quivering violently from Ethan Phillips being inside her. Her back formed a perfect semi-circle as her incredible orgasm caused it to arch dramatically. The waves of pleasure seemed to coarse through every muscle fiber in her body triggering violent spasms along the way.

✍

As Summer yelled these words, Ethan climaxed too, and as Summer was screaming, Ethan erupted inside her, yelling, "Ahhhh! Ahhhh! Summer! Summer! Ohhh, Summer!" Ethan unleashed numerous relentless and power-ful waves of pleasure into her. Each pulse of pleasure from him exploded savagely into her body. It felt so good to give himself to her, he thought.

After the final waves of his orgasm had passed, he was speechless and eased down to lay on her for several minutes. He was exhausted and he felt like they were two lifeless bodies piled atop each other.

✍

Eventually Summer broke the silence after about five minutes and was first to speak. She looked at him and said, "I love you, Ethan. I'm sorry for hurt-ing you."

Ethan smiled back at Summer and said, "I love you, too, Summer, and

I'm sorry for being so stubborn. Be gentle with my heart. You hold it in the palm of your hands, and I'm entrusting you with it. Please don't hurt me again."

"You have nothing to worry about. I will cherish and protect it as long as I live and love you the rest of my life" Summer replied as she gazed deeply into Ethan's eyes. They lay in each other's arms for another few minutes when Summer looked back at Ethan and gently said, "I'm glad you're home."

Ethan smiled happily and said in return, "I'm glad to be home, too."

Epilogue

$\mathcal{E}$THAN AND SUMMER'S whirlwind romance resumed right back where it ended, only this time around, each had learned from their previous mistakes. Ethan learned he needed to talk with someone about Emma and what she did to hurt him so that he could truly get over the pain and move forward.

He decided to first tell Summer everything that happened with Emma and see if just simply talking about it with her and getting all of it out in the open would be enough to move on with his life. He was prepared to see a counselor, if necessary, but it turned out he didn't need to. Ethan told Summer the whole sad story between him and Emma. Those discussions with her and her insight proved enough to allow him to genuinely heal from the pain Emma wreaked on him.

❦

After Summer learned of all that happened to him, it gave her a sense of understanding of why he had reacted as he did when they broke up. Summer, for her part, had learned a valuable lesson as well, to trust her heart when it came to Ethan Phillips and not doubt her feelings for him. She, too, had allowed someone from the past to affect her and her relationship with someone she loved. She resolved to trust her feelings, and Ethan vowed to do the very same thing.

❦

They resumed dating, but now they made every effort to see each other at least three times a week. Both were much happier with this arrangement, and young Jake was thrilled to see Ethan again. He welcomed him back as if no time had passed between them.

Summer had kept Jake in the dark about all that transpired between Ethan and her during the breakup. She had simply told him that Ethan had accepted a new job in New York and was forced to move away. She also told him that Ethan wouldn't be able to return to Valdosta for a while and that they wouldn't be seeing him for some time. She had hoped and prayed that 'some time' didn't become 'ever again,' and at the end of the day her prayers were answered.

They dated for about three months after their passionate reunion and could stand it no more and chose to elope at the most special place on earth to them, Rosemary Beach. It was a small afternoon wedding with only Ethan, Summer, and Jake in attendance, along with the local justice of the peace who performed the ceremony. They chose to keep the wedding simple to make their lives easier before the ceremony, and it was a decision they never regretted. In addition, both of their families were happy for them and completely understood their eloping on a second marriage.

The entire time they had resumed dating and through the wedding ceremony, Ethan had kept secret the fact that he had purchased the home in Rosemary Beach that he and Summer shared those magical moments in. Before the wedding, Ethan had asked Summer where she would like to honeymoon, and naturally, she said right there in Rosemary Beach. Ethan then surprised her after the ceremony with the news of the house, and she was ecstatic.

Ethan and Summer stayed for a week in Rosemary Beach in their new home away from home and had the most passionate and romantic week a couple could possibly have. It was so passionate, in fact, that about nine months after they returned from their honeymoon, Summer gave birth to a son. They gave him the only name that seemed to fit, William Sebastian Phillips. Will, as he would be called by everyone, bore the names of the two influential men who would not give up on Summer and Ethan, even when it seemed the two of them had.

⤦

Sebastian remained a close friend of Summer, and now Ethan, for the rest of his life. He continued to live in Rosemary Beach and was able to see Ethan and Summer often, as they would spend as much time at their home there as was possible. Sebastian continued to find and forward to Summer potential event planner clientele, and her business was soon popular in not only Rosemary Beach, but the entire panhandle of Florida, as well as South Georgia. In return, Ethan, through Michael and his other New York contacts, managed to keep Sebastian well supplied with tickets to musicals and plays on Broadway.

∝

Willie managed a quite remarkable recovery from his heart surgery. Despite all the doomsday predictions from his physicians, he managed to live another seven years after the heart attack. He became close to Ethan and Summer's son, Will, and treated him like the grandson he never had. He also finally met Summer and grew close to her as well before his death. He felt as if he knew her already when they first met because of all he heard Ethan say about her.

Once Willie met Summer, he was sure the dream about Rosemary Beach and the call he received from his Atlanta friend the next day were indeed the work of God. Finally, Ethan spent as much time as humanly possible with Willie over his final years, and their friendship only grew stronger. The two of them more than made up for the two years they lost during Ethan's hiatus in New York. By the time Willie passed away, both he and Ethan had decided everything had happened according to God's will and for the best.

∝

Ethan was never able to work again in New York. After he and Summer's explosive reunion night, he knew what he had to do, and that was return home to Valdosta. He called Michael the next day and only said he was coming back in a few days to sit down and talk.

Once Ethan had made that return trip to New York, he explained to Michael all that had transpired between him and Summer and discussed their reunion. He informed Michael that he could no longer work in New York and would have to move back home to Valdosta.

∝

Michael, ever the salesman, tried to talk Ethan into staying and simply flying home on the weekends, but Ethan couldn't do that. Michael listened as Ethan informed him that he had to see Summer more than that, and it would be impossible for them to build their life together if he continued to work in New York. Michael ultimately understood and allowed Ethan to return to Valdosta and didn't hold Ethan to the contract he had signed. Michael had grown close to Ethan, much as Willie had, and he wasn't about to keep him from his happiness in Valdosta.

❧

Ethan and Summer chose to live in Ethan's cabin in Valdosta. Ethan had just enough room for him, Summer, Will, and Jake when he would stay with them. The cabin was centrally located between Valdosta and Thomasville and allowed Summer and Ethan to both have a reasonable drive to the cities where they worked. They also stayed at their home in Rosemary Beach whenever possible, which turned out to be at least one week per month. Both of their careers permitted them to work from home at times, and they took full advantage.

Ethan and Summer cultivated their love and friendship for the rest of their lives. They both returned to church, which was important to each of them. They involved Jake and Will in church, as well. They both felt it was the least they could do to repay God for not giving up on their relationship and working through Willie and Sebastian to bring them back together.

Over the next twenty years, Ethan would manage the lone hedge fund in Valdosta he had started with Willie's help. His performance managing the fund was second to none, and the investors rewarded him generously for as long as he managed it. Ethan was so happy to be managing only the Valdosta fund again, even if it was for less money. He was thrilled to be back home and building a life with the woman he absolutely adored and with their sons. He never looked back and never again doubted Summer's love for him.

END

CPSIA information can be obtained
at www.ICGtesting.com
Printed in the USA
FFOW04n0146300916
28107FF